RELIGIOUS DRAMA:
ENDS AND MEANS

RELIGIOUS DRAMA:
ENDS AND MEANS

Harold Ehrensperger

GREENWOOD PRESS, PUBLISHERS
WESTPORT, CONNECTICUT

Library of Congress Cataloging in Publication Data

Ehrensperger, Harold Adam, 1897-1973.
   Religious drama.

   Reprint of the 1962 ed. published by Abingdon Press,
New York.
   Bibliography: p.
   Includes index.
   1. Christian drama--History and criticism.
2. Theater--Production and direction. I. Title.
[PN1880.E48 1977]   792   77-22986
ISBN 0-8371-9744-9

The preparation of this book has been made possible by a grant from the Lilly
Foundation, Inc., of which G. Harold Duling is executive director.

Under this grant William T. Thrasher has made a major contribution to the editorial
work. Yolanda Reed has assisted. The author's appreciation is expressed to these
persons.

Originally published in 1962 by Abingdon Press, New York

Reprinted with the permission of Abingdon Press

Reprinted in 1977 by Greenwood Press, Inc.

Library of Congress catalog card number   77-22986

ISBN 0-8371-9744-9

Printed in the United States of America

FOR

Winifred Ward whose life has established
a standard of excellence which is seen
in her work in creative dramatics and
children's theatre

Robert Scott Steele whose life and work have
exemplified the values to which this book
is dedicated

PREFACE

Conscience on Stage was published in 1947. Because much progress has been made in religious drama, it has needed revision. The idea of drama that communicates values both by way of its content and the production experience has gained status in the last twenty years. A book has been needed to indicate this advance and to make definitive the meaning of this growing concern. The revision of an old book seemed like patchwork. A book with a new approach and larger scope seemed to be the solution.

This book has been written with a hope that the area of contemporary religious drama could be dignified by its consideration in the long history of drama. The unfortunate aura of offensive amateurishness that has hung over religious drama has so clouded it that artists and craftsmen of the theater have shunned the term and the experience that would relate them to it.

This book is an effort to change this attitude. If its content can clarify concepts and spur professional and nonprofessional theater practitioners to have a concern for good plays well produced, then it will have fulfilled its purpose.

The growing interest in religious drama has its alarming aspect because more time is needed to create plays that will be admirably and deeply religious and to prepare theater-arts craftsmen who can surmount the difficulties of formal and informal dramatic production outside the commercial theater. Until more and better plays are written and trained leadership and artisans are available, little progress can be made. When good plays are produced, the audience for religious drama will be found.

The conjunction of these three necessities of effective drama—plays, producers, and consumers—is the goal of those committed to the serious and intelligent dramatic statement which is worthy of being called religious.

The contributions of many people have given this book whatever inclusiveness it may have. Lucy Barton contributed bibliography on costume, Winifred Ward on creative dramatics, Joseph Gifford on dance, and Mrs. Evangeline Macklin on speech. Others have contributed material for which credit has been given. No person has made a larger or more telling contribution than has Dr. Robert Scott Steele of the School of Communications and Public Relations of Boston University. To Mrs. Clare A. Burke fell the task of copying the manuscript—a project which became much more than a job of mere copying. Her judgment and experience are reflected in the text of this book.

HAROLD EHRENSPERGER

Boston, Massachusetts

CONTENTS

PART TWO

PART THREE

B. SCENERY

C. PROPERTIES

D. COSTUMES

E. MAKEUP

F. LIGHTING

APPENDIXES

    HISTORY

    INTRODUCTION TO DRAMA, THEORY, CRITICISM, REVIEWS

    PLAYWRITING

    DIRECTING

    ACTING

    PRODUCTION

    LIGHTING

    COSTUMING

    MAKEUP

    ARENA STAGING

    SPEECH

    CHORAL SPEECH

    DANCE

    PAGEANTRY

    CREATIVE DRAMATICS

    CHILDREN'S THEATER

    DRAMA IN EDUCATION

PSYCHODRAMA, SOCIODRAMA, AND PLAYS USED FOR
DISCUSSIONS
COMMUNITY THEATER
RELIGIOUS DRAMA
    Meaning and Development
    Handbooks on Production in the Church
    Use in Religious Education
    Biblical Material

WORSHIP

Part one

The three laws governing religious drama

We always have control over the means and never the ends. The end grows out of the means. As the means, so the end. The means may be likened to a seed; the end to a tree. And there is the same inviolable connection between the means and the ends as there is between the seed and the tree. If one takes care of the means the end will take care of itself, and the realization of the goal is in exact proportion to that of the means.

> —G. N. Dhiwan, The Political Philosophy of Mahatma Gandhi (Bombay: The Popular Book Depot, 1946), p. 49.

This is the first law of religious drama

The distinction of means and ends arises in surveying the course of a proposed line of action, a connected series in time. The end is the last act thought of; the means are acts to be performed prior to it in time. To reach an end, we must take our mind off from it and attend to the act which is next to be performed. We must make that the end.

> —John Dewey, Human Nature and Conduct (New York: Henry Holt & Company, 1922), p. 34.

This is the second law of religious drama

There is only one means and there is only one end: the means and the end are one and the same thing. There is only one end: the genuine good; and only one means: this, to be willing to use those means which genuinely are good—but the genuine good is precisely the end. In time one distinguishes between the two and considers that the end is more important than the means. One thinks that the end is the main thing and demands of one who is striving that he reach the end. He need not be so particular about the means. Yet this is not so, and to gain an end in this fashion is an unholy act of impatience.

> —Purity of Heart by Sören Kierkegaard. Translated by Douglas E. Steere. Used by permission of Harper & Brothers.

This is the third and final law of religious drama

14

Chapter I

THE MEANING OF THE DRAMATIC

BECAUSE ITS RAW MATERIAL IS THE TOTAL HUMAN BEING, DRAMA IS THE most alive of all the arts. Human beings are presented to other human beings in situations of movement, action, and change. Drama is life in motion seen at times of especial significance. The dramatist puts movement and action on a stage and holds it there until we have had a good look at it. It is housed in a building, fixed in a frame, or held at a distance so that it is sufficiently arrested for us to grasp it. By way of dramatization we get some beginning, middle, and ending out of segments of ongoing and ephemeral life. This view of a selection from life in action enables us to see the extent of our own aliveness or deadness and consequently to walk away from an experience of drama more alive than we have ever been before.

The dramatic performance is primarily visual, but it cannot achieve maximum effectiveness without support from the spoken word. Verbal language announces the meaning of movement and action; also it illumines and clarifies. Decisions resulting from the experience of meeting life in action are arrived at before an audience. Speech divides the ambiguous from the nonambiguous. The words of a drama help man to make and transmit man's decisions. Therefore, drama is a unique art form because it presents life in action culminated in decision-making which makes it possible for this action to lead to more life in action.

Drama is also unique in that its substance is embodied in flesh, blood, bone, and voice. The artist is a creator of symbols. The dramatic artist uses symbols that are human beings. Symbols in painting, literature, and music are created of a nonhuman substance. Therefore, more interpretation is needed for these art forms. The drama speaks to the audience most directly. We in the audience are met directly by the

15

minds, expressions, gestures, and decisions of the performers. Their acts and decisions readily become ours. The substance from which the symbols are created is the same substance of the audience. Performers and audience are one in the raw material and the subject matter of the drama. Contrasted with other art forms little translation or interpretation of the symbols is necessary for the performers and the audience to participate as an organic whole in perceiving the portend of the life depicted in the drama. Readily we see, hear, feel, understand, believe or disbelieve, and accept or reject what the dramatist says to us about life.

Because of the closeness of experience in the drama to that of the audience, because of its directness and immediacy, it can be easily forgotten that drama is not reality. Drama, more than other art forms, can reach us in ways that seem astonishingly real and true. Yet drama must never be confused with or strive to pass for reality. If this happens drama ceases to be drama and its value is lost. No matter how real the performers may seem or how lifelike their problems, actions, and decisions, drama to be drama must always be the illusion of reality. This nonreal, illusory, and artificial nature of drama explains its power, worth, and necessity for us. Great drama is never a record or photograph of ourselves but a re-creation of ourselves by way of the mind of the dramatist. This allows us to see ourselves from his point of view.

Drama exists only in performance. Because its life is fabricated and fictionalized, selected and organized, contrived and controlled, it can happen only in the shape and form of a created object—the play. It is not something we encounter on the street; it is the creative work of the dramatist. It does not exist in the mind of the reader of a script. Its existence is in the tangible, physical life in action mounted on a stage. It is a production that has emerged from expanding, compressing, and arbitrarily creating. The play is an artistic expression that has reality, and it is more real than reality itself. The reality of a play is fabricated from the most meaningful and significant moments of many moments, of many lives, of millions of words. It is a created nexus of movement, crisis, and language which has the power to condition the future living of those who experience the play. By way of living persons who interact upon each other in such a way that they interact with the audience it unfolds a story. The participating experience of the audience is so important that drama can be complete and alive only in the presence of an audience. A play is designed for performance, and it is born when it gathers more life to itself by way of the response of an audience. Response resulting from the sharing of the experience is integral to the reality of the drama. This sharing of the meaning of the play by the actors with the audience provides the essence of drama. The spectator ceases to be spectator as the play gets under way, because he projects himself imaginatively into a participation with the destiny of the characters in the performance.

This sharing takes place by empathy. A member of the audience does not feel merely sympathetic for the characters and identify himself as an observer of the crisis or problem; he is actually *in* the crisis to such an extent that the crisis is his, the problem is his, the dilemmas and potentialities of the characters are his, and the actors are himself. His projection into them and their introjection into him result in the experience being an organic whole. The response of the audience may be hisses or bravoes. The response that is the result of the sharing, whether it be rejection or acceptance, makes the miracle of drama take place. By this empathic experience, according to Aristotle, as well as to contemporary psychological thought, man is purged of the emotions of pity and fear. To this classic concept of catharsis and its function in the theater John Gassner adds "enlightenment" to pity and fear. "In tragedy," he writes, "there is always a precipitate of final enlightenment —some inherent, cumulative, realized, understanding . . . a clear comprehension of what was involved in the struggle, an understanding of cause and effect, a judgment on what we have witnessed, and our induced state of mind that places it above the riot of passion." [1]

The spectator is so much a participant that he is emotionally aroused and later intellectually able to rise above passion to make a judgment. The director of a dramatic performance is aware of this end to be sought; he is involved in the action on the stage, and yet he maintains an awareness of the feeling and enlightenment of the audience so that he may direct the moment when passion is transformed to judgment. He is responsible for the final enlightenment following the understanding of the cause and effect working in the play which will bring about a verdict in the lives of the audience. The emotions shared by the audience, the purging that has taken place, the enlightenment, the residue of judgment, and the decision making that takes place are culminated in a re-creative experience. By way of the experience cast in a creation of the dramatist, the member of the audience experiences its re-creation in and for himself; this constitutes the aesthetic experience of drama. The efficacy of the play is derived from the depth and extent of the sharing of the performance. The member of the audience leaves the theater as a re-created human being. Because of the creative work of the dramatist and performers the audience becomes changed human beings. Participants have been re-created, and the power and permanence of this re-creation is the yardstick for the measurement of the greatness of the dramatic experience.

The form of the drama from which this re-creative experience is distilled is called a play. The root meaning of "play" is illusion; literally, the word means "in play" (*illuderi*). Drama happens when we are in play.

From infancy play is vital for us. We cannot grow into human beings without an abundance of play in our lives. It must go on from birth to death. Children play being grown-up. By way of the enlightenment they receive from play, they learn, experience, and grow into maturing human beings. Child's play is acting which has a social function.[2] It is a voluntary and craved activity which incorporates movement, action, conflict, and language. Play is fabricated from tensions which result from the eagerness to achieve the ends in view. Play has form and rules. In play a boy may stab his sister with a rubber knife, but play is over when the weapon ceases to be an imaginary one. Play remains play as long as it is of an illusory and imaginative nature. Masks and disguises are essential to play. They represent the creation of an image or symbol or the realization of a desired appearance which substitutes for the real. ("Only the drama, because of its intrinsically functional character, its quality of being actions, remains permanently linked to play." [3])

Advanced chronological age does not take away the need for play. Adults also must play, participate in make-believe, and open floodgates of re-creative activity. Because of this need we have had art with us from the beginning of time. Art is man's play. We do not find any people anywhere at anytime whose culture is devoid of some kind of expression that seems to serve no function other than art for the sake of art. Much activity serves religious needs, but we also find decoration and artistic expression that serve no function other than the need to express. Art, therefore, is no luxury to be engaged in in times of leisure or peace. It is a vital part of life, whenever we find it.

Dromenon, from which the word "drama" comes, was something acted in a performance or contest. It focuses our attention on the play as action, as illusion, and as expression of our enjoyment. The play, the form of drama, therefore is an illusion of life which is acted out as if it were actuality. It shows action rather than talks about it. It does not paint life but sets it before us. It shows man's interior nature working itself out as an objective fact.

"Man's interior nature working itself out" indicates the uniqueness of dramatic expression as contrasted to theatrical expression, if by theatrical expression is meant spectacle and the spectacular. Louis Adamic suggests that the drama of things is the truth of things to the extent that if one perceives the drama of a thing one perceives the truth of it. To write truthfully, then, is to write dramatically. The dramatic is our interior nature expressing itself truthfully in the apparent symbols of human beings.

To write truthfully, and therefore to write dramatically, means that the theatrical may be a blind alley. The production aids of lighting, scenery, costuming, and makeup may enhance a dramatic presentation, but they are aids to help create and sustain the illusion. Drama can come into being with a minimum of these so that sometimes by an excess or misuse of production aids drama is obliterated.

Theatrical is identified with theater—an institution that has emerged in most civilizations. Since the beginning of recorded time, in every culture the essentially dramatic of existential experience has sought a place where it may be presented. The production aids of theater are largely the results of the needs of the place where performances occur. The play can come alive both in the theater or outside the theater; in fact the miracle can happen anywhere. Strolling players who performed in the open, the masques presented in English and French courts, and space-staging which uses all sorts of playing areas are evidence that a theater building is not necessary. The truth of the idea, theme, characters, and conflict can be so potent that the audience may be unaware of the presence or absence of aids. Drama can exist without the theater but the theater cannot exist without drama.

For the fullest enjoyment of theater, however, all production aids may be of value, and for pageantry and spectacle they are essential. They can enhance and enrich the power of the dramatic experience. Their cumulative effect lends excitement that only theater can have. Yet, despite their value, they remain auxiliary to the necessities of drama as an art form. The theatrical in the drama is present to the extent that it is essential. Production aids are to be used to the extent that the dramatic form may have its finest support and expression, so that it may best communicate to performers and the audience.

The theater may be a vehicle for the presentation of truthful and spiritual subject matter, but frequently it is an institution surviving on trivia. To make it more marketable bits and pieces of showmanship used for titillation are tacked onto a play. When great drama is presented in the theater, or away from the theater, the subject matter is so integral that it cannot be tampered with. It is an entity, a reality in itself. Great drama should not be victimized by peripheral theatrics or showmanship. The uncompromised taste and judgment of the writer is combined with the taste and judgment of the director in order to create a vicarious experience for members of the audience. The production aids of the theater, along with the producer, the director, and the actors, are tools for the realization of the intention and purpose of the dramatist.

A play which is a work of art has its own truth, and it must be re-created and judged in the light of its truth. As a created object it awaits interpretative insights from the mind of the director to give it actualization in physical space and time. The good play effectively rendered captures attention and holds an audience in an attitude of responding. The play may concern itself with a small segment of life, but this small segment, in some way or another, has pertinency to a large framework of experience. It allows one to walk with common men and kings, to become one with the great and small of humanity, and to have a re-created perspective on all of life. The play, like other art forms, rids men of differences which, despite their superficiality, may blind them to each other. Morals, politics, and time and space distances may be perceived in perspective and set aside by way of art which unites human beings on an instinctual, intimate, and universalizing level.

This responsibility for perceiving truthfully in order that we may present and experience truthfully is not limited to dramatists of the past. To get the truth of a French dramatist of the twentieth century, we must see him and hold him in those limiting aspects of his culture and milieu. To judge the contemporary playwright of Japan in the context of American drama or vice versa is absurd and false.

The greatness of drama lies in its capacity to contribute to the spiritual growth of man. It can succeed in uniting the whole man with the whole of another man, so that the result of the encounter will be growth of many kinds. The subject matter of the play and the content of the dramatic experience provide the bridge between the performer and the audience or between man and man. By way of this bridge communication that is profound and relatively total takes place. Communication that takes place fulfills the original meaning of the word "communication," which is the sharing of suffering, wealth, property, and experience until they become one. Ben Jonson spoke of "the thousands who communicate our loss." When sufficient life is made common by way of the experiencing of drama, communication is restored to its original meaning, "communion." The consequence of persons meeting persons in such a way that actors and audience commune results in their being transformed into a community. When one feels this is happening in a theater, a school, a church, or under a tent, he can know he has experienced the miracle of drama. When drama communicates truth and results in spiritual growth, revelation and rediscovery of meanings and values in life are taking place.

Drama, then, like other arts, is that which keeps us from wasting our minds, energies, and lives. It shows us a way to a better way and puts us to work saving what is worthy of being saved that we and others possess. Because the dramatic experience has shown how the redemption of life takes place we are saved from the stupidities and losses of our past selves. Drama, both in and out of the theater, can lay its stern and uncompromising reality upon us, irritating and arousing us to the realization of the way we must go in doing our duty to fulfill our destinies. This is a religious experience.

The danger of theater is greater than that of other art forms. When the raw material and subject matter are one—that is, the human being is the vehicle of the art form—reality of the human being and reality of the dramatic experience come threateningly close. They so mingle that the hazard of substitution of realities is precarious, and it is fatal to both when fusing exists. The creators of dramatic experience may unknowingly substitute their reality in life-as-it-is for life-in-the-theater or in dramatic experience. This paves the road for an escape from reality. When this happens drama has lost its value, and its practitioners are our enemies. The unrealized perfection we can experience by way of the drama is confused with perfected reality and the illusion becomes delusion. Drama and theater fail us when they become so satisfying that we are content. The power of the drama lies in its capacity to arouse, to stimulate, and to irritate.

Drama shows us what ought to be. It is on the move toward perfection of the individual and the social order. It presents the will of man in conflict with the yet-to-be-created or the already-created which is destroying man. This is also its miracle. By way of dramatic experience we can have a sense of fulfillment and delight. It can be so powerful and so wonderful we are jolted when the curtain comes down and the spell is broken. This hypnotic experience of how life could be or what it is yet to be, despite its being made today frequently in negative statements, can carry us off into constructive or destructive fantasy-making. Drama can fill or empty us. No other art form can so bewitch or inspire us.

The purpose of this book is to explore ways in which drama can find its deepest meanings and realize them in dramatic terms. When this happens drama will have religious meaning wherever it is born.

Notes

[1] J. A. Withey, "Action in Life and in Drama," *The American Educational Theatre Journal*, X, N. 3 (October, 1958) 234, quoting John Gassner, *European Theories of the Drama*, ed., Barrett H. Clark (Rev. ed.; New York: Crown Publishers, 1947), p. 550.

[2] For a full treatment of the play theory of life see Johan Huizinga, *Homo Ludens, A Study of Play Element in Culture* (Boston: Beacon Press, 1955).

[3] *Ibid.*, p. 144.

Chapter II

THE PLAY

A. Structure

A PLAY IS THE ACTUALIZATION OF A SEGMENT OF LIFE IN A TIME SEQUENCE brought to life by characters whose action and speech are relevant to the crisis moment in which they have been caught. The form of the play can be defined by episodes that are called scenes and acts. These are usually arranged in an order of rising action to culminate in a climax.

Contemporary playwrights are not overly concerned about traditional techniques of playwriting. They are, nevertheless, still concerned about the adequate realization of the story in a form that uses action and dialogue and that has a beginning and rising action culminating in an end when the tension or tensions giving rise to dramatic action are at least temporarily resolved. That many contemporary plays do follow this formula is only evidence of the vitality and freshness of the dramatists.

Aristotle in the *Poetics* suggests six components of a good play. He gives as his leading argument a worthy theme. This can often be expressed in a sentence which might be called a topic sentence. It is the idea of the play, the subject, the dramatic situation, the idea behind the tension situation that is being treated. The use of the word "worthy" is significant because it defines the subject matter in a particular way. For Aristotle tragedy has to have a sublime, elevated theme.

The second characteristic of a good play is that it shall have convincing characters. By this is meant characters in which the audience can believe, whose semblance of reality is sufficiently apparent to make them convincing. In Greek drama the characters were likely to be legendary heroes or gods whom the audience knew. The dramatist was bound by this knowledge and had to use it convincingly.

The next component was a well-knit plot, which can be explained as

23

a plot that holds together, that is fastened by events which lead from one to the other so that the audience is kept interested and attentive. This is inherent in Aristotle's concept of the unity of action.

The concept of memorable diction is less appreciated today because we would probably not use the word memorable. We would suggest that the diction in a good play ought to be characteristic, that it ought to belong to the characters. This does not mean that it cannot be memorable. Unfortunately our idea of memorable diction is likely to be related to its use by Shakespeare or one of the other great classical dramatists. So it should, but it should also cause us to look for the approximation of this in all plays. Too much of our dialogue is undistinguished and commonplace.

Contributing melody may mean either the melody of the words themselves as they are spoken or the use of melody accompanying the words. Just to hear Greek spoken gives an idea of what melody could have meant. Music was used in the theater as an expression of the mood and feeling of the play. We have revived music to express emotion which words alone may be unable to do. Along *with* action and dialogue, not merely as accompanying action and dialogue, music contributes to the play. Our stage has been the poorer because we have lost the melody of language as well as the melody of music.

Aristotle's last component is attendant spectacle. This allows for spectacle as an inherent aspect of theater. One can readily understand this in the Greek theater. Its size, its needs for physical proportions in the actors, and for the use of masks all lent the air of spectacle to the performance.

A play is an art form—a form which can be described in terms as distinctive as those in architecture, graphic arts, or music. It is a form that is characterized by dramatic limitations prescribed by the tension which the writer is treating.

The tensions that cause dramatic situations may be between the "selves" in a man, between what is often called his "higher" and his "lower" self, between the positive and the negative, the healthy and the unhealthy forces in his own personality. Tensions also arise in man between his will and that of another because of antagonisms, ambitions, et cetera. A play can also show the tension between a man and his ultimate destiny, between what he is and what he wants to be.

In Greek drama the tension was often between a man and his fate—

as, for example, in *Oedipus Rex*—or between a man, however great, and his gods—*Prometheus Bound*. Most contemporary plays actualize the tensions between men seen in social situations in the home, in business, or in politics. We are no longer able to blame the gods or our fates for the dilemmas through which our tensions are expressed. Psychology has explained these in terms of variations from norms and in conditionings which can be understood and dealt with. Many of our tensions arise today out of ignorance of their causes or out of our unwillingness to face them and seek their resolution. Drama uses these to the best advantage.

Characters

Tensions are always expressed through characterization in emotionally charged situations even when their origin has been intellectually conceived. Shaw "discusses" many things in his plays, but conversations on any questions are never dramatically interesting until they are emotionally expressed. Characterization simply means the way in which the dramatist has shaped the persons who are the people of his story.

In ancient drama the characters were usually well-known figures. They acted according to their known characteristics—the hero like the personage known in the story, the king according to the legend which has been built around him. All kings had much in common. Any minute differentiation in character that made for idiosyncracy was practically unknown. It could not be communicated under the conditions of the classic theater.

Later drama was to present persons as types; this is seen to an excellent advantage in the commedia dell' arte of Italy and in the morality plays of the Continent and England. The morality plays used characters that represented moral qualities or conditions or outstanding characteristics of human beings—vices and virtues. Some of the more recent plays of the contemporary stage are also endeavoring to focus attention on qualities and situations rather than on the idiosyncracies of the characters.

Some of the post-World War I dramatists, particularly writers like Georg Kaiser, Elmer Rice, and a few of the Soviet playwrights, named their characters as numbers—for example, Mr. Zero—or by the generic title Man, Woman, Child. They were able to universalize them so that they became symbols rather than individuals. They often represented classes of men, such as the manual worker or the white-collar worker, with the characterization conceived in broad strokes with little sense of a particular person. This seemed good for social drama where conflicts concerned classes of people rather than individuals. It served certain kinds of drama which were written to convict on social issues. Too much individualization in character may cause the audience to "look at" a person and to miss the overall social meaning. It is often easier for the audience to identify itself with broader characteristics of mankind or with social groups rather than with individuals in the group. Too often the audience can escape identification by insisting that the character is peculiar, a unique person, and therefore unrecognizable. (Witness reaction to the characters in Tennessee Williams' plays.) There is no empathy when this happens, no identification, no realization of "There, but for the grace of God, go I."

The epic theater of Bertolt Brecht takes another interesting point of view by distrusting the emotions when they are used merely for the sake of emotions. The spectator does not experience empathy, although he must be awakened in order to make decisions. The theater, for Brecht, communicates knowledge by *putting action in front of the spectator.* Each scene in a Brecht play exists for itself, and its social reality determines what man thinks. These concepts have aroused the contemporary dramatist and have made Brecht a highly controversial figure. The traditional idea of the play has been challenged by an extraordinarily intelligent playwright and man of the theater.

In the Renaissance the figures in a play began to take on real characteristics identified by their individuality. Hamlet was a prince; he acted like a prince, and everyone knew him as a prince. But what a unique person Hamlet was! What a different sort of prince! Characters in tragedy were usually of the upper classes or of royalty. Not until a century after the renaissance of drama in England were tragedies written about ordinary men, about the common man.

American drama today is not only the drama of the common man; it is also the drama of man exhibited with idiosyncracies, with evidences of difference from rather than likeness to his fellow men. So far has this gone in some realistic plays that audiences are likely to leave a performance asking where such characters came from or where they live? Are they not the pathetic inventions of the diseased mind of the dramatist? Is the theater a clinic for psychological analysis? We have so individualized characters, so made them into freaks, that there seems to be little universality in them. They are not the common man because we have nothing in common with them—that is, unless we are ready to admit that all mankind is sick and that we are freaks instead of individuals.

The dramatist is limited by the need to introduce his characters speedily and yet thoroughly. A person appears and by his speech and action assumes a character. As persons act and speak in a play, their characters are revealed. They must be true to their characters, and the dramatist is compelled to make them "develop" because they are the people they are. The inexperienced writer is likely to be guilty of over-simplification of character and of thereby making people fit an idea or fulfill a role. When an actor begins to bring a character to life the audience can readily see whether the dramatist has been honest, whether he has made this man or this woman speak and act as they do because they are the people they are. Development of character calls for clarifi- · cation as well as revelation.

Careless dramatists are likely to oversimplify all characterization—a minister has certain characteristics, he speaks and acts like a minister; a doctor, a teacher, or a lawyer all speak and act like the professional figures they represent. This leads to caricature rather than characterization. Perhaps the reason why such caricatures are disappearing from drama is that they are disappearing from the contemporary scene. There is no typical doctor, apothecary, lawyer, and—lingeringly and slowly on the way out—no typical teacher or minister.

Characters are distinguished by appearance and by speech. What they are is revealed and clarified by what we call their characteristics—their appearance, speech, and action. What they are outwardly, however, is the revelation of what they are beneath the surface. The dramatist must know his characters thoroughly, so that he can let them reveal themselves through what they look like, what they say, and what they do. This, as has been suggested, is a process of clarification as well as revelation.

Plot

Characters are related to each other and reveal themselves through what is called a plot—the structure of the story that has enmeshed the characters. A plot is a contrived, connected narrative.

Plot is revealed at the beginning of a play by the exposition made possible through characters in a given situation. The exposition is executed by means of characters who may be a prologue or by any group of characters important to and integral to later, connected events in the story of the play. The dramatist must interest the audience at once. There is no opportunity in contemporary plays to lose time, to talk or act without motivation that leads directly into the tension situation with which the play deals. Greek plays used the chorus for exposition; Elizabethan playwrights often introduced minor characters to give information to the audience. All plays must tell the events that happened before the play began which lead up to the action of the play, so that the audience knows the circumstances of the action. They must know why the dramatist chose this beginning and why there could be no other.

Plot is introduced by the opening exposition to establish the beginning action and to introduce the people related to the action. It develops by revealing the tension, or what has been called the problem of the play. The development of the plot in most plays proceeds to a climax which usually has been foreshadowed by a series of crises. These crises build up to the heightened tension moment *to* which the plot moves and *from* which it moves to what we call the end. The end is merely the resolution of the main tension or problem that the plot has treated. It is not necessarily a solution of the problem although it may be. It is, however, the resolution of the particular tension, the settling for the moment, at least, of the problem that has been the basis of the plot.

Dialogue

Dialogue is manipulated conversation. It is conversation with a purpose. If one considered how much of his conversation is without any main purpose he would realize that when conversation is used for dialogue it must be cleaned up, condensed, and pointed. Our conversation is not ordinarily consciously pointed, and, therefore, it needs pruning to give it the compactness and direction necessary for a play.

Every word spoken in a play should have a necessary function. Words are active in a play just as bodily action is, and they constitute one of the distinguishing characteristics of drama. The function of dialogue, like that of action, is to move the plot forward and to reveal character. In what are often called "literary" plays dialogue takes on importance as poetry or prose, and the play may have literary as well as dramatic significance. The plays of Shakespeare, as well as those of T. S. Eliot, Sean O'Casey, and Christopher Fry of our own day, contain dialogue that is dramatically sound and yet strikingly effective as literature.

Obviously, good dialogue "belongs" to the character; it is characteristic of the person speaking it. It reveals the period of the play, the social status of the characters, and the geographical area from which they come. It is actually the most revealing thing about the characters.

B. Types of Plays

Dramatic form has been distinguished by four major types: Tragedy, comedy, farce, and melodrama. None is easy to define exactly, and none is a tight compartment which excludes other forms that are closely related. At various times and with various types of plays, dramatic historians have distinguished plays as histories, as problem plays, as "serious" plays that are not tragedies, as tragicomedies, as farce-comedies, as farce-melodramas, and as burlesque. The four main forms do call for a fifth—a play which is not strictly speaking a comedy and yet is not a tragedy. This type of play is serious and usually centers around a problem. More than likely it is a serious play that is motivated by characters in a situation which is not intrinsically the stuff of comedy and yet, at the same time, is not tragic. We have no name for such a type of play. It is often referred to just as "a drama." Shakespeare's *Merchant of Venice,* Ibsen's *The Doll's House,* Shaw's *Saint Joan,* and T. S. Eliot's *The Cocktail Party* are interesting examples of serious plays that are not strictly speaking comedy. Even the four main forms have been defined differently in various periods of the history of the drama.

Tragedy [1]

The oldest and most often quoted definition of tragedy is that of Aristotle in his *Poetics:* "Tragedy is an imitation of an action that is serious, complete, and of a certain magnitude; in language embellished with each kind of artistic ornament, the several kinds being found in separate parts of the play; in the form of action not of narrative; through pity and fear affecting the proper purgation of those emotions."

This classic definition covers the essential characteristics of all good drama—action, serious treatment, completion, certain magnitude of worth, good language, and empathy that causes the spectator to be purged especially of certain emotions. "Tragedy," says James H. Clay, "is a closed form. The last scene of a tragedy is not merely the establishment of balance; it marks an absolute terminus, to which a sequel is unthinkable." [2]

John Gassner suggests that in tragedy the characters play "for keeps" rather than for the audience. We have come to associate high seriousness, motivated human conduct having social as well as psychological causation, with tragedy. The calamity may be a means of "achieving significant revelations concerning character."

The conflict in a play that leads to tragic consequences is characterized by the quality of the antagonists and their proportions as men. When man is overcome so that he is defeated by evil forces against which he struggles his is a tragic fate. He may fight against his baser self; he may be in conflict with other men or with groups of men in society. He may combat powers higher than himself and be overcome by them. He may defy God and be defeated.

W. H. Auden said:

> Greek tragedy is the tragedy of necessity; i.e., the feeling aroused in the spectator is "What a pity it had to be this way"; Christian tragedy is the tragedy of possibility, "What a pity it was this way when it might have been otherwise"; the *hubris*, which is the flaw in the Greek hero's character, is the illusion of a man who knows himself and believes that nothing can shake that strength, while the corresponding Christian sin of pride is the illusion of a man who knows himself weak but believes he can by his own efforts transcend that weakness and become strong.[3]

Tragedy used to concern itself only with lofty or exalted characters; the subject matter was also always lofty. The certain "magnitude" in Aristotle's definition is a different way of stating this. In a few plays before the nineteenth century and in most plays since Ibsen we have accepted ordinary people as persons of tragic dimensions. Some contemporary plays that are either intrinsically tragic or have overtones of tragedy of the ordinary man are Ibsen's Ghosts and Hedda Gabler; Strindberg's The Father; Tolstoi's The Power of Darkness; Gorki's The Lower Depths; O'Neill's The Hairy Ape, Desire Under the Elms, Mourning Becomes Electra, and The Ice Man Cometh; Giraudoux's Electra; Cocteau's The Infernal Machine; and Maxwell Anderson's Winterset and his Elizabethan trilogy.

Death is not inevitable in tragedy. To live may be more profoundly tragic than to die. One should not feel depressed after seeing a great tragedy. The exalted tragedy of Greek drama leaves one with a sense of the splendor of life, its magnificence and its stature. Tragedy demands great characters in significant tension situations.

Contemporary drama, as we can see from the plays we have just enumerated, has produced tragedies. These may be fewer in number because theater as escape or a commercial commodity demands pleasant plays that entertain in a particular way. In his play *Marco Millions* Eugene O'Neill has Marco voice the dilemma of the modern theater:

> There's nothing better than to sit down in a good seat at a good play after a good day's work in which you know you've accomplished something, and after you've had a good dinner, and just take it easy and enjoy a good wholesome thrill or a good laugh and get your mind off serious things until it's time to go to bed.[4]

The popular problem play may have tragic implications, but its characters usually are not of the stature to be capable of tragic consequences. They are, more likely than not, little people caught up in little problems. Too often the theme capable of tragic proportions has become thesis. The characters are manipulated to satisfy the problem situation. The audience never gets to know or understand them—they are too busy working out the problem!

The lack of tragedy today may also be indicative of our surface living or of the numbing of sensitivity in a world where death and violence are accepted passively on both a small and large scale. The tragic consequences of Hamlet pale before the colossal potential tragedy of the atomic age. When one of today's major playwrights takes death and destruction for granted, having lived through two world wars—it is obvious that life for him can only be seen as ironic. The absurd, in Camus' phraseology, is characteristic of so much of life today. When a genuinely sensitive writer is able to get perspective on man as he is and as he might be he will almost be forced to write out of the anguish of his soul, and his drama is likely to be tragedy.

Comedy

No form of art is more vague in definition than comedy. To the plays of Aristophanes and to the most recent farce, the term comedy is applied. All plays except tragedy are broadly comedy. An examination of some characteristics of the comic may help to clarify the meaning of comedy.

Comedy is a matter of perspective, yet it is a certain kind of perspective. What is funny depends on where you stand. A pathetic old woman may be tragic when she is viewed as a social derelict or as a lonely, disregarded person. She may appear highly amusing when she is seen as a beggar acting the role of a choosy old woman. A drunk can scarcely be called a comic character; yet from Shakespeare to the present time some of the finest comedy scenes have involved characters who are inebriated. Comedy often results because the surface view is funny when beneath the comic the scene is serious and many times tragic.

A matter of perspective and knowledge! What happens to characters on a stage may be sad to them and highly humorous to the audience because the audience sees and knows much more than the people involved in the scene. Some of the funniest scenes in drama are humorous only because the spectators are aware of situations which the characters themselves cannot possibly know. The humor of most comedies of situations comes from this possibility. The ludicrous is very often the incongruous.

Older tragedy, as we have said, needed royalty and high birth for its characters. From the beginning of drama, comedy has treated all types of characters. Certain characters have been considered too sacred or too serious to be humorously treated; yet the medieval plays indicate that even God may have a sense of humor and that the most sacred characters can be funny. The fact that Satan was so often the source of humor may be the reason why sin and vice have many times been the source of comedy. Contemporary realistic dramatists are likely to take sin and vice seriously, to treat them in a sociologically analytical fashion and to find in them theological importance. Humor often depends on the accepted status of persons and their positions in a given society. Court fools are difficult to understand today and seem too often sad and pathetic. Strangely enough, this was the condition of the court fool—he was at once a brilliant wag and often a slightly unbalanced mental case. This mixture of personality is seen in the Fool in *King Lear*, a very comic and yet tragic figure.

To poke fun at anything is to criticize it. The line between comedy and satire is often difficult to see. People laugh at satire which holds up to ridicule and derision individual or social follies or shortcomings. When the ridicule is broad and obvious satire becomes burlesque. Satire is used to intensify incongruities, usually with an intent to provoke change for the better. Vice can be exposed and discredited through satire. When something is burlesqued it is so exaggerated that it is likely to be less severely criticized—in fact burlesque is less cruel, less trenchant than satire. Aristophanes, Shakespeare, Molière, Gay, Gilbert and Sullivan, Wilde, and Shaw are the authors of some of the world's great comedies, and they are the greatest of satirists.

Humor gives new perspective and thus presents fresh points of view. The humorous scenes in Shakespeare's *Henry IV* show Prince Hal and Falstaff with their disreputable friends. Hal in these scenes is an entirely different person from the man who meets Hotspur in battle or his father in the king's chamber. The humor fills out an all-around portrait and makes Hal one of the most intriguing characters in all Shakespeare. Hamlet with the gravediggers takes on new dimensions of tragic importance because of this comic interlude.

Divisions of comedy into high and low comedy, sentimental comedy, and comedies of manners and of character are not important except as these names indicate the special comic emphasis. A study of Molière, probably the greatest writer of comedy, reveals all types of the comic form.

Farce is comedy which treats improbable and impossible situations as if they were probable and possible. Farce is laughed at because it is improbable, and yet it is presented as if it could actually happen. It becomes hilarious because the audience knows its absurdity and yet enjoys seeing it presented.

Studies of contemporary comedy indicate that dramatists like Ionesco and Adamov are humorous because of the devastating satire which underlies the surface situation. This is humor of a high quality. Unfortunately, most humor today is on a lower level. It is obvious and often insulting to the intelligence. Where it is found, it may take its measure from the cartoon or comic strip. It is broad and lacks subtlety. A culture may be characterized by its humor. Drama from 1890 to the First World War had many excellent writers of comedy. Certainly, the comedies of Henry Arthur Jones, Arthur Wing Pinero, Oscar

Wilde, George Bernard Shaw, the early Noël Coward, and John van Druten are some of the best in English literature. Comedy declined after the Second World War as it became an escape from the tragic realities of life. It has never regained its status in the theater.

The lack of humor in religious drama is one of its most serious deficiencies. A good sense of humor is an adult accomplishment. It indicates a security that is without fear of ridicule. Humor humanizes and changes —and it is necessary in a sane life. It is a catharsis that religion and the church need.

Melodrama

The play in which the story dominates is called a melodrama. Character is subservient to story. What happens, "how the story comes out," is all-important. Unfortunately, the form has been identified with a type of play popular in the nineteenth century—the sentimental, over emotionalized, unrealistic drama found in *Uncle Tom's Cabin*, *The Girl of the Golden West*, and *Ten Nights in a Bar Room*. For the most part melodrama has been taken over today by movies and television because these media can tell a story with greater detail and with better facilities. The mass-communications media cater to the tastes of the public because they "who live to please must please to live." Soap operas and wild-west stories which once belonged to the theater now have found a better home.

Melodrama is also characterized by action; slowing down kills it. The form of drama which we now call melodrama comes from the plays of a century ago that used music to arouse the emotions. Music has disappeared, for the most part, but the adventure and the thrills are still characteristic of the melodramatic play. Detailed characterization impedes the story and, therefore, is not wanted. Type characters are easily recognizable and speed the action. Episode follows on episode, and pace is all important.

What must be emphasized again is that most plays embody several types of dramatic treatment. Shakespeare's tragedies contain comedy scenes which only heighten the dramatic impact. Many plays have elements of melodrama, so that character is subservient to plot. It is important only to recognize the great variety of forms, to appreciate the merging of forms in one play, and to enjoy the way drama has used all these forms in the involvement of face-to-face relationships.

Notes

[1] For a detailed analysis of Greek tragedy see Chapter I, Francis Fergusson, *The Idea of a Theatre* (Garden City, N. Y.: Doubleday & Company, Inc., 1953). In this book Professor Fergusson discusses the tragic rhythm of action, the actor and the theater of reason, the actor and the theater of passion, and the analogy of action, using *Oedipus Rex*, *Bérénice*, *Tristan and Isolde*, and *Hamlet* as examples of these forms of action. Various critical writings on tragedy are excellently condensed in Barret H. Clark, *European Theories of the Drama* (New York: Crown Publishers, Inc., 1947).

The best discussion of modern tragedy is found in John Gassner, *Theatre at the Crossroads* (New York: Holt, Rinehart & Winston, Inc., 1960). See especially Chapter V, Parts I and II.

[2] James H. Clay, "A New Theory of Tragedy," *The American Educational Theatre Journal*, VIII, n. 4 (December, 1956), 296-97.

[3] From the book review section of the *New York Times* (December 16, 1945). Used by permission.

[4] Act II, scene 1. Used by permission of Random House.

Chapter III

TYPES OF DRAMATIC EXPRESSION:
FORMAL DRAMA

A. The Formal Play

FROM THE GREAT GREEK CLASSICAL PERIOD TO THE PRESENT TIME THE dramatic form has been known as a "play." Significantly enough, a play is a form that has grown and changed throughout the history of drama. It is always a representation of life—always life seen through the imagination of the writer. A play differs from all other art forms in that it is an action using characters in a situation which begins at a certain time and continues until the situation undertaken leads to another or is completed so that further action is impossible. A play is action at a particular time of tension in the lives of the characters. The action continues until the tension is resolved—until the specific tension or tensions for the time being are released.

Tensions may arise so that the outward acting of the play is largely taken up with the internal struggle in a man as he makes a choice between a constructive or a destructive action. It may be an action that consists of a struggle with conscience or with whatever a man conceives as his god. For the Greeks the tension was often between the gods and man or between man's fate and his own will. Medieval drama developed plays on biblical themes, using the story of the fall of man, the sacrifice of Isaac, the sufferings of Job, the birth of Jesus and its meaning in terms of the ultimate revelations of God and the redemption of man, and the events of the Passion of Jesus. All of these were used because the tensions between constructive and destructive forces were evident and capable of being put into action.

A play may be founded on real situations, but, as we have suggested,

36

it is more than reality itself. The dramatist takes the situation he wishes to treat, cuts away all unnecessary material and presents the action through a scene or a series of scenes in which the characters act by means of physical movement and speech. The only physical movement that can be shown must be within the confines of the playing area—a room, a street, a place in a road, or some location, real or imaginary. The action is circumscribed by the limitations of the space and the verisimilitude of the movement as it might be in real life. The action of a play usually has a coherence in that it must begin, rise to some kind of climax, and then resolve itself in the denouement of the story. To be most effective, it must be designed to be interesting, utilitarian, and graceful. The performance of a play has always been a visual thing. It is what the audience sees. For this reason the playing space must be lighted to enable the spectators to see the action and to transmit the necessary dramatic information about the scene—the time of day, the mood of the play.

The formal play is intended to be produced before an audience that not only sees but also participates vicariously in the action. The dramatist labors for others as well as for himself. A work of art, says Ernest Grosse, presupposes a public just as much at it does an artist. "It seems safe to say that no art form would have come into existence if it were not for the hope of an audience, real or imaginary." [1] A play is always to be judged by its technical excellence, by the way in which, through action and dialogue, it presents the situation and holds the interest of the spectator and involves him in the action.

By being involved in the action, the audience, it is understood, will feel the effect of participation or "empathy." Empathy has been defined as *Einfühlung*, a feeling into, when one's own personality is merged and fused into that of some external thing. When one has sympathy for something, he is feeling *for*; when he has empathy, he is feeling *with* —he has the sense of being merged in the object or emotional experience.

Formal drama calls for a finished performance. This is discussed in other parts of the book. What is necessary to insist upon here is that the adjective "finished" characterizes the quality of the performance. Obviously no production in its first performance is ever finished. One could wish that any play carefully and sincerely produced might have more than one performance so that actors could grow in their roles, and the ensemble playing could take on the unity that is characteristic of the truly finished performance.

Too often plays done by amateurs are presented before the cast has learned its lines or before the actors, because they have been occupied with memorizing lines, have a sense of their characters. Too often production problems hinder a finished performance. The costumes have been completed just in time to wear for a dress rehearsal, yet all actors know that historic costumes may be strange and unwieldy when they have not been lived in. Lights may also cause confusion when actors find themselves in the places where the blocking of the action has been rehearsed but where lighting has not been prepared for. The actor finds himself in the dark and moves not out of necessity for the meaning of the play but out of the necessity to have his face seen.

A finished play is arrived at by a process that can be mapped out as definitely as an itinerary of a trip. In the chapter "The Play Comes Alive" a rehearsal and production schedule is given. Productions of formal plays will take longer, and less concentrated work can be done. Rehearsals will have to be worked in and around all kinds of activities. The director knows that in the weeks before the performance much time will be needed, and unless the actors and production crews can manage to give this time formal drama to be acted before an audience must not be undertaken. Dramatic activities which take less time, play-readings and role-playing, should be substituted. There is no shortcut to good performances, just as there is no shortcut to any other artistic endeavor.

B. The Pageant

Religious drama has often been condemned because it brings to mind the old church pageant which was usually given at Christmas time, on children's day, or on whatever occasion called for the participation of the whole church school. When these ill-conceived performances were derisively called "nightgown nightmares" they were aptly named. Usually the participants were either too embarrassed to want to be associated with them or enjoyed them at the expense of the serious purpose of the activity. Many of us remember some of the most humorous episodes of our youth in relation to the church pageant.

Pageants, however, have played a major role in the history of drama from the Roman era to the present. The form has been used to celebrate major events in history as well as events in the lives of people who have shaped our civilization. Most of the great Passion plays are pageants. Celebrations of Christmas and Easter can probably be most effective as pageants.

The form calls for expansive techniques, with effects which are designed to impress. Color, movement, and music have been the chief characteristics of the pageant. Its effects are scaled to larger areas than that of the formal play. At best, because of its usual size, it shows characters in situations but allows for little development of the character in the course of the action. Like Greek drama, and for the same reason, it uses both singing and speaking choruses. It usually relies on a narrator or interlocuter to weave the story together and give it unity. It cannot have much of a plot because it must rely on episodic rather than unified, well-knit action. It causes one to wonder, to be astonished, and to be excited by its effects. It is a display rather than a development of an idea or story. It impresses rather than convinces. Its glory is still seen in the opening pageants of the circus which may portray the Cinderella story or the *Wizard of Oz*. The revival of outdoor pageants in North Carolina, Tennessee, Virginia, and Kentucky has been one of the major events in contemporary theater. *The Lost Colony, Unto These Hills, The Common Glory, Wilderness Road*, and *Horn in the West* are current examples of the historical pageant.

The decline of the pageant is due to the growth of the motion picture and its facility to present great numbers of scenes involving many people on wide screens with tremendous effects. This tends to dwarf any attempt to present a pageant as a "live" show. Thousands of people in gorgeous costumes and innumerable scenes with striking theatrical effects are now characteristic of the big feature films which have been associated with the names of D. W. Griffith and Cecil B. DeMille. What a far cry this is from the medieval mystery plays performed in the city square! These were called pageants, and the wagons on which they were performed were called pageant-wagons, their name being derived from the idea that they were movable scaffolds or stages.

Pageants have always been associated with celebrations. Today when a church wishes to celebrate some anniversary, it is likely that a historical pageant will be the first suggestion. Some highly liturgical churches use pageant techniques to celebrate great feast days of the church year. The Greek Orthodox Church employs pageant techniques on

Easter eve with processionals and hosannas sung when the tomb, represented by a room at the back of the altar, is found empty. In liturgical churches the blessing of the palms on Palm Sunday is a beautiful and meaningful spectacle.

The Church needs to rediscover ways to celebrate the great events of her history and the significant days of her calendar. What techniques will be evolved with mass-media communications remain to be seen. Until these techniques are perfected, ways of celebration by music, procession, dance, and speech should be experimented with. The Church must find her own pageant techniques and learn again the value of this form of celebration.

C. The Masque

The masque in the sixteenth century was purely a form of entertainment. It came into England as an imitation of the older Italian pageants. Royalty used the masque as a form of private entertainment until it became so elaborate it was used publicly. Allegory or mythology furnished much of the subject matter. Ben Jonson, the Elizabethan dramatist, was certainly one of the foremost writers of masques, although many of the Jacobean writers, including John Milton, tried their hands at masques. Milton's *Comus* is an excellent example of a later development of the form. Costume designs and plans for machinery and scenery are extant, so that a good idea of the techniques can be understood today. The masque is a small pageant, less episodic, and much more highly developed in subtle artistic effects that appeal to smaller and more sophisticated audiences. Someday perhaps the Church will celebrate important days and other events of the church year with a new kind of masque.

D. The Mime and Pantomime

Mimicry or miming has been generic to the peoples of the world. The word "mime" comes from the Latin word derived from the Greek verb meaning "to imitate." On the Roman stage it had a farcical or low comedy use, but it was a favorite form of entertainment. Augustus on his death bed is supposed to have asked his friends whether he had played well the mime of life. Mime is pure dramatic action. Language has been called the extension of gesture because action does speak more definitely even if not more loudly than words. Contemporary amateur actors often concentrate on the memorization of words when the words really should be the extension of something that is felt and is expressed in action.

The story material of the *mimus* was usually built on stock characters who were drawn in bold characteristics by the actors. No words were used in the later mimes, so that today we associate the word with actors who use facial movement and gestures as their means of communication. Experiments have been made in the use of miming in situations where people cannot understand the spoken language of the actor. Understanding subtle miming requires great concentration on the part of the spectators, as faces of actors must be seen and their smallest expression must be appreciated. When it is effectively used it is one of the greatest arts. At his best, Charles Chaplin was a master of mime, and there are great artists in the French theater who use only movement and facial expression in their performance. This has been vividly illustrated by the greatest of all mimes today, Marcel Marceau.

Children use mimicry before they use words. Many leaders in creative dramatics with children insist that the children mimic the action before they use words. Teachers of acting are likely to begin acting lessons by the use of pantomime. In the school of the Moscow Art Theater eurythmics and pantomime are the beginning studies.

Pantomime is fun for groups who wish to test their skills in demonstrating emotions such as joy, fear, anger, confusion, apprehension, deception, or affection. The capacity to express these in action is the beginning technique of the still greater accomplishment of adding words to the action and fulfilling the art of the actor.

E. The Play-reading and the Walking Rehearsal

Great plays are literature as well as theater. Furthermore, the moment a play comes alive before an audience is a brief one. After the performance, the moment is gone forever. In many cases, however, the text of the play is ours to read. Part of the value of the play remains for us to enjoy by reading.

Many of the great plays of the world, both ancient and modern, are too difficult for amateur production. Where can they be seen? Kenneth Thorpe Rowe has rendered a singular service by telling us that we can have a theater in our heads. By this, Rowe means that we can read plays, imagining them as acted before us. His book, *A Theater*

in Your Head, is an admirable exposition of the essential principles that
need to be known about production as well as about the technical structure of the play.² This book should be used as a guide for both private
and group play-readings.

Plays are satisfying reading in that they can be read at one sitting.
The world of the theater is available for us in easily accessible books.
The publishing of current plays in America is an event of the last fifty
years. In the early part of this century few contemporary plays were
printed until they had proved themselves enduring classics. Now groups
can have admirable libraries of paperback editions available to everyone.
Ignorance of the background of drama and the lack of understanding
of plays that can come only from reading need no longer be a problem.
An extensive list of plays for reading is given in the Appendix. Many
of these are in inexpensive editions.

Play-readings are valuable for giving a group familiarity with dramatic
technique or with the history of the drama and the dramatic forms
such as tragedy, comedy, et cetera. A play-reading can be held every
month for a group that may not be able to produce more than one or
two major productions a year. One thinks immediately of many plays
that are not likely to be produced by a church group because they are
too difficult. Reading these plays will make them familiar and will
give the group more knowledge of drama than any number of lectures
or discussions.

Many suggestions have been given to make play-readings effective.
Readers may sit on one side of a table, or they may be seated on stools
before music racks on which the script is placed. Solid racks are necessary so that scripts can be handled effortlessly. When the actors enter
and leave the scene, care must be taken that their entrances and exits
do not distract from the reading. Most directors of successful readings
insist that all the readers be in sight, merely indicating by some physical
posture when they are "on." Actors actually engaged in a scene may
lean forward while reading. When they are out of the scene they may
lean back as if unconcerned. If the director wishes, the persons in a
scene may rise to read, returning to their chairs or stools when they are
not in the scene. The use of music stands for this type of reading is
felicitous because it gives the idea of a concert rather than a play. A
walking rehearsal is a reading with scripts that includes as much of the
action as possible.

Platforms effectively lighted by spots are good for short scenes when the play contains a number of these and the action must continue from one scene to another. A narrator is often necessary, particularly if the play has been cut for reading or if the stage directions are necessary to the understanding of the dialogue, but under no circumstances should stage directions be read. A narrator may give the setting and tell what must be known of the staging. The actual movement and action are up to the reader to indicate by his voice and by the timing of the lines.

Hand props should be avoided in play-readings, as it is most difficult to handle properties along with the script. A subtle suggestion of costume can be effective in the use of a shawl, cloak, coat, or hat. This must be done with judgment and skill so that there is no ludicrous situation or foolishness on the part of the readers.

Play-readings may be used for group discussions or for testing out plays that are suggested for production. They furnish a good way to let an entire group know the play. If the group is large enough these play-reading casts can give readings of the plays that have been selected as possible production scripts. Hearing them read, the group will be more intelligent about selecting one of them. Likewise, a director can hear the entire group read and can make judgments about individual abilities.

Many "plays with a purpose," particularly scripts produced by the United Nations, UNESCO, the Society of Friends, or the Anti-Defamation League of B'nai B'rith are not strong as dramatic writing; yet these plays, as well as those published by the Friendship Press and the National Association of Mental Health, are good for reading and discussion. Their presentation of a "cause" through a dramatic situation will compel almost any group to discuss the material presented. Thus, as informal drama they are valid and have a place in the church program. (See the list of plays for reading and discussion in the Appendix.)

How to Prepare and Present Play-readings and Walking Rehearsals

(Suggestions used by the Religious Drama Workshop of the National Council of Churches at Green Lake, Wisconsin)

I. Advantages
   A. A play-reading or walking rehearsal needs only two or three rehearsals; actors do not have to memorize lines

B. A play-reading or walking rehearsal does not need scenery, costumes, properties, or lights; little experience involved
C. A play-reading or walking rehearsal does not involve royalty if outside audience is not invited to attend
D. More plays and types of dramatic experience can be presented to the group

II. Requirements
  A. An adequate number of scripts
    1. One for every two persons in a play-reading (preferably one for each reader)
    2. One for each person in a walking rehearsal
  B. An adequate number of rehearsals
    1. Two rehearsals for a play-reading
    2. Three or preferably four rehearsals for a walking rehearsal
    3. Rehearsals should be an hour or an hour and a half long for a one-act play; two and a half hours for a longer play
  C. A supervisor or director
    1. An adult or responsible young person who will supervise the rehearsal
      a. Preferably a person with drama training
      b. A person who will help the actors interpret their characters with thought and feeling
      c. A person who commands the respect and co-operation of the group and takes the work seriously
  D. An adequate place to rehearse and perform
    1. For the first rehearsal there must be a place where actors can be
      a. Physically comfortable
      b. Free from interruption
      c. Accessible to informality and discussion
    2. The second and last rehearsals must be in a place that is
      a. Preferably the place where the reading or walking rehearsal will be held or a room that approximates the place of performance so that actors can check.
        (1) Volume—whether they are too loud in the more vigorous scenes or too soft in the quiet scenes
        (2) Diction—whether the words of the actors are clear and understood
      b. A place where the actor's face and body can be seen
        (1) A raised platform is preferable but not absolutely

necessary; the end or middle of a room is adequate; the audience's chairs may be staggered to increase visibility

(2) Adequate number of chairs

III. How to choose actors

    A. Everyone who wishes should have a chance to read throughout a year's time

    B. The supervisor or director, or the group may choose the people; they should be chosen for the following reasons

        1. They will take rehearsals seriously

        2. They read well

        3. They are "cast" so that they

            a. Vocally sound like the character

            b. Are not physically too different from the part

            c. Have insight and understanding of the part

            d. Will not become too inhibited before an audience

            e. Will co-operate and "act" with the other members of the cast

IV. Things that must be clear to the audience

    A. A narrator—or an actor—should describe the following things at the opening of the performance and between scenes (if there is a shift of locale and time)

        1. Place—a vivid description sets the mood; all opening actor's lines that mention place or setting should be clear and read in the proper mood; all entrances, exits, and vital properties should be mentioned by the narrator or clearly "pointed" in lines or pantomime

        2. Time—as with place should be established through narration or lines

        3. Characters and their relation to each other—most of this will be in lines, but at times may be introduced at the beginning although never during the middle of a performance

            a. This may be helped by

                (1) Important characters sit in the middle of the seating arrangement; lesser ones on the outside

                (2) Actors moving, rising, or sitting on the important lines sit beside each other

                (3) Actors should face each other when reading; bow head and shoulders and look away when not sharing the scene with other actors

   b. In a walking rehearsal this may be helped by
    (1) Important actors say important lines in the most em-
     phatic position—not blocked from the audience's view
     by each other
    (2) The actors moving, rising, or sitting on important lines
    (3) Actors looking at each other as much as possible, listen-
     ing to each other when they are not speaking
    (4) Actors not shifting or moving while others talking
    (5) Actors not getting too crowded
    (6) Actors standing out of view of audience when they are
     not in the scene or "on stage"

 B. When the play ends
  1. Actors may stand still a moment after closing lines; then leave
   in character

V. Rehearsal procedure; copies of plays have been ordered well ahead of time;
 rehearsals should get under way two weeks prior to the performance;
 rehearsals should be close enough together so that actors do not forget—
 one week is a good time span.
 A. First rehearsal
  1. Everyone reads the play through without interruption except
   to ask questions about pronunciation of words and names; strike
   out all printed stage directions; if a walking rehearsal, determine
   movements
  2. Everyone discusses the meaning of the play; questions about the
   background of the play; work on characterization
  3. Read through the play stopping to discuss and make suggestions
   about character—work for understanding and feeling the part;
   go through movements if a walking rehearsal
  4. If there is time read the play straight through again
 B. Second rehearsal
  1. Read straight through watching for
   a. Volume
   b. Articulation and enunciation
  2. Pick up lines quickly so there isn't too much time between lines,
   unless this is necessary and called for—don't let the reading
   drag
 C. Performance
  1. Go on and off stage, platform, or to seating arrangement in
   character

2. Actor never looks at audience when reading or not reading (unless he is the narrator or the part calls for looking at the audience)

Notes

[1] Herbert Sidney Langfeld, *The Aesthetic Attitude* (New York: Harcourt, Brace and Company, 1920), p. 268.

[2] New York: Funk & Wagnalls Company, 1960. See especially Chapter 9, "Through Literature to Meaning," and Chapter 11, "Principles of Evaluation."

Chapter IV

TYPES OF DRAMATIC EXPRESSION: INFORMAL DRAMA

A. Creative Dramatics for Children

"ALL WORK AND NO PLAY MAKES JACK A DULL BOY" IS A TRUTH THAT IS now being revived in educational circles, but for reasons which our ancestors who first coined the phrase would never have used. The play theory has been broadened into a life theory, so that books are now appearing with the theses that play is the natural employment of man and that work is merely play taken too seriously. Whatever this theory of play may mean for philosophers and psychologists, it has great significance for the educator and particularly the religious educator.

To play a life situation, whether it is ancient classical lore, biblical story, or contemporary problem is to put it into action. For children this is a most natural way to express ideas. Words gain meaning as they are lived and experience gives them importance. Actions do speak louder than words for children, and they speak a language that is understandable. Young imaginations visualize a story as it is being told; to suggest that it be put into action is merely to suggest to them that it be expressed—that it be made real.

We do not need to be reminded that a child begins life by discovering his body and playing with it. He continues to play with himself and for himself until the older person intrudes with his world that is consumed with work, so that play becomes a duty and is made a requisite of health and well-being. Child's play is all consuming and all important. It is a living process. When it reaches the stage where persons other than the child are involved, he plays with them, taking them into his world that is played real. Only when others come into watch the play does the child shift his attention from play for itself to play for others.

48

When this happens the child plays for others and not for the mere joy of playing.

To create an environment for playing, for putting an idea into action, and to confront the child with ideas and situations that it can make come to life in its play is the problem that faces the teacher or leader of children. Anthropologists believe that play is integral to life, that it is more than an instinct. They suggest that the curtailing of play and the changing of it in the artificial living of our day is likely to have something to do with man's unhappiness and his frustration in the midst of his hectic life. Certainly, we need to return to free play, to expressing ourselves joyfully, and to social playing where we are not organized as players and coached as to how we ought to play. Our play, like our work, has become professional.

The child can begin his understanding of life by playing. If this is a free, happy experience he can carry the pattern into his adult life. Self-consciousness may be described as a kind of absence of the play spirit. The most successful adult enjoys his work; he brings to it a play spirit. Unfortunately, we have associated irresponsibility and casualness with the concept of play. Actually the highly skilled and genuinely artistic person gives himself to his work with the abandon of play, and he enjoys his work as if it were play. This is true of the skilled surgeon and of the true artist. "In the joy of the actor lies the sense of any action" can be amended to read, "In the joy of the player."

The leader of children in religious education can use their play tendency in life to achieve the greatest possible growth. A number of years ago a delightful artist by the name of Dugald Walker was confronted with the problem of directing the activities of children at Christadora House on the lower East Side in New York City. The children were not easy to handle; many were from an environment that created delinquency and lawlessness. Furthermore, there was no money for equipment. Dugald Walker found, however, that all the children had one thing in common—a joy in playing. So he decided to play a city, allowing each child to be in his imagination what he wanted most to be in life. Thus was created the "The Invisible Village." Firemen, policemen, garbage collectors, ash men, mayors, and businessmen sprang up all over the hall in which they played. Never was there anything like this in the settlement house, and for some months the recreation problem was solved; the children played the roles they longed to be. Each child in his time played more than seven ages; he played roles in an imagined life.

When drama is played by children for themselves with their own group as the only audience, it is a creative experience that has many possibilities for religious education. When disciplined into a compact form which we call a play, it is not a complete experience until it is reacted to by an audience or congregation. Drama, then, as an art form is action reacted to. Both action and reaction are necessary to it as an art.

Creative dramatics, or drama that is played by the participants without regard to any reaction except that of those taking part, is used in elementary schools and junior-high schools throughout the country. Winifred Ward's pioneering work in Evanston, Illinois, has spread to many school systems and is now a definite part of the educational process. The use of the creative method in church schools, however, is still in the early experimental stages. The reasons for this are not difficult to understand. The time element is perhaps most serious. To tell a story or create one and to have the children dramatize it and give it takes more time than the usual short period of a church-school class. The extended class period can help solve the problem of time. Very brief episodes can be done in an extended period and with some difficulty recalled and re-created another time.

Another major stumbling block to the use of the creative method is the lack of adequately prepared teachers. To keep a balance between control and spontaneous creative work is not easy. The teacher must know dramatic values and how they can be achieved naturally, and at the same time he must know how to allow complete freedom in the creative process. Above all, he must know the child and must be able to think and play as a child without superimposing his adult life and thinking on what he is doing. He must know what it means to have religious ideas come alive in action, and he must be able to meet the awful honesty and forthrightness of the child who wants his religion to be meaningful, natural, and related to everything else he is doing.

What the child dramatizes, makes come to life, will not be forgotten. What he learns in the application of life principles to contemporary settings will be much more lasting in value if he acts it out. This is a method that can be unique in an age of television. Creative dramatics, as well as formal drama, allows the child to experience a life situation in action. When he creates the story and brings it to life he is not likely to forget it. He is not merely looking at life, he is participating in it. Religion, even for the little child, can come alive through this method. Difficult words and remote stories that are sometimes connected with the Bible need no longer frighten or bore him. Some things cannot be dramatized by children because they are adult concepts and experience. In an interview for the *New York Times* Miss Ward suggested that creative dramatics is fun. When fun comes back to the church-school classroom, enhancing the meanings of the materials in the curriculum, the time on Sunday can be anticipated with joy by children.

For younger children through the junior-high-school age, formal plays are educationally open to question unless they are skillfully directed. For this reason the creative method is suggested, building upon the play tendency in all children, guided, to be sure, until the child is old enough to understand the allurements of showing off in a formal play presented before an audience. The child, as we have said, must act for his own joy and for his fellow players until he is old enough to understand the reaction by others who are not actually participating in the creative act and who, unfortunately, in theater are known as audience.

There is still little written on the use of this method in the church school. *Let's Play a Story* by Elizabeth Allstrom, formerly supervisor of the primary department of Riverside Church in New York City, concerns story-playing for the primary and junior departments of the church school. The new revised edition of Miss Ward's definitive book *Playmaking with Children* has a chapter on the use of creative dramatics in the church. The principles set forth in this book are to be applied to the teaching methods in the church. The Lake Forest Workshop on religious drama and others like it throughout the country have included courses in the creative method, and many colleges and universities offer creative dramatics.

Miss Ward has condensed her definitions and techniques in the following outline. Teachers who are taking seriously the use of the creative method will need to consult the books listed at the end of this chapter. The techniques of creative dramatics should be used only by persons who understand them. After carefully studying this outline and following its suggestions, they may be successful in simple experiments, but in order to guide children with any degree of skill they will need to read further and, if possible, take a course in creative dramatics.

What is creative dramatics?

It is any type of drama created by children and played with spontaneous action and dialogue. It begins with dramatic play-living in which little children play out experiences they have had and "try on" the characters of the people around them. Under the guidance of an adult, older children in church or vacation schools plan plays or worship services based on ideas, experiences, or stories, leaving the specific action and dialogue to the individual players.

This is a different aspect of drama from the memorized, directed, rehearsed drama designed for the entertainment of an audience. It develops from the ideas of the children. Because it is improvised, it is never twice the same but is developed further each time it is played.

It influences the personal development of the children who participate by giving them:

A constructive use for their creative imagination.

Experience in working together in situations which strongly motivate co-operation.

Sensitivity to the thoughts and feelings of others which is the basis of understanding.

Controlled emotional release through playing all kinds of characters.

A heightened appreciation of the material studied.

Leadership training by way of thinking on their feet and expressing their ideas fearlessly.

It has the power to bring alive for children dramatic stories in the Bible and other literature. Also it can help them to see both sides of current problems through role-playing.

What material is good for creative plays?

Dramatic play might begin with an idea; the beginning of things, i.e., spring, homes, time, happiness, how God cares for his world.

If it is a story, it should have a central idea which is meaningful to the modern child. It should have emotional appeal, involve decisions, and offer opportunity for plenty of action. Only literature of good quality should ever be used. (Good examples of Bible stories which have these qualifications are The Good Samaritan, Joseph, and the incident in which David spares Saul's life in the cave.)

How may creative dramatics be introduced?

Before beginning any creative activity there must be a friendly, relaxed, confident feeling in the group set by the leader. Without this there can be no creative drama.

For primary children:
1. Dramatic play—the make-believe in which children learn much about themselves and others as:
   A. Playing on things constructed from blocks: Houses, boats, planes, et cetera.
   B. Playing out situations in preparation for real experiences, as: Greeting visitors, welcoming new members to the class, introducing parents.
   C. Playing out ideas of such things as love: The mother bird's care of her young, a human parent caring for a baby, God's care of nature—the snow, rain, seedlings growing up and blossoming.
2. Rhythms with music or percussion instruments. An accompanist who can improvise on the piano, one who is sensitive to the ideas of the children, is highly valuable in creative dramatics by setting a mood for their playing and guiding their dramatic rhythms. Without such an accompaniment, the leader can use drums, bells, or other percussion instruments. Records, although less satisfactory, are available for almost any activity. The RCA Victor Record Library for Elementary Schools, especially those called "Rhythmic Activities and Basic Rhythm Programs," are useful.
3. The sharpening of sense awareness, important for drama, to say nothing of its significance in life itself.
   A. The leader calls to the children's notice the beauty of colors and combinations of colors—including, perhaps, stained-glass windows if there are beautiful ones in the church—sounds which are pleasing and those which are not, objects which are interesting to the touch, flowers which are fragrant, and foods that appeal to the taste.
   B. Such questions may be asked as: "What does the color yellow make you think of?" "What is the most beautiful thing you ever saw?" "And heard?"
4. Dramatizing very simple stories, such as "Why the Evergreen Trees Keep Their Leaves in Winter" and "The Little Pink Rose." (In

Stories to Dramatize, edited by Winifred Ward.) Very few
Bible stories are suitable for dramatization by primary children.

For older children: (VACATION SCHOOL)
1. Pantomimes of activities as preliminary to story dramatization:
    A. Something you especially like to do—the others guess what
       it is.
    B. Activities at camp or at a picnic.
    C. Exploring a cave.
    D. Searching for something. After looking in many places,
       find it. Show by your actions where you are, how urgent
       the search is, what it is that you find.
2. Characterization. (*Always* from the inside out!)
    A. Be some definite person who finds a purse. What do you
       think? What do you do?
    B. Enter and sit on a chair by a table as if you were a prim old
       aunt who has come to spend the day and knit. Or as a
       boy who is afraid he is going to be scolded. Or as an old
       person with rheumatism.
    C. Be the Witch in "Hansel and Gretel."
    D. Be the Egyptian princess when her handmaidens find the
       baby, Moses.

How does one guide a group into dramatizing a story?
1. The leader sets the mood for specific material by:
    A. Capitalizing on the feeling of the group induced by the
       season, a holiday, or a recent experience.
    B. Arousing interest by a picture, music, an experience, or a
       question.
2. Presents story with enthusiasm. Before the children can create
   from it the story must reach inside.

An example of procedure in creating a play from a story: FOR JUNIORS
(CHURCH OR VACATION SCHOOL)
    The leader may introduce the idea of good neighbors. "What do we
mean when we say a person is a good neighbor?" Children discuss this
in terms of their own experience.
    One time when Jesus said, "Thou shalt love thy neighbor as thyself,"
and a man asked, "Who is my neighbor?" Jesus told the parable of
the good Samaritan. The leader tells the story in his own words, making

it very alive and understandable to the children. He has informed himself concerning the geography of the country, its dangers, the customs, and the feeling between Jews and Samaritans. He relates it to the children's experience in some way, such as: "Now it was only twenty miles from Jerusalem to Jericho, and today we wouldn't think that was much of a trip, would we? We'd go in a car or on the train. But in those days there were no cars and no trains. When people traveled, they either walked or rode on donkeys.

"This man had no donkey, so he was going to walk the twenty miles, starting out early in the morning with his bundle of lunch and his stout stick, expecting to reach Jericho that evening."

After telling the story as vividly and effectively as possible, the leader might say, "When Jesus had finished the story, then many knew the answer to his question, 'Who is my neighbor?' Do you?"

In the ensuing discussion, the leader might ask, "If you had been traveling along this road and had seen this wounded man, why might you have hurried past without helping him?"

Various answers will doubtless include, "I might be afraid the robbers were still around," or "He was a horrible sight and I wouldn't want to touch him." "I might be afraid people would think I had beaten him."

"Let's all of us be passersby in order to get the feel of people who for one reason or another do not stop to help him."

With some groups of children, it is better at first to use a coat to spread down for the wounded man so that there will be less chance of self-consciousness. Each one imagines and tries to show how he feels when he sees the beaten man. Perhaps one will pause as if inclined to help, another will be horrified, and still another will be fearful. Several volunteers may then try on the character of the Samaritan and his reaction to the situation.

After a discussion as to how each felt in the situation, they may play the scene with only the three passersby and the Samaritan, as well as the man who was hurt.

It is a matter of choice as to whether they begin at the beginning of the story and play it all the way through or use only the latter part of it. Sometimes children begin before the Jew leaves his home, and his wife is fearful and anxious that he wait until he can travel with others. Often, they want to start as the Jew is walking along the dangerous road, just before the robbers attack him. The Samaritan will, of course, be introduced this time, and point is made of the fact that while he has far more reason to pass by without stopping, he is the only one who does stop and help the Jew. It is always better to play a story in short units at first, putting it together afterwards.

The children often do the first playing in pantomime, adding words later. After each group plays the scene, there is an evaluation, not only by those who were not playing but by the players also. Unless the children make all the points which should be made, the leader should by all means ask questions which will cause the group to think about what was real and sincere, and what they can suggest that the scene needs.

Give the children freedom in playing.

Choosing the casts: Who would like to be the Samaritan? (The robbers will be the choice of some of the boys, and it may be the means of making dramatization fun for them.) Try to combine in each cast one or two of the freer, more imaginative children with others who are shy or less imaginative. Every player should have a feeling of achievement each time he makes a sincere effort. As often as possible, let many children play at once.

If any child is burlesquing a character or in any way spoiling the sincerity of a scene never allow the scene to go on. Without taking the child to task, call the children together and talk with them about the need for staying in character from beginning to end. That is one of "the rules of the game."

Guide them in evaluation.

Allow no negative comments at first. Instead, ask a question such as: What did you like? Or, what new ideas were added? Later ask, How can we give this scene more meaning? If the group is made up of juniors or intermediates detailed evaluation such as the following should be used:

1. Was the story clear? Was it real?

2. Were the players thinking and feeling like the characters in the story?

3. Was there good teamwork? Was everyone in the story all the time? Did each react to the others in the scene?

4. Was the action true to the story?

5. Was the dialogue true to the characters?

6. Did they make the meaning clear?

Then ask, How can we make it better? After the children have had a chance to tell how the scene can be improved, another cast is chosen —from volunteers always—and the scene is developed further. After each scene has been worked out as well as the group can do it, the whole story is put together.

Throughout the whole process in creative dramatics the leader guides the children by asking skillful questions to stir their thinking. There is little talk by the leader after the material is presented and the children are never directed or told what to say. Above all, each child is encouraged to contribute what he can and is given credit for every sincere effort.

These books will be of direct help to the teacher or leader:

Allstrom, Elizabeth. *Let's Play a Story.* New York: Friendship Press, 1957.

Brown, Jeanette Perkins. *The Storyteller in Religious Education.* Boston: Pilgrim Press, 1951.

Siks, Geraldine B. *Creative Dramatics: An Art for Children.* New York: Harper & Brothers, 1958.

Ward, Winifred. *Playmaking with Children.* Revised edition. New York: Appleton-Century-Crofts, Inc., 1957.

————, editor. *Stories to Dramatize.* Anchorage, Ky.: Children's Theatre Press, 1952.

Role-Playing for Adults[1]

Role-playing is a form of dramatic play, which, unlike creative dramatics, requires reaction from players and audience. In this form of activity people spontaneously act out problems of human relations and analyze the enactment. It is as old as certain kinds of charades in which often there is role-playing, and it is as new in its application as the forms to which it is most closely allied—sociodrama and psychodrama. Both of these newer forms require not only players but an audience which helps the players interpret their roles. Sociodrama may be defined as a form of role-playing which portrays interactions of people with other individuals or groups as carriers of some specified cultural role such as supervisor, leader, mother, father, employee, et cetera. The situation always involves more than one person and deals with problems a majority of the group faces in their lives.

Psychodrama is concerned with the unique problems of one individual and forms release for these problems built up in the personalized world of the actor. *It is a form of dramatic expression which should not be experimented with except under the guidance of a therapist.*[2]

Role-playing, on the other hand, can be a delightful group activity. It is primarily a discussion technique, since its purpose is to stimulate discussion by the group which observes the technique. It is, in fact, one of the best methods to get a group involved in the discussion of a subject. As is true with any dramatic technique, role-playing brings a subject to life and thus makes a given situation more real than any description of it could be. The actors as well as the observers "live through" the situation presented. With this emotional involvement, the participant, both actor and observer, is able to test his knowledge and judgment about the situation, and to have this checked by the experience of the group. In this way, individuals may gain new skills for dealing with problems in human relations. A contrived situation may not apply to the specific problems faced by the group. It is only when the group has set up the problem as one real for itself that it will appreciate the relevance of this method in dealing with social problems.

Role-playing also allows many different attitudes and feelings to be expressed, so that as they are objectified their validity can be tested. In a meeting of the National Association of Foreign Student Advisors on one of the campuses of America, a delightful afternoon was spent showing by role-playing the right and wrong methods of dealing with many of the problems of foreign students when they came to this country. Students from other countries were used in the playing so that their individual grievances, as well as the mistaken theories of some of the advisors, were aired. What was particularly interesting was that everyone agreed that the method made much more impressive what needed to be known, and the discussion following each role-playing episode was more lively than any of the discussions in the conference. Some of the group became so involved that they decided they should demonstrate the right methods of dealing with their problems.

How does a group go about using role-playing as a learning device? Like most dramatic presentations, role-playing needs a director who is responsible for all the procedural aspects involved in the process and who helps the actors and other group members (observers) become emotionally involved with the situation to be acted out. The director may be the group leader or some other member who is familiar with the role-playing process. Unlike a director in a legitimate theater production, however, whose main function is to help actors interpret already written lines and characterizations, a director of role-playing is mainly concerned with helping the actors to be spontaneous in presenting the characters they are portraying and with helping the audience-observers to analyze the situation and behaviors presented in order to increase their insights into problems and their knowledge of how to deal with them effectively.

As an educational technique role-playing involves more than the simple acting out of roles. It is made up of a series of steps, of which the actual acting is only one, and it is the director's job to see that all these steps are taken care of in every role-playing situation and that the function of each step is understood by everyone in the group. In practice, these help the group understand the significance of each of them. In brief, the steps in the role-playing process are: Defining the problem, establishing a situation, casting characters, briefing and warming up actors and observers, acting, cutting, discussing and analyzing the situation and behavior by actors and observers, and making plans for further testing of the insights gained or for practicing the new behavior implied.

Most groups will welcome a suggestion to try role-playing in their meetings, as most people like opportunities for dramatic expression and like to try new ways of bringing content into their group meetings. Some groups, however, may be hesitant about role-playing or even frightened because they do not see themselves as "actors" or because they are afraid such spontaneous expression and exploration of problems may get too close to personal anxieties and problems.

Groups which appear hesitant will quickly learn to feel at ease by starting with a simple situation which can be initiated by some problem with which the group is dealing. One member of a discussion group, for example, might be having a heated argument with another over the right of farmers to receive production subsidies. The first member insists that the second member cannot look at the problem objectively because he has a farm background and will always be in favor of anything that helps the farmers, whether or not it hurts the rest of the country. A third member of the group, or the group leader, could easily introduce role-playing as a way of helping each party to this argument get a better understanding of the other's point of view. He might suggest that each of the contenders stops the argument and portrays the other person, seeing how accurately each can represent the other's point of view. After a few minutes of this attempt to reverse roles, each person could be asked to describe how he felt in the role of the other, or if he thought he might have been oversimplifying or stereotyping the other's position. This simple but effective way of using role-playing has the advantage of needing almost no preparation. It automatically briefs and warms up the participants. After such an experience, some other uses of role-playing could be described to the group.

Generally, when role-playing is used for the first time, the situation selected should be simple enough to allow group members to discuss it profitably. It is important that group members have the experience of discovering that with the leader or director's guidance they can explore a problem, break it down into factors which may be causing it, and construct ways of meeting the problem through changing the situation or their behavior. It is also generally true that while an experienced group leader can take on the job of directing role-playing readily, an inexperienced group leader may feel too burdened to charge himself with sole responsibility as a director and may want to involve group members in this task with him.

Overpersonalization of Problems

The role-playing director can do much to help a group steer clear of psychodramatic situations and analyses by being on the alert to avoid situations and roles which lead to personal exposures or are so closely related to personal and private feelings that psychodramatic expression can hardly help. The director sets the tone for portrayals and analyses in introducing briefing and discussion by pointing out that the job of the observers is to look at the actors in terms of their roles. It should be made clear that each actor is playing a specified role in a specific situation and is merely giving his spontaneous interpretation of how such a character would be likely to respond in such a situation.

Overuse of Role-Playing

Groups which are new to role-playing as an educational technique sometimes get very interested in it and begin to use it as a cure-all. Such inappropriate overuse may lessen its effectiveness when it should be used. If role-playing is to be an effective training tool it must assume its proper place among other educational methods in the group's reper-toire. It is wise to remember that role-playing is useful in dealing with a very distinct group of problems only—that is, problems involving human relations. There are many other procedures which are sufficient to meet the educational requirements of many group situations, and sometimes it is wise to reserve role-playing only for those situations where it is crucially required.

Finally, when role-playing is used it can be enriched and varied by adapting variations and new forms to the basic structure. Groups that have gained some experience with the basic technique will want to build new or more complex structures for getting at specific problems. Some such ideas—the use of alter-ego techniques, consultants to the actors, et cetera—are described in the literature on role-playing, but many groups will be able to invent these adaptations in relation to their own specific needs. In fact, the basic role-playing technique offers one of the best opportunities for exploiting the inventive abilities of any group.

The design of role-playing is always dependent on the learning out-comes desired or needed by the group. The planners must always work with the training purpose of role-playing uppermost in mind.

There are several ways by which situations can be designed:

1. A subcommittee can plan the situation and bring it to the group.

2. The total group can make up a situation on the spot.

3. A member or the leader can suggest an actual case which illustrates the problem. (If this method is used care must be taken to see that the scene doesn't get clogged up in details about what really happened.)

The responsibility for defining and casting characters may be taken by the total group or delegated to certain members. The planners must think about what kinds of characters will have meaning for the group and will contribute to the group's understanding of the problem. If the director or planners are not well acquainted with the group mem-bers and do not know how they would feel about taking roles in the play it is probably wiser to ask for volunteers or suggestions from the members during the meeting rather than to assign parts in advance. In general, persons should be chosen because it is thought they can carry the role well and are not likely to be threatened or exposed by it.

Regardless of what method is used for casting, no one should ever be asked to take a role unless he is definitely willing to do so. If an individual plays a role under forced circumstances, he is likely to give a constricted and nonspontaneous portrayal of the role.

If a role has unfavorable characteristics, it is wise to assign it to a person who has enough status in the group or enough personal security to carry it without stress, or if the group is a new one, its leader might be asked to take this role to get things moving.

When dealing with beginners at role-playing it may be wise to start them in roles in which they feel at home and confident. Soon, however, they should also be assigned roles which will help them stretch their perceptions and insights.

If the situation is simple, it may be better to depend on oral briefing. Because spontaneity is such an important element in role-playing, over-preparation may restrict the players or even cause them to ham their roles.

No attempt should be made under any circumstances to use the briefing or warm-up process to structure what the actors are going to say or do in the action.

When the role-players have no hidden motives, they can warm up by talking among themselves about their parts, setting up the physical properties on the stage "in role," by saying, "This is our house. We have lived here forty years. This is the door, et cetera."

One of the most important responsibilities of the director is to see that everyone moves into the role-play at the same time. The mood of the play can be destroyed after the action has started if one of the actors begins to talk as himself rather than as the character he is portraying.

A common tendency is to let the scene go on too long. Generally, role-playing should be cut when:

1. Enough behavior has been exhibited so that the group can analyze the problem it has set for itself.

2. The group can project what would happen if the action were continued.

3. The players have reached an impasse because they have somehow been miscast or misbriefed.

4. There is a natural closing.

The director must always be alert to see that the discussion relates to the original problem.

Sometimes the players are asked to comment first, and sometimes the discussion is started by the observers. The advantages of the former in some situations is that it allows the players to set the tone for constructive criticism. If the players show by their own observations that they are unselfconscious because they are analyzing the characters portrayed and not themselves the observers are more likely to feel free to express their full reactions.

It is important that the observers steer clear of comments that evaluate the acting ability of the players or the convincingness of the players' interpretations of their roles. The discussion should be focused on what the play can contribute to their understanding of the problem they were trying to solve.

The observers should try to bring into the discussion what they saw and heard, rather than commenting on what should or should not have been done.

If the diagnosis of the problem opens up a whole new way of working at things the group might try a different role-playing situation to see if their generalizations hold true in more than the specific case, the leader or director might suggest readings for the group to explore the problem further, or the group may plan to have a future discussion on other aspects of the problem.

Notes

[1] The author is indebted to the Adult Education Association of the United States of America for much of the substance of this discussion. A fuller treatment will be found in Leadership Pamphlet Number 6 which can be secured from the association or from the Service Department, The Board of Education of The Methodist Church, Box 871, Nashville 2, Tenn.

[2] Dr. J. L. Moreno has been the pioneer in the use of psychodrama. His book on psychodrama should be consulted for the explanation of its use. *Psychodrama and Sociodrama* (Boston: Beacon Press, 1946).

Part two

Chapter V

WHAT IS RELIGIOUS DRAMA?

ELIGIOUS DRAMA IS NOT A KIND OF DRAMA, IT IS A QUALITY OF DRAMA.
is produced like any other type of drama, but the quality of the pro-
ction is judged both by the artistic and theatrical results as well as by
quality inherent in the process of production itself. Religious drama
esupposes a standard of work that is religiously oriented. It is dramatic
tivity in its finest expression, since it is concerned with persons both
the characters in the play and as persons who are bringing the char-
ters of life in the production. It is, therefore, potentially a genuinely
igious activity.
Drama is not religious because it uses material that comes from
igious books or from Judeo-Christian sources in the Bible. It is not
igious because it dramatizes so-called religious themes. These may
e religious significance to the material, but they are not its only
irce. Drama is truly religious when it shows meanings and purposes
life that grow from the revelation of the highest values conceivable.
seeks to relate man to the totality of his being. When these values
translated into living situations which cause conflicts with lesser
anings and purposes, then religiously effective drama may occur.
hen life situations are filtered through dramatic imagination they may
presented in terms of the perspective of the ultimate concerns and
rposes of men or they may be presented merely as experiences in a
oratory of life. The former is likely to be the framework of religious
ma, the latter that of realism which may or may not have religious
aning.
Plays may have ethical and moral values because they probe into
tivations. In a very real sense the religious value of a play grows from
motivations which drive the characters to action. The deeper the

67

motivation for action, the more likely it is that the play will have religious significance. This does not mean, necessarily, that the play will be a good play because of its concepts. A good play is judged by dramatic standards. The finer and sounder the subject matter, the more likely will the dramatist be able to create a good play. *Religious drama presents characters in action in situations where faith and belief are tested in lives of people at tension moments.*

The Stage Manager in the last speech in Thornton Wilder's *Our Town* looks up at the stars while he makes the observation that scholars seem to think that none of the other stars is inhabited: "Only this one," the earth, he adds by way of benediction, "is straining away, straining away all the time to make something of itself." Religious drama is *man's straining away trying to make something of himself* because he is endowed with this capacity by his creator.

Plays that bring to an audience a depth experience of conflict which is not artificial and not fantastic, with a story that is accepted because its plot and characters come out of genuine life situations and call for emotional responses that are constructive and elevating, is religious drama. By this definition many of the plays of Ibsen, Shaw, and other continental dramatists, as well as those of T. S. Eliot and Christopher Fry, have given new dimensions to the meaning of religious drama. Christian, Muslim, Hindu, or Jewish drama are specific kinds of religious drama.

Religious drama, furthermore, deals with characters, situations, and themes that are clarified by means of religion, by man's relationship with his God, with himself, and with his fellow man because of the nature and meaning of his God. It should have high seriousness of purpose whether it is comic or tragic. It derives its meaning from man's struggle to fulfill his destiny to the best of his ability. It communicates life on its deepest level.

Roderick Robertson suggests three basic areas of human experience which religious drama may treat.[1] In the first area drama deals with man's state as unrelated to God and may be called the *drama of religious alienation.* Eugene O'Neill's *Days Without End* is a play of this type. In the second area it deals with the process through which man goes in order to achieve his relationship to God and may be called the *drama of the religious experience.* Ronald Duncan's *This Way to the Tomb* belongs in this category. In the third group are dramas concerned with the person who has found a successful orientation to God, or the *drama of the religious hero*. Shaw's *Saint Joan* immediately comes to mind as an example of a play which has this kind of heroine.

The attempt to arrive at a definition of religious drama is a continuing project. Some clarification has been possible in definitions arrived at through group processes and through the research that has taken place in colleges. The Religious Drama Project of the American Educational Theatre Association framed the following definition:

Religious drama includes not only a literature but also a body of acts and skills religiously inspired and motivated. Religious drama, as literature, is based upon a centrally religious theme and has a religious impact upon its participants and witnesses. This may include experiences of worship, plays for entertainment, educational drama, and creative dramatics. It is not concerned exclusively with propaganda and/or edification. It is not limited to acts of worship and chancel drama, although it may be of these things. Religious drama is written, produced, and performed in a spirit of reverence and with concern for the enrichment of its participants, church, and community.

In a Religious Drama Workshop held at Boston University, in the summer of 1959, other suggestive definitions were formulated. Some of these are given here to show the range of thinking and the broad scope of the kind of drama called religious.

Religious drama is action involving man in the ultimate concerns of his relationship with man and God for the purpose of aiding him in his search for maturity.

Religious drama is the enactment through staged action and dialogue of human situations that convey men's concepts about ultimate reality; and the transcendence of that enactment into a relationship that involves the participants (actors and audience) with the concepts presented.

A religious drama is any drama which allows man to discover or deepen his own relationship to the ultimate, or God.

Religious drama is a peculiar attempt to communicate through involvement of writer, actors, and audience by means of psychological, physical and mental action, man's endeavor to respond with his whole being to that which is most real and most important.

Another definition contributed by Marvin Halverson pinpoints Chris
tian drama:

Drama is an art form which has evocative and communicative power whic
causes one to confront the human situation—and one's self. This is true o
Greek tragedy and contemporary skeptical drama. Christian drama, howeve:
points beyond the depths of tragedy to that fulfillment of life which is see
in Jesus, the Christ. Christian drama, like corporate worship, derives its co
tent as well as its structure from the drama of the biblical story, and pa·
ticularly, the Incarnation, ministry, Passion, death and resurrection of Jesu
Christ. Such drama makes men experience not only pity, fear, and catharsi
but also guilt, judgment, and the forgiveness of God which brings the "peac
that passeth understanding." [2]

Christian drama mentioned in this definition has certain specific cha·
acteristics. E. Martin Browne, writing in *motive*, suggests some of them

The most important thing of all about drama for us Christians is: *that*
partakes of the nature of incarnation . . . that the coming of God to eart
as man, the Word made flesh, is the climax of all human development in a
fields. . . . So we see the Incarnation as God's use of the dramatic form i
human history, as God's action in human life. The word drama itself simp
means "doing." [3]

The Danish dramatist Kaj Munk in a ringing declaration written f
the program of the first production in 1938 of *He Sits at the Melting Po*
expresses in another way the significance of Christian drama:

The Christian God is a great God. He is so just that he cannot do with le
than a God as stoker at his foundry. It is the God of hell who shovels in t
coal under God's melting pot. That is why the heat is so terrific, and has ·
be, in order that the dross may be cleansed away. . . . Will it be cleanse
away? What does mankind know? . . . Christianity robs life of none of i
thrills. *It is the religion of drama.*

Preston Roberts has further illuminated the meaning of Christi
drama. He suggests that Christian dramatic tragedies turn upon t
theme of man's idolatry and pretension rather than upon the themes
man's suffering nobility or piteous abnormality. "They move from fa

to freedom, from defeat to victory, from doom to grace, and from tragedy to peace." [4]

A Christian tragic hero may abuse the radical freedom which is his— he is free to respond to God, to others, to his own conscience, to forgiveness, to God's grace. The effect of the Christian play on the audience is that of judgment and forgiveness rather than a sense of pity and terror as in Greek plays or despair as in the modern, skeptical play. Dr. Roberts points out that the meaning of Greek and modern plays is "despair, virtually complete and unmitigated, whereas the meaning of a Christian dramatic tragedy is that life and history are redeemable in principle and are in part redeemed at certain crucial points and moments in fact." [5]

More and more persons have come to respect the French dramatist Henri Ghéon. In the preface to the collection of his plays, *Saint Anne and the Gouty Rector*, the translator, Marcus S. Goldman, suggests that Ghéon sought to express his Christian faith in all his writing. He had a sensitive, artistic conscience, but he did not believe that piety and good intentions could make up for poor writing. He felt that his highest duty as a dramatist was to write plays which would act well and entertain the public. His first purpose was not to teach but "to delight." As an artist, he regarded with horror and scorn the pious theatrical performances usually presented under ecclesiastical auspices. He referred to them as *bondieuseries*, a word that can be translated as "goodgoderies" but which probably ought to be translated as "goodie-goderies," the pious, goody-goody plays he sought to run from the scene.

Ghéon used humor in all his plays. What a cleansing, revitalizing thing it is in religious drama! The medieval writers used it, too, as we can see in *The Second Shepherd's Play* of the Townley cycle of mystery plays. Ghéon felt that religion, and specifically Christianity, had a place in the theater. If an actor could be asked to take the part of a Homeric hero or a Greek god, why should he not be asked to take the part of an Old Testament prophet or a disciple of Jesus? Laughter can be mingled with true piety, however, and this along with a true dramatic sense, was Ghéon's great contribution to religious drama. His plays are some of the best we have.

Morality is not only doing right; it is discovering what is right. Moral problems are those arising out of sincerity and conscience, not those created out of living according to moral law. Drama helps us to discover what is right by showing us people who do the right or wrong things. Ernest Toller, the German dramatist of the First-World-War years, reminded us that artists were not to serve the tastes of their day, but were to serve the eternal powers of life, truth, justice, joy, beauty, freedom, the mind, and the spirit. These are the subject matter of true religious drama. The Italian artist Enrico Prampolini has gone even further by insisting that the future theater will use time and space as dynamic elements to serve the function of "spiritual education."

Shelley, in the preface to *The Cenci*, speaks of the illuminating power of the drama when he says: "The highest moral purpose aimed at in the highest species of the drama, is the teaching of the human heart, through its sympathies, the knowledge of itself." Thus, drama in the theater can reveal the human heart to itself. It can also reveal the human heart in its leap to immortal things and "show the trace" in the lives of men.

Fräulein Schmidt in Kaj Munk's *He Sits at the Melting Pot*, a vivid, melodramatic play written at the height of German occupation in Denmark, says: "Then *let it be play-acting, and let this be the great idea of the play—that we may be allowed to come out of our narrow selves.*"

The capacity of drama as it comes alive in performance to let human beings "come out of their narrow selves" is one of its most important functions. This is what is meant by perspective, by vicarious experience that drama alone can give. It can also do this by "purgation," as Aristotle called it, or by release that can be found in delight and enjoyment. It is important to understand that significant drama or religious drama is characterized by its possibilities for *illuminating* the private world of the spectator—illumination that allows him to come out of his narrow self. Any drama or theater that can do this will have religious value.

In drama one can walk with kings and not lose the common touch, or one can associate with individuals and groups that are not accessible even to the most cosmopolitan person. In the theater one can see history come alive and ideas take shape in human situations, and one can see revealed what never was revealed before—the inner working of the mind outwardly and the insights of the imaginative artist demonstrating themselves in human forms.

The essential religious values of any play are found first of all in the subject matter of the script. When these are communicated to the audience in performance, a dimension of religious significance is added to the theater.

In other parts of this book religious values in the total activity of producing a play will be discussed. These relate to the leadership in the group, the significance of the director, the "atmosphere" of the church as a producing center, and the effect of the play on the audience. These are all important aspects of the religious-drama experience.

Notes

¹ "Toward a Definition of Religious Drama," *The Journal of The American Educational Theatre Association*, IX, n. 2 (May, 1957), 99.

² Quoted from Marvin Halverson at the National Council of Churches Religious Drama Workshop, Greenlake, Wisconsin, 1955.

³ (April, 1958), p. 10.

⁴ Preston Roberts, "Christian Theory of Dramatic Tragedy," *The Journal of Religion*, XXXI, n. 1 (January, 1951), 7.

⁵ *Ibid.*, p. 13.

Chapter VI

A BRIEF HISTORY OF RELIGIOUS DRAMA

ONE FINE SPRING DAY MILLIONS OF YEARS AGO ONE OF OUR LESS HOUSE-
broken ancestors looked out upon the primeval forest and the unculti-
vated plain. The warm sun had returned again, and he felt the sense
of returning life in the world. He had learned to recognize certain
plants as good to the taste. He saw these coming out of the ground
that morning, and he felt instinctively glad. He knew that the sun caused
the plants to grow, that rain was necessary, and that frost and cold
retarded growth. Naturally, this primitive man wished that the sun
would shine, that the warm rain would come, and that the plants would
mature. He gave utterance to this wish, perhaps in the form of a song
or an uttered petition to the unknown powers he felt were responsible
for the sun and the rain and the wind.

His plea was repeated, this time with other men like himself, and
the place where the plea was raised, especially if the supplication was
answered, became for them a sacred place. It might have been at the
top of a hill where the sky could be clearly seen. It might have been
at the base of a cliff where protection from the wind and rain would
have been possible. Wherever it was, it became the place of petition
to the powers that be, and for the time being it was set apart for that
purpose. This may have been man's first shrine. Here he uttered his
first sincere petition. Here at the time of harvest, he sang his first song
of thanksgiving. Here, too, he may have come when hunting was not
good, when hurricanes struck, when wild animals devoured his stores
of food or killed those with whom he lived. With the other men
women, and children he came to this shrine. Together they raised
their petitions in songs, the rhythms of which gave them incentive

74

to walk in a procession, and finally they delegated to certain persons duties and action that were particularly significant in the worship.

Man lived in a hostile world where survival of the physically strongest was the rule. Even at this early time he was seeking some way to understand the universe and to put himself more completely into harmony with it. He had learned that to defy nature was suicide. Yet he had not sufficiently learned the laws to understand how they might best be used to make for life and not for death. This long process of learning is still going on, and even after millions of years man is confronted with the struggle of life that eventuates either in tragedy or comedy, depending on the way he plays his role.

To please the powers that brought heat and moisture, we can imagine primitive man erecting a stone structure on which he placed gifts he thought the powers might like—the first fruits of his harvest or the finest specimens of his hunting. Nature was often cruel. Frosts killed the early growth and stunted the fruit, and animals filched the store of the hunting. Man was opposed by nature. To overcome this opposition, he thought that more appeasement was necessary. Soon he made images of the powers of nature and gave them human form and human characteristics so that by talking with them, humoring them, bargaining with them became easier. Quite by accident he discovered that when he did certain things certain other things resulted. By this trial-and-error method he came to find the right ways of dealing with the powers and the more advantageous procedures that would guarantee his success. As he transferred human characteristics to the powers or gods, he found himself struggling with them. Their jealousy and ambition were pitted against his jealousy and ambition.

As the spring came we can conjecture that he learned to construct a little story about the return of mother nature from some hidden place where she had been held captive during the winter. He re-enacted this story as a greeting to the spring, putting it into action, performing it with his fellows at the time that was formerly given over to incantations and petitions. Everyone, including the powers of nature, he felt, liked this, and stated occasions for such action became popular. Because the acted story took more concerted effort and used more persons, co-operation was necessary. The struggle of the powers of darkness against the powers of light and life was dramatized in the story of the return of spring. Certain individuals developed abilities to perform the story more effectively and thereby gained popularity. In the course of time man set apart these favorite places where creative dramatics began to solidify into formal drama. Soon the places were to be further marked by playing spaces and by shelters against the weather. The world was to know its first play, its first theater, and its first place of worship.

Worship and drama were probably born together. The emotional expression of a petition, the emphasis upon a word, the manner of walking, the pattern of a celebration, and finally the story of the conflict between the forces of good and evil—all these were to become the dramatic elements of this primitive worship. As these "occasions" became more interesting, man created devices to appeal to larger groups. Words spoken together were easier to understand, and words sung together could raise greater emotional response from the group. Action spoke more effectively than words even at this early time, symbols carried meanings when words confused, and silence often seemed filled with emotion while noise seemed to distract.

At this early stage in primitive civilization, all dramatic expression had form; it was structured, however crude, with a beginning, a sequence in time, and an end. There was a sense of progression, of climax in every performance. Something special that was anticipated, something that differentiated it from the ordinary round of life made it a break in the customary routine. It became celebration.

The drama of native peoples was developed by the people, and the ceremonies recaptured group experiences of earlier days. Song, dance, myth, and poetry were all integrated in the performance. Masks were created by primitive graphic and plastic artists, as were costumes and other paraphernalia for the celebration.[1]

Obviously, there is no line of demarcation between primitive and civilized drama. "In beauty of physical movement, richness of costuming, effectiveness of music, impressiveness of masks, primitive drama is often superior to the drama of culture; in literary expression, subtlety of thought, mechanical equipment, and organization, the latter is obviously superior."[2]

Primitive man believed in a sympathetic magic. He was surrounded by the mysteries of nature, and as Glenn Hughes has pointed out, he lacked any adequate explanation of them. Thus the theory that imitation is a "potent act" has evolved. The act of imitation is as old as man—it is the art of acting. And acting that evoked magic was essentially a religious act because magic itself was a divine process since it was related to forces and powers greater than man.

Other essentially religious concepts occur very early in drama. Penance and sacrifice are characteristic dramatic rituals in the earliest known celebrations. The early Greeks offered the lives of virgins to their deities; later they substituted sheep and other animals. The later sacrificial, symbolic rites developed from the more primitive ones.

Primitive drama, the expression of the communal or religious life of the organic human group, the tribe, had spontaneously the unity of a pure art. There may be two hundred actors dramatically dancing the conflict of winter and spring, but all that all of them do in that drama springs from one shared fund of feelings, ideas, impulses. Unity is not imposed on them by the will of one of their number, but comes from that deep level in the spirit of each where all their spirits are one.[3]

The ancient Egyptians had a dramatic statement of the rebirth of life from the ground that is interesting to study in its relation to the concepts of Easter. The overflow of the Nile meant plenty or famine. The Nile was called Father Osiris, and the land was known as Mother Isis. The annual overflow was the embrace of Mother Isis by her spouse, during which he impregnated her with the life that was to be born during the harvest. The overflow depended upon the melting of the snow in the mountains by the moon, by the sun. The sun was Horus, less powerful than Osiris because the sun could not give life, since he shone in the desert where all was dead, while life bloomed wherever Osiris touched. Therefore they depicted in their great mysteries, the death of Osiris at the hands of the demon Drought, his entombment and Mother Isis' waiting for him, Horus searching for his father and restoring him to life by his magic eye, the sun, and the happiness of Egypt as a result. This was the basis of those splendid and shadowy dramas which filled Heroditus with awe.

Glenn Hughes maintains that while the Hebrews, Egyptians, and Turks never advanced beyond "a rudimentary sort of theatrical expression," the Greeks, Hindus, Chinese, and Japanese achieved elaborate and extraordinarily effective theatrical systems. "The nontheatrical races are only cases of arrested development."[4] Certainly the Jews were not without a dramatic sense in their elaborate feasts, their ceremonials, and their symbolic national role of a chosen people. The Egyptians excelled in dancing which obviously had its dramatic significance, and the Turks were famous for shadow puppets, if not for live drama. Their lives were full of dramatic incident that still needs to be put into dramatic form.

For anyone who has lived in India drama seems a natural mode of expression. The love for ceremonials, the passion for celebration, both religious and secular, and the inherently dramatic events in the lives of most of Indian deities are generic to the Hindu way of life.

The Indian theater is supposed to have grown from the conception of Brahma, the creator, in his meditation as a means of bringing joy to all people. He inspired Bharata to write the Upageda, which is a treatise on dance, drama, and music, which forms the religious-philosophic cornerstone of the many-faceted art of the dance in India. Dance in India is three or four thousand years old, and it is so integrally bound up with drama that the two cannot be separated.

Religion is meaningful to the Hindu in a very real way through ceremonials. His interest has been fostered and kept alive through the celebrations which occur on all days and seasons set apart to pay homage to the deities. All later drama in India—seen best in the performances in villages on the birthday of Krishna or local deities—is largely re-enactment of legend or history in the form of dramatized myths. Music, dance, and pantomime belong in the Indian theater, and all are highly developed in intricate ways that baffle the Westerner but give enduring delight to the Indian. In many ways the village drama of India is similar to the medieval mystery plays. These are India's educational dramatics.

Theorists of the Hindu theater have classified many modes created by dramatic presentation; these include the exotic, the comical, the pathetic, the tragic, the heroic, the hateful, and the miraculous. They have discovered 48 types of heroes, 385 types of females, and many varieties of villains, comedians, and confidants. Contemporary student groups enjoy nothing more than the performance of both Eastern and Western drama. Remarkable, too, is the way in which dramatic interest has found an outlet in the motion picture; India now ranks among the three or four leading producers of movies in the world. Many are founded on religious myths and heroic figures, and all integrate pantomime, dance, and music into the fabric of the myth or history that constitutes the story of the play.

Only recently has the drama of other oriental countries attracted our attention. How interesting it is that in Java none of the arts exist independently of the theater! The intricately carved and beautifully painted shadow puppets have been used to evoke the spirits of ancestors. Originally each family had its own puppets; then the puppets passed to the priests and finally to professional manipulators who still remain among the most skilled artists in the world. Here again we see the secularization of the dramatic art along with the secularization of the subject matter of the plays.

When live actors were substituted for the puppets the physical movements of the puppets were imitated. Today in Jakarta one can see the ancient religiously oriented shadow puppets, as well as modern dramatic forms with live actors, and all are artistically presented with dance and music native to the performance. Theater historians are now suggesting that in the history of the Javanese theater we can see the evolution from religious ritual to secular art in a striking way. We shall also observe the same evolution in all the Western countries.

Before the Christian Era—some historians suggesting as far back as 2000 B.C.—the Chinese were developing a theatrical art. In temples and palaces religious festivals were held in which spectacle and dramatic rituals were recorded in drawings and paintings. The oldest extant specimens of Chinese dramatic literature go back only to the sixth century A.D. In the Yuan dynasty (1280-1368) at the time of the Mongol emperors, well-developed plays existed.

In ancient China, dramatic writing was placed in a category lower than poetry, philosophy, and painting. Interestingly enough, this was because drama was thought of as writing in the vernacular, somewhat more vulgar than the delicate statement of poetry. Then, too, drama was not written in classical Chinese, which is quite different from the language of conversation.

In the golden age of Chinese culture during the Ming dynasty (1368-1644)—corresponding so remarkably with the Renaissance in the Western world—dramatic literature flourished. Cycles of plays divisible by four, some reaching the length of forty-eight plays, were written. Four of these were always performed at the same time.

Chinese plays ought rightly to be called operas, for they are acted to music and are sung. The subject matter is myth and legend. To the Westerner they seem terribly verbose and slow. They are written to amuse and to instruct, with good triumphing and evil always defeated. All scenery and properties are symbolic. They leave everything to the imagination of the spectator. A table may be a mountain, and a journey of a thousand miles over rivers and mountains can be taken back and forth across the stage. The stage manager, always present, plays a singularly important role in the performance.

The Chinese drama came from ritual, and it has never lost its ritualistic character—it does not represent nor does it cope with reality. It is a unique, distinct art form.

Religious dances with masks, accompanied by chants and music, were given in the temples of Japan at a very early period, but the literary drama of Japan does not seem to have been recorded and solidified until sometime in the fourteenth century. A shogun, Yoshimitsu, enjoyed the dancing of a priest, Kwanami, and brought him to the court in 1375. Kwanami developed the art of dramatic representation and with his fellow priests arranged the first real dramas of Japan. They dealt with religious subjects, but their appeal was aesthetic because the gestures, postures, and rhythmical movements of the dancers were based on a symbolic system. This classical performance was called Nō which means drama or something done.

Nō plays using elaborate costumes and headdresses are short and often are merely efforts to establish a mood or set forth a poetic atmosphere. Buddhism dominates many of these early plays so that they are understandable best by adherents of Buddha and his many interpreters. In this sense these are truly religiously based plays, without comedy and completely unrealistic. Some critics suggest that the Nō plays are the most significant specimens of ritualistic drama in the world today.

Popular theater aimed at entertainment did not appear in Japan until two centuries after Nō was established. The doll-play and Kabuki are both famous examples of the popular theater, the former being a puppet theater where music and narration are used. Kabuki began with a religious dancer, in this case, a woman. Her dancing was soon to veer away from its religious origin and to become secular. She assumed the role of warriors and, with her Samurai husband as her composer, established what was to be called Kabuki. The interchange of sexes in the actors and the fact that less high-minded artists were attracted to this performance caused Kabuki to be shunned by respectable people. The abolition of women's companies gave older men a better chance, with families establishing their reputation as actors, and the form was gradually given status. It is still enormously popular in Japan today. The contemporary stage in Japan also includes Western styles of acting and production. Motion pictures have been highly developed, with some of our best pictures originating in Japanese studios.

Ancient Greek drama may have sprung from funeral dirges, from the celebrations of the Eleusinian mysteries, from the concept of the "year spirit," or from satyric drama. The spring season was symbolic of the spirit of rebirth and coincided with the chief worship period of Dionysus, who was also known as Bacchus, the god of wine and fertility. The ode in honor of Dionysus, expressed through song and dance, was known as the dithyramb. This may have been improvisation at first, but certainly by the sixth century B.C. it had become a regular form of literature with a chorus of fifty dancing and singing in a formal composition. In the festival in honor of Dionysus in 534 B.C., there was a contest in tragedy as the chief feature of the program.

Tragedy in this sense was an action that was serious. The satyrs, dressed as goats, give us the word tragedy which originally meant "goat song." Greek tragedy was a music drama or sacred oratorio. The place where the dithyramb took place, the theater of this event, was the place of worship for Dionysus where the only scenery was an altar. When one of the actors dressed himself as the god Dionysus and had the other performers become the god's followers, impersonation was established and acting began.[5]

The state produced the religious festival which gave birth to drama. Dancing was highly important in worship. It was genuinely a social activity co-ordinating music and the muscular control of the body. "It bound reason and emotion together and expressed them, through music, in physical movement."[6] From the beginning the drama was to ask questions about human existence and human destiny. The theater where this took place brought together masses of people and became a great social as well as educational institution.

The great festivals of Greece lasted for several days, with two or three days given to the dramatic contests. These began at daybreak and continued through the day. The winning playwright was crowned before the audience and was highly respected by the people. The open air performances in the great arenas demanded the use of masks and a chorus as well as song and dance to illustrate and emphasize the words of the play. The Greek chorus acted as an "ideal spectator." Arion of Methymna introduced spoken voices into the chanted dithyrambs, and some hundred years later Thespis decided to hold a conversation with his chorus and thus become the first actor.

In one century Athens gave the world four of its greatest dramatists. Aeschylus (525-456 B.C.) was the eldest and in many respects the most somber and magnificent. His plays are filled with foreboding and doom. Of the ninety plays attributed to him only seven survive. He introduced the second actor, differentiated the chorus and the actors by costumes, and elevated the actors by a boot which was called a *kothornos*.

A priest—as were Aeschylus and Euripides—and a man of great affairs, Sophocles (496-406 B.C.), wrote what critics have often called the greatest tragedy of all time, *Oedipus Rex*. The story and characters of the play have meaning for twentieth-century America. His *Antigone*, too, has been adapted by playwrights throughout the history of drama, and his plays have occupied the contemporary stage both in Europe and America.

Euripides (fifth century B.C.) won his first dramatic prize at a city Dionysia when he was thirty-nine. He is generally considered the most modern of the three writers and is often called a writer of psychological drama. Certainly he is the most contemporary in the way his plays delve into the motivation of men; his tragic heroes are no longer merely the victims of the gods or of their fates. He carried the drama a step further not only by celebrating the greatness of his fellow men but by exploring their shortcomings. He seems to have wanted to bring in a new day of social betterment, of honesty, and of rights for all men. His plays are a kind of social drama.

Comedy in Greece came from the Comus song or revel which was often connected with fertility. In contrast to tragedy, comedy presented all of the action on stage. It had much more relation to the audience so that it became popular as a form of commentary on manners and morals. It burlesqued many of the conventions of tragedy such as the use of the messenger, and it gave the audience a sense of participation in what may have been the thought of the spectator that had never been expressed. In this sense comedy is more closely related and intimately concerned. In Aristophanes' *Knights* Demosthenes says:

"Would you I told the story to the audience?" Whereupon Nicias re-
plies:

"Not a bad plan; but let us ask them first
To show us plainly by their looks and cheers
If they take pleasure in our words and acts."

Plato in the *Ion* classes the actor with the poet as an interpreter of
the gods. "In like manner," he says, "the muse first of all inspires men
herself; and from these inspired persons a chain of other persons is
suspended who take the inspiration." The actors were looked upon as
ministers of religion and their persons were sacred and inviolable.

In his book, *The Story of the Theatre*, Glenn Hughes gives this
summary of the importance of the Greek theater:

It can be readily seen that the theatre held an important place in Greek
life. Its motives were religious, patriotic, educational, and aesthetic. Devoted
in its early days to mythology, it came soon to embrace recorded history, and
finally to interpret and evaluate contemporary life. Its tragedies plumbed the
very depths of human emotion; its comedies subjected life to the most pene-
trating rays of human intelligence. Rising from orgiastic ritual during the
sixth century B.C., it developed in the course of a hundred years into magnificent combination of poetry, acting, and pageantry. After the fifth century B.C.
tragedy declined, but comedy persisted and flourished until the end of the
fourth century B.C., when culture moved from Athens to Alexandria, and
Greek civilization gave way to Roman. Probably the first well-organized
theatre in the world, the Greek remains one of the most inspiring.[7]

The Roman world found its drama in wars and conquests, and the
instinctive form of amusement was athletics. Classics of the Greek stage
were performed in Rome, but they were altered to exhibit more
spectacle and more entertainment. Seneca, one of the famous tragic
dramatists of the first century, followed Greek models. Although he
was popular during the Renaissance, it is doubtful if his plays were
performed in Rome during his lifetime.

Rome liked festivals, and her games were called *ludi* or plays. She
was also the originator of the circus where gladiatorial contests, animal
fights, races, and gymnastics vied with each other for popular support.
The remains of the ancient arenas where these took place can still be
seen in Italy. By the fourth century after Christ the Roman calendar
was mostly holidays—101 days were given to plays, 64 to chariot races,

and 10 to gladiatorial contests. Rome loved the pantomime with the actors in masks and the mime which degenerated into a bawdy show that satirized almost everything.

Man's struggle with man, his absorption in the trivia of life, and his living unto himself in a society that gradually evolved into a mad, competitive scramble had its effect on drama and theater. The theater was soon to become the place where man's lowest and meanest characteristics could be seen. In his own natural weakness man liked to see the weakness of his fellow men. From the Greek theater—a place of worship in the time of Aeschylus—to the arena orgies of the later Roman theater is a long development. It is the history of a theater that ceased to have serious and significant meaning. It represents the dilemma of much of the theater today, but the story of this modern development deserves more elaborate telling.

When the theater had degenerated until its effect was only to divert man, a new force had arisen in the world. In the catacombs of Rome little bands of men and women formed an underground movement that advocated a new way of life that stood above any government which might try to impose limitations upon its adherents. In the struggle that was to grow around the early Christians the world was to see the material for new drama. The earthly life of Jesus, the moving spirit of this new interpretation of an old religion, was dramatic. He stood out against the powers of a corrupt secular world; he lived as if God were not some remote force or some idiosyncratic human-divine idol, but a father, the Being who had brought him into life, who provided a world for his food, shelter, and protection; truly the kind of father who would search all night if his child were lost. This Father God of Jesus was an indwelling spirit that lifted all men into a new relationship and that made each life sacred and of equal worth. Here was a concept of man and of God that was to create dramatic struggle as it came against the crude life of the later Roman empire. It is still the material for drama as it comes against the ruthlessness of modern society in the world as we know it.

By the time of Tertullian or by the second century the leaders of the new religion had come out against the institutions which were disregarding the worth of human personality and were corrupting men by exciting their sensual natures. The theater was one of these institutions. Marcus Aurelius sat publicly in his box but averted his eyes to a state paper or a book. Arius, the leader of one of the greatest heresies of the early church, talked of setting up a Christian theater in rivalry to the pagan theater. In his *De Spectaculis* Tertullian said:

If the literature of the stage delight you, we [Christians] have literature in abundance of our own. . . . Would you have also fightings and wrestlings? Well, of this there is no lacking, and they are not of slight account. Behold unchastity overcome by chastity, perfidy slain by faithfulness, cruelty stricken by compassion, impudence thrown into the shade of modesty: these are the contests we have among us, and in these we win our crowns. But would you have something of blood too? You have Christ's.

Tertullian called the theater the devil's church. The later church fathers and Augustine, specifically in his *City of God*, distinguished between high and low drama and praised the use of high drama in education. In A.D. 400 he said, "The theaters are falling almost everywhere, the theaters, those sinks of uncleanness and public places of debauchery."

The early Christians are often given credit for the destruction of the theater. The truth is that the world was changing and with it the theater had to change. The Lombards came in 568, and after that the theater really ceased to exist as an institution of any consequence. "The drama as a living form of art went completely under at the breakup of the Roman world. A process of natural decay was accelerated by the hostility of Christianity, which denied the theater, and by the indifference of barbarism, which never imagined it." [8]

Remarkably little connection seems to exist between the classic stage of Greece and Rome and the medieval drama. For most historians the medieval drama represents a new beginning. The wandering minstrel, acrobat, juggler, or wild-animal trainer took the place of the actor of the Roman theater. The street was the natural place for these amusements. At the same time, however, religious poems were composed. The Dark Ages are dark only by comparison with more brilliant periods of history. One of the surviving representatives of the early religious poem is *The Harrowing of Hell*, written in dramatic form but probably intended to be read. Dramatic dances, folk games, and folk plays also existed from a very early period. The May-day games and dances, as well as the more formal morris dances, come from very ancient times.

Plays connected with these—particularly the Robin Hood plays—were improvised as mummings. The mumming of Saint George in the Saint George play is a typical example. They are genuine folk plays. Roswitha, the Benedictine Abbess of Gandersheim in Saxony, emulating Terence, wrote six plays in Latin for the edification of her nuns. These were written to be read, not acted.

Medieval drama is usually said to originate in the Church. Part of the ritual of the early church is characteristically dramatic. The ritual of Gallican origin, used at the dedication of a church, is an interesting example of this early dramatic form.

The bishop and his procession approach the closed doors of the church from without, but one of the clergy, representing the evil spirit, is inside. Three blows with a staff are given on the door and the anthem is raised: "Lift up your heads, O ye gates; and be ye lifted up, ye everlasting doors; and the King of glory shall come in." From within comes the question: "Who is this King of glory?" The reply is given: "The Lord of hosts, he is the King of glory."

Then the doors are opened, and as the procession sweeps through, the evil spirit who was concealed within slips out. The dramatic expulsion of the spirit of evil takes place so that the church is consecrated to God and purified through the use of holy water and incense. The host is then introduced and the altar becomes a sacred place. In the Roman Catholic Church such was and still is the finely dramatic service that opens a church.

E. K. Chambers in *The Mediaeval Stage* says:

Dramatic tendencies of Christian worship declared themselves at an early period. At least from the fourth century, the central and most solemn rite of worship was the Mass, an essentially dramatic commemoration of one of the most critical moments in the life of the founder. . . . Some scholars attempt to show that the earlier gospel narratives of the passion, those of Saints Matthew and Mark, are based upon a dramatic version . . . on classical lines, and to have been performed liturgically until about the second century, when it was dropped in deference to the ascetic views of the stage then prevalent. The gospel narrative is, no doubt, mainly a "presentation of dramatic action and dialogue. . . ." The earliest liturgical dramas, even in the Greek Church, and those only guessed at, are of the fourth century.[9]

Antiphonal singing seems to have been introduced into Italy from

Antioch by Ambrose of Milan. It is from this antiphon that the actual evolution of liturgical drama starts. Often the melodies used in these antiphonal exercises were not sung to words at all but to vowel sounds. Then texts were written later. These were called tropes. The earliest extant tropes are from the ninth century and are found in a manuscript which shows that the monks of Saint Gall had improvised words to the old liturgical chants. Later in the same century, Benedictine monks added action to part-singing. The method was extended to the Christian story, to other parts of the New and Old Testaments, and to the lives of the saints. The *Quem quaeritis* of Easter Day is the finest example.

We can imagine how this early trope was written. Probably one Easter season some of the younger brothers went to the Superior to suggest that on this great feast day some additional feature should be added to the regular service. The superior, being a stickler for tradition, told the young men that they might sing something additional— an extra number for the occasion. Despairing lest they might not get to do even this, they decided to accept the offer and worked out a choral addition to the music of the introit of the Mass, that is, the procession with which the Mass began. The addition was an instantaneous success.

The following description of the trope used at Winchester around A.D. 970 will give some idea of its simplicity:

While the third lesson is being chanted, let four brethren vest themselves. Let one of these, vested in an alb [a white linen vestment], enter as though to take part in the service, and let him approach the sepulchre [a place on the altar, bare except for the cross, surrounded by a veil] without attracting attention and sit there quietly with a palm in his hand. While the third response is chanted, let the remaining three follow, and let them all, vested in copes [hooded cloaks], bearing in their hands thuribles [vessels with incense], and stepping delicately as those who seek something, approach the sepulchre. These things are done in imitation of the angel sitting in the monument and the women with spices coming to anoint the body of Jesus. When, therefore, he who sits there beholds the three approach him like folk lost and seeking something, let him begin in a dulcet voice of medium to sing *Quem queritis* [Whom seek ye?] And when he has sung it to the end, let the three reply in unison, *Ihesu Nazarenum*. So he, *Non est hic, surrexit sicut praedixerat. Ite, nuntiate quia surrexit a mortui* [He is not here. He is risen, as he said. Go announce that he is risen from the dead.] At the word of this bidding, let those three turn to the choir and say *Alleluia! resurrexit Dominus!* [Alleluia, Christ is risen!] This said, let the one, still sitting there, and as if recalling them, say the anthem *Venite et videte locum.* And saying this, let him rise, and lift the veil, and show them the place bare of the cross, but only the cloths laid there in which the cross was wrapped.[10]

This simple action proved so popular that the dialogue was enlarged and some real dramatic action was included. Finally the action was divided into scenes, and then other characters were included. In one version Pilate places a watch before the sepulcher, an angel sends lightning, and the soldiers fall as if dead. Then the Marys appear and sing songs of lamentation. One scene introduces a spice merchant from whom the women buy spices to anoint the body, a character who was to become humorous in a still later version of the play in Germany. At first the properties were extremely simple, for example, a pile of service books on the altar for the tomb. There were no costumes to distinguish the characters, although later both costumes and other realistic accessories were added.

One of the happiest examples of medieval drama is the play *Adam* which dates from the twelfth century. This play, divided into three parts, treats the fall of man, the first shedding of blood, and the foreshadowing of the redemption. Its unity is religious but not dramatic.

The miracle play *Daniel*, which dates from 1140, has had some successful revivals in New York and Boston in recent years.

The popularity of the trope caused some trouble. At Christmas time the same technique was introduced, and at Holy Innocents' Day and Epiphany dramatic performances were added. Ascension plays became part of the repertoire. Finally, to give more room for the staging and to allow more people to see, the priests presented the dramatizations in the open yard where platforms had been erected. These spaces, too, became crowded; therefore, the plays were taken to the streets and market places. The church could not hold the crowds, nor could the Church keep the secular and humorous elements from being introduced. When the plays left the church, they began to include a great many scenes that had no place in the church. The separation of the Church and drama was taking place. For many hundreds of years thereafter, the drama, which had begun originally in religious rites and had been resurrected in the worship of the Church, stayed out of the Church.

When drama left the churchyard its control passed to the municipal authorities and into the hands of lay groups which were called guilds. These fraternities of men pursuing the same crafts took over the plays, each guild performing one of the scenes in the longer plays. The plasterers put on a play, *The Creation;* the shipwrights did *The Building of the Ark;* the fishmongers and mariners, naturally, were adept at *The Flood;* the goldsmiths were a natural for *The Adoration;* and the bakers worked at their own trade to put on *The Last Supper.* The language was changed from the Latin of the Church to the vernacular of the country. Scenes that had no relation to the Bible were introduced into biblical stories. Herod and Pilate became very important characters; Noah's wife became a shrew; and Mary Magdalene became the heroine of elaborate shows of profligate luxury. The plays of the Church were secularized, nationalized, and localized. Likewise, in the metamorphosis they became theatrically effective. They were genuine folk plays.

In order to show the various parts of the play in sequence the guilds put the scenes on stages or wheels. These pageants usually had two floors, the lower for the dressing room and the upper for the stage. On great feast days, such as Corpus Christi, the plays formed part of the procession. Finally, the lower part of the wagon became the place for hell. Great cycles of plays were shown in one day. The York plays are a cycle of forty-eight plays and were all given on one day, with the performances beginning at four-thirty in the morning.[11] Plays on saints' lives came to be called miracle plays.

No sooner had the liturgical drama been taken up by secular groups than the Church began to realize the danger in what had happened. Opposition was set up and grew in intensity. In an anonymous sermon in 1375 these arguments for and against miracle plays were given:

Arguments for: (1) Played to the worship of God. (2) They do not pervert but by force of example turn men to God. (3) Move men to tears and this in turn leads them to compassion and devotion. (4) They often lead those men to God whose hearts have been proof against all other approaches. (5)Men must have some sort of relaxation, and miracle plays are better than other kinds of amusement. (6) It is lawful to paint pictures of miracles; it is lawful to act them; the dramatic method is more effective for teaching holy Scriptures.

Arguments against: (1) Played not to the worship of God but to the approval of the world. (2) Men are converted by miracle plays just as evil

90

can be cause of good, i.e., Adam's evil cause of Christ's coming. More people perverted than converted. Plays are condemned by Scriptures. (3) Men weep, not for their own sins, not for their inward faith, but for their outward sight. It is not, therefore, allowable to give miracle plays but reprehensible. (4) Conversion is an act of God—motive for conversion can come from miracle plays, but only feigned conversion. If truly converted would hate such playgoing. (5) Recreation should consist in doing works of mercy for one's neighbors, not in false vanity. Wicked deeds of actors and spectators prove plays' worthlessness. (6) Painting, provided it is true, Christian and restrained, may be as a book to discover truth. But acting is an appeal to senses. Good men, seeing that time is already short, will not want to spend it in playgoing.[12]

In the course of time moral allegories in the form of plays came into popularity. These were called morality plays. Personifications of virtues and vices were used as characters. The Seven Deadly Sins, Charity, Flesh, Learning, Mind, Will, Youth, Age, Holy Church, and Riches are all characters found in this type of play. The earliest morality recorded is a dramatization of the Lord's Prayer, Paternoster, dating from 1387. The play is concerned with the results of the seven deadly sins and the petitions of the prayer in the form of a contest for the soul of man between these sins and the Christian virtues. Everyman is the best example of the morality play extant. It has been performed continuously from the time it was translated from a Dutch play of the same name until the present time. The famous performance under the direction of Max Reinhardt in the cathedral square at Salzburg, Austria, the performance by E. Martin Browne in England, and innumerable productions in this country have made it one of the most often produced plays of all time. It is still one of the truly great plays that needs to find production in the Church today.

At a still later time, a new type of play called the interlude came into popularity. It is a play with two or more characters in which the author invents much more freely, uses comedy, sets his scene in the near and familiar, and is realistic. The farcical episode of Mak, the sheep stealer in The Second Shepherd's Play, is one of the happiest examples of this kind of play. The subject matter of this mystery play is the nativity story in which low comedy is used to interest the audience in the story of the birth of Jesus.

A medieval farce that should be revived is Maistre Pierre Pathelin by Guillaume Alécis. This comedy of situation is delightfully funny today when it is not overdone. It is a farce of subtlety and wit showing the knavery of Pathelin as a lawyer.

The transition from the humorous interlude to modern comedy is a natural one. Thus we see the play which began as part of the Mass pass through a popularization and secularization until it becomes a completely secular play. The farcical material which was used to enhance the religious part became the purpose of the play. With the plays of John Heywood, who was born before 1497 and died before the time of Shakespeare, the drama became the instrument of pleasure without serious or religious responsibility.

The history of religious drama from the beginning of the Elizabethan period to the present time is the story of the development of theater and the increasing richness of playwriting. Singular examples of great plays with profound meanings come to mind. Marlowe's *Dr. Faustus* and Goethe's *Faust* treat in different ways man's search for truth, the understanding of good and evil, and the need for redemption. Shakespeare's *Hamlet, Winter's Tale, Othello*, and *King Lear* are some of the world's great dramas that reveal new insights with each reading.

A study of Allardyce Nicoll's *World Drama* [13] with its numerous quotations from plays will show that many plays of genuine religious significance are found in England, France, Germany, Italy, Russia, Scandinavia, and Spain. The list of plays for reading and study in the Appendix of this book is a long one, but its richness only suggests again how many great playwrights have turned to the great tensions of life that have to do with man, his meaning, and his relation to values and purposes that are fundamentally religious.

The drama of the contemporary world beginning with Henrik Ibsen has often been called the drama of social significance because it has treated social problems as they are seen in the lives of ordinary men and women. Certainly *Brand, A Doll's House, Ghosts, An Enemy of the People, The Wild Duck, Hedda Gabler*, and *Rosmersholm* deserve the new translations and the fine revivals they are being given. They still remain the contemporary world's greatest plays.

Scarcely less significant is George Bernard Shaw (1856-1950) whose plays are now read for their cleverness and wit and for the profound comment most of them make on the strengths and weaknesses of contemporary man and his society. *Arms and the Man, The Devil's Disciple*,

Androcles and the Lion, Man and Superman, Major Barbara, and *Saint Joan* are all plays that provide delightful reading and enjoyable study. John Galsworthy's problem plays are still valuable as sociological studies. St. John Ervine's *John Ferguson* has been called a kind of book of Job. Christopher Fry's *The Boy with a Cart, The First Born,* and *A Sleep of Prisoners* are beautiful, meaningful plays in a poetic language that is often dramatically alive. T. S. Eliot's *Murder in the Cathedral* and *The Cocktail Party* are two of the genuinely fine religious plays of this century. James Forsyth's *Emmanuel* and his version of Ibsen's *Brand* are becoming increasingly better known.

The contemporary Irish theater has produced poet-dramatists like William Butler Yeats and Sean O'Casey whose passion has been expressed in language that makes them two of the great artists of the present-day world.

France has continued to produce playwrights of astonishing versatility and power. Brieux, Rostand, and Becque have been followed by Jean Giraudoux, Jean-Paul Sartre, Jean Cocteau, and Jean Anouilh. The richness of the plays of these artists is hardly challengeable.

Gerhart Hauptmann's *The Weavers* was one of the finest examples of contemporary naturalism in Germany. Bertolt Brecht (1898-1956) came to international attention through his *Berliner Ensemble.* His concepts of epic theater must be understood to appreciate his plays. His is a theater calling for intellect rather than emotion, for directness rather than illusion, and for alienation rather than empathy. Critics agree that his *Mother Courage* may remain one of the great plays of the contemporary world.

Nor should one miss the plays of Karel Capek of Czechoslovakia, Luigi Pirandello of Italy, or Federico Garcia Lorca of Spain. Tolstoy's plays, together with those of Chekhov in Russia, complete a listing of European playwrights whose work should be read by anyone who wishes to understand religiously oriented drama.

America, too, has produced plays of consequence from the rousing propaganda of *Uncle Tom's Cabin* to the most recent plays of Thornton Wilder, Arthur Miller, and Tennessee Williams. Eugene O'Neill, Maxwell Anderson, Elmer Rice, Clifford Odets, Lillian Hellman, William Inge, Robert Anderson, William Gibson, Archibald MacLeish, and Edward Albee are familiar names to anyone who has read drama or attended the theater in America in the last thirty years.

With the founding of the Drama League of America under the leadership of Mrs. A. Starr Best, religious drama was revived in the Church, in schools, in colleges, and in the professional theater. The National Catholic Theatre Conference, the Religious Drama Project of the American Educational Theatre Conference, and the drama committees in two divisions of the National Council of Churches have continued and strengthened the movement. The pioneering work in the School of Theology and the Theatre Division of the School of Fine and Applied Arts of Boston University, the work at Christian Theology Seminary in Indianapolis, the drama courses offered at Union Theological Seminary in New York City, together with work at Redlands University and at Scarritt College in Nashville, are evidence of the attention the Church is giving to drama.

What this new interest will mean is a matter for the future. Certainly, the concern of colleges and seminaries and the intelligent work of Methodist and Presbyterian churches is an addition to the interest in Britain where the Religious Drama Society, which has carried on for many years, has had the attention and respect of the professional theater, as well as that of the churches, for a long time. What this should mean is that the day of the concept of religious drama as the silly nightgown pageant in the church is over and that the new day of understanding the depth of religion and its concern for the good life is coming to focus in the drama.

Notes

[1] Glenn Hughes, The Story of the Theatre (New York: Samuel French, Inc., 1928), p. 8.

[2] For a fuller treatment of this subject see Melville I. Herskovitz, Man and His Works (New York: Alfred A. Knopf, Inc., 1950), Part V, Chapter 25.

[3] Quoted from George Cram Cook in the first program of The Provincetown Players.

[4] Hughes, op. cit., p. 4.

[5] For a provocative discussion of the origin of the theater see Benjamin Hunnigher, The Origin of the Theatre (New York: Hill and Wang, Inc., 1961). This is available in a paperback edition.

[6] Philip A. Coggin, The Uses of Drama (New York: George Braziller, Inc., 1956), p. 3. Used by permission.

[7] Hughes, op. cit., p. 78. Copyright, 1928, by Samuel French. Copyright, 1956 (In Renewal), by Glenn Hughes. All Rights Reserved. Reprinted by permission of the author and Samuel French, Inc.

[8] E. K. Chambers, The Medieval Stage (New York: Oxford University Press, 1903), II, 2. Used by permission.

⁹ *Ibid.*, II, 3. For a more modern use of this idea see the *Passion According to St. Matthew* by J. S. Bach. The idea here dates from an early attempt to sing the Gospel and make it dramatic.

¹⁰ *Ibid.*, II, 4.

¹¹ The whole of the forty-eight cycle plays condensed into an acting version was put on in 1951 at York in England under the direction of E. Martin Browne. The *Introduction* in Mr. Browne's selection of mystery and morality plays in *Religious Drama 2* (New York: Meridian Books, Inc., 1958) should be required reading.

¹² Coggin, *op. cit.*, p. 51. Used by permission.
This book is an excellent source for the history of religious drama and the attitudes toward drama by the church and churchmen.

¹³ New York: Harcourt, Brace and Co., 1950.

Chapter VII

THE USES OF THE DRAMATIC

A. Drama as Celebration

IN THE ANCIENT WORLD MEN AND GODS AND THEIR DEEDS WERE HONORED by sacrifices and ceremonies in designated places. The Greek world was a world of such celebrations. To a degree this is true in the world where the Church has become the place for the celebration of events in the life of Jesus and the saints of Christian history. Great movements in church history for the Protestants, likewise, have been memorialized in services of commemoration.

An interesting example of this kind of celebration—among its other meanings and purposes—is found in the Protestant concept of Communion. The immediate friends of Jesus met to "remember" him in the Last Supper. Later the friends of the friends, the group of the fellowship of the followers of Jesus, met to commemorate his last meal with his disciples. As this ceremony was observed by taking food or wine and bread, the eating was done in memory of him. How interesting is the apostle Paul's statement of the meaning of the Communion: "As often as ye eat this bread, and drink this cup, ye do shew the Lord's death till he come." It was the core of early Christian worship, and it was a dramatic ceremony in every sense of the word because it was a *showing forth*, a *representation* of an event which had deep and real significance. It was an action performed. We *celebrate* Communion.

In the process of this development, confession of sins and forgiveness, as well as praise and thanksgiving, were made a part of the ceremony. Around this core of the service grew all the other characteristic aspects of worship. It was "right, proper, and a bounden duty" to give thanks. How pathetic it is that the contemporary Christian in the evangelical church has lost his capacity to express thanks. He allows the minister

95

to do this for him. He is likewise limited in his ability to praise. He sings songs of praise in a desultory fashion, and hallelujah sticks in his throat. He finds no excitement in praising God and in expressing his thanksgiving. Praise and thanksgiving are now largely offered by choirs expertly trained musically to feel for him and express for him.

The Church must regain its function for celebration of worship if it is to be unique as an institution. It must afford men a chance to worship, to give themselves in public corporate ceremonies to something higher than themselves; it must allow them to express their feelings in acts of worship so that the meaning of these acts will be constantly clear and understandable to them. It is through worship that the dramatic can re-enter the Church.

The Church must learn how to celebrate great historical events and the personages of whom these events may be the long shadow. To celebrate an event is to dramatize its meaning. The European church has been more effective in keeping these events alive. *La Festa el Missterio,* held yearly at Elche in Spain on the day celebrating the Assumption of the Virgin Mary, is an event in the life of the Spanish church. Anyone who has been present to see the Virgin taken to heaven by being drawn up through the dome of the church and has been part of the shouting, laughing, and crying mob knows that for that time, at least, something has happened, something has been vividly alive for several thousand people. *The Mystery of Elche* is a dramatic reality, and it cannot be forgotten no matter what may be one's attitude about its theological implications.

The Church needs to regard baptism, marriage, admission to church membership, and death as times of celebration. The meaning and purpose as well as the quality and means of celebration will differ, but the fact of celebration will prevail. This is an instrument of the Church which gives it uniqueness in a modern society.

Nowhere is celebration more likely to be needed than in the great events of the church year. Christmas and Easter should be celebrated; so should Advent, Epiphany, Ash Wednesday, Good Friday, All Saints Day, Whitsunday, and the lesser days which have been dropped from the "free church" Protestant calendar.

The reason why many of these days have dropped from the calendar may be due to a lack of proper ways to celebrate them. The Church has no real means to celebrate birthdays or what on the church calendar are called feasts. Here dramatic means can make a contribution, but it will need to be means that are not yet improvised. There is need to remember, and to remember by calling attention in effective ways to events in the life of Jesus as well as in the lives of the apostles and saints who have made Christianity the vivid, living thing it can be. Here again, Christianity has been demonstrated by these men and women, and the demonstration is something that the Church needs to see today.

Obviously, the lives of most of the saints are matters of legends and myths, and some of these are forgotten or at least have never been kept current for the Church today. Only recently has a writer in the *Saturday Review* suggested that the vitality of a religion can be judged by the freshness of its myths.

Lawrence Housman has kept the legends related to Francis of Assisi alive in the delightful *Little Plays* which are listed in the play list in the Appendix. The body of material relating to the events of the lives of the saints is enormous. Much of it is too ridiculous to be of any use, but again and again there are stories which cry out for dramatization.

Contemporary Protestantism is without the rootage of tradition, and particularly without the charming legends which make so vivid the meaning of much of the witness of its heroic figures. Furthermore, the evangelical branches of the Church have almost totally neglected the church calendar. As these events are brought into focus for one day, the Church has attempted to resurrect some of the meanings.

An example of this may be found in the revival of a day to celebrate the meaning of the Reformation. When the makers of curriculum began to probe into history and to find what events in the life of the Church, to say nothing of the life of Martin Luther, were available, they discovered that except for a feature-length film and innumerable books very little had been done with a subject that ought to be kept alive and fresh. Nor have denominations founded by exciting figures been any the more ready to celebrate the contributions made by these men. The Baptists have only recently looked into the highly dramatic life of Roger Williams, and the Methodists have looked, but have done very little about John Wesley or Francis Asbury.[1] Still more important is the need to give a sense of the Church to contemporary churchgoers. This can be done, in part, by celebrating the Christian year.

Christmas

Most Christmas celebrations in the Church are neither educationally sound nor dramatically effective. Merely to put into action the events surrounding the birth of Jesus is not to present an effective pageant or drama. A pageant may often lift a congregation because of its mass effects, its use of group movements, and its pictorial devices.

What we should celebrate at Christmas time is what Jesus of Nazareth stood for. We commemorate his birth by rededicating ourselves to what he taught. What could be our finest dramatic celebration has been made into a rather meaningless, sentimental celebration of the birth of a baby and the attendant wonderful events that surrounded it.

We can give thanks for the advent of Jesus by the use of drama and music which glorifies and interprets the significance of the life of Jesus. The traditional carols can be used to show the extent to which the birth of Jesus has affected the world.

The play list in the Appendix gives a few good plays to be used at Christmas. They should initiate worship experiences which grow out of thinking and out of emotional reactions that remind us of the meaning of Jesus for us. Christmas must be made a day for considering the worth of individuals and also of the family of all the children of earth to whom a man came to bring a gospel of peace and good will. Simple scenes relating these ideas to contemporary life can be given. Projects which look to a better community, as well as to better world relationships, need to be emphasized. The season should be one of emphasis upon the value of each person and upon the need for concern on the part of all for every other creature. Pageants that show the effect of Christianity through the ages can be given. Music, drama, choral speech, and interpretive dancing are all ways in which the meaning of the religion of Jesus can be interpreted.

Lent and Easter

The Easter season is the most dramatic of the church year, but the events and their meaning for us are so great that we can scarcely condense them into one unified play. This is perhaps the reason why most of the Passion plays are undramatic. They try to give too much and usually succeed in treating much of the material with little thoroughness or dramatic intensity. Maundy Thursday has something to say that can come through no other day. Good Friday needs drama to give a sermon-interpretation of the tremendous events of that day. Easter Sunday should be the outburst of joy and thanksgiving that can come only when the spirit of God has so illuminated a man that he knows no death.

Drama can help to reinterpret the meaning of Easter and of Holy Week for the Church. Music, speaking choirs, and effective dramatization may call us again to follow the example of a completely consecrated man whose redemptive message for the Church needs to be heard now. The dramatic representation need not be given on the day of the celebration—it should be a part of the church educational process.

Drama in the Church must not be used to dress up an occasion merely to give it prominence or popularity. Drama should be a tool of the ministry of the people in the church who feel that their interests, capacities, and abilities can best be used through this particular medium. *It should be used any time when what needs to be said can best be said through drama.*

Many times during the year something needs to be said dramatically. Christian history is full of events that show the forces of light battling against the dark, reactionary effects of evil. From ancient times to the present men and women have lived lives that have stood against wrong. Sometimes their lives have been recognized, and they have been sainted. Other lives have been recorded in modest ways and with little publicity, but the deeds have stood. The contemporary church can lift up these witnesses to truth and justice through dramatic episodes in their lives and show the contemporary Christian what living in the Christian pattern has meant and still means.

Fearless prophets and more ordinary men today are trying to live their faith. The Church needs to give effective expression to the dramatic incidents in the life of Mahatma Gandhi, Toyohiko Kagawa, Albert Schweitzer, Jane Addams, Muriel Lester, and other men and women whose names are not so familiar but whose lives have given exciting witness of religious living. No better episodes for drama could be found than the intense moments in the lives of local figures who have been pioneers in just and honorable living.

B. Education Through Dramatic Production

Most educators agree that to be integrated, personality must be motivated by an ideal. For the Christian this is the ideal of a life that finds its source of power in God as he is revealed through Jesus. This means that each Christian can find a relationship to God and through the precepts and the example of Jesus can find a right relationship to man. The integrated personality is "at home" in the universe; it belongs. It should not, however, be satisfied with things as they are. Once a person has understood the meaning of the religion of Jesus he can never be content with what man has done to man. To become effective in changing the state of man, he needs to organize his own life into a harmonious whole. Education becomes for him the process whereby he gains a complete conception of life. As he sees life in this way and as he grows into an integrated person at the same time, he becomes an adult.

The growth process in personal and social education needs imagination to comprehend goals. The dramatic instinct is peculiarly the instinct that uses imagination, for it enables a person to put himself in someone else's place. The capacity to imagine the thoughts and acts of another person begins in earliest childhood in imitation. It is then transferred to the play stage—first with one's self and then with others—and finally it gives each older individual the ability to create characters while he is working in a co-operative group process. The more dramatic instinct is cultivated, the larger the perspective of the person is likely to be. He gains perspective by understanding other people. In this way he gains a conception of life that sees things in proportion, and he can more readily belong.

Religion needs imagination and the dramatic instinct. If we are to be persons who are sensitive to other men, if we are to relate ourselves to God, if we are to worship and pray effectively, we must have the capacity to imagine these things, for no matter how wide our contacts and our life span, we cannot know all of these things through direct experience. The ability to put ourselves in the place of others will alone help us create the brotherhood of man. How much insight with imagination it took to see a common fisherman and know that he could be Peter the disciple! How much understanding and imagination it takes at the present time to forgive one's enemies, and what dramatic instinct is necessary to sympathize with and understand the situation of people less fortunate than ourselves! To create a new world we must have these assets, for without vision a people will perish.

In the program of Christian education the need for the cultivation of the imagination and the dramatic instinct is at once apparent if we are to identify ourselves with life situations and have the vision to put them into action. All the fine sentiments which we accumulate in religious education will be wasted unless we cultivate the sense to see them in situations which most of the time do not exist except in imagination. Furthermore, to understand the past and to have a sense of its relation to the present is a matter of imagination as well as knowledge. The Bible is a book singularly lacking in exact description. Not even the figure of Jesus is described with accuracy. To reconstruct the person of Jesus through the records, imagination must be brought to bear upon the records.

In the presentation of the formal play the whole process can be an educational experience, and in the church it should also be a religious experience. This can only happen when we recognize that the uniqueness of drama in the church arises out of what the activity does, both to the actors and the production crew as well as to the congregation that comes to participate. Creating a character, no less than creating a scene or lighting a playing space on a stage, requires technical skill. Without a sense of the dramatic, however—the objectification of our dramatic instinct—imagination and creativity in the lighting and scenery still will not be used to best advantage. These, then, are the two primary prerequisites. If a child has grown up under the creative dramatic process, he will have both of them. He is likely to be the person who will also appreciate the insights of religion because he knows the way to actualize them in everyday experience.

One time we thought that educational dramatics was principally concerned with the people backstage. We said boldly that the play was being done for them and that if an audience was present it was inconsequential. Our purpose was to produce a play for the benefit of those who were participating as cast and as production workers. The director was concerned primarily with the development of these individuals, and the success of the experiment would be judged solely by their growth.

The project might be a simple play dealing with the concern persons should have for their neighbors—with the theme, let us say, of the Good Samaritan story. If the educational dramatic method worked, the person cast as the Good Samaritan would have been through a sound educational process; he would have learned not only the teaching of the parable, but also the historical background of the story. Every character in the cast would have learned something about the period of the play and would understand the ethical values inherent in the story.

This method is attractive and desirable largely because it means that persons with little or no ability may have an opportunity to act and to participate in the production. The idea is that the method can also allow a director less concern for perfection. Yet without the stimulation of an audience plays do not come alive nor can the "miracle of the theater" ever take place. Formal plays are not best suited to the educational technique. The creative dramatics method should be substituted for children and role-playing for adults.

A child or an adult creating any part in a play ought to go through an educational process. The depth and effectiveness of this process is determined by the depth of the actor's feeling as he assumes the character. It is also determined by the way in which the character is developed so that it becomes a reality both to the actor and to the participating audience. If the dramatic process for young people and adults does away with audience participation it lops off one of its most valuable potentialities. There is no consummation or completion in a performance until an audience comes alive to the play.

Since the production of a play is a group process, unity and focus can obviously be achieved only through competent direction. If each person in the production disregards the others chaos will result. Likewise, the selfish person will find that expression of his own desire must be submerged in the good of the majority. The young person who is over-assertive will soon understand that the success of the project will depend on his doing his part with a minimum of his habitual expression. Boys and girls who have never learned to work with other children will in time find joy in this co-operation. *The purpose of the play, not the director, should be the unifying element.* The enthusiasm and energy of the group can be captured in the ideal that has been set up. The director is the person who holds the group to this ideal and who helps each person achieve his maximum effectiveness.

Drama is being used in many types of therapeutic work. In a sense drama in the church is likewise used for this purpose, for in this kind of drama each person associated with the project is important both as a person and as a contributing factor in the co-operative process. In ordinary play production when an individual interferes with the procedure because of personal shortcomings he is quickly dismissed. In our use of the drama we must be determined to find a place for each person's assets. We cannot be psychiatrists, nor should we attempt counseling on difficult matters of personality adjustment. We do know, however, that the process of producing a play can help even antisocial personalities find a constructive outlet for their energies and a place in a co-operative venture that makes all persons lose their individual selves in the working toward final group achievement.

We know now that the educational process is as continuous a process in the theater as it is in life. Nowhere is this demonstrated more effectively than in the growth of students in high school and college. The drama gives an actor a chance to understand characters that can never come into his actual experience. Through his imagination he may appreciate historical characters that by reading in a book he can understand only dimly. He becomes the person while at the same time he has a perspective on that person which actors alone can get. He must be able to put himself into the life experience of a person whom he can never possibly meet because of his restricted environment and limited experience. We have already suggested that drama frees an individual from the confines of the narrow circle of his experience. Today he may walk with kings, or he may feel the common touch of a person whose social experience is completely out of his life. The good director is the one who helps the actor and all of those concerned with the production to understand sympathetically and intelligently the background of the play, the characters, and the experiences that they will interpret.

If the process of producing a play has been truly an educational one the miracle of the theater takes place in that the audience joins with the actors and the production crew in the experience of the performance and in an amazingly short time goes through the experience of the play firsthand. How good the educational process has been can be judged by the sincerity of the actors and their capacity to "get over" to an audience the thing that they represent—that is, to translate to the people in the audience an experience in which they are participating.

If the director is forced to use persons who have little capacity to interpret the parts, and if he knows that his performance is to be ragged because he has tried to work with an inexperienced group, he should then be bold enough to announce this fact to the audience. It should not be done by way of apology, but it should be done as a matter of explanation so that there is no misunderstanding on the part of the audience as to what the director is trying to do. Every audience has the right to expect the best possible production of a play. Any performance that falls short of that standard must be explained.

Education during the process of production takes time. It cannot be done in a hurried, shortcut rehearsal period. It is in a real sense the method that is used in the continental theater, particularly in Russia. It means that all persons in the production are given chances. The director must be willing to work for long periods of time with the weaker members of the cast. He does not resort to typecasting even though it would be an easier method. Much more patience and understanding is required when the educational approach is used. In the professional theater typecasting too often is used largely because of the element of time, and because the director has neither the skill nor the patience to work with people who are less obviously suited to the character which they must create. In the amateur field the educational process simply means that in the entire project the person whose work is sincere, who is willing to work, and who is also willing to spend sufficient time will be rewarded by a director who in turn will try to help this person achieve the thing he sets out to do, so long as the production is not harmed by incompetence and lack of some ability. If the children used "show off," the process is not an educational one, and the resulting detrimental effects cannot be laid at the door of drama. The blame should be placed on the director for his lack of understanding.

The education of an audience is a new idea in the theater. In 1911 the Drama League of America was established specifically to educate audiences for better plays. The League had a playgoing committee which sent out criticisms of all the new plays. Local centers of the organization then took these comments to their constituency so that theatergoers could be aware of the type of play they were seeing. When an especially good play was given an audience was organized to support the play. This was audience education at a time when there were audiences for professional productions outside New York City.

In every church there are people who are willing to do something if somebody else will just take the initiative. The technical aspects of play production offer invaluable opportunities to get this kind of leadership.

Theater work has such scope that there is a place for each person, re-gardless of his interests or aptitudes. Then a group begins working together. The cutting out and sewing of costumes, the construction of a tree stump or a rock, the painting of scenery, the rigging up of lights, and the mimeographing of programs are activities which can be rich in co-operation, in recreation, and in the friendships which they foster. Under a skillful director many people can work together and have a good time all along the way if there is a common goal. The worth and the interest of the work can prove to be a forgetting ground for petty rivalry, self-assertiveness, and bickering which are sometimes present in churches.

The whole work of technical production can be made even more worthwhile if it is done regularly for other groups. The play can be pre-sented before clubs, organizations, and other churches, or the stage crew of the church may pitch in and help other amateur organizations of the community in their productions. People find themselves in work to which they can give themselves. The scope of work involved in dramatic production is intriguing for many people.

If plays in the church are to succeed in being something more than shows the people who come to the play must be willing to help create the response that is part of the process. Only as they are aware of their purpose will the play come alive. The wise director will do everything possible to help in the education of an audience. If the play is an experiment, or if it is being done as a project in co-operative work, a short speech before the play begins can introduce the meaning of the project and can ask the co-operation of the audience. If printed programs are used some intelligent notes may point out the purpose of the play and its value as a project in the church. A drama group may also have "afternoons" when they can present informative talks on plays. The more understanding the audience has, the more certain will be the success of the play from a religious point of view.

We have said that the entire process of producing a play should be an educational project. If a play has values, if it is carefully interpreted, and if it is performed sincerely and intelligently before an audience that comes to enjoy the experience, it will inevitably be an educational process for the cast, for those who helped in the production, and for the audience that comes to participate in the experience as it comes alive.

C. Drama as Recreation

Our forefathers understood the meaning of "enjoy" as experiencing. Drama has the capacity to re-create through enjoyment. Its capacity to give perspective, to let us see ourselves as others see us is more evident when one assumes a role in a play. Through the portrayal of a character an actor is given insights into character that can come in no other way. The character must be brought to life. This means that the actor must live the character until he walks, talks, and feels like the person he is representing. This can be true recreation. To play is to become a part of, to re-create. Recreation through drama is a way of throwing one's self into life and not escaping from it. If plays are produced for recreation and by recreation is meant escape from life, the group will be disillusioned. Even a superficial characterization requires some understanding of life. Drama lets one see life and by seeing life understand contrasting values and concepts.

Drama for recreation allows one to laugh and to have the healthy, cleansing experience of enjoyment. Naturally, the value is conditioned by the kind of laughter. "Gypsy laughter from the bushes" is of dubious value. Likewise, laughter which arises from the exhibition of bad taste, of catering to sensual experience as a thing in itself, has no place.

As a group process "putting on a play" requires the time and talent of an amazing variety of people. That the production of a play can use all talents, that it is always a co-operative venture, and that it is successful only when everyone connected with it has had fun make it a contribution to any institution when these values are wanted. What must be stressed again and again is that the production of a play is not easy, that it will be disappointing and disintegrating as an experience unless time and ability are freely given. The better the play, the more expert the production, the more certain are the positive results. If a play is worth doing, it is worth doing well. The amount of recreation is proportionate to the amount of effort that is put into any production. There is no shortcut to worthwhile enjoyment.

Notes

[1] Information about the film on the life of John Wesley can be secured from the Radio and Film Commission, 1523 McGavock Street, Nashville, Tenn. Donald Mauck's play on Francis Asbury, *Glory in the Land*, can be secured from Dr. Mauck at the University Methodist Church, Columbus 10, Ohio.

Chapter VIII

DRAMA AND WORSHIP–CHANCEL DRAMA

A. Dramatic Worship

DRAMATICALLY EFFECTIVE WORSHIP SUCCEEDS IN LIFTING THE WORSHIPER out of himself and in bringing him into the spirit or presence of something higher than himself. This may be from a source within himself or from something he feels outside himself. True worship establishes a relationship with this presence or spirit. The enduring quality of the relationship and the intensity of the reality are tests of the validity of the experience. In this sense, then, true worship is the recognition, identification, and relationship to the noblest, the highest, and the best that one can conceive. It is a coming into the presence of God and remaining there.

Worship is this relationship in progress. The effectiveness of worship can always be judged by the way in which the self is prepared for the experiences of this relationship to the highest and noblest and by the resultant effect on the self. It is, therefore, a two-way experience. It is the soul and spirit of the individual going out to a higher spirit, the opening up of the avenues of approach and, at the same time, the coming in of the influence of the greater spirit. Like all experiences, it is at first self-conscious. The more one comes into the practice of it, the more certain does the experiment become natural and spontaneous. It is always possible to have the experience of worship immediately and without even the consciousness of an attempt. When this happens it is one of the supreme experiences of life—a moment in eternity when the physical is broken through and the self enjoys a spiritual existence. As man succeeds in discovering this spirit world, as surely he must in his progress toward higher levels of living, the union and relationship with the supreme spirit will become the truly noble and energizing experience of his life. It will, of course, color every other experience and grow to be a more continuous process in his every activity of life.

The technique of practicing the presence of God demonstrated by Brother Lawrence is in a very real way perfection of the technique of practicing worship. Worship is an extraordinary thing or an unusual experience only because it is not continuous. In the progress of spiritual life it should become more continuous so that all life becomes a worshiping experience.

On the other hand, the very complexity of living, the distractions of the materialistic world, and the busyness of life are all characteristics that make the true experience of worship all the more unique. This does not mean that worship should be an escape or that it is a running away from day-by-day experiences. On the contrary, it should be the means whereby these ordinary experiences are given meaning and are elevated to the distinction all life should have. The necessity to "be still and know" is a prerequisite to strength, poise, and inward peace. As one prepares himself and comes into a relationship with the spirit of life he is participating in preparation for and the experience of worship. When the union between the spirit of man and the spirit of God becomes complete true worship takes place.

The dramatic is always the genuine because it arises from within and expresses itself in the truly sincere. It is always an experience from the inward outward. It is the expression of depth feeling. Its expression reveals its origin. Dramatic speech is characterized by its sincerity, by its depth of feeling, and by its meaningful expression. To test the dramatic quality of speech one must evaluate the sincerity of its origin as well as its effect. Like produces like. The dramatic should cause depth reactions. Deep calls to deep. The end of worship is so much a depth experience—in fact, it should be the deepest experience of life —that it should always be dramatic. *All effective worship is dramatic.* It arises out of a deep feeling of relationship, and it succeeds because it establishes that relationship.

The Leader of Worship

Unless the leader of worship himself is having the experience of worship there can be little hope for a worship experience on the part of an individual being lead. The leader must, therefore, feel genuinely everything he does. Through the experience he transmits his own feeling. He is not playing a role; he is not assuming a position. He is worshiping. He is part of a total process.

This means, therefore, that in group worship the worship leader must prepare himself for the worship period as surely as the worshiper in the group is prepared. Dramatic group worship can be effective only when the group itself is prepared for the experience and is helping in the participation. This same principle applies to all those participating in the worship—the assistants, the choir, the organist, and those in charge of seating or administering any part of the service. The entire personnel in leadership as well as those in the congregation must be in a unified worship atmosphere. Distractions caused by interruptions by insensitive worshipers can destroy the dramatic effectiveness of worship.

This is particularly true because dramatic worship is always unified worship which begins with the entrance into a receptive attitude and continues as the worshiper is raised to that point of unity and relationship with God which is the end of dramatic worship. It continues until the experience is completed. The object of worship should be the creation of an experience that can be carried out and continued after the group is disbanded. The more one becomes experienced in worship, the more fully he will learn the ways in which the experience is continued.

Dramatic unity is always achieved by recognizing a beginning, a rising action, a climax, and an end. These are not artificial markings. They are essential elements in the structure of a worship service. For this reason the place of worship, the establishment of the atmosphere and mood, the call to worship, the participation leading up to the climax of the moment of emotional and intellectual unity in the spirit, and the holding of that until it is established and becomes reality are all component parts of the total dramatic worship experience.

Ways to Dramatic Effectiveness

The setting of a worship service can be either dramatic or theatrical. If it is theatrical the trappings will call attention to themselves. A dramatic setting never calls attention to itself. It always becomes part of a total picture. When lighting, costuming, setting, and atmospheric conditions call attention to themselves they obtrude so that they distract from the purpose, and the dramatic element may be lost and the service may end in a theatrically impressive but superficial experience. Anything new may often be considered theatrical. It must be introduced with explanation and through an educational process. Changes in an accustomed service are oftentimes so distracting that they negate any chance for betterment. This does not mean that worship needs to be stereotyped or that changes cannot be made. The way in which they are made is important, however. Worshipers must be prepared for changes, or worship is likely to be theatrically exciting but not dramatically effective.

Dramatic unity which has the structure of a beginning, a rising action, and a climactic ending is not an artificial structure. The tone and intensity of worship should obviously not be the same at the beginning as at the climax. There should be rising action or intensifying feeling as the service progresses. The worshiper comes into the atmosphere and experience from myriad distracting influences. Each person coming into group worship is coming from a different kind of distraction. In the theater the lowering of the lights, the magic moment before the curtain rises when the audience is stilled, the use of music, and the device of a curtain are all means to galvanize a group into a whole and to prepare it for a unified dramatic experience. The church has no such opportunities. Yet it must use lights and setting and create moods even more effectively than does the theater.

As the theater recognizes the distractions from which the audience comes so must the church. It should not ask people to come immediately from a distracting world into the sudden experience of worship. For that reason, if the congregation can be brought into a service at the beginning, the auditorium should not of necessity be dimly lighted nor all of the setting of worship completely established. If a congregation is friendly and chatty it is much better to introduce worship gradually. This can be done by means of lights or by the use of music or by the preparation of the altar or worship setting which will be the visual objects on which the worshiper will concentrate. The ritualistic churches do this by lighting candles after the congregation has assembled. If there is a worship setting the worship leader as well as the congregation should be facing it. Nothing is more absurd than the average Protestant procedure of introducing a worship setting and then having the minister or worship leader sit with his back to that setting. It should be the focal point to hold the attention of the congregation so that there is no distraction. Dramatic worship appeals to all the senses, for it is a complete experience. It appeals, therefore, to the sight and to the hearing. In certain churches the atmosphere is equally important, and the purification by holy water and by incense is not accidental.

Dramatic Unity

Dramatic unity in a service is related directly to the movement of the service. Once the mood has been established and the service has begun there should be a continuous development. The intensity may be relaxed at moments in the service, but the unity should never be lost. The qualities that will hold attention, direct thought, and supply the feeling of spiritual relationship must be arranged in logical progression.

The preparation of a group for worship has been grossly neglected in non-Roman churches. The preparation of the setting of worship, the establishment of a mood, and the call to worship are fundamentally important if the dramatic values are to be initiated. From distractions and noise to quiet concentration is the aim of the beginning of the service, for the service begins whenever the congregation is directed toward a setting and attention is concentrated on the purpose of the participation. The call to worship should be truly a call to worship. This does not mean a few mouthed lines that have little or no meaning to the congregation; it does not mean a superficial call. The call is dramatic only when it is genuine, when it pulls people out of their distractions and reminds them of the purpose for their being present. Here as much as any place in the service creative ability needs to be introduced. A good call to worship that has become established in a church can help enormously to bring about an effective total group experience. The individual preparation takes place in meditation and prayer.

A dramatic service will rely on experiences that are familiar to a congregation as well as those that are new. A familiar call to worship and familiar hymns have genuine value and place, just as certain litanies, creeds, and prayers have significant contributions to make. The introduction of new material can have appropriate significance because of the meaning of the day, the time, or the purpose of the worship. Obviously this is best illustrated in the use of the materials for Christmas, for the celebration of various days in the church calendar, or for the particular needs of the congregation.

Dramatic Prayer

Dramatic unity is accomplished also by the maintaining of a mood and a spirit. The offering can be as dramatically effective as the reading of the Scriptures and the prayer, provided it is thought through in terms of the mood of worship and of its place in the service. How it is introduced and carried out is, of course, of great importance. The repetition of prayers and the use of litany familiar to a congregation are not dramatically effective simply because they are well known or are repeated often. Their effectiveness will depend on the way they are repeated. In a prayer every phrase should be fraught with meaning and considered seriously, not ruined by meaningless repetition. The repetition of the Lord's Prayer should be one of the high moments in a service of worship.

A prayer can be theatrical or it can be dramatic. If it is words spoken to gain effect or to flatter the capacity of the leader to coin nice phrases it is of little value. The dramatically effective congregational prayer is one that is spoken out of the needs of the people, and it is said with sincerity and felicity in phrasing that comes out of effective praying. The success of the pulpit prayer is measured by the praying congregation. When the congregation prays with the minister the prayer is successful, and it is dramatically effective. For this reason, the great prayers of the Church are obviously better than individual attempts by the minister.

Inherent in a dramatic experience is the sharing process. Unless the worship group becomes one with the participants in the leadership of the worship, and unless there is a total shared experience, there is likely to be little dramatic effectiveness. Each person out of the mood and each person who does not succeed in becoming one with the total experience is a distraction. The leader may be the chief distraction.

B. Music in Worship

Music is not an adjunct to worship; it is a means through which one worships. The so-called mood music at the beginning of the service, like music in other parts of the service, should not be the occasion for the mere display of skills. It is the beginning of worship. Like the worship leader, the organist must be a worshiping participant. He must feel the mood, enter into the experience, and have the privilege of helping to direct it. For this reason, therefore, the music in the various parts of the service, forming almost a continuous structure, may be the foundation unifying all the service. Growing out of it but never separate from it should come the spoken as well as the silent meditative parts of the service. There is no place for prima donnas either in the pulpit or in the choir. Special numbers are a tragic holdover from the concert hall and are likely to be distractions rather than contributions to a worship experience. A solo can be expertly and technically effective and at the same time a genuine part of the worship provided the artist is a part of the experience himself. The choir as well as the soloists must be worshiping participants. When a soloist stands out from the group and when he centers attention upon himself and distracts the worshiper from the setting to the individual, the dramatic unity of the service is likely to be jeopardized. The organist, the choir leader, and the choir as well as the worship leader—who may be the minister or his associates—all play a part in the total dramatic unity. One is as important as the other if there is to be an organic whole.

Group singing can be dramatic or theatrical, or it can be merely meaningless activity. If it is singing that arises from the true spirit of worship and gives utterance to thanksgiving, to petition, or to an affirmation of faith, it can be an integral part of the service and heighten the worship to give effectiveness to the whole experience. The use of traditional folk music with religious overtones may have values for fellowship. It has no place in dignified worship.

All of these aspects of dramatic worship must be made important to the congregation through the educational process, through classes in worship, through instruction in the church school, and through practice in the main worship service. The main service, however, is not the place for untested innovations and experiments. The young people's meeting, the church school, family nights, and worship interest groups are the places where experimentation should take place. When a technique has been perfected until it is related to and becomes a part of the unity of the service it can be brought into the main worship service of the church.

Dramatic Leadership

Obviously the success of any service will depend upon the persons who lead the service—the minister and his associates, the choir, the director, the soloists, the ushers, and any others who participate in the activities of the service. Unless there is a common understanding and purpose in this leadership group there is little hope for dramatic effectiveness. This unity can be brought about through conferences, through discussions, and through the give-and-take that must of necessity be brought into the picture if there is to be a real attempt made to worship.

The worship leader, more often than not the minister or his associates, is the pivotal person. If he does not have a sense of the dramatic, if he has no real depth experience and does not understand worship, there can be little hope that the whole service will in any way be dramatically effective. If he leads in prayer it must be because he is praying. If he reads Scripture effectively it must be because he understands the Scripture, because he has read it and reread it, and because it has meaning for him which he wishes to transmit to the congregation. *If the spirit does not come alive in him it will not come alive in the congregation.*

This all applies with equal importance to the sermon. It can be an exhibition, a theatrical stunt, a dull academic recitation, or it can be depth thinking arising out of depth living spoken in terms of present-day life and experience measured by the witness and the revelation of the spirit of God. If the sermon is this kind of exchange of experience and is a real exposition of insight gained through consecration and study it is certain to be a part of the dramatic unity of the total worship service. The way it is spoken will either be distracting, theatrically annoying, or will evidence sincerity in its dramatic effectiveness. The Protestant pulpit has too often been the place for bombast, for ineffective and poor public speaking. Until the preacher is trained in speaking there is little chance for dramatic worship.

Dramatic Timing

In a service of worship there must be time for the experience to begin to find its place in the life patterns of the participants. If the service ends rapidly, if it is disturbed by people going out of the auditorium, if there is not silence and prayer, it is likely to be ruined at its most important moment. The most effective dramatic worship allows the heightened moment at the end of the sermon or prayer to have time to sink into the consciousness of the participants. The benediction the offering, and the choral amen are all distinct attributes to dramatic worship.

This matter of time and silence is, of course, an important part of the entire service. Time has always been important in the theater, and so-called timing of speaking and action is one of the first techniques that is learned by an actor. In the church timing must be a natural, spontaneous thing. It must grow out of feeling and become effective because it has genuine purpose. The speaking of lines effectively may mean that they are broken in the center by silence or by inflections that give them heightened values. If this is done superficially it is theatrical. If it is done with feeling it is dramatic. Timing, therefore, in a service of worship is a matter of feeling the sense of the meeting. If a moment of silence after the prayer is needed it must not be neglected. This is a matter of testing, judgment, and feeling.

Silence is a dangerous thing. For most people silence is distracting. Only after long training can it be used effectively. More and more it is coming into Protestant worship because of the experiences of the Friends. It should be brought back into worship but it must be used with judgment; it can be so effective that there is no other device comparable to it, or it can be so distracting that it dissipates the entire feeling and allows the mind and emotions to wander. There is no rule for silence. Its use and its values grow out of the feelings one must have and the sense that a leader can gather in knowing how much is necessary. Nothing is more dramatic when rightly used.

Dramatic worship will grow through experience. It may take upon itself techniques that come directly from the need of the moment, but it is likely to be effective only when there is consultation, co-operation, and a continuous educational process. Dramatic worship is possible in the smallest church and in the largest congregation. Its success will depend upon how much worship is understood, how sincere the leadership is, and how much time and preparation are put upon this integral part of the religious experience. It is the most unique contribution that the Church has to make to the needs of people, for it combines the total congregational group experience with the spiritual relationship without which life is indeed poor. Unless nonliturgical Protestantism takes its worship more seriously and develops the opportunity for genuine worship experiences the Church will become, more and more, merely a social institution and will lose its most important contribution to society.

C. Using the Chancel as a Playing Area

The theater is the theater and the church is the church. Each has its own distinct function in our society, and each must make its contribution in its own form, revealing its purpose in its best expression. The church must never seek to become theater, nor must the theater preach. Yet both have contributions to make to each other.

Good theater is dramatic. It has the capacity to stir the emotions on a deep level through the imagination which is more than fancy and superficial make-believe. The Church—particularly the Protestant churches—needs to express its Gospel dramatically if it is to make the hard core of its revelations a living reality in the lives of men today.

The chancel of the church is the place for this inspiration. Here, through worship, power can be released that will enable men to make the Gospel come alive in their lives. The fact that the sermon is often thought of as the only instrument through which this power can be stimulated is evidence of the failure of the Church to use the dramatic elements inherent in worship. The Church has been robbed of means that have constantly offered themselves to religious celebration.

If the Church is a place of worship and instruction, shows have no place in the sanctuary. The parish or community hall used by church members may have a stage or a playing area where good plays can be produced. As a means of providing wholesome and worthwhile recreation this is entirely legitimate.

A place set apart for worship should have been built for that purpose. It furnishes few aspects of a stage even though the rites and ceremony of the church are performed on it. It is a place of reality, not of illusion. Communion is most intense drama, and it is a drama that is participated in by everyone. There are no actors in sacraments or in general orders of worship. What is done in costuming, properties, and scripting is not to give a semblance of reality. Each costume worn, whether it be a choir robe or a vestment, is put on with meaning so that it becomes not a costume but a symbol in an act of reality. In real worship the spirit of God is present—not the illusion of his spirit.

For this reason drama performed in the chancel should be drama which invites all worshipers to participate. The processional, the act of genuflection, and physical evidence of praise and thanksgiving are most real when they are dramatically sound, that is, when they are actions which grow out of completely sincere motivation.

A place of worship should not be reconstructed as a theater. The play which comes alive in a chancel should be played in the chancel as it is, unless the chancel is ineffective for worship and needs reconstruction to be effective for its true function. This limits what can be done in a sanctuary. The physical limitations of a sanctuary must always be given primary consideration in planning any kind of dramatic presentation.

In many instances, however, the chancel may be used as a stage for appropriate dramatic presentations, depending on the attitude of the denomination toward the meaning and use of the sanctuary. If the chancel of a church is regarded as a platform for a sermon a play can be produced on this platform. Theater-in-the-round has shown us that backdrops, curtains, and footlights are not necessary for good dramatic performance.

Such productions require skilled technicians and even more skilled directors. When theater aids are taken away the actor becomes much more prominent. The quality of the acting is primarily important in any sanctuary play since the surroundings are more intimate and revealing than in the theater.

The direction in this type of drama is all important. If the play is to come alive in a worship setting the director must have a sense of worship. He must have a feel for the place that will give his direction a tone and quality different from that of a secular production. He must be a better director because he is conditioned by the place, and yet he must direct expertly under these conditions.

Not all plays with church interiors as settings are appropriate to give in a church. For example, the setting of Christopher Fry's A Sleep of Prisoners is a bombed-out church, not a sanctuary designed for worship. The right setting for this play is a stage. Similarly, despite its name, T. S. Eliot's Murder in the Cathedral belongs in the theater. Plays ideally suited for the sanctuary have yet to be written. A new technique may evolve when the conditions and purposes of the production are thoroughly understood. Movement may be the chief characteristic of this new form, with rhythmic movement as a distinctive contribution. The voice and the speaking chorus must play a much larger part. Music will come back as an integral part of worship, not as an accompaniment. It is possible that the new form may return to some of the earliest forms of the drama in Greece and that an integration of the arts of dance, music, and acting may produce something which will be called chancel drama. Much exploration and experimentation are needed before we can define this type of drama and determine its contribution to religious expression in the Church.

Few plays have been written for sanctuary presentation. Biblical stories that have values leading to deep searchings of soul, as well as meditations, may be dramatically presented. *The Sign of Jonah*, by Gruenter Rutenborn, may be given in the chancel. With good actors and good direction it creates a mental and emotional situation that is both highly dramatic and soundly religious. *Christ in the Concrete City*, by Philip Turner is another play that can be presented in the chancel, though it is less direct and forceful than *The Sign of Jonah*. The medieval morality play *Everyman* is excellent in the chancel as an acted Lenten sermon.

Part three

Royalties: Authors are human enough to like to be treated kindly and to respond kindly if they are. It is as well to remember that not only courtesy, but the law, gives copyright-holders certain rights and controls. They have the right to be paid for the loan of their property, and they have a right to protect it from mutilation or other ill usage. Most authors have a very natural concern for what happens to their work when it falls into the hands of strangers. Their plays are far more to them than merely "property" (or even merely a livelihood); they are the offspring of their labor, their experience, and their imagination. But authors like nothing more than to share these things with those who show that they appreciate them. And the fact always remains that both you and the author want the same things on the play's behalf: that it shall be performed as honestly and as effectively as possible; that it shall reach the minds and hearts of its audience. Mundane considerations are certainly not everything, but sound business arrangements with authors, like sound rehearsals, are part of the necessary foundation upon which sound performances are built.

—R. H. Ward, "Agree With Thine Adversary,"
Christian Drama (Autumn, 1953), p. 14.

Chapter IX

STANDARDS FOR CHOOSING A PLAY

A GOOD PLAY FOR THE CHURCH IS NOT EASY TO FIND. UNFORTUNATELY, the Church has not been willing to look with sufficient honesty on the major problems of life so that they can be acceptably produced in the church with any general agreement. Drama should deal directly and honestly with problems; consequently, it may be somewhat disturbing. So was the gospel of Jesus in his day! The time is rapidly coming when the Church will be able to speak frankly, freely, and truthfully about sex, marital relations, the home, delinquency, war, exploitation, labor, imperialism, and discrimination of all kinds. The better plays of Ibsen, Shaw, Hauptmann, O'Neill, Wedekind, Arthur Miller, and Tennessee Williams discuss these subjects. Most of these plays cannot, however, be put on in the church at the present time.

To discuss conflicts that arise from the evils connected with these life situations calls for honest, straightforward attitudes. The attempt to treat them in any kind of watered-down, parlor-talk fashion makes them unreal; it accentuates the very thing that the person opposed to this subject wishes to avoid. This is not a plea for realism as such, nor is it a wish for a washing of dirty linen in public. Certainly it is not a desire for dignifying back-of-the-barn talk by bringing it into the parlor.

The drama, we must emphasize, is always real in that it seems real; yet at the same time it is always the art of illusion. Art is never real in the sense that a replica represents the actual thing, nor is it real in any photographic sense. It is always the real thing filtered through the imagination of the artist. In order to win audience response the group producing the play brings this realism to life by means of the art of production which includes direction, action, scenery, lighting, and costuming.

121

The good play is not shocking in any moral sense unless the audience is prudish to the point of disliking honesty. It is never real for realism's sake or just for exhibiting something that can be better produced as a replica or as a picture. A good dramatist aims at a semblance of realism. This makes the audience believe in the authenticity and veracity of the situation and of the characters because they have the appearance of reality. What is important is that the person in the audience thinks the action on the stage is authentic, that it does not offend his sense of truthfulness, and that it appears real to him.

Too many plays for the church are weak and vacuous; they are pale and insipid treatments of situations and problems that cry out for strong, forthright presentations. Furthermore, they lack dramatic effectiveness— that quality of drama which presents a problem in a conflict moment, carries it to a tense moment of decision, and then holds the emotions of the audience at this climactic state. This is characteristic of all emotionally effective drama. If a play lacks dramatic effectiveness it ceases to fulfill its unique function.

Plays that are dramatically effective are not easy to find. Scenes in which forces are pitted against each other and the audience is sympathetic to the one or the other make situations for good drama. The best plays have closely knit action so that they seem to have a tautness that is felt whenever any scene is diagnosed. Technically expert plays are so condensed that scenes often seem underwritten. Many so-called religious plays are overwritten in dialogue and complication of plot so that they lack the compression that will make them effective on the stage.

Many biblical plays seem unimportant and appear to have little relation to problems of the present day. We are not aroused, shaken, or inspired by them. They leave us cold. The cast and stage crews cannot get excited over them, and this means that the audience is never moved.

Some plays written to be performed in the church not only lack these dramatic qualities, but they are also preachy and moralistic. Nothing can —and should—kill a play more rapidly. The moral or the point of the play should grow out of natural or real situations, conflicts that are met constantly in life. Plays should never attempt to preach a sermon. They are different art forms and have a different function. They must demonstrate life situations through action.

A play must be chosen first of all with the needs of the congregation in mind. The play-choosing committee must try to understand what these needs are and how plays can minister to them. A play ought never to be chosen just because a director likes it. A director should like the play he produces, but he should like it because it meets needs and demonstrates situations which can be shown effectively in no other way, and he should make the group understand his enthusiasm.

What are the needs of the congregation? Let us suppose that the church is in a relatively prosperous neighborhood and that the members are in the business world or in professions. It is likely that this congregation will have little understanding of the problems of labor and labor unions. A need here would be for plays that show the situation of labor and its fight for collective bargaining and organization. In a city church there may be a need to know something about rural situations and farm problems. Also plays dealing with peace and with race relations are needed everywhere. These needs arise because of the little experience most of us have with groups or types of life different from our own. The director must use judgment in selecting plays on these subjects. They must never be merely propaganda plays. On the other hand, *Back of the Yards* by Kenneth Sawyer Goodman can arouse a smug community to think and do something about the conditions in the slums. Galsworthy's *Strife* and Shaw's *Major Barbara* used for reading may awaken a congregation to situations in the struggle of labor and capital.

The process of choosing a play can be a continuous process in a group. If the director of a group will guide the reading of plays so that the group is constantly looking for plays to produce the process can be a genuinely educational experience. Members of a drama group need to get into the habit of reading plays. The search for plays for Christmas should have started in January, and as plays are discovered they should be passed around for reading. Probably by fall there may be ten plays which for one reason or another seem suitable for the particular church and the particular occasion. By careful analysis at meetings of the group, a play can be selected for production. The group will have learned about plays and will understand the reasons for choosing the play that has been selected.

A further advantage of this process is that the director will learn much about the taste and judgment of the group and will know how great the need for educational development is throughout the production of the play. If the group should fail to agree on the selection of a play, then the director must exercise tact and judgment in making the final choice.

The director must have the privilege of saying what play should be done. The aid of the director of religious education and the minister may be needed, but their authority should be resorted to only in a case of a deadlock in choosing. They should know the play that is to be done and their support should be sought in the project.

Chapters in this book on "The Play" and "What Is Religious Drama?" should be read carefully. They give the chief characteristics of a play and indicate what is generally meant by religious drama. The following tests are to be used by a play-reading committee in choosing a play for production by a church group.

1. A good play is one which moves an audience to participate emotionally and to respond to the conflict.

2. The subject matter of the play should be worthy of the time and consideration of the actors and of the audience.

3. The plot and setting of the play should be so related or pertinent to an audience that the situations and conflicts will be valid.

4. The plot will begin at a point that will elicit immediate interest; it will carry the story to the place where the audience will feel satisfied that the particular episode has been completed. It is compact and knit together so that it holds interest.

5. The characters must have a reality which makes them believable to the audience.

6. The action must be honestly motivated. It should begin in the "midst of things," rise to a climax, and complete itself as far as the story is concerned.

7. The dialogue must seem right for each character. It must never seem artificial or oratorical. It differs from conversation in its economy of words and in its directness. It is never rambling or leisurely.

8. It must have literary merit.

9. A good play may present its ideas through humorous situations. The humor should always grow out of situations that are accepted as probable and natural. Improbable situations treated as probable create farce, while exaggeration leads to burlesque. The value of a play will depend on how well it succeeds in being the kind of play it is supposed to be.

10. It must come within the range of abilities, equipment, and purposes of the producing group.

When the group and the play-choosing committee has reviewed the tests for a good play and has familiarized itself with the dramatic technique so that standards of judgment have been established, the actual process of choosing the play may begin.

Anyone interested in drama in the church will always be on the lookout for plays and scenes from plays that can be used. Radio, movies, and reading will furnish ideas. An alertness to need is the one essential.

Lists of plays are printed in the Appendix. The first list is of plays that are likely to be difficult for the average group. Directors who have produced the plays have been asked to point out good and bad aspects of the script as well as suggestions for direction that come out of their experience with this play. The second list is made up of less difficult plays, many of which are standard plays that have been used in the church.

Catalogues of play-publishing companies should be in the library of every church group. New plays are constantly being published so groups will want to keep informed about the new announcements and releases. Significant plays in the commercial theater and new plays from publishers may be reviewed regularly at the meetings of the drama group. A special committee should consider this its main function. Plays should be discussed and filed with complete notes on reactions so that they may be referred to and brought up when there is a need for a play.

Playwriting is a profession which deserves adequate compensation. A playwright is dependent on income from the royalty on his play. The publisher of the play likewise needs to get some return so that he can continue to print plays. The net profit to a publisher on a playbook which sells for fifty cents is obviously small. If cast copies are bought the profit is a little larger. Since it is illegal to duplicate copyrighted material, copies for the entire cast should be bought.

The author's royalty is likely to be a sum that is small compensation for all the work he has put into the writing. Church groups are notoriously careless about paying royalty. Good plays should be paid for, and good writers should be encouraged to write plays that will bring adequate incomes. The royalty notice is usually found on the back of the title page of a play. If there is no royalty notice it is likely that the play has no royalty, but the director should write to the publisher if there is any question. It is deliberately dishonest to change a title of a play or to change the lines in any way so that the play is called a new version. It is dishonest to think of producing a royalty play without paying the fee regardless of the cause for which the play is produced. A religious or charitable benefit is no reason for waiving the royalty unless the author and publisher consent. The fact that tickets are not sold does not make any difference. Unless the royalty notice specifically says that the fee is different if there is a collection rather than a ticket sale the fee must be paid. Many plays are royalty free or have reduced royalty fees if there is no admission charge. This will be noted in the write-up of the play in the publisher's catalogue or in a play list.

Not to pay a royalty when it is stipulated is cheating a writer out of his honest wage. It must not be the practice of church groups. To change the attitude of publishers toward church groups on this matter is the duty of every drama-producing organization in the Church.

Lists of plays for the church are available through the following publications:

1. *Plays for the Church*—a list compiled by The Commission on Drama, Department of Worship and the Arts, National Council of Churches of Christ in the U.S.A. Secure from: Office of Publications and Distribution, 475 Riverside Drive, New York 27, N. Y.

2. *Best Plays for the Church*—compiled by Mildred Hahn Enterline. Secure from: The Christian Education Press, Philadelphia, Pa.

3. Lists in the Appendix of this volume.

Chapter X

THE PLAY COMES ALIVE

WHEN THE PHRASE, "THE PLAY COMES ALIVE" IS USED IT IS NOT MEANT TO
suggest that the script is dead. The script is waiting to be born, and it
comes alive only when the director, the actors, the production people,
and the audience come together for that magic moment which is known
as the "performance." After all the work which has gone into a production it may seem strange to call the moment of performance magic.
Yet, even though what happens has been planned and worked on by a
co-operative effort on the part of a large number of people, the actual
thing that takes place in the performance of a play is something of a
miracle. This is not meant to be facetious, because the word is used
by directors whose group is not ready to perform and whose feeling
about the whole affair has been that if it comes off at all it will be a
miracle.

Quite a different sort of miracle does happen when a good script
comes alive before an audience in a performance. John Mason Brown
says of Robert Edmund Jones that the "theatre for him [Jones] was always an exceptional occasion." Roy Mitchell described this as "miracle"
and his meaning is the substance of his book, Creative Theatre.[1] No
matter how many plays a director may have done, each production is a
miracle because no one quite knows what the moment of coming alive
may mean. It is true that the director has seen dress rehearsals with
the production functioning—the lights, the scenery, the costumes and
the actors ready for the opening, but when the first performance takes
place there is an audience, and with an audience present all aspects of
the production take on new dimensions. What happens happens for
the first time and will never be repeated again in exactly the same way.

What does happen? A play that has been a script, with dialogue and stage directions, becomes a living experience to be shared by the persons who have worked to make the words become flesh and live in the confines of the human experience that make up the plot of the play. A play, furthermore, that has been a script—a one-dimensional, flat surface with words in it—has become a three-dimensional reality. It has taken on proportions: A room is no longer a word, it is an illusion of a room, defined as playing-space, and it has dimensions and proportions. Yet it is more than a room; it is the room in which certain people have lived and which now lives—and only for this space of time—because people who were descriptions, and who were dialogue now move about and live through a tense moment in their lives. Rooms are strange things. One can see them in houses and admire them for their decorative values or historic witness. In a play a room may still be a room, but it will be the room in which Nora in A Doll's House has lived and from which she has broken away. Trees may fit every requirement for a forest; yet in the magic and miracle of the theater trees become more real, something more than forest because it is the forest in The Blue Bird or the trees of The Cherry Orchard.

Still more of the miracle is seen when an audience lends its imagination to what actors and technicians have created and another kind of creative experience takes places. Every lover of theater knows the magic of the moment when house lights dim and there is the hushed expectancy of an experience waiting. It is then that the sense of wonder becomes a reality and "an extension of life, not a duplication, a heightening rather than a reproduction" takes place. The world of any number of people is suddenly extended and expanded, and a new experience shared by new people takes place. No other art galvanizes a group of people and takes them together into such an experience. The only other experience similar to this is found in a service of worship, but because of the difficulty of joining together people with differing concepts and differing theologies the service may not unify, and the miracle of relating all of the persons to God may not take place.

What does happen in this miracle of the theater? The secret may be discovered if a consideration is given to the place and contribution of the director, what the actor furnishes, the work of the production staff, and other means that are used to bring the play to life.

A. The Director and Directing

A good director is a trinity—a technician-artist, a diplomat, and an organizer—and like a trinity, he is three in one, for he must be first of all, an integrator. It is in his imagination that the play is seen as a whole; it is he who sees it in its totality and in all of its parts. He works with a designer and technical aids to conceive the vision he has of the play. He must be able to share his ideas and to communicate with his technical staff. In the working out of the action, as well as in the interpretation of the lines, the director must know what he wants because he has imagined the action. With the actors he becomes a benevolent dictator, while he is at the same time a diplomat who knows how to listen to his advisors, to take what is good from their advice, and still to keep in his mind the overall pattern he is seeking to bring alive.

He is the pivotal person in any production. A good play imagined in action by a director is the epitome of theater. While it is hazardous and probably unwise to suggest it, the quality of dramatic imagination of the director is the most important prerequisite for a good production. It is the one thing necessary. Positions on stage, timing, and interpretation of lines can be worked out. If, however, the director is lacking a sense of dramatic movement, a sense of the dramatic values in a play, and ability to picture the total performance and know what is wanted from the play no amount of technical excellence or acting ability will be able to cover up the primary lack in direction. Too many directors are merely manipulators of actors in felicitous positions on the stage. Too many are merely absorbed in the interpretation of lines. These are important aspects of direction, to be sure, but they are secondary to the total dramatic unity. Unless the director has the capacity to envision this, unless he knows what he wants, then all the other techniques he may have learned will be frustrating to him. The director is an artist, and like all artists he must know his craft. This comes by knowing the fundamentals of play-directing and from experience in using them.

For this reason the contribution of the director in religious drama is all the more important. He is not producing a play to preach to an audience, yet he is working to express the deepest and finest meaning in the play. He is producing this particular play because he believes in what it has to say, and he wishes this to be said effectively as drama. He knows that the meaning must become an actual experience both for the actors and for the audience. In religious drama, therefore, he is concerned about meaning. He must decide on this by careful study of the play. The more subtle the play and the more it is good drama, the more certain must the director be of the meaning he wishes to actualize. He studies the play. This does not mean that he reads it superficially a few times. It means that he digests it, that he lives with it, that he pictorializes it in his imagination. It means that he lives with the story and the characters until they are realities to him. Unless they are real, imaginatively real, unless he is able to experience their situations himself, he will never be able to help actors bring them to life.

He begins by reading the script carefully. He tries to condense the point or meaning of the play into one topic sentence. He says, "This play is about such and such," and he then spots the sentence which seems to say this. He finds the scene which is the essence of this idea and decides that this scene is the heart of the play. He finds how the rest of the action contributes to the making of this scene. He traces the action of the play from its opening scene noting the way in which the dramatist relates the action to the climax. He studies carefully the relations of the characters to the action, what each contributes by the person he is and, therefore, by the words he speaks.

The director places himself in the milieu of the play, trying to understand the period and its meaning in the historical setting. He reads all he can about the period, especially books that make the period live. He investigates the manner and customs of the time of the play, resorting to books and, still better, to museums where he can see costumes and properties as they were. He knows that these are probably not to be reproduced but that they are to be simulated, to be represented in such ways that they will seem authentic.

He learns everything he can about the dramatist's interest in this play—why he wanted to write it and what he hoped it would mean to an audience. How fortunate he is if the play happens to be one of George Bernard Shaw's! In the elongated prefaces—many longer than the play itself—Shaw states his reasons for wanting to write the play and much of the mental process through which he went in the collecting of materials as well as in the actual working out of the plot. Even with these prefaces, however, there is still much research to do.

Histories, especially those with prints and pictures, encyclopedias, other plays of the period of the type, pictures found in histories of art, biographies, diaries, letters, essays, in fact, any form of recorded experience which will spur the imagination, are needed by the director.

The play may be written in a form that is peculiar to a period, or it may be experimental and, therefore, without precedent, or it may seem novel only because the director does not know other dramatic forms from which it derives its novelty. How significant, for instance, are the styles of some contemporary continental plays when one knows the technique of the Nō plays of Japan, or how illuminating can be the understanding of the free techniques of contemporary dramatists when one knows the well-made play of the nineteenth century and can see the straitjacket from which it is a revolt.

A sense of the history of drama is necessary for any director who wishes to actualize the greatest meaning from plays. To produce a contemporary comedy one should know the types of comedy that have been historically important. To direct a contemporary problem play one should know the difference between the effect of tragedy and the effect of the presentation of a problem in which character has been sacrificed to the need for statement of the problem. One needs to know what epic drama means—and especially Shakespeare—before one is able to comprehend what Bertolt Brecht has done. Certainly one needs to know the tradition of melodrama if he is to understand the escapist drama that occupies much of the contemporary theater comedy and the television soap opera.

The director needs to be an observer of life, keenly aware of the nuances of character, yet not so absorbed in the idiosyncracies that the common and universal qualities are overlooked. He needs to know people both from the inside, where he finds motivations for actions, and from the outside, where he observes and records in his memory the action patterns that make people unique. He is an alive person, above all a sensitive person, so that he feels and knows through experience when an action is authentic and when it is bogus.

The director must be able to communicate his sense of these things by the most subtle methods known, perhaps, only to the theater. Directing is easy when a director merely shows an actor what to do. How many amateur performances are evidence of a director who has told the actor how to say a line and has directed his action so that it fits into a pattern, whether or not it is intelligently felt and thought out! The good director communicates by creating emotional and intellectual problems, and when the actor is not getting the right approach stimulates him by creating questions that he must answer if he is to find satisfaction in the part. This is probably the most difficult aspect of direction, for the director may discover that the actor does not have the capacity to comprehend what is wanted, or he may lack the sensitivity to feel what must be felt. The director cannot create these qualities when they do not exist, but he can so stimulate that the actor will go far beyond what is expected of him or what he thought he might give. When this happens the process is truly educational.

A director must be constantly growing if each play is to be actualized for its greatest values. If a director decides after a successful production that he knows how to direct he may stop growing. Each play is a new direction problem, and each play challenges the director to new insights and new imaginative experience. The director can learn basic concepts of stage positions, but the mastery of dramatic movement is a matter of visual imagination and feeling for pictures that is gained by trial-and-error methods, if, to begin with, he is given a sense of the dramatic.

The repetitive use of the phrase "sense of the dramatic" has not been unintentional. Its meaning ought to become clearer as one understands and feels the meaning of theater and the dramatic form in its expression. It has to do with mind as well as imagination; it comes about through experience as well as through insights and inspiration at the time of production; it grows from understanding plays through continuous reading of plays and through the habit one must form of visualizing the plays when they are read. A director always sees each play as a stage performance, and his mind becomes the stage. This truly is the "theater in your head." Yet theater is never realized until it is out of your head. This process the director guides, and this process is the "borning" of a play; the technicians and all the other related people— including the audience—are the company of wet nurses, as well as the "relatives," who participate in the birth with imaginative expectancy.

The director in the final analysis must be a person who can work through people. He works with the people in a cast, to be sure, but his most important job is to work through them. What he works through them is the play—the story and the characters—so that these are filtered through the actors and the production people to become what has been referred to as the miracle of the theater. The capacity to work through people means, as has been pointed out, that the director does not give direction to be carried out nor action to be imitated. His work involves both of these under certain circumstances, but basically he creates through people, motivating and expressing through them what he sees with them in the script for the audience to experience imaginatively.

All directors must have concern for the personalities of the actors. In the church this ought to be one of the major aspects of the director's job. The production of a play in the church should always be an educational experience because the people participating are usually amateurs in the obvious meaning of the word. They are often people with no experience of theater, not even as audience. They are amateurs not because they love theater but because they have a feeling that they might like it. Their knowledge of acting is in terms of movie stars or television actors who seem compelling and attractive. They are probably the people who say, "But I don't have any ability. I'd be scared to death to appear before an audience." Yet here they are offering themselves as actors in a church play. The director needs a keen insight into the personality of the actors as well as into the characters who are to come alive. *Both must come alive if the play is successful.* Often the director will find that his main and too often his insurmountable problem is that he just does not have people with enough sensitivity and imagination to be actors. He must work with what he has, good and bad. He can feel for and relate himself to the actors, but he cannot make them into artists.

What does he do? If the actors are so inexperienced that they cannot even learn basic techniques of acting in the time allotted for the rehearsal of a play he can suggest that the play be done as a reading and that the major emphasis be put on interpretation of lines. He can suggest that a simpler play be done first, perhaps only for the members of a group or for friends of the cast, and that this be a learning experience for the actors. He can steel himself to go on with the production, with the understanding that a note will be put in the program or a prologue with a humorous meaning will be added to the performance to say that this is a first attempt and that, whatever its faults, it is the result of serious and sincere effort. Dramatists of the past have been fond of explaining through prologue situations that they think ought to be faced, and they have asked the audience to be kind.

The text of a play may have to be edited or adapted to the peculiar situation in the church. This does not mean that it may be warped into the meaning desired nor that the realistic language may be watered down to fit the moral climate, whatever that may be, of the church. There is in some contemporary plays language which is strong and possibly offensive. Some changes may be necessary. Here taste and judgment are the only criteria. The fewer changes made, the better. It is true that plays may often be simplified in production by combining scenes or by cutting. In general, this again is a dangerous procedure. It is much better to do the play by simplifying the scenery so that a forestage can be used and the scenery kept to a minimum. The use of screens and platforms is advisable. More will be said about this under production.

Good books on directing are available to be studied. The important thing to remember, however, is that directing, like swimming, can be learned only through experience. The novice should begin with simple scenes, progressing to longer plays only when basic concepts have been thoroughly tried. The director has perspective on the play; he sees it as each person in the audience sees it. No actor, regardless of the quality of his imagination, can comprehend the total scene; or even if he develops a complete sense of his own role he cannot also visualize the other actors in relation to him. While experienced actors sometimes assume the position of director of a play, this is dangerous and risky for even a more-than-competent actor.

The primary direction of any play is dictated by the plot and the suggestions of the dramatist. In Shakespearean plays practically the only stage directions given are exits and entrances. The rest is left to the imagination of the actor and the director. With the open-ended stage of the Elizabethans, only the presence on the stage of the dandies and the rabble in the pit—our orchestra seating section—confined the actor.

Stage directions in any play are conditioned by the playing space which will eventually be used. How important it is, therefore, to define this space and the physical characteristics of the scene from the beginning of the rehearsals! This should be understood at once so that the actors know precisely the area in which they will work.

Most significant both for the director and the actor is the delineation of character basic to the plot of the play. This must be given primary consideration for it is the essence of the working arrangement of the whole play. The director needs to become so familiar with the script that he has lived it in his imagination. He sees it with his inward eye, as well as in the visual picture. He is constantly aware of the picture that is created while the actions are creating the situations in the play.

The director must also understand the play in terms of its rising and falling action, where emphasis is to be placed, and where pointing up needs to be done by his direction. The director can be compared with the leader of an orchestra. The musician knows the score, but it is the director who guides him so that he does not play too loudly or go too slowly or too fast. The director hears the play as well as sees it, and it is his ear as well as his eye that guides the harmonious movement of the actors.

The play director guides through the comprehension and understanding of the actor. Through consultation at the beginning of the rehearsals and throughout the play he leads the actor into a relationship to the character that requires concentration and genuine devotion. He helps the actor realize the role not by manipulating him but by directing him to an understanding of it.

Blocking is a word heard constantly in the direction of a play. It indicates the positions and movements of the actors within the playing space so that audience sight lines are good, and the actors' movements do not block each other from the sight of the audience. Blocking should be done only after the play has been read and discussed and the actors have a picture of the movement and understand what it means in relation to the story or plot of the play. Blocking is necessary because inexperienced actors cannot see themselves; they cannot feel deeply the parts they are playing if they must think constantly about where they are and how they are turning. Once the actor knows his relative positions on the stage he is free to think about and become the character he is portraying.

The director is always dependent on several other persons related to the production. A stage or production manager is responsible for all the physical properties on the stage. He sees that the scenery is ready and is placed so that it can be changed with expedition; he is familiar with the movable properties, and he organizes a crew to get props on and off a set; he checks the costumes to see if they are what the director wants; he works with the light technicians to see that the light plot is carried out and that the cues are on time. He is a very important person on whom rests the efficient running of the play. He may make the promptbook unless it is done by the director.

Sometimes a director is given an assistant who acts as a liaison person with the stage manager and other crew chiefs. He may be given the responsibility of the prompt book and may call all rehearsals and in some cases take over line rehearsals and individual coaching when action and interpretation have been established by the director.

In the church the backstage duties are usually assumed by committees which in the theater are called crews. In the professional theater these separate crews are in charge of stage and shop work, the building of sets, and stationary props; the electrical crew in charge of lighting; the prop crew in charge of all movable props; the costume crew; and the front-of-the-house crew. In churches there should always be a public-relations committee which has to do with the publicity for the performance. The business aspects of the project can be handled by a treasurer or a business manager. No matter how small the production, a comprehensive budget should be drawn up, and all persons related to the play should adhere to this budget in consultation with the director and the business manager or treasurer.

B. Casting

Casting a play in the church may be one of the most difficult aspects of the project. Too often the director in a church is told that Mary or John should be cast in the play because he has been faithful in attendance or has been tireless in his attention to duties in other projects. What the director knows is that he must use whatever acting and technical ability is available. Most of the time there is little choice except in the major roles. Here there may be a problem. If the play is to be performed before an audience and is sufficiently good to warrant the effort it takes, then the best possible cast should be chosen. This does not mean that actors should be recruited from the outside or that the same leaders must of necessity be cast again and again in a play. It may be the very thing to develop workers who have not discovered an interest in other kinds of work. In the last analysis, however, the play deserves the best acting and the best production possible, and persons must be chosen who can fulfill their oblgations.

While it is true that all work in the church should have educational as well as religious values, it is apparent that a singer must have a trained voice before he is asked to sing in a church service and an actor or technician must have ability and skills that can be developed. If the

Christmas pageant requires only pantomime and a minimum of that while music and reading are used, characters may be chosen who "deserve" parts, and the director can cast the play with only size and carriage as factors. In any case, with young people the director of religious education and/or the minister should be consulted before casting is announced. It is possible that the best actor may be the most serious problem child. It may also develop that casting him in the play is the way to find his loyalty and direct it. Good judgment with a good amount of trust and faith are prerequisite to any skills of the director, and the capacity to size up situations and handle them is as necessary as any knowledge of directing techniques.

The value of the play and its best performance must be given first consideration if it is to be done before an audience. In the process of production the skillful director can contribute much to the lives of the persons involved in the production, and by minor parts and by all sorts of duties connected with the staging, growth in responsibility and in talent can be encouraged so that the project can have genuine educational as well as religious significance.

The play may be the "thing" in the sense that it must come alive, but unless the people in the group process come alive for richer, fuller experience under the capable leadership of the director, the project in the church is not achieving the best results. The director in the church is first of all directing people—both the persons in the play who are waiting to be born and the persons who as individuals will bring the characters to life. In this sense the whole experience is one related to people, and the person who directs must first of all be a person of unusual quality. In the educational process perhaps no one is so closely related to the people with whom he works as is the director of a play.

Not the least important asset needed by a drama director is a sense of humor. The church group works on a voluntary basis. It may be made up of old and young. It is often working on borrowed time when actors and crews are tired. It may be made up of young people who have not been initiated into the serious business of producing a play. They are probably in the project just for fun. The director is the person who must have sufficient perspective to understand all of these things, to appreciate them, and yet have the patience to "let down" with the group and then pull them back up again. He must be able to laugh with the cast when the release of laughter may save the situation. He should know that a good sense of humor may be the most effective means of insuring discipline that will keep a group at work. The steady grind of rehearsals or crew work can be lightened by it. Whatever else may be prerequisite to directing, a sense of humor is a saving grace.

The director must feel himself a part of the institution through which he works. The belonging sense is fundamental if the drama program is to be related to the general educational program of the church. Furthermore, the director needs to know the congregation. The intelligent minister would not preach without knowing something about his congregation. Yet directors in the church are often asked to produce a play without any knowledge of the congregation. The result is that the play usually fails to come alive at the crucial moment of performance.

The church should not build its program on the work of those experts who make one contribution and then lose interest. The church must learn how to compel the concern of experts—of artists of all kinds —so that they make their contributions willingly. No apology need be made in asking for their services. The giving of one's talent, ability, and experience to the church should be a privilege. It should be a distinctive part of the stewardship which everyone ought to feel.

Knowing an audience personally and having a sense of audience relationship are quite different. The director, to direct, must have this sense of audience relationship. Until the audience is actually present, their needs and tastes rest with the director alone. Seasoned actors will have a sense of the audience, but most amateurs lack it entirely. How is the audience sense acquired? Certainly one of the best ways is experience gained by being in an audience. Therefore, the good director is one who has spent many hours sitting in audiences; he has watched not only the show but also the reactions of the audience. For him the lines of Emily Dickinson are delightfully true:

> The show is not the show
> But them that go.
> Menagerie to me
> My neighbor be.
> Fair play—
> Both went to see.[2]

If drama in the church is to succeed in stirring a congregation this audience sense is imperative for the director. In the church the congregation-stage relationship has greater significance than in the regular amateur or professional theater. If the director in the church is to succeed in "putting over" his play he must know exactly how he wishes the congregation to be affected.

The good director producing a play in the church will be cognizant of both the means and the ends which he uses—one must not suffer at the expense of the other. The educational procedure of rehearsal and the religious impact of performance are both to be preserved. While adequate attention given to the means will demand more time and patience, the effort necessary for the effective, determinative quality of the end will be worthwhile.

The church is part of community life. This means that all its activities must be considered and evaluated in terms of their contribution to community values. The director must have this community sense if the project is not to be dwarfed into a little outlet for a clique in a church. If the Church is to have a sense of mission—without which it cannot truly exist—this popular activity of drama must be considered as integral to this mission. Drama should bring people with all types of skills into the church in the producing group, and into the audience it should attract persons who might never come to the church for any other reason. This then makes drama an outreaching arm of the Church. The director should be aware of this if he is to make the most of it. One danger of drama in the church is that it becomes an ingrowing process that is thought of as the interest of a small and often smug group. A good director should be community-minded and should have a sense of mission to give the experience of a play to the largest group possible.

Of course, no one person will have all the qualities of the director analyzed here, but this fact will not discourage the dedicated director— it will spur him. As he grows, he can foster more growth for those who come under his direction. As he fosters their growth, he expands and intensifies the whole ministry of the Church.

C. The Promptbook

The promptbook of a production is an essential aid. While it is true that most churches are not likely to produce the same play within a short period of time, it is also true that the keeping of a promptbook will help everyone related to the production. If for any reason the director or the stage manager cannot be present the promptbook becomes an invaluable asset. Because it contains any cutting or changes made in the text, it is used as the source book if minor characters are without books.

The promptbook should be made up of nine-by-twelve pages with one page from the printed copy of the play pasted on each sheet. Two copies of the printed play will be needed to make the promptbook. There should be wide margins on all sides of the text, with the inside and bottom space used to note movements, positions, changes in text, tempo, and interpretations. In the top and outside margins should be written warnings for entrances and cues for lights, curtain, music, and sound. The prompt cues should be in different color pencil than the directing changes and cues.

The book should include carbon copies of rehearsal schedules, the scene and light plots, the property lists, program notes, publicity releases, and photographs. If a church takes its drama program seriously, these books will be added to the library and will be available for lending to other churches that may want to do the play.

D. The Actor and Acting

The actor is the center of attention in any play. His creative work differs according to the style of the play. His chief assets are sensitivity and intelligence, or what the great nineteenth-century American actor Joseph Jefferson called "the warm heart and the cool mind." An actor is an artist whose basic material is himself—his body, muscles, hands, feet, and voice. The Russian director Stanislavski divided the work of the actor into two spheres—the work on himself and the work on the role he is creating.

Pantomime was perhaps the first dramatic action in the world. Men acted out an idea before they put it into words. Acting was probably the first art of communication learned by man. Certainly, in the theater acting antedates the written play. As we all know, many profound emotions can be easily represented in action, but to give them words is indeed difficult. The obvious and yet most interesting example is the emotion of love, which can be naturally expressed by action, and yet can be very awkward and oftentimes foolish when it is expressed in words. Christian in Rostand's *Cyrano de Bergerac* was breathless in the terrible emotion he felt for Roxanne, but he was not poet enough to express himself. The charming love scenes in As You Like It are further examples of the same dilemma.

The kind of acting that grows out of premeditated planning is the kind needed in drama in the church. It must always be action which results from thoroughly worked out ideas motivated by deep and real emotion. Superficial action has no place in the church, nor has representation. Acting in a play in the church, therefore, becomes something more than a technique. It must truly be an experience. Its sign is sincerity on the part of the actor.

How then are we to get actors who are willing to take the time to study and understand a character in order to bring about this kind of action? Understanding must come first if a character in a play is to come alive. There are no insignificant characters in drama in the church. The smallest part is a reality or nothing. It must be thought through so that it becomes part of the larger pattern of the play. If it is badly or superficially done it will weaken the whole play. Characters in a conflict situation at a climax are so closely woven together and so interdependent that the failure of anyone weakens the whole structure. If this is not true the technique of the play itself is bad; it will not hold together, much less hold the interest of the audience.

Acting must always be more than acting; it must be interpretation. If a character is to come alive, he must be something more than the skeleton structure of words and positions on the stage. He needs the studied action that gives him life—the intellect and the emotions both adding to his quality. Interpretation, likewise, is something more than saying words well. Interpretation means bringing out the subtleties and the nuances that give idiosyncratic reality to a person. Parts in plays must become persons. The dramatist can give only the words, and while these may be entirely adequate to give an idea of the character, in the last analysis the actor makes the character become a person.

The material of a part is filtered through the mind and imagination of the actor and of the director. The play should be read carefully at least four or five times just to get the total picture. One of the great faults of the amateur is neglect of preliminary study for the relation of his part to the whole.

The amateur imagines that a casual reading of the play will supply the meaning, and that a line-perfect performance will be a successful one. He will soon learn that the better the play, the more care must be taken. The part to be created must not be considered as a part to learn; it is a part to be brought to life. This is no easy matter, and it cannot happen unless the actor is willing to spend a great deal of time understanding the character and the part the character lives. Everything about a character must be known. How he looks, walks, talks, sits, stands, gestures, eats, relaxes—all these must be known completely before the creative part of acting can begin.

What a man says is important, yet one only needs to think of a person he himself knows well to realize that what his friend says is merely an outward and audible indication of the real person. The actor must imagine the character outside the play as well as in the play; he must know background. Certainly he must know what the character would do in many different circumstances. The wise director will spend a long time talking out the character with the actor. Too often the playwright gives too little of the character. This always makes the actor's job much more difficult. Tragically enough, learning lines is often the only accomplishment of the actor, and plays in the church too frequently have unreal characters who speak lines but never actually live the experience. An audience must feel impelled to respond to the actor. It cannot do this in the religious sense if the characters in the play are not created by the actors.

The process of creating a character is not a simple one. An actor must live with his "part," and he must live with it intimately. This requires time, and it means that long before a part is learned it must be understood. The actor needs to walk and talk the part. He must give himself to it with a devotion that is rare in amateur drama. If our problem were simply to amuse an audience superficial acting might be condoned. If our theater were an escape from life, as some theater and movies are, the job of acting would not be difficult; however, when we propose to affect an audience so that it is elated and inspired, then the work before us is of great importance. Sincerity, honesty, and understanding will call forth that sort of response.

The actor's art, however, is not all good intentions, nor is it merely sincerity and understanding. He must learn to watch people, to see their reactions. He must be awake to living people if he is to create them on the stage. He must be willing to take time to think about the character until it becomes quite familiar to him. This process begins and continues by reading the play again and again. The character is from the play, and it must never be unrelated to the circumstances that gave it birth. An actor will always need to know more about the part than is given in the play. He will need to understand the environment, the setting, the way of life of the times, and all the historical relationships possible.

Most of us can act characters who are like what we think we are like. The problem of understanding characters who lived at times about which we know little or nothing is still more of a problem. For this reason plays founded upon biblical material are very difficult to interpret. To create a part like the apostle Paul the director and the actor will need to do research, to read books about Paul and his times. The more interesting and exalted the character, the greater will be the problem of the actor. In Oberammergau the citizens of the community are selected to take the roles in the Passion play by popular ballot. If a woman wishes to play the part of Mary she needs to live so that her neighbors will elect her to the role. This is a process of understanding that reaches into the living of people and calls for interpretations that are not artificially taken on in the hurried days of preparation for the play.

The actor needs to remember, too, that he is playing only a part of a whole; acting is always a co-operative process that can never be at its best when a prima donna usurps the stage or plays alone to an audience. The days of this sort of conceit are passed and should never be revived. Each person in the entire production is important to the finished product. By playing together—because the play is a closely knit unit— the achievement of an artistic whole is possible. This capacity to play with others is one of the truly educational aspects of drama in the church. The egocentric actor who is concerned only with his own success has no place here. Plays in the church need people who are willing to sacrifice all their selfish ends for the greater good to be accomplished by the play.

The Russian theater furnishes an admirable example not only of ensemble playing but also of the group process at work. The Moscow Art Theatre will spend months and even years bringing a play to life before it is ready for an audience. In this theater all people are important. The theater is an educational institution as well as one designed for entertainment. The peasant can get the idea through a play if the play is so well done that it will have precisely the desired effect upon the audience.

When the Moscow group was rehearsing Gogol's *Dead Souls*, for example, one scene was given an extraordinary amount of attention. Some twenty actors were on stage seated at a banquet table stuffing themselves with food and drink. The story of the play deals with the tax abuse and the old system of tax collectors. Into this banquet scene, unannounced and with alarming suddenness, walks a collector. Each one of the guests must register by his action and facial expression what his conscience feels at the appearance of this man. Guilt, innocence, unconcern, scorn, fear, threat—each of these must be shown according to the reaction of the individual, and it must be shown immediately. A long, careful analysis was made of each character seated at the table. Many of the actors had no lines to speak, and a large number did not appear in any other scene. Here was a problem in acting. To see the Moscovites work on the scene with the patience of truly great artists, to see them go over and over the action until each character was as nearly right as possible, is an experience which makes a person realize what is required of an actor.

Almost anyone can act if he acquires the techniques and comes under good direction. He may act, but he may not act well. Almost anyone can play tennis, but the Davis Cup winner is a player who has practiced longer than most people know, has had the discipline to make himself work, and has worked with coaches who know how the game should be played. The great player will still have his individual serve and his way of receiving the serve; he will always be the product of all his playing and coaching plus the something which is distinctively his own. So, too, the good actor will learn by doing, by understanding the technique, and by studying all that can be learned about acting. The average amateur will not be a good actor under these standards. Yet the more he can be encouraged to try, the more the quality of playing in a church will be raised. Good books on acting are available and should be studied carefully. Practice scenes are valuable for the beginner.

Although much good advice on technique can be learned from books, the actor must have the guidance of a good director. Most amateurs have not learned how to stand or how to walk—in other words, they are awkward. Acting shows up all these defects, so the director will watch the person's posture and his ability to use his body gracefully and expeditiously. The actor must be able to make his body do what he wants it to do. Awkwardness is unnecessary for anyone, and even minor physical defects need not keep one from acting. Some of the greatest actors have noticeably bad defects. To overcome these, the interpretation needs to be all the more subtle. Simple physical exercises will help. When a group can secure leadership, eurythmics is invaluable to help gain control of the body and to rid it of stiffness and awkwardness. High-school and college groups are giving much more attention to posture, and in many instances eurythmics is part of the physical-training program.

A good voice is equally necessary for the actor. Americans are likely to have ugly voices largely because they have never taken the trouble to train them. The voice, like the body, can be made effective by practice. Almost any community can find a high-school teacher who has had work in voice training. The person should be prevailed upon to work with the group. Choral speaking and speaking choirs are excellent ways to create interest in voice work. The actor should realize that his training must take in the total person—the body, the mind, the voice, and the personality. To create characters, all of these must be trained.

No substitute can be found for training and for hard work. Acting is not something that one does just naturally. Some persons have more than average ability to mimic. Nevertheless, even this talent needs training if it is to be an instrument in the co-operative process of bringing a play to life. The most supple body, excellent voice, and fertile imagination will be of little use if the possessor of these assets is not willing to work extraordinarily hard. To gain any kind of efficiency in acting takes time. The amateur is eager to accomplish what for professionals has taken years of work. In Russia the actor, like the ballet novice, begins as early in life as possible. The training continues all his lifetime. Madame Chekhov, the wife of the great dramatist and one of Russia's Honored Artists of the Republic, at seventy was still willing to take minor parts to get new insights into characters. To have this opportunity, she said, enabled her to get perspective on the leading characters. This is the attitude of a truly great artist.

The actor needs to learn how he can best memorize lines. Before the actor turns to work on actual lines his major work on characterization should be completed. If he were to speak in character impromptu, he would know the right pitch, tempo, cadence, rhythm, dialect, or speech provincialism of his character. Most actors find the job of memorization easier and more dependable if they work from general familiarity to specific line memorization. If the play is in three acts, the competent actor will first familiarize himself with all the play. Then he will pay particular attention to his lines. He will then become familiar with his lines by acts and by scenes.

At the same time he memorizes the idea or thought behind the dialogue. The grasp of the thought will pull the whole act or scene together for him. It will facilitate the actual memorization of words. It will enable the actor to enter into the real purpose of the scene. It will prevent him from forgetting "which line comes next." His thought throughout the entire playing of the scene can be given to the point of the scene, not to fumbling in his memory for the exact word. Only after these steps in the memorizing process have been taken is the actor ready to become letter-perfect in his lines. Most actors find they memorize better by "walking it out." This technique has an integrating quality; it pulls together the movement and action of the play, the bodily manifestations of characterization, and the actual speeches. It prevents one's remembering that he should walk to the table, pick up the book, and say, "So this is the new book." Instead, in his subconscious mind he has routed his movement to the table, and as he moves toward the table in performance, he can't think of anything but the line which motivated the movement. This walking helps make for thinking which motivates movement and the consequent speech explaining the movement. Most actors also "talk the lines out loud to themselves" as they memorize. This utilizes the sense of sound in memorization. After all these steps have been taken actors learn their cues so that the sound of these words calls out their speech.

The drama group should devote meetings to acting, to trying out scenes that have been selected for that purpose. Katherine Kester's *Problem Projects in Acting* is a valuable book for this purpose. It gives short scenes from plays that can be used for the various problems in acting. The organization that makes up the drama project should spend many of its meetings in this kind of activity. New recruits can be used in this way, and abilities may be discovered. The group should have in mind constantly that it is a workshop organization and that its time between plays should be taken up with training for the various aspects of play production. A drama group should be working continuously yet with interest and devotion which will be characteristic of the people who love drama and believe in its distinctive contribution to the Church.

To sum up, then, the group should start its training in acting by simple exercises in patomime—the expression of fear, anger, pleasure, distrust, love, and other emotions. These lead naturally to scenes from plays. Part readings of plays for the sense of the character are always advisable, and walking rehearsals will help in the understanding of what make a play dramatic and how characters can come alive even in this crude process. When the actor begins to feel at home with a character, or as if the character "belongs," then the art of acting is becoming real. An actor will soon learn that all action in a play must be motivated. There is no other kind of intelligent action in a play. Actors simply do not move at will. Every action has a reason or it is not valid. Part of the skill of the actor is to discover the pattern for action and, with the director's aid, work that into the total picture of the stage. That the actor works with the whole group cannot be said too often. The director is concerned with the action so that its flow in the performance is smooth. In the church the actor is the interpreter who knows that through his creation a character will come alive to affect a congregation of people and carry them with him through common experiences.

Notes

[1] See the note in the Bibliography in the Appendix of this book.
[2] From *The Poems of Emily Dickinson*, edited by Martha Dickinson Bianchi and Alfred Leete Hampson, published by Little, Brown and Company.

Chapter XI

ORGANIZATION AND REHEARSAL SCHEDULE FOR THE PRODUCTION OF A ONE-ACT PLAY

THE SITUATION: THE DIRECTOR OF CHRISTIAN EDUCATION OF A PARTICU-
lar church has interested the Commission on Education in the use of
drama in the annual Christmas celebration. They have enlisted the assistance of Mr. Stanley, a young businessman who has had experience in
a college dramatic group. The following is the procedure which Mr.
Stanley, the director, followed in producing the play for the Christmas
celebration.

Procedure: First Mr. Stanley confers jointly with the minister and
the director of Christian education to establish exactly why the play is
wanted and what is expected from the production. This meeting is held
on Saturday, November 3, and several dates are suggested by the minister as possibilities for the production. In order to give the maximum
amount of time the tentative date of Sunday, December 23, is set for
the performance. From this meeting comes this statement of purpose:

To add a fresh enthusiasm to the yearly program of activities of the
Christmas season.

To involve the entire church membership in the performance.

To use this first endeavor as a sort of inquiry into the possibility of establishing a program of dramatics in the church.

The next move is to announce the plans for the project to the entire
church membership. A space is given in the church newsletter which is
mailed in time to reach members before the weekend of Sunday, November 11. The announcement is given on that Sunday morning and to
various groups meeting in the evening. This is the announcement as
it appeared in the weekly newsletter:

148

THIS YEAR'S CHRISTMAS CELEBRATION TO INCLUDE DRAMA

In addition to our annual Christmas music by the choirs, this year we are reaching out into a new area of the fine arts—drama. Believing that this is the right time to provide such an opportunity for people in this parish who are interested, the Commission on Education has encouraged the production of a Christmas play for this season. We are fortunate to have the assistance of Mr. Stanley, who has accepted the responsibility of the direction of the play.

If you are interested in being a part of this production in any way, will you attend the first meeting of the project on Monday evening, November 12, at 7:30 P.M., in the church auditorium? If you are interested, but are unable to attend this meeting, notify Mr. Stanley between the hours of 5:00 and 7:00 in the evening at his home, CE 8-9078.

Remember, there are many jobs connected with the production of a play beside those of the actors—costumers, painters, electricians, publicity people, and especially the audience. In other words—there's a role for everyone in our parish.

Choosing the play: On the evening of the first meeting, Monday, November 12, the director takes charge. He passes out mimeographed forms which he has prepared in order to get information concerning particular interest and ability of those attending the meeting. The form contains this basic questionnaire:

Name: Vocation:
Address: Phone:

Interests in drama: Experience in these:
  Acting   —
  Directing—
  Scenery   —
  Lighting   —
  Properties—
  Costumes—
  Makeup   —
  Publicity   —
  Other   —
Would you like to see a regular drama group formed in this church?
Further comments:

The director has chosen five plays which he thinks are possibilities.

The plays have been read and approved by the minister and the director of Christian education. The next step is the forming of a reading committee from this group, with each member of the committee taking one play, reading it carefully, and reporting on it to the entire group at the next meeting on Friday, November 16. The report should contain a description of the play as to length, setting, characters, and period; a summary of the plot; an analysis of the content and timeliness of the play and an evaluation of things most important in it; and a statement of its simplicity, difficulty, and suitability for this church.

On the evening of the second meeting, November 16, nearly all the people in the original group are present to be part of the work of choosing the play. The reports on the plays are given and after discussion—and not without subtle advice from the minister and the director of Christian education—the play is decided upon. The director then conducts a reading of the play, making certain everyone who wishes to read a part is allowed to, and announces that the cast will be decided upon from this reading and will be revealed in a supplement to the bulletin on Sunday, November 18. The first rehearsal for the cast will be on the next day, Monday, November 19. At this second meeting of the entire group the director also determines the heads of the production crews and gives them the names of the people who indicated an interest in that particular aspect of the project. The director will shortly be meeting with each of the crews to outline the plan of work.

The director casts the play, and it is announced in the Sunday bulletin as planned.

Rehearsal schedule: The director knows the importance of setting goals for the production—every meeting, every rehearsal should have a purpose, a goal. But it is just as necessary to adapt to the accomplishments of each, so that the project steadily builds on what work has been completed. Care should be taken not to postpone any facet of production or rehearsal for long because all parts of the play must get attention.

FIRST WEEK

First Rehearsal—Monday, November 19:

Goals: Talk to cast about the policies of the director.
                    Set the rehearsal schedule.
                    Read the play.

Accomplished: All but two of the cast are present. This is a good time for the director to talk about responsibility to the thing to which these people have agreed to do. He explains that he knew about and had okayed the two absences, since they were due to previous engagements that could not be broken. At this time he tells his people what he expects of them in the matter of co-operation and attendance at rehearsals. They discuss the kind of involvement that will be necessary if this play is to be a success, and each of them describes his particular schedule and responsibilities that will have effect on the rehearsal schedule. Then the rehearsal schedule is set, with the exact days and exact times of rehearsals through to the day of performance, which has also been approved by the cast. The schedule takes the major part of the time on that evening. Mr. Stanley explains that he had hoped to read through the play, but since there is not enough time he asks them to read through the play as many times as they can for the next rehearsal. (The rehearsals were scheduled generally on Monday, Wednesday, and Friday, with only a few variations from week to week and individual rehearsals with members of the cast).

Second Rehearsal—Wednesday, November 21:
 Goals: The first reading of the play for its story and its meaning.
    Discussion of the play.
    Minor changes of the cast.
 Accomplished: In the first reading there is no real concern with interpretation or characterization. After the reading there is an opportunity for questions from the actors and for the director's interpretation, plans for production, and especially for the director's suggestions for the most intelligent methods for the actors to work up their parts.

Third Rehearsal—Friday, November 23:
 Goal: To block Scene 1.

Accomplished: (Since the play is not divided into scenes as it is written, the director divides the play into two scenes for the purposes of blocking and rehearsing.) In blocking the movement of the actors on stage it is necessary that they learn how to move around in "the place" where the action takes place and yet to be aware of the need for being seen and heard by the audience. They should begin to co-ordinate their bodily actions, their spoken lines, and the ideas with which they are dealing. When the blocking is completed for the first scene it is set by immediately going through the scene at least twice. The actors write down their movements in their scripts so that it will be easier to remember them at the next rehearsal. At the end of the first blocking rehearsal the actors are familiar with their movements onstage and with the overall movement of the first scene.

Since the hall in which the play is to be performed is in constant use by various groups in the church, it is necessary to rehearse elsewhere until the last weeks of rehearsals. The director has scheduled the use of another room and has marked off a similar area which will give the same space as the stage. This had to be worked out carefully with the church calendar in order to eliminate any conflicts in the use of the hall.

SECOND WEEK
Fourth Rehearsal—Monday, November 26:
Goal: To block Scene 2.
Accomplished: Before this is done a brief run-through is made of Scene 1 to be sure that the blocking is set, to allow for any changes the director wants to make, and to get the actors working in the area in which they will be blocking the second scene. The procedure for blocking Scene 2 is the same as that of blocking Scene 1. The additional concern here is that the climax and end of the play occur in this

scene. Therefore, the blocking is done with the end of the play in sight.

Fifth Rehearsal—Wednesday, November 28:

Goal: A complete run-through to set the blocking for the whole play; to get a feeling and understanding of the overall movement of the play.

Accomplished: The run-through reveals to the actors the unity of the play as a whole. This leads into the work on timing. (At this point all the rehearsals for the next two weeks are more or less the same kind of rehearsals, all of them working mainly on the timing—the co-ordination of speech and movement —working out all the many difficult spots in the play, attempting to make all of the action and direction work for the actors so that it becomes natural for them, discussing important words and ideas that must be communicated and how best to do this. During this time the lines and blocking are memorized. The director must insist on specific dates for this memorization.)

(It is during this time also that the director meets with the production people. The first meeting includes all the people involved. All of them must have a thorough understanding of the interpretation of the play and what is to be achieved in the completed production. Dates are assigned when the various production crews should have completed their work. The director tells when he wants them at rehearsals and warns them that the last week will be the one of major responsibility to the play. They must understand that the progress and ultimate success of the play now depends on their co-operation and their production of what is needed. Possibly the director has chosen an assistant director who will help him out in rehearsals and who will especially be responsible for production, checking with the production people, helping them do what they must, and being sure they meet their deadline. A devoted person as assistant director cannot only be an extremely important part of the entire production, but can also relieve the director of unnecessary responsibility so that his work with the actors can be more effective.)

THIRD WEEK

Seventh Rehearsal—Monday, December 3:
Goal: Scene 1 lines memorized.
Accomplished: The director insists that no scripts may be used and the actors are prompted as they miss lines. This scene is gone over several times. The director makes certain that there is no misunderstanding of lines. Any questions about meanings are discussed at this time.

FOURTH WEEK

Tenth Rehearsal—Monday, December 10:
Goal: Scene 2 lines memorized.
Accomplished: The same procedure as that used for Scene 1 is followed. (In the third and fourth weeks of rehearsals primary attention is given to the overall movement of the play: it should begin to run smoothly and should not drag; a certain pace should be felt and worked out until it becomes natural and dependable. Any elements necessary to co-ordinating the play, or bridging it, such as narration, music or other sounds, are introduced now and worked into the overall movement and mood of the play.)

During this next week, then, the demands of the play have doubled; therefore, the time spent on the show will necessarily double. Everyone should be well prepared for this period. The production people should be ready to go—now is the time to mount the show.

At the end of this week of rehearsals there is one week until the performance.

FIFTH WEEK

Thirteenth Rehearsal—Sunday, December 16:

Goals: The set is up.
The cast rehearses on the complete set for the first time.

Accomplished: Any changes in set, properties, et cetera are made.
The cast can feel what they will be working with.

Fourteenth Rehearsal—Monday, December 17:

Goal: Technical work set.

Accomplished: The lighting is tried out for the first time.
Technical rehearsals are always long and tedious and are more concerned with setting the technical aspects of the production than with the acting.

Fifteenth Rehearsal—Wednesday, December 19:

Goals: Costumes.
Experimentation with the more complicated makeup requirements.

Accomplished: The costumes are completed and fitted to the actors outside the regular rehearsal time, for the rehearsals must be devoted to putting the various elements to work, trying them out under lights, and letting the actors become familiar with their clothes. Doing as much of the experimentation as possible at this time will eliminate further stopping and interruption in other rehearsals that should be devoted to polishing the play.
The following rehearsal period is the most rigid and intensified period of work on the play.

Sixteenth Rehearsal—Thursday, December 20:

Goal: Line rehearsal.

Accomplished: The director is concerned with the actual text of the play—checking for correctness, emphasis on important factors in delivering lines, re-emphasis on the important places in the dialogue. He then lets the actors go early—they need the rest!

Seventeenth Rehearsal—Friday, December 21:

Goal: Run-through with production details.

Accomplished: A complete, careful run-through with complete costumes and technical work is conducted. A few people are invited as a try-out audience. They comment on the production and the director takes advantage of any valuable suggestions. The visitors are dismissed and the cast goes back over the rough places that need work.

Eighteenth Rehearsal—Saturday, December 22:

Goal: Dress rehearsal.

Accomplished: The final, polished rehearsal is conducted as a preview for a few people invited just like the Friday audience. Preview audiences can be extremely valuable to amateur actors though they may become problems as far as the director is concerned. They do, however, make "opening nights" a less frightening experience, and they give the actors an idea of the audience response to expect from the play.

SIXTH WEEK

The Performance—Sunday, December 23:

Goal: Curtain at 8:00 on an artistic performance.

Accomplished: (The wise director calls his cast and his production people at just the right time before the performance. He must not insist that they come so early that they wear themselves out before the performance, yet they must have time enough to dress and be made up at a comfortable pace and not be rushed before the performance begins.)
Performance!

Chapter XII

THE PRODUCTION

A. Organizing for Production

THE ACTUAL BUSINESS OF CHOOSING AND PRODUCING A PLAY WILL REQUIRE organization similar to the following:

1. Director
2. Play-choosing committee
3. Casting committee
4. Technical director and production staff

A. Art director
B. Building crew
C. Stage manager and stage crew
D. Properties crew
E. Lighting crew
F. Costume crew
G. Makeup crew

5. Business committee

A. Business manager
B. Ticket committee
C. Publicity
D. House
E. Program

6. Prompter

1. Director. (See The Director and Directing, pp. 129-36.)

2. The play-choosing committee: The duties of the play-choosing committee have already been listed. (See Chapter IX.) The members of this committee should be reading plays constantly and should be storing away suggestions for other projects. They should be on the alert for names of plays that groups in other churches are producing. Church papers are an excellent source for this kind of information. The director always works closely with the play-choosing committee. His recommendation of plays should receive first attention, and he should be consulted before any plays are suggested to the group for production.

3. The casting committee (three persons and the director): The casting committee should act in an advisory capacity. Its first business is to see that on the date set for the tryout as many candidates as possible appear. Everyone with any ability should be urged to tryout. The committee can be of great help to the director in seeing that casting is done with all consideration and fairness. The director should have the final decision about any candidate. Because he is to direct, he must be able to work with the people in the cast. The committee should never try to dictate to the director or try to prejudice him. The group must always keep in mind that the production of the play in the best possible manner is the goal of the project. All effort should be bent toward that end.

Casting should not be considered final until after several rehearsals have been held. A person may read well in tryouts and yet have nothing to give in rehearsals. Several candidates may be chosen for the same part, and the best person selected early in the rehearsals. If the spirit of the group is right each person will find his place to work. In the co-operative venture of the church production of a play each job is of utmost importance.

4. The technical director and the production staff: This group turns the backstage wheels. The technical director is chosen by the production staff and the director. Next to the director the job of the technical director is most important. He is responsible to the director for all aspects of the technical production. The production staff (chairmen of the various crews) is responsible to the technical director for each member's particular part of the work. The technical director must be the integrator of the production. He follows the play script during rehearsals. Next to the director, he knows the play most thoroughly. Consequently, he is responsible for helping to make the director's promptbook—the complete record of the production showing all movement and stage business used, light plots, ground plots, costume and makeup charts. The stage manager is responsible to the technical director for the co-operation of the crews.

A. The art director may design both the set and the costumes, but usually two people are secured to design the sets and the costumes When the set and costumes are not designed, he creates the ideas for whatever costumes and sets are used. If costumes are rented or borrowed he makes sure they are right. His job is to see that the scene ery, properties, and costumes are in good taste and are historically authentic.

B. The building crew is responsible to the technical director and the art director for the building of the scenery. When no scenery is to be built, the duty of the crew is to furnish the screens, drapes, and set pieces that may be used. For church productions this committee needs to be ingenious. Many times the facilities for producing a play do not allow scenery to be constructed. Often the play will not permit movable scenery. In these cases the committee will devise ways and means of representing the scene and of changing it. Excellent books on production are available for learning ways of constructing scenery. Persons mechanically inclined or those adept in the use of tools should be members of this committee.

C. The stage manager and stage crew are responsible for placing the set and for changing the scenery. The stage manager is responsible to the director for getting the stage ready for all action. He picks and directs a stage crew, whose business it is to follow his direction in changing the setting. He must be a good manager and must be systematic in his work. The smoothness of a production will depend upon him. He should have a floor plan for each scene and should organize his stage crew so that scenery can be changed in the quickest possible time.

D. The properties crew should get a list of all the properties from the director. Properties are all the movable things used in a production other than scenery. These are both set pieces and hand properties. The list should show when the props are needed. The committee should assemble the props early and should have them available for the cast as soon as possible. Any prop that has to be "worked" should be tried out in the rehearsals to see that it is in good working order. The chairman of the committee should be artistically inclined.

E. The lighting crew is extremely important in the whole setup. If at all possible, someone trained in lighting should be secured as chairman of this crew. Certainly care should be taken to see that no unauthorized person touches the lights. The physical dangers are at once apparent, and fire may result from ignorant meddling.

F. The costume crew may be large or small depending on the number and period of the costumes. A good chairman can often borrow costumes. If he has artistic ability he can make them cheaply.

The costumes should be ready sufficiently early so that the actors can become thoroughly familiar with them and can feel at home in them. There should be few last-minute changes and remodeling. Suggestions for books on costumes will be found in the Appendix.

G. The makeup crew must be organized so that at the last minute it functions smoothly and speedily. Before the dress rehearsal the committee should make whatever experiments are necessary. During the dress rehearsal the committee should sit in the audience and note any changes that need to be made under lighting. Religious drama often requires difficult makeup, and the committee should start work and experimentation very early in the rehearsal period. Several good books on makeup are available.

5. The business committee (the business manager and his assistants): The business management of a play is obviously important. Here is an opportunity for those who may not be artistically inclined but whose talents and interests lie in the field of business.

An estimate of the costs should be made and a budget drawn up. The director's fee, the royalty, the printing, the production costs, and the house expenses must be included in the estimate. A reserve fund should always be kept for emergencies such as loss and breakage. Every person spending money should get a receipt for what he spends. This should be kept with his statement to be turned in to the business manager when the production is over. The business manager should submit a complete and final report of all money taken in and expended. All bills, including royalty, should be paid promptly.

A. The business manager must be the head of a three-ring circus —tickets, publicity, and house. He must be a person with clever ideas, yet he must always be practical in his dealing with the rest of the organization. If tickets are to be sold he should map out a campaign for publicity and ticket-selling. He must also work with the entire stage staff in keeping down the costs of production.

B. The ticket committee has entire responsibility for the sale of tickets. Never make the ticket sale a nuisance in the church. It is an important part of the process of play production and should be kept on a dignified plane.

C. Publicity: A good publicity chairman and committee are invaluable assets to a performance. Publicity in a church should be an ed-

A Very Cold Night by Dennis J. Weaver, as produced by Union Theological Seminary, New York City, Robert Seaver, director

A Sleep of Prisoners by Christopher Fry, as produced by Baylor University Theatre, Waco, Texas, Paul Baker, director

It Should Happen to a Dog by Wolf Mankowitz, as produced at Union Theological Seminary, New York City, Margaret Lightfoot, director

Christmas in the Market Place by Henri Ghéon, as produced by the Scarritt College Players, Nashville, Tennessee, James Warren, director

The Lark by Jean Anouilh, translated by Christopher Fry, as produced by the Boston University Theatre, Boston, Massachusetts, John Ransford Watts, director

Movement for Actors, Creative Dance Class, Martha Cornick, Instructor, National Methodist Drama Workshop at Scarritt College, Nashville, Tennessee

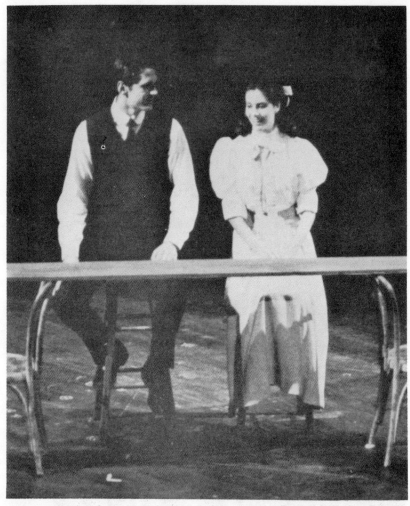

Photo by N. Bleecker Green, Dallas, Texas

Our Town by Thornton Wilder, as produced at Dallas Theatre Center, Paul Baker, director

Photo by Hugh Wilkerson

The Blind Men by Michel de Ghelderode, presented as a graduate thesis production, Division of Theatre Arts, Boston University, Boston, Massachusetts, Donald Knaub, director

Photo by Betty Jane Nevis Photography, Berkeley, California

A Masque of Mercy by Robert Frost, as produced by the Bay Area Religious Drama Society, San Francisco, California, Wayne Rood, director

Photo by Stu Lang, Twin Cities

The Crucible by Arthur Miller, as produced by Hamline University Theatre, St. Paul, Minnesota, James Carlson, director

The Journey of the Three Kings by Henri Ghéon, as produced at The Church of St. John the Evangelist, Boston, Massachusetts, William Thrasher, director

Grab and Grace by Charles Williams, as produced by the Methodist Student Movement in the Canterbury House at Southern Methodist University, Dallas, Texas, Paul Blanton, director

Photo by Tim Harden, Nashville, Tennessee

God Still Speaks, an unpublished script by James H. Warren, as produced by Scarritt College Players, Nashville, Tennessee, directed by the author

This Way to the Tomb by Ronald Duncan, "The Masque," as produced by Denison University Theatre, Granville, Ohio, William Brasmer, director

The Mystery of Mary, Lincoln Cycle, as produced at St. Mary's College, Notre Dame University, Notre Dame, Indiana, E. Martin Browne, director

Photo by Avery Willard, New York

The Book of Job by Orlin Corey, as produced in the nave of Christ Church (Methodist), New York City, Irene Corey, designer, directed by the author. The production was originally performed at Pine Mountain State Park, Pineville, Kentucky. Mr. Corey is on the staff of Centenary College, Shreveport, Louisiana.

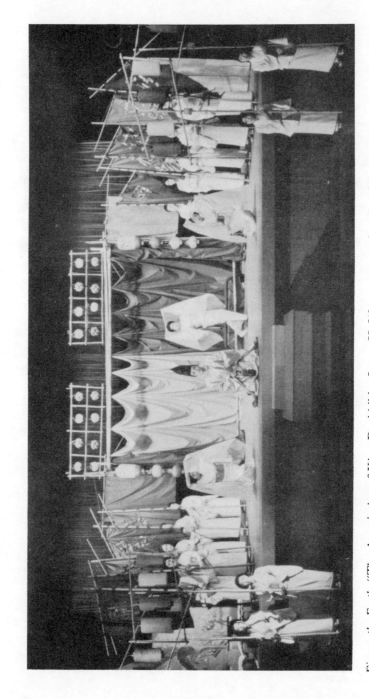

Fire on the Earth, "The Annointing of King David," by James H. Warren, as produced at Seiwa Tan Dai, Nishinomiya, Japan, by the students at Seiwa Tan Dai and Kwansei Gakuin, directed by the author

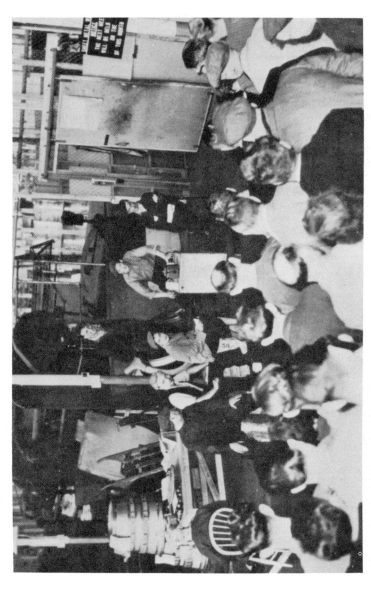

T' Other Shift by K. M. Baxter, a play especially written for the Religious Drama Society of Great Britain and particularly designed for evangelization in industrial areas, as produced by the Pilgrim Players in an English factory

Noah, by André Obey, as produced by Hamline University Theatre, St. Paul, Minnesota, James Carlson, director

ucational process. The committee should know the play thoroughly, should attend some rehearsals, and should understand enough about the play in its period to be intelligent about it. Their effort should be to make people want to come because attendance will be worthwhile. The facts about the play, the plot, comedy, characters, will make good sales talk. Interesting news about the director, actors, and stage crews will also make good material. Bulletins, posters, letters, newspapers, and talks should all be used. A short, colorful scene may be presented before organizations to show something of the play's charm and value. The publicity people should be alive to every opportunity to give news of the play. Experience in news writing can be gained in this way. To secure newspaper publicity feed the paper a series of articles giving different aspects of the production. Give a general idea of the play first. Then follow with an article about the cast, the director, the artists, and the stage crew emphasizing all the types of persons taking part. Names make news. Keep some new ones for each article. Keep the play before the people and make them conscious of it at all times.

D. House: The house committee takes care of everything in the auditorium on the night of the performance except the sale of tickets, which is in the hands of the ticket committee or business manager. Ushers may make the whole performance seem better to the audience. Neat, alert young people should usher. The house manager should also see that the auditorium is properly ventilated.

E. Program: If a printed program is to be used be sure that someone is appointed to supervise the printing. Every name should be spelled correctly and each person serving in any capacity should be listed. Each person's contribution is important, and everyone should be given credit. Drama in the church should not feature actors above the others in the co-operative venture. Use the largest type for the name of the play. Never feature a player. Give the director credit on a separate line. Be careful not to make advertisements in a program a community nuisance. In most communities this should not be undertaken at all. Allow a small amount in the budget for the programs and make them as attractive as possible.

6. The prompter is to note the action as it is mapped out. He should write it down in the promptbook so that the action will be recorded

in case an actor forgets, another actor is substituted, or a dispute concerning action arises. The prompter should give undivided attention to this book. This is an important job; consequently a very intelligent person is required. The prompter must be present at all rehearsals. He should also note pauses in the dialogue and be careful not to prompt unless the actor has really forgotten his lines. His promptbook becomes a valuable part of the drama library when the play has been produced.

In drama in the church curtain calls should not be customary, and under no circumstances should gifts to the cast or the director be passed over the footlights or be made obvious backstage.

After the play has been produced, the stage cleared, the properties returned, the scenery and costumes stored away, and the whole house set in order, the director and his organization will want to check up on the results. In a church performance there is little chance for professional criticism, but every church organization should plan for an accounting. Just as a complete financial statement is necessary, so it is also desirable to look at the net results after a performance. This may be done in several ways.

A few competent persons should be asked to give a criticism of the production. The director and cast, as well as the producing group, should be told that this is to be done for the benefit of future productions and for the education of the persons taking part. If the persons selected do not want to appear to give their criticisms they should be asked to write them.

A meeting should be called within a week after the final performance. The president of the group, or some other official of the church, should state the purpose of the meeting. Then the cast, the crew, and the director, together with members from the audience, should be asked to state their criticisms as honestly and as frankly as possible. If this is done in the right spirit it will be a thoroughly educational process. The criticism of those invited or of anyone interested should then be given. These should be carefully discussed and digested. Suggestions as to what was wrong and what can be done to better the next production should be considered with great care.

The whole process of producing a play in the church should be an experience of religious proportions. As a co-operative experience it gives to the participants the opportunity of learning to work with a group, of being able to take directions, of being creative both artistically and mechanically, of playing together, and finally of learning to take criticism to improve one's self. It should be a genuinely educational process fraught with happy experiences and worthwhile results. Until it reaches this standard, drama in the church is not achieving its real ends nor is it being the activity that it rightly deserves to be.

B. Scenery

The art of scenic production has never been more advanced than at the present time. It is the work of specialized artists as well as famous painters such as Pablo Picasso and Salvador Dali. The scenic designer makes visible what the dramatist has in mind for the setting of the play. In this process of visualization he is joined by the director of the play who sees the action within the limits of the stage or playing space. The scene designer, therefore, is limited by the original idea of the playwright and the need for movement in the direction of the play.

In the older concept of scenery the stage was dressed to represent the scene by scene painting. A backdrop was painted to represent the perspective of a forest or a hall while the flats in the wings were painted to give a continuing sense of the place, allowing for the acting area with its need for such stationary props to fulfill the actualization of what came to be known as the set. In recent years the scene designer working with the light designer has inherited a much more different role. Robert Edmond Jones calls scenery the "environment" factor.

Modern conceptions of scene design date from the work of Gordon Craig, who in the first quarter of this century maintained that scenery should be the visual expression of the dynamic spirit of a play.[1] The other great pioneer of stage space design was Adolphe Appia, who, along with Craig, cleared the stage for vistas, for light, and for action that was free and flowing, adding to the vitality of the action. The contemporary artists in scene design have followed these lines, freeing the stage to present best the action of the play as it is visualized by the director. The concept of scenery as establishing *visual environment* dates from Appia and Craig and it has been agreed to by most scene designers. The idea of environment proposes the placing of a scene and the imaginative suggestion of the place without actually imitating it. In this use of scenery, the spectator is made to feel the place without actually having it shown.

Another contribution that scenery can make to the action of a play is the presentation of the idea without the forms so that a style is achieved. Some character or style of the play is given visual representation in the scenery. Scenery of this stylized nature was used in both Eugene O'Neill's *The Hairy Ape* and *The Emperor Jones*.

Contemporary artists are also freeing the stage of representational scenery so that the playing space is indicated by set pieces or architectural forms such as walls, platforms, and steps. In such space-staging the actor is released to use the freedom in space, but he is called upon to make his action much more telling because he is without the benefit of pieces that might define for him the environmental assets of realistic scenery. He may have little to lean on, nothing to support his words, and he will need to control his body since its movements are much more obvious when they are "in the open."

In the Greek and Elizabethan theater there was little or no scene building. The actors played against a background which probably was the same from scene to scene. This type of setting has again become popular in the contemporary use of outdoor and arena stages. Many schools present plays on a stage that is defined by a cyclorama or curtains against which scenes are played. This "accepted environment" is used for many plays of different types.

What is important to remember is that the scene designer is faced with the limitations of the size of the playing area, that he must suggest by his scenery the place and the mood of the play, as well as its time and its opportunity to allow the actor to create the scene that is called for in the script of the play.

Informal staging, used now in theater-in-the-round, is not informal. It may be more flexible staging because it is viewed from many angles. It is often more difficult than ordinary picture-frame staging since it must allow movement in a variety of directions and allow actors to face the audience which is often on all sides of the playing space. Picture-frame staging does not expose a room by taking off the fourth wall, as is so often suggested. Even picture-frame staging is theatrical in that it exposes a room to the best advantage to an audience looking at one side of it. Even David Belasco could not make an audience believe that one side of a room had been removed. The room had been arranged by the scene designer to allow actors within it and to show this action to the audience.

In arena staging or theater-in-the-round walls disappear and scenery as such is scarcely ever used. This type of setting uses stationary and movable props and depends on lighting for the definition of the playing space. It can be used to great advantage in parish halls and in rooms where a stage is not possible.

Screens, in two-or-three-joint sections, are useful for chancel drama. They can be moved easily, set at a variety of angles, and arranged in interesting designs. They can be made of profile or fiberboard. They should be painted some neutral color, perhaps the walnut finish of the chancel furniture or a shade of gray or tan. They are often used for the mounting of pictures or hangings. Their size should be determined by the size of the playing areas and the auditorium. Screens must be sufficiently wide to stand firmly when jointed with another section and should be sufficiently heavy not to be in danger of upsetting should they be hit by an actor. They should be thick enough to prevent light from behind seeping through. Because of their extreme flexibility screens are very useful for church drama.

All scenery and properties used in space-staging should be so planned that they can be placed before the service begins. There should be as little shifting of screens or set pieces during the performance as possible.

It is important that a satisfactory place be designated for the storing of all equipment. This storage room or closet should be kept orderly. Crews should be trained to return each piece of equipment to its proper place. A good director will help his crews to feel pride in the systematic way in which all scenery, properties, costumes, and lights are cared for.

The Appendix lists books which deal with the designing and construction of scenery for the parish house and chancel.

C. Properties

Properties are those parts of equipment which are used by actors and which decorate or complete the setting. The business of the property chairman and his crew is to gather props and see that they are in the hands of the actors at the proper times. If a play has a large number of properties and a large cast, the surest way of supplying an actor with his hand props is to assign a crew member to be individually responsible for one or more members of the cast. After the performance the property crew should see that all borrowed items are returned. Those properties bought or owned by the group must be listed and stored for possible future use.

Properties should not be merely gathered at the time of a play; they should be obtained whenever they are available. In the spring and in the fall it is a good idea to put a notice in the church bulletin saying the property and costume committees would welcome all donations of hats, canes, furniture, clothing, and white elephants. Auction sales, salvage stores, old trunks, and attics are all good sources of properties. Collecting and care of properties can become an interesting and worthwhile facet of dramatic productions in the church.

D. Costumes

Milton Smith calls costumes "scenery worn by actors," and certainly many of the principles determining the use of scenery in chancel drama are applicable to the use of costumes. In chancel drama costumes should be as simple as possible providing they portray the character.

Difficult costumes should be worn by actors in rehearsal as early as possible. Many times biblical plays are ruined by actors who are embarrassed and self-conscious about their costumes. The clothing must seem as natural for them to wear as their lines in character are to speak.

In biblical plays a great deal of attention must be given to costumes. Costumes should be authentic; however, authenticity should not be carried to an absurd extreme. Dress that causes a congregation to laugh thwarts the purpose of religious drama to give greater understanding and appreciation for nations and peoples.

The church groups will want and need a costume wardrobe. As in the case of properties the alert group will collect costumes from the church members, the community, and rummage sales.

E. Makeup

In chancel drama a minimum of makeup should be used. Makeup is used to accentuate the features so that from a distance they will appear natural. When makeup is overdone it detracts from rather than makes for naturalness. The intensity of the lighting, the distance of the actors from the audience, and the difference in the facial characteristics of the actor from those of the person he is portraying will determine the amount and accentuation of makeup. Superficial manuals on play production are not the source of satisfactory guidance in the art of makeup. Some of the capable practitioners of this art have thorough books on the subject. With the aid of these books the amateur may learn a great deal about the techniques of makeup. Beards, wigs, and graying of hair are all dangerous in unskilled hands. Bad jobs will call attention to themselves and will spoil the effectiveness of the drama. Rather than risk an incompetent makeup job, a group should work without makeup. For difficult makeups there should be much experimentation. Actors using wigs and beards should wear them in as many rehearsals as possible. The director will need to watch carefully to see that actors do not appear in performance with their own jewelry or makeup. For example, a director must see that a prophet of the Old Testament does not wear a wrist watch and that Mary the Mother of Jesus does not have lacquered fingernails.

F. Lighting

The lighting of a play is perhaps more difficult than any other phase of its production, and it determines the effectiveness of the presentation perhaps more than any other aspect. Under proper illumination cheap material in costumes may look rich. Lighting, enabling one to see facial expressions, makes the difference between interest and dullness. The correct use of lighting can make for power in any performance. It is not a dress rehearsal consideration. The lighting facilities of an auditorium will figure in choosing, directing and acting the play.

Effective and safe lighting demands the services of an electrician who knows stage-lighting and the lighting needs of the particular play. A lighting designer must have experience enough to know what can and cannot be done in stage-lighting in order to achieve desired effects. He must know the mood, purpose, and quality of the play. He must have attended enough rehearsals so that he knows the location and size of playing areas and the exits and entrances. He must study the ground plan of the playing area. It is conceivable that a group might have one person who fulfills these three needs, but usually it takes more skills than one person possesses.

Those in charge of lighting should insist upon having the auditorium for technical rehearsals. They must test their lighting from various parts of the auditorium and be sure that the light is not so harsh or so weak that the audience will have to strain to see.

The purpose of lighting is to make the play visible. The person untrained in lighting often makes the play almost invisible. Care should be taken that, while a mood is maintained through the lighting, the actors remain easily visible. Lighting also serves to establish the time and locale and to intensify and objectify the mood of the scene. For example, an abundance of straw-colored, surprise-pink, and steel-blue light will tell an audience that it is daytime—and the more straw color in the light, the more cheer in the mood. Other colors of light, of course, convey other times of day and other moods.

In space-staging lighting serves as a curtain. It also focuses the audience's attention, guides their eyes, and affects their feelings.

Specific illumination is desirable for drama in the chancel. For this type of illumination the lighting instrument is so constructed that it controls the shape and size of the pool of light which it casts. The spotlight, which gives specific illumination, is the most useful piece of lighting equipment for the church. Lighting equipment is expensive; nevertheless, because good lighting can make poor costuming and scenery effective, and poor lighting can destroy the effectiveness of good costuming and scenery, it should be the primary production consideration. Professional-theater lighting equipment is most desirable. It is far better to have one safe, efficient, and dependable piece of equipment than a whole collection of shoddy, inefficient, carelessly constructed equipment. The technical director should get catalogues from dependable manufacturers of theatrical lighting equipment.

Groups should add to their lighting equipment. A goal might be to add a spotlight with each new play or one every six months. It is far wiser to spend money for a good piece of lighting equipment than for elaborate costumes or sets which may be used only a few times.

Above all, lighting equipment for the church should be flexible. A lighting instrument which may be used in only one way and for one purpose is a loss. For example, it would be foolish to buy floodlights, border lights, and footlights. By removing the lens of a spotlight, we have a floodlight. By using a battery of spots, we have borders or foots. In addition to being flexible, equipment should be light in weight, durable, and should give as much light as possible for its size and wattage. In time, good cables should be bought to replace the traditional extension cord. Colored gelatines should be bought in quantities rather than just enough for each play. Stands, clamps, and any special rigging needed to solve the lighting problems of a particular auditorium should be secured. Extra fuses should be on hand at all times.

Quantity and quality of lighting instruments are not the sole solution to the difficult task of lighting chancel drama. The architecture of most churches makes the placement of lighting equipment a real problem. Only through the ingenuity of the light crew working in their own auditorium can the final solution be found. The following suggestions, however, may be helpful to a few groups. Crosslighting, originating from the sides and converging at the playing area, is more desirable than frontlighting. It may be that in some churches both cross- and frontlighting will be desirable and possible.

If a church has a balcony which follows around the side walls of the auditorium, lighting is comparatively simple. Powerful spots may be used opposite each other at the front of the church; their beams may meet and pass through each other when they reach the playing areas. If a church has a balcony only across the rear of the auditorium, spots at both sides or a single powerful spot, centrally placed, may serve the purpose. If a church has no balcony and if there are no pillars or ceilings from which spots may be rigged, light instruments may be clamped to stands and placed behind screens at each side of the playing area. If the playing area is sufficiently elevated, spots may be placed between the chancel rail and the first row of pews; or in some instances spots may be used on standards placed in the front pews. Masking of all visible instruments must be effective! Lighting from the sides or rear of a balcony or from the front of the auditorium will throw shadows upon the wall back of the playing area. Unless a shadow is used purposefully and dramatically, it must be eliminated. Otherwise, the flitting, grotesque shadows of actors will destroy all possibility of concentration upon the play. One way of solving this problem is to throw light upon the back wall. Spots with lenses removed or bucket lights can be used for this purpose. If the play is such that some kind of hanging is desired on the back wall, it will serve to absorb the shadows.

Because outlets may be great distances from the instruments, many cords and cables will be needed; where they cross entrances and exits they should be tacked down and covered with carpet.

It can be seen that the lighting of drama must be planned and experimented with long before the presentation. Nothing should be left to chance. If it is impossible for the person who operates the switchboard to see the actors or hear the cues, he must be given much practice in taking the cues from someone else. Even though the operator has had thorough rehearsal, the tenseness of the performance may cause him to forget. Cue sheets should be made for lights. Diagrams and charts should be worked out to show which instruments control which playing areas. The connections and switches controlling all instruments should be as simple as possible. It is highly desirable to have all instruments as well as auditorium lights controlled from one place. In some instances the building of a portable switchboard may be necessary. Circuits should be so set up that the throwing of one or perhaps two switches will make all the light changes necessary for one change of scene. Care given to the lining up of circuits makes for smoothness and infallibility of lighting. During dress rehearsals when lighting is used the light chairman should sit in the auditorium to check the lighting. There will be times when, due to lack of equipment or the angles or distances from which instruments are rigged, acting areas may have to be shifted in order to keep all actors in the light pool or to have sufficient light on their faces. The light chairman should also be alert to check upon the actor who has not developed a sense of the importance of staying within the lighted areas.

Lighting like scenery is right in proportion to its subtle intensification, its unobtrusiveness, and its lack of theatrical effects. Lighting should be an integral part of the whole composition of the chancel drama. Attention should be given to getting the feel for the right lighting changes between the end of a play and the time for the audience to leave. It may be that the same lighting is used after the drama which was used before the play began. Then after a few moments the coming on of a few wall lights and lights in the vestibule will indicate to the audience that they may leave when they wish.

At times it may seem as if there is little to show for the infinite patience, the perseverance, the hours of labor, put into the technical aspects of dramatic production in the chancel. To many people there is little to show for all the hours involved. Yet because the work is concentrated in building moods and feelings, production for chancel drama can be satisfying and rewarding.

Notes

[1] Craig's main contribution is recorded in his book On the Art of the Theatre (New York: Dodd, Mead & Company, 1925).

DEVELOPMENTS IN RELIGIOUS DRAMA IN THE UNITED STATES: HISTORICAL PERSPECTIVES AND CONTRIBUTING ORGANIZATIONS

Historical Perspectives

IN THE FIRST DECADE OF THE TWENTIETH CENTURY PIONEERS IN THE CHURCH both in New York and Chicago began to look for ways in which religious experience could be given dramatic expression. The Drama League of America was founded in 1911 and from its start sponsored an interest in drama in the church. By the third decade of the twentieth century, in 1924, the Federal Council of Churches had created a committee on religious drama, and in the same year the first volume of *Religious Dramas* was published under the committee's sponsorship. Some years before this, the Drama League under the leadership of Mrs. A. Starr Best and Rita Benton had published lists of plays for community and church uses and had investigated the use of the dramatic method in religious education. Rita Benton's two books of Bible plays were published in 1922, and Helen Wilcox's *Bible Study Through Educational Dramatics* was published in 1924. Another early book in this field was Grace Sloan Overton's *Drama in Education*, published in 1926.

By 1920 significant drama experiments were being carried on by Hulda Neibuhr in New York, and by Mrs. Best and her Pilgrim Players in the First Congregational Church in Evanston, Illinois. Dr. Walter Russell Bowie was experimenting with dance interpretations in New York City, and Elizabeth Edland had published her *Principles and Technique in Religious Dramatics* as a result of experiments she had carried on in New York City.

Actually the interest in the educational use of drama and the beginnings of drama groups in churches were approximately at the same time. Phillips Endecott Osgood in St. Mark's Church in Minneapolis was one of the pioneers. His book Old-Time Church Drama Adapted contained a preface which is still an excellent statement of the meaning of the revival of drama in the church. Much of the theory he expounded is still valid today. His work in the Episcopal Church helped to make that denomination a pioneering church in this whole area.

The Methodist Episcopal Church began its Department of Plays and Pageants under the direction of Lydia Glover Deseo about 1927. With the depression, most of the drama organizations ceased to function, and it was not until 1934 that the Methodists revived the Department of Plays and Pageants and kept it going until 1939 under the direction of the author of this book. A dramatic organization within the Methodist Student Movement known as the National Society of Wesley Players was founded in 1924. As the only student religious drama organization it flourished until 1960 when it was taken over by the Department of College and University Religious Life of the Church.

Fred Eastman began his interest in drama in the early twenties, and the department at Chicago Theological Seminary, along with the one at Boston University, were among the first of such departments in this country. Fred Eastman's interest was logically in writing because plays were needed. His relationship to this whole field has left a residue of material which is significant as a pioneering venture. Along with Fred Eastman's contribution in plays was that of Dorothy Clarke Wilson who had turned out some sixty plays, many of which have become extremely popular. Other writers who were effective in this field were Edna Baldwin, Mary Hamlin, Anita Ferris, Helen Wilcox, Rosamond Kimball, Marshall Gould, Tracy Mygatt, Dorothy Leamon, Marion Wefer, Elliot Field, and Louis Wilson.

The revival of the interest in religious drama after the depression was significant because of the pioneering work that was done in several local churches. Amy Loomis' leadership in her work in the Fountain Street Baptist Church in Grand Rapids was outstanding. Perhaps no other church achieved so complete a program and carried on for a longer time with such a high standard. The educational use of drama in the Riverside Church in New York under Hulda Neibuhr's leadership, Mrs. Best's pioneering venture at the First Congregational Church in Evanston, and Von Ogden Vogt's work in Chicago with both worship and drama are examples of the way in which drama had come back into the church.

Carolyn Joyce's productions at the Hennepin Avenue Methodist Church in Minneapolis were consistently good over a long period of time. The Allen Richardsons have worked in Webster Groves, Missouri, and valiant groups have done good work both in the churches of Des Moines, Iowa, and through the Protestant Players in Detroit. Ruth Winfield Love's work with the Wesley Foundation in Nashville was another notable achievement. Nor should the leadership in their respective communities of other people go unmentioned: John Patterson, Arthur Risser, Margaret Barnes, John Heineman, Reece Hearn, Daryl Montgomery, Ormal Trick, Nels Anderson, Angus Springer, Roberta Anderson, Pearl and Allison Long, Marie Roper, Verna Smith, Iva Wonn, Louise Massey, Edna Alee, Cecil Wry, Mr. and Mrs. Harold Sliker, Edith Steed, Georgiann Goodson, Martha Odom, Mrs. Chester Prince, Sue Ann and Carl Glick, Jon and Phyllis Baisch, and Margaret Huffman—these are some who have believed and have worked.

In 1936 Harold Ehrensperger was asked to construct a dramatic calendar for churches for the *International Journal of Religious Education*. The days of the month were to be celebrated by plays, and from September, 1936, to July, 1937, the *Journal* published a dramatic calendar with descriptions of plays for various days in the Christian year, as well as plays that celebrated biblical characters and outstanding figures in church history. The whole calendar was reprinted as a pamphlet, and it went through several printings before it passed out of circulation.

Religious Drama in Colleges and Seminaries

The department established by Esther Willard Bates at Boston University's School of Religious and Social Work was among the first such departments in American universities. Fred Eastman's department at Chicago Theological Seminary was also a sign of the new awakening. In 1927 a department was organized at Garrett Biblical Institute at which the author of this book was professor of drama. Hulda Neibuhr transferred her work to McCormick Seminary in Chicago, and later Dr. Alfred Edyvean began his work at the School of Religion at Butler University. Boston University School of Theology began a drama department in 1953. In 1958 Boston University offered a master's degree in fine arts in religious drama with courses jointly in the Division of Theatre Arts and in the School of Theology. In 1955 through a grant from the Rockefeller Foundation, Union Theological Seminary in New York initiated its drama project under the direction of Robert Seaver, bringing to this country E. Martin Browne whose work has been the professional direction of all T. S. Eliot's plays and the sponsorship of much that has gone on in England's revival of interest in religious drama. Tom Driver who is best known as the drama critic of *The Christian Century* offers courses in the department at Union.

Courses in drama in the church are now found in many colleges and universities. Mildred Hahn Enterline has worked in many different parts of the country and at Elizabethtown College in Pennsylvania. The work of Albert and Bertha Johnson at Redlands University has been exemplary, as has been the basic work of William Brasmer at Denison University in Ohio, Paul Baker at Baylor University in Texas, and Orlin Corey at Georgetown College in Kentucky. The work at Lon Morris College in Texas under the leadership of Zula Pearson is well known, as is the department at Huntingdon College in Alabama. At Scarritt College in Nashville, Tennessee, James Warren has become an acknowledged leader in taking drama to the small church in the rural areas. James Fiederlick at Drake, Charles C. Ritter at Stetson University, and the consistently good work at Hamline University under James Carlson's direction are other examples of directors and centers that have made serious drama have large dimensions.

Drama at Catholic colleges and universities has had a long and important history. The early work at Loyola in Chicago, Catholic University in Washington, St. Mary's at Notre Dame in Indiana, along with many drama departments in secondary schools and colleges, has been the backbone of the National Catholic Theatre Conference.

The Drama Trio

In the spring of 1954, the president of the University of Redlands asked the drama staff, Albert and Bertha Johnson, to form a mobile drama unit that could move about the country unencumbered by scenery, properties, costumes, and a bus load of actors. Johnson, an established playwright, was working on a play about Roger Williams at the time. Premiered that fall in the First Baptist Church of Los Angeles, the play *Roger Williams and Mary* was the debut of the Drama Trio.

The popularity of the new medium demanded that the University of Redlands have two trios, both of which play weekend engagements in churches, schools, and clubs, and both of which make annual extended tours.

The medium calls for the utmost skill and careful training on the part of the actors and makes ingenious demands of the director. Reading performances of the plays can be given, but that is not the main purpose of the group. One of the assets of the Drama Trio is that it can perform anywhere at any time. Performing without scenery or properties and with no special costumes, the three young players rely on the spoken word well spoken and the art of pantomimic movement to project provocative plays pertinent to current religious problems.

The Chapel Players

The Chapel Players are a group of professional Broadway actors who present serious drama as a form of worship at the five o'clock Sunday vesper services of the Broadway Congregational Church at Broadway and Fifty-sixth Street in New York City. The Players were organized in 1953 by Bill Penn and the Rev. Joseph D. Huntley, advisor to the Players. The work of the Players is the result of this initiative, supported by the encouragement and co-operation of the Tower League of Young Adults. Two productions are presented yearly for ten Sundays each.

Productions have included *The Boy With a Cart* and *Thor, With Angels* by Christopher Fry; *Noah* by Andre Obey; *In April Once* by William Alexander Percy; *The Hour Glass* by William Butler Yeats; *Thunder Rock* by Robert Audrey; *A Box of Watercolors* by G. Wood; *Tobias and the Angel* and *Susannah and the Elders* by James Bridie; *The Marvelous History of St. Bernard* by Henri Ghéon; *The Potting Shed* by Graham Greene; *Fugue for Three Marys* by Jay Thompson and *Women at the Tomb* by Michel de Ghelderode; *The Miracle* by Manuel Mendez-Ballester; and *The Bible Salesman*, a folk musical by Jay Thompson based on a short story by Alma Stone.

The Bishop's Company

The concept of The Bishop's Company and their drama-in-the-church program began in 1939 in the mind of the founder-producer Phyllis Beardsley. In 1952, with the advice and approval of Bishop Gerald Kennedy, the present company was formed and has performed continuously since. An invitation to appear at the Second Assembly of the World Council of Churches in 1954 prompted the beginning of national touring, and the company became an independent organization.

The productions are designed for any type of church architecture. The chancel and the sanctuary itself become the playing area. The company employs no scenery and only the simplest properties and costumes. Some stage lighting is used. The players have appeared in churches of different denominations throughout the country. They have also played in many colleges and universities.

The Role of the National Church Bodies

Presbyterian

For the purpose of encouraging, correlating, and strengthening the interest in drama, music, and art on the part of overseas churches, the Commission on Ecumenical Mission and Relations of the United Presbyterian Church in the U. S. A. incorporated a portfolio of fine arts into its structure in November, 1957, with Mrs. Jeanne Carruthers as administrative director of its art projects.

An important feature of the unfolding program in religious drama is the Barn Playhouse at Stony Point, New York, established in 1959. A renovated barn near the Ecumenical Training Center for missionary candidates has made possible seasons of summer stock in religious drama. In the resident group of actors there have been national leaders and missionaries from Ethiopia, Brazil, Germany, Pakistan, Japan, and Thailand. Participating also were people from Stony Point and nearby communities, short-term missionaries, and others from the Ecumenical Center.

The Barn Playhouse was created to serve as a drama workshop and training center for missionaries and national church leaders, and as a "showcase" for original scripts and for dramas suitable for translation and production by Christian groups elsewhere in the world.

Centers of creative and significant work overseas are developing. Mr. and Mrs. D. L. Swann, United Presbyterian missionaries, have been released to do full-time work in religious drama in northern India, and Miss Joyce Peel of the Anglican Church is doing similar work in southern India.

The only Protestant seminary in Thailand has already made an important contribution to the United Church of Christ in Thailand through its newly established fine arts department. A trilogy of dramas covering some events of the Old Testament and incorporating indigenous Thai music and dance have been written, produced, and taken on tour throughout the country.

Lutheran

The Lutheran Foundation for Religious Drama was founded in October, 1958, at Holy Trinity Lutheran Church in New York City. The organization, officially incorporated in 1959, has on its Board of Directors prominent clergymen, laymen, and theater professionals. Its advisors are drawn from leaders in the church, business, and theater worlds. An independent, nonprofit production and study group, the Foundation is supported mainly by the voluntary contributions of churches and individuals in the New York area.

In 1960 the organization staged its first professional production, an adaptation of Henri Ghéon's *Christmas in the Market Place.* In 1961 the group received its first foundation grant in support of its activities.

Protestant Episcopal

Within the past ten years in the Department of Christian Education of the National Council of the Protestant Episcopal Church an active awareness has sprung up of the need to consider informal and formal drama as two separate branches of the same body, distinguishing their purposes and uses within the church.

Starting eight or nine years ago, it was recognized almost at once, coincidental with the writing of the new curriculum called the Seabury Series, that creative dramatics had wide application for teachers throughout the church. Mrs. Emily Gillies was appointed as consultant in creative dramatics to the department. Sections on the uses of creative dramatics and role-playing were written into the teachers' manuals by editors of the curriculum on various age levels. One result of this exploration in further possibilities of informal drama within the church pointed to the need for a teacher-training workshop in creative arts, to train diocesan leaders of Christian education to carry out workshops of their own. This workshop was held at Seabury-Western Seminary in Evanston, Illinois, in August, 1959, using a staff of leaders who had worked on the pilot projects combined with specialists from Northwestern University, who also introduced new aspects of formal drama such as Chamber Theatre.

Church of Jesus Christ of Latter-day Saints

The drama committees of the Young Men's and Young Women's Mutual Improvement Associations of the Church of the Latter-day Saints are remarkably active in community drama that includes most of the Mormon Church groups. Their unique *Play Production Handbook* is described in the bibliography.

The Southern Baptist Convention

The Southern Baptists began an organized program of church drama in 1954. At this time the responsibility of promoting drama in the churches was assigned to the Baptist Sunday School Board with headquarters in Nashville, Tennessee. Emphasis has been given to leadership training and to the publication of drama materials.

Drama festivals are held in various states and include the presentation and evaluation of plays and discussion-demonstration session in costuming, make-up, lighting, and other technical area. Six festivals are held annually.

Summer workshops are held at Ridgecrest Assembly, Ridgecrest, North Carolina, and at Glorieta Assembly, Glorieta, New Mexico.

Through the Broadman Press the Southern Baptists have begun the publication of religious plays. Future plans include a nationwide playwriting competition and the publication of books on producing the church play. Cecil McGee acts as drama consultant.

The Methodist Church

The Methodist Church initiated its drama interests in 1927. Under Argyle Knight's leadership, the Methodists have held two summer drama workshops at Scarritt College in Nashville. In 1957 a unique experiment was carried out at the Lancaster Camp grounds under the sponsorship of the Ecumenical Voluntary Service Committee of the National Council of Churches. A small company of players organized as a work camp under the direction of Jay Buell presented plays on Friday afternoon and evening and on Saturday evening. A first performance of Donald Manck's play on Francis Asbury, *Glory for the Land*, was given. In 1958 the Youth Department of The Methodist Church joined with the Bishop's Company to hold a second drama work camp at Lancaster with both Buell and James Warren as directors. Another unique contribution of the Methodists was the Religious Drama Caravans, manned by college students, which flourished from 1954 to 1958. Argyle Knight was executive director of the caravans, and James Warren was the dramatic director. The teams trained for ten days and then served for one week in six different communities. More than five hundred churches participated with approximately two thousand persons engaged in the project.

Although The Methodist Church does not have a drama department at the present time, the Student Department and the Youth Department through Argyle Knight's work still carry on various drama projects and co-operate with the National Council departments and other organizations.

The National Catholic Theatre Conference

The National Catholic Theatre Conference was organized in 1937 by directors and sponsors of Catholic theater groups to provide a channel for the exchange of inspiration and information among groups and individuals interested in fostering and spreading Catholic theater. Its members, drawn together by their common Catholic faith and their love of theater, represent the most diverse phases of theater activity from professional writers to the lowest high school amateur. Yet the original purpose of the Conference defined at the first meeting—i.e., the dissemination of Catholic theater in harmony with Catholic spirit and philosophy—continues to be the guiding principle of all members.

The further subdivision of the twelve geographic regions into conveniently located units has also increased local interest in Catholic theater and strengthened the organization. Both regional and unit drama meets and play festivals have helped to solve local theater problems, and the evolution of the NCTC noncompetitive festivals with the system of a Critic Judge has helped to trained appreciative audiences and to raise local standards of play selection and production.

Over 700 member groups representing at least 14,000 members participate directly in the work of the conference. The greatest numerical growth has come with the increased number of high schools. These have grown from 4 memberships in 1941 to 460 in 1958, with over 3,000 high school students individually affiliated as members.

The maintenance of a lending library of over 2,000 published and manuscript plays available for examination by directors and play-reading committees enables directors to select plays for production on the basis of actual reading, rather than merely on catalogue information. Postage is the only cost to members who wish to borrow plays from the NCTC collection at Immaculate Heart College, Hollywood. A list of recommended plays, revised in 1959 by Mrs. Christopher Wyatt and Anna Helen Reuter as the *Blue Book of Recommended Plays*, also guides members in the selection of suitable plays and of plays which have positive Catholic values.

The monthly publication, *Catholic Theater*, since its first publication in 1937, under the editorship of Francis MacDevitt of the NCWC News Service, has continued to supply members with information concerning professional and nonprofessional theater and forms the connecting link between regional and national activities.

From 1945 until 1957 an annual *Bulletin* was published in order to present individual reports and pictures of productions by member groups as well as significant articles by leaders of theater. In 1958, with the administration of the Rev. Gabriel Stapleton, S.D.S., the *Bulletin* was replaced by *Drama Critique*, a critical review of theater arts and literature published three times yearly. In connection with this scholarly journal a contact-placement service was established to assist in the staffing college and university departments with trained Catholic personnel. *Drama Critique*, moreover, has established a medium for the exposition of Catholic truth and principle as applied to theater in many secular colleges, universities, and libraries.

Throughout its history NCTC has encouraged the writing and production of original Catholic plays. Since its very first published original manuscript, a translation of Ghéon's *Old Wang* by Sister Mary Constantia, B. V. M., Clarke College, Dubuque, Iowa, the NCTC has worked for the rediscovery of the Catholic tradition of theater and for high standards of religious drama. Continuing its tradition of encouraging production of plays by Catholic playwrights such as Claudel and Ghéon, the Religious Drama Committee with the translating ability of Mother Fiske of Manhattanville College of the Sacred Heart, has made sixteen plays of Ghéon, as well as his book *The Art of the Theatre* and Claudel's essay "Theatre and Religion," available in English.

NCTC also maintains a Catholic Playwrights Circle wherein both professional and amateur benefit from the study of original scripts. Other committees maintained are College, High School, Community Theatre and Children's Theatre Committees; a Grants and Scholarships Committee, which annually obtains for talented students approximately $30,000 in drama scholarships to Catholic colleges; a Career Guidance Committee, and other organizational committees such as Audit and Budget Awards Committees.

The growth and development of NCTC can best be traced through a study of its biennial conventions, since at each convention a progress report is presented, plans for the future are discussed and voted on, and a program of speeches, discussions, and demonstrations is offered. Fr. Gilbert Hartke has been the guiding head of the organization.

The National Council of Churches of Christ

The Commission on Drama, Department of Worship and the Arts

The Commission on Drama of the Department of Worship and the Arts of the National Council of Churches was established in 1954 in recognition of the historic relationship existing between Christianity and the drama. The purpose of the Commission on Drama is that this relationship may achieve overt and significant expression in the culture in which we live.

The purpose and work of the commission are predicated upon two fundamental assumptions, the twin principles of judgment and service: That the Lordship of Christ extends over man's entire life; that it is the task of the church to minister to the common life of man. In a culture impoverished by an exaggerated concern for scientific analysis and a scientific approach to life, the commission believes that the drama is not only a valuable but also a necessary part of the life of the whole man. It believes that the drama needs the sustenance of religion and that its ultimate welfare is of concern to those Christians who would assume a responsible role in society.

For drama within the church, the task of the commission has been:

A. To help the church interpret the place of drama in the Church's life.

B. To aid the churches in achieving and maintaining fitting standards for drama in the church

C. To encourage and promote the writing of new plays which reflect the religious concern of contemporary Christians.

For the theater at large, the commission will seek:

A. To assist church members in understanding drama and the meaning of drama for man's life.

B. To establish communication between members of the theatrical community and Christian thinkers, in order to discover grounds of common concern.

C. To assist members of the theatrical community in recognizing the religious dimensions of the theater and in perceiving the theater in its potentiality as a vocation in the Christian sense of the word.

D. To provide opportunities for playwrights to communicate a Christian understanding of man and history.

E. To advise and co-operate with persons in the mass media by studying the role of drama in these media in the light of the commission's general purposes.

F. To suggest such other plans as may seem advisable to further the general objectives of bringing the historic relation of church and theater into significant expression.

The commission has published a list, *Plays for the Church*, available from the Commission on Drama, Department of Worship and the Arts, National Council of Churches of Christ in the U. S. A. Marvin Halverson served as secretary of the Department of Worship and the Arts.

The Drama Committee of the Division of Christian Education

The first Religious Drama Workshop was held at the American Baptist Assembly, Green Lake, Wisconsin, in the summer of 1949. The founder was Amy G. Loomis, who served as the director of the project for the first eight years. The workshop, first sponsored by the Baptists, became a project of the Division of Christian Education of the National Council of Churches. Helen Spaulding of the National Council became the codirector. Miss Loomis was succeeded by Blaine Fixter who acts as the council codirector. Miss Loomis was succeeded as workshop director by A. Argyle Knight in 1957. In 1958 the workshop was moved to Lake Forest College, Lake Forest, Illinois.

The aims of the Religious Drama Workshop across the years have been to provide training experiences in various aspects and forms of religious drama; to help delegates find deeper meaning and insight in the Christian faith through participation in drama work groups; and through informal opportunities to share experiences, insights, and resources with faculty and other delegates. Each delegate may participate in two work groups, one in the morning and one in the afternoon.

Work groups included at various times in the workshops include beginning and advanced acting; beginning and advanced production; beginning and advanced directing; creative dramatics for children and youth; creative movement for children, youth, and adults; informal drama (play readings, walking and rehearsals, use of play cutting, et cetera), lighting and designing, costuming and makeup, and in more recent years, a seminar for leaders and a productions studio for more advanced delegates.

About one hundred delegates have attended each year. They have included persons of experience as well as beginners. It has been the primary training enterprise available to interested people in local churches with the focus always on the local church.

One of the tangible results has been a strong religious drama committee which is one of the standing committees of the Division of Christian Education of the National Council of Churches. This committee is made up of representative staff members from national boards of Christian education of the various denominations holding membership in the National Council of Churches. There are in addition elected members who are active in the field of religious drama. The committee in enlarging the scope of its work to include other projects. The meetings are held annually with various subcommittees working on special projects throughout the year.

Manhattan Division of the Protestant Council

The Religious Drama Council is an integral part of the Manhattan Division of the Protestant Council. It was begun in 1959 by a group of persons from various churches of Manhattan for the purpose of sharing ideas, problems, resources, and techniques related to religious drama on the parish level. It has thus far confined itself to a smaller geographical area until its usefulness is demonstrated.

The American Educational Theatre Association

The American Educational Theatre Association represents the activities and study programs not only of colleges and universities, but also of grade and high schools, of children's theater, and of community theater. It is the largest active theater association in the United States. It provides the most inclusive channel for communication and action. Its work is carried on through divisions representing various expressions of drama, and through projects.

Interest in religious theater has found expression in at least four of the organizational activities of the AETA.

A. The publications of the association have carried articles of direct and indirect relationship to religious concerns in the theater. The *Educational Theatre Journal* is the quarterly of the association.

B. Special sectional meetings concerned with religious drama have been included in the programs of both national and regional meetings of the association.

C. A Religious Drama Project was set up by the Association in 1957 under the chairmanship of Harold Ehrensperger. The first meeting began an exploration of concerns in the area.

It defined the following investigations which it proposed to undertake:

1. Leadership training opportunities in religious drama in colleges and universities and other agencies.

2. Material on religious drama in periodicals.

3. The use of creative dramatics, discussion drama, and role-playing in religious education.

4. Field work and internship opportunities in colleges and universities.

5. Employment opportunities offered by churches in the field of religious drama.

The "Next Steps" Conference at Boston University

The Conference and Consultation on the Next Steps in Religious Drama, held at Boston University on July 3-5, 1959, was sponsored by the Department of Creative Arts of the School of Theology and the Division of Theatre Arts of the School of Fine and Applied Arts of Boston University in connection with the degree program in religious drama.

The Religious Drama Project of the American Educational Theatre Association at its meeting in Chicago, December, 1958, had proposed a meeting of leaders in religious drama in colleges and universities to discuss the next steps to be taken. The Drama Committee of the Commission on General Christian Education of the National Council of Churches had planned a meeting for February, 1960, to consider the next steps in religious drama. Boston University was happy to find that both of these significant committees were willing to co-operate in the conference and consultation.

The conference and consultation were held during the sessions of the Religious Drama Workshop at Boston University. The Workshop brought together thirty-nine students from eighteen states. The Institutional Division of the Board of Education of The Methodist Church made it possible for five directors of drama in church-related colleges to attend the workshop. A grant from the Lilly Foundation, Inc., of Indianapolis made possible a workshop fund for students, as well as the expenses of persons who served as faculty and special lecturers, both in the workshop and in the conference and consultation.

A report of the consultation, Next Steps in Religious Drama, is available from the Boston University School of Theology, 745 Commonwealth Avenue, Boston 15, Mass.

The Bay Area Religious Drama Service (BARDS)

The Bay Area Religious Drama Service (BARDS) was formed in the spring of 1960 by a group of ministers who felt that the time had come for the San Francisco Bay Area of California, with its rich artistic traditions and a newly vigorous Protestant churchmanship, to have a religious drama program of its own. Wayne Rood of the Pacific School of Religion has been the organizing head.

The idea came from within the church, and the aim was both educational and experimental. For example, each of the churches inviting the players agrees to conduct a study of the Book of Jonah in preparation for the performance of *Jonah*, adapted from *Jonah and the Whale* by James Bridie. The purpose is not to import theater into the churches, but to give churchmen an opportunity to produce for themselves drama of high artistic quality and religious significance. The BARDS project is an experiment in the direction of bringing together the realistic word of the theater and the redemptive word of the Church.

It is the hope of BARDS that plays given in the church will be an integral part of the Christian education program. Their plays are not thought of as isolated events but as focal points for study in groups already meeting or in new groups which may start because of interest in drama.

Boston Area Religious Drama Service—BARDS East

Boston Area Religious Drama Service (BARDS East) has been formed on the historic assumptions that the truths of the Gospels and of the Old Testament can be expressed dramatically. Man receives wisdom not only through his intellect, but also by means of his imagination and his emotions; the drama is an effective way of confronting man, churched and unchurched, with his relation to God.

Concert play-readings are given in churches which request them. Consultation is given on dramatic material and production; workshops are held on techniques of play reading (choosing and cutting a script, direction of dialogue, theatrical aids to presentation, handling discussion).

BARDS East is an interdenominational team with co-operating members from various churches in the area and representatives from Andover-Newton Theological Seminary, Boston University School of Theology, Emerson College, Episcopal Theological School, and Harvard Divinity School.

Service fees are charged at cost. Overall operating expenses depend upon the support of churches, seminaries, and individual memberships. Individual members receive the periodic *Newsletter*, with a calendar of religious drama activities in the Boston area. They may take part in weekly exploratory play-readings, try out for concert play-reading performances, and attend them without charge. Chouteau Chapin has served as executive director, with William Thrasher as associate.

DEVELOPMENTS IN RELIGIOUS DRAMA
OUTSIDE THE UNITED STATES

The Religious Drama Society of Great Britain

THE RELIGIOUS DRAMA SOCIETY OF GREAT BRITAIN ORGANIZED IN 1929, IS AN interdenominational society whose aim is "to foster the art of drama as a means of religious expression." The society is the authoritative national body. It works with all Christian churches, with the theater, with social organizations, and in association with S.P.C.K. (Society for the Promotion of Christian Knowledge), which gives it generous help.

The Society organizes an annual nine-day summer school with classes in all aspects of production. In addition, schools and conferences are held and lectures given. It is possible to arrange for visiting lecturers and tutors to advise and direct productions. Some of the other services of the society are:

Choice of plays: Free advice is given to all members. Classified catalogues are published and sold to members at a reduced cost.

Library: The Society has an extensive collection of plays and reference books; single copies and sets may be hired by members.

Advice to playwrights: Plays are considered for publication, and written criticisms supplied for a small fee. Return postage must be sent with all manuscripts.

Christian Drama: A magazine free to all members is sent out three times annually.

Flash: A newssheet giving details of forthcoming events is sent free to members.

Publications: Plays and pamphlets are published by the society and by S.P.C.K.

Youth Work: The society offers stimulating instruction in play production to youth organizations so that club members may enjoy the magic and excitement of drama. Short courses can be arranged for youth leaders.

Decor: Advice is given on scenery, costume, and lighting.

International: The Society is the only national interdenominational body of its kind in the world and is in close touch with Christian communities of many nations.

The Christian Drama Council of Canada

In response to an increasing interest and activity in religious drama throughout Canada, the Christian Drama Council of Canada was formed in 1954 as a national body to serve the Christian churches and all who promote religious drama. From the beginning the council gained the approval and active support of all major denominational groups, as well as that of members of the professional theater. Slowly at first but then with gathering momentum, the council has made its influence known and felt across the land until it is now recognized as the major source of inspiration and leadership in the resurgence of drama in the service of the church and its ministry.

The purpose of the council is "to foster the art of religious drama as a medium for the expression and communication of Christian truth" by bringing together in a common service the skills of the theater, the faith of the Christian church, and the peculiar insights of each into human character and experience; by using every available means to support the highest standards of choice of play, of direction, of acting, and of presentation; by exchanging information, making available resources known, and providing a full range of services which shall include both practical guidance to those who are compelled to work on the simplest and most economical lines, as well as expert advice and direction to large-scale presentation; by encouraging the writing of plays of sound dramatic value which explore and interpret the Christian way of life; by promoting the use of drama and the dramatic form in Christian education.

The Council offers many services to members:

Lending Library: The largest library of religious drama in Canada is available to provide members with plays for reading purposes, references, and technical books. A small borrowing fee is made to cover handling costs.

Advice on play selection: Lists of recommended plays for seasonal and general use are available. These indicate the type of play, cast required, degree of difficulty, publication details, and other information of assistance to the prospective producer.

Production and technical service: Questions answered on matters of organization and on directing, acting, costuming, lighting, presentation, et cetera.

Traveling advisors: The service of a traveling advisor may be arranged for periods ranging from two days to one month.

Drama workshops: Workshops are arranged from time to time throughout

Canada as a means of helping local groups to improve their techniques and to discover the latest resources. In addition, annual summer workshops lasting from one week to two weeks are held in various parts of the country.

Advice to playwrights: Arrangements may be made to evaluate and give constructive criticisms of scripts. A fee is involved.

Christian Drama: A magazine containing reports on significant dramatic ventures and resources, as well as giving practical help, is sent out periodically to members.

An International Conference on Christian Drama, Royaumont, France, 1960

The purpose of the conference held at Royaumont near Paris for five days in July, 1960, was to continue the work begun at the Oxford Conference in 1955. Its aim was to bring together Christians of many nationalities and denominations who are concerned with the promotion of modern religious drama in various ways. It was made possible through the generosity of the Rockefeller Foundation of New York and the Cultural Fund of the Council of Europe.

Fifty delegates came from twenty countries, including the U.S.A., the Dominions, Great Britain and most of Western Europe, Greece, India, and Japan. From the ecumenical point of view this was an almost unique achievement, one not even attained by the World Council of Churches, for the delegates included Roman Catholics, Anglicans, Greek Orthodox, and Protestants.

Plays showing great diversity of style were presented in the evenings as examples of contemporary Christian drama. Both lectures and plays gave rise to lively discussions in which professional theater directors, playwrights, and amateur producers contributed.

The following resolutions were proposed and carried unanimously:

A. That this conference accepts with much gratitude the offers from Holland, Sweden, and Berlin of secretarial exchange services for an initial period of one year, to be continued if interest warrants it.

B. That the delegates invited to this International Conference on Modern Christian Drama are convinced that future meetings at intervals of not less than five years would be of great creative value: that they intend to prepare, by the exchange of material, by local organization and by study, for such meetings; and that they accordingly ask foundations sympathetic to their aims to consider favorably assisting the organization of such conferences.

Reports presenting the work of churches in Europe are printed in Christian Drama, Vol. 4, No. 4, Winter, 1960.

The address of the Conference is that of The Religious Drama Society of Great Britain.

THE DIRECTORS' PLAY LIST

Introduction

THE SEARCH FOR THE RIGHT PLAY IS AN INTEGRAL PART OF THE TOTAL PROCESS of play production. Yet descriptions of plays in catalogues and, indeed, in the supplementary list in this book are often of necessity so short that they do not greatly help. Most directors choose plays because some person they respect has produced them, or they hear about a play from a friend. This directors list is the codified "advice" of the people in the country who have done the best work in religious drama.

Here are the answers to the questions: "What play have you produced that you think worthwhile?" "What are its strengths and weaknesses?" "What are the things to look out for in directing it?"

The answers to these questions are the statements of the directors. This is their confidential advice! A study of the comments will furnish a rather complete discussion of the problems of choosing plays and producing them in the church.

Aria Da Capo, Edna St. Vincent Millay

Poetic fantasy-satire; 30 minutes; a stage set for a harlequinade; 4 m., 1 w.; Baker's Plays; royalty $15.00.

The idea of the play: Through satire, Aria Da Capo reveals to us the stupidity of war.

The director's suggestions: This play is an interesting one to produce because of the new meanings and implications that continuously come from the lines. Each performance was interpreted quite differently. We would often finish by saying, "I never knew that line could mean that!"

Timing is very important in this play. We found that creating suspense, that is, waiting a split second before giving the next line, was a good technique. The play can also become very complicated in the matter of stage properties. Keeping them as simple as possible served our purposes for church sanctuaries. The actors found difficulty in being convinced of what he or she was saying.

Since the play is "abstract," it is hard for the player to remain in character and to remain coherent. Each line, we found, had to be said with extremely good diction due to the abstractness of thought line.

After each performance we discussed the play. There were lines of comedy relief that we did not discover until the first performance. But in the second, third, et cetera, the reaction was not the same to these lines. There needs to be a slight hint of comic relief in this play.

The production should be kept simple. It can be done in modern dress, but we found it to be best in harlequinade costume. Begin ahead of time for more *reading-of-line* rehearsals and *line-interpretation* rehearsals to find every possible meaning and interpretation for each line and the play will be a more rewarding experience.

It should be presented by older youth or adult groups.

Leon Albert
Director of Christian Education, Grace Methodist Church, Blue Island, Illinois

Billy Budd, Louis O. Coxe and Robert Chapman (based on the novel by Herman Melville)

Modern morality; 3 acts; on board a ship at sea; 24 m., extras; published by Princeton University Press and Dramatists Play Service; royalty $50.00, $25.00.

The idea of the play: *Billy Budd* is regarded by many as the outstanding Christian tragedy in American literature. The story involves two seamen, one the embodiment of good and the other the embodiment of evil.

The director's suggestions: *Billy Budd* interests me because it points with great beauty to the central historical events upon which the Christian faith rests. In terms that are real to modern man, it grapples with the biblical themes of suffering, evil, and forgiveness. It is theatrically interesting to actors and technical crews. Audiences show deep involvement from great irritation.

Like many plays made from novels it suffers from too many scenes. The all-male cast presents some difficulties. The fights are fascinating, but require careful blocking and rehearsal. Casting is of supreme importance. It should be done by young adults or adults.

Records of sea sounds, a swinging lantern, and scenes such as the burial, Claggart and Billy, Captain and Seymour, built into the rhythms of the ship's movement, help establish the sense of movement so necessary to make the sea a symbol of nature upon which the small society is afloat.

It is extremely important that the director do thorough research on Melville and the period of the story. Melville's descriptions of the characters and of the death of Claggart must be studied carefully. There is much written on Navy law, impressing sailors, the treatment of children on ships, and the effect of the mutinies on England which will help directors, actors, and crews. But most important is for everyone related to the performance to experience the profound metaphors of the play.

RUTH WINFIELD LOVE
Director, Projects in the Christian faith and the Arts, Europe, 1951, 1953, 1956, 1959; Director, Wesley Intimate Theatre, Nashville, Tennessee, 1949-1957; Assistant in drama, Boston University School of Theology, 1961

Calvary, William Butler Yeats

Easter verse play; one-act; can be found in Yeats' Collected Plays, published by Macmillan; royalty on request from the publisher.

The director's suggestions: There are three "musicians" and six other characters in the play. They wear masks. The play requires music; there are songs which should be set to music or spoken against music. Three of the characters, the soldiers, perform a short dance.

Yeats' short play in verse is an intriguing work for the Christian theater for two reasons. It presents a provocative—and unorthodox—reaction to the events of Calvary. Christ is confronted by Lazarus who protests his resurrection because in death he had found solitude, safety, peace. Judas submits that his betrayal was his only recourse because freedom demands that absolute authority be challenged. The soldiers dance indifferently about the cross asking nothing in their world of caprice. The play is opened and closed by a chorus which underscores the loneliness of Christ.

The play is also an interesting example of Yeats' effort to achieve a kind of dramatic concentration through the use of verse, music, dance, masks, and other theatrical devices. He seeks a kind of ceremonial experience that will revivify ancient stories and legends and their power to revive the human spirit. Calvary is not orthodox in its theology, indeed it is perhaps heretical, but it is intellectually provocative and worshipful in feeling. Like the didactic plays of Brecht, it is an instructive work for those who seek to recover the Christian spirit in the arts.

JAMES CARLSON
Director of the Theatre, Hamline University, St. Paul, Minnesota

The Captains and the Kings, Channing Pollock

40 minutes; 11 characters; Baker's Plays; royalty $10.00 if admission is charged, $5.00 if no admission is charged.

The director's suggestions: This play is an interesting one to produce because it concerns a theme that is very timely, but there are certain things to watch out for in the production. It is a static drama, but with good direction it is very challenging to an audience. Be careful not to overplay the acting. The lighting can add to the effectiveness of the presentation greatly, as can authentic costume.

The play is best performed by adults.

MILDRED ENTERLINE
Director of Drama, Elizabethtown College, Elizabethtown, Pennsylvania

A Child Is Born, Stephen Vincent Benét

A serious modern drama of the Nativity; 30 minutes; interior of the inn in Bethlehem; 4 m., 2 w., extras; Baker's Plays; royalty $10.00.

The idea of the play: *A Child Is Born* points out the futility of mankind's renunciation of God's purpose for us in life in favor of materialistic pursuits and ambitions.

The director's suggestions: The play's timeliness as to theme, definitiveness of the characters, strength of the thief's role, small cast, simplicity of staging, eloquence and beauty of Benét's poetry—worthwhile from a playwright's standpoint, applicable theme to our times, the challenge this play offers a producing group; all these things make the play interesting to me. The climax graphically points out what happens when mankind wholly and with faith receives the Son of God.

Proceed with caution! Make thorough study and exploration first!

On *A Child Is Born,* remembering that it was originally written for radio, the director must be inventive as to the movement and action so as to keep the play from being static—but also be careful to suit the action to motivation of situation or lines. This need not be an unsurmountable task for the director who does his homework thoroughly before rehearsal time. As you study the play you will find opportunities for movement harmonious with the dialogue and mood. It is difficult to keep the tempo and rhythm, especially with inexperienced actors—this is a talky play, thus utmost care needs to be taken in regard to phrasing and timing.

The direction needs creative imagination. Know the casting and staging limitations, although staging can and should be kept simple. We found the more sophisticated or experienced audiences more responsive to the play. It is important to be sensitive to preferences, needs, and limitations of the congregations and to have skillful mature readers.

The play is suitable for either chancel or auditorium. Lighting can be simple but effectively used. Biblical costumes are suggested, but other periods may be used, with discretion. Costumes designed to be timeless may also be tried—that is, the costume may not belong to any set period, but it is universal in design. A musical background is suggested with the use of a choir, perhaps, and an introductory prelude. Consult your organist.

Produce other well-written plays before presenting *A Child Is Born*. Don't start off with it! Read and study it; have your group read and discuss it; explore the avenues of presentation; know what you as a director want the play to say, what the playwright has in mind as you understand it; be sure your group understands and is sympathetic toward poetic drama. Again, know casting limitations, your objectives, and the needs and desires of your congregation.

While it should be produced by adults, it is possible for advanced young people, but proceed with care here.

> Mrs. Andrew B. Montgomery
> Director of Drama, Mount Lebanon Presbyterian Church; Chairman of Drama Commission, Council of Churches, Pittsburgh Area

Christ in the Concrete City, Philip Turner

Modern verse drama; 1 hour; a bare stage; 4 m., 2 w.; Baker's Plays; royalty $15.00.

The idea of the play: A narrative of the crucifixion of Christ with contemporary reflection on the event. Shows how we daily crucify him and the potential of resurrection.

The director's suggestions: *Christ in a Concrete City* is a modern verse drama patterned after the writing styles of Henri Ghéon and R. H. Ward. One must say that Turner's plays have a style all their own, however. The application of modern vernacular thrusts and realistic present-day situations contrasted with the historical characters from the Bible give this drama a freshness not often found today.

The interest value of the play may be noted first in the potential catharsis for the local church situation. It has a dynamic effect on most audiences. One sees real therapy at work here as the audience identifies with the actual events of the passion of our Lord with the life they now live. It becomes a process of self-examination for each individual who is willing to become emotionally and intellectually involved. In terms of therapy for the actors it has a noticeable effect. They become involved in a depth analysis of the play both philosophically and theologically. They examine themselves in terms of their own growth or lack of growth in Chirstian awareness. One may find this soul-searching going on whether the group is a more mature high school class, seminary students, or more mature adults.

It is imperative that the actors have some understanding of the Christian tradition and particularly Christian theology. The production ought not to become so stylized or sophisticated that they lose the essential and honest throb of the play.

The director must provide for a lot of movement both individually and groupwise or the play will have a static quality about it. Avoid underplaying the historical characters. Build the mood and the tempo, especially in the last scenes, with music, and if possible, skillful choreography.

> DR. ALFRED R. EDYVEAN
> Professor of Communications, Christian Theological Seminary, Indianapolis, Indiana

Christmas in the Market Place, Henri Ghéon

> Nativity play; 1 hour; 3 m., 2 w., 2 carolers (optional); Baker's Plays; royalty on request.

The idea of the play: The story of the Annunciation and the birth of Christ is acted out in a village square by a troupe of gypsy strolling players with bits of their own humor and personal gypsy philosophy thrown in to give the play sparkle and a rather unusual freshness.

The director's suggestions: One of the most interesting aspects of this play is the relief provided by the play-within-a-play structure in which it is written. The five actors required portray nineteen different characters needed for the re-enactment of the Annunciation and the birth of Christ in addition to their own gypsy roles. For the director with amateur actors this can be at once a blessing and also be fatal. It does not require extensive work on developing a meticulously created role of one character, but it does require enough versatility for the actors to portray a variety of roles under the certain character-type of their original roles.

Both sides of the footlights will find the self-consciousness that is "built in" to the play refreshing. The awareness of the actors as "actors" and their play as a "play" puts the audience to ease and allows for a great deal of informality in the presentation which can simplify your staging. Ghéon has written the play in this manner to help in bringing to life for modern audiences the familiar Christmas story. It is important that you disarm the audience at the very first, making them realize that you are really playing to them and that you want their response as your "sixth character"—the audience! Otherwise they will remain somewhat timid and nervous about the whole thing and your show will walk off with all the prizes for "greatest embarrassing moments."

One of the characters, Joey, is more responsible than the others for this audience-actor rapport, and this means that this actor must be a real "winner" at disarming the audience.

Each of the five characters is intriguing and each contributes a major part to the ongoing story. They are not only 100 per cent people, but also 100 per cent gypsy, uninhibited virtuoso performers in the commedia dell'arte fashion who, nevertheless, present the events of their play, "The Sacred Mysteries of the Childhood of Our Lord," with deep regard. As the play progresses and the audience has a chance to see more facets of each of the five personalities on stage, so do the historical characters "act out" increase in interest and significance.

Staging the show can become a problem unless you give your imagination free reign. The set requirements can be stripped to a certain extent, but not at the expense of the necessary atmosphere, namely, a village square with a portable stage surrounded by the aura of a rather primitive "show business." Almost any place can effect the village-square idea with some sort of impro-vised stage and the necessary paraphernalia in costuming, set pieces, et cetera. My suggestion is to achieve as much informality in your arrangement as pos-sible, especially in seating the audience. This is not for the church sanctuary.

Almost any age group can understand and enjoy the play, but it should be acted by rather mature people who can cope with the humor required. Well-trained teen-agers could do an admirable job with some of the roles, but the two older people should really be acted by adults.

The play is a good one to present rather early in the Christmas season.

WILLIAM THRASHER
Associate Director, BARDS East, Boston, Massachu-setts

The Coming of Christ, John Masefield

A Christmas play in verse for the sanctuary; long one-act; 13 m., 1 w., chorus; Baker's Plays; royalty $15.00 each performance; musical score also available from Baker's Plays; music royalty $4.00 each perform-ance.

The idea of the play: John Masefield presents the story of the Nativity in a manner that emphasizes the deep spiritual values that the coming of Christ has for all peoples.

The director's suggestions: If this play is well done it will reach any audience, but it will speak more fully to people of some intellectual and artistic background. It should not be attempted by an inexperienced director. The choir director and play director must work together closely in order to co-ordinate the action and the choral interludes.

The play proposes several challenges to the director:

1. The beauty of the poetry in which the play is written does not come through unless the actors are well trained.

2. The music by Gustav Holst requires a well trained choir.

3. It is difficult to treat the spirits of Power, Light, Sword, and Mercy in a manner that distinguishes them from the spirits that are to become human. It should be presented by adults.

> ARTHUR C. RISSER
> Architect, Theatre Consultant, Professor of Engineering
> Graphics, University of Wichita, Wichita, Kansas

The Crucible, Arthur Miller

A tragedy; full length; Salem witch hunts—interiors and exteriors; 10 m., 10 w.; Dramatists Play Service; royalty $50.00, $25.00.

The idea of the play: It is a highly dramatic account of the hysteria of 1692.—the Salem witch hunts. The conflict between good and evil is illustrated by the struggle in the soul of John Proctor to maintain his own integrity and not to compromise or submit to expediency.

The director's suggestions: To produce this play one must have actors who understand the art of sincere characterization. It dare not become melodrama. Act II must not be allowed to drag. The director should study Arthur Miller's own comment on the play, both those in his introduction to his *Collected Plays* and also his remarks at the beginning of Act I. In our production we used a narrator who spoke the introduction to Act I.

There are several things to watch out for in directing this play:

1. Tituba must not become a stereotype or a comic figure.

2. The Court Trial (Act III) must not drag; it must build to the hysterical climax of the young girls. Danforth must dominate the courtroom.

3. The humanity of Elizabeth and John Proctor, as well as that of Rebecca Nurse, must shine out in contrast to the other characters.

Our high-school audience was most attentive, and students have often commented on the play since. As it comes out of our own national history,

most audiences find it moving. We did not use the scene in the forest between Proctor and Abigail which one finds in later versions of the play, and
it seemed just as effective without it, and certainly more suitable for high-
school audiences.

Directors should certainly know their own audiences and should be prepared if necessary to "tone down" some of the seventeenth-century diction if
it might give offense to modern ears. Effective substitutes can easily be found
in the literature of that day.

Note on production and costume: We found the staging to be relatively
simple, using a set of black drapes. Benches, table, stools, et cetera, were made
by a stagecraft class. In Act II we used an imaginary fireplace in the "fourth
wall," but had real andirons, rack for the cooking pot, the musket, et cetera,
and the red glow from the imaginary fire. This made for effective movement
and grouping with the actors' faces bathed in the firelight always visible to
the audiences. Our costumes were made from Indianhead and denim (black,
grey, brown, dark greens, with white collars and cuffs) by a group of parents.
It should be produced by senior high-school age to adults.

WILLIAM H. CLEVELAND, JR.
Director of Religious Interests, Director of Drama,
George School, George, Pennsylvania

Cry, the Beloved Country, Felicia Komai (from the novel by Alan Paton)

Inspirational problem play of South Africa written in verse; 3 acts;
South Africa (interior and exterior settings); 15 m., 7 w., 2 boys,
extras; Friendship Press; royalty on application.

The idea of the play: This dramatization shows that Christian commit-
ment exempts no one from the agonies of life and death and yet it does supply the power with which to face them.

The director's suggestions: In many respects the play does capture the
mood and meaning of the fine novel by Alan Paton. With judicious cutting
it can well project the simplicity and beauty of the original. The verse style
is well written and adapted from the novel.

The play should probably be cut—at certain points within particular pas-
sages, and even some entire scenes can be deleted. I do not believe that too
much effort should be made for realistic setting. Because of its episodic nature
the flow of action can be achieved through effective lighting and use of various
stage areas—or chancel—for these separate scenes. Above all, there should be
no lapses between scenes.

There was good audience reaction to this particular production. The play was cut to just one hour, which I feel is good time for the presentation. The character of Stephen Kumalo carries so much of the play that great care must be taken to assure a strong person in this part. The other parts also offer a real challenge. Narrators are particularly important. The play should be produced by adults.

Do not be afraid to make cuttings in the play and keep staging to a minimum. The play adapts well for chancel presentation. Effective lighting is the most important single staging factor. It should permit spotting of stage areas quickly and flexibly. Great care must be taken with lines. Don't let a cast be awed by the fact that it is written in verse. The main thing is the meaning of the lines.

This is a good play to work on with an adult cast. Even small bit parts when seen as a part of the whole offer great opportunity. It should not be undertaken, however, unless there are several good strong actors of ability to take the central roles. The play offers good opportunity for discussion and concern about problems of interracial and intergroup conflicts.

In productions I have directed we did not attempt makeup for the African natives.

> DONALD M. MAUCK
> Author, Minister, University Methodist Church, Columbus, Ohio

Cry Dawn in Dark Babylon, Philip Turner

Modern verse drama; full length; a bare stage; 4 m., 4 w.; Baker's Plays; royalty $15.00.

The idea of the play: Much of what has been said about *Christ In The Concrete City* applies also to this drama, as it is identical in style and treatment. Instead of four men and two women, we have four men and four women. There is a particular emphasis toward individual characterization in this play in the characters of Mr. and Mrs. Jones and the Vicar. *Cry Dawn in Dark Babylon* has a consistent thread around which the various sub-themes center in the Jones family, which has lost a child, and in the Vicar's struggle with them in terms of their image of the church.

The director's suggestions: We found this play interesting because theologically it took some probing to arrive at the inner meanings and implications, and yet when one arrived it was satisfying. This play should be followed by a discussion.

The director must watch out for the dangers of too much burlesque of scenes which may destroy the dignity of the piece. There must be a careful pointing of certain lines to retain the original meaning of the author. An objective handling of the scriptural accounts is called for in this play, as they are treated in somewhat of a different manner than in *Christ in the Concrete City*.

As in *Christ in the Concrete City*, there must be expert chorus work. The actors playing Mr. and Mrs. Jones and the Vicar must be especially competent.

The main difficulty with producing Turner's plays seems to be an understanding of these plays as good theater because they are so deliberately religious drama. The director must work for much movement and color throughout the production. Musical backgrounds, both organ and instrumentation, may be very effective. Costumes may be simple, yet colorful.

> DR. ALFRED R. EDYVEAN
> Professor of Communications, Christian Theological Seminary, Indianapolis, Indiana

Family Portrait, Lenore Coffee and William Joyce Cowen

> Dramatization of the story of the family of Jesus; 3 acts; Nazareth and Jerusalem, 2 interiors, 2 exteriors; Samuel French, Inc.; royalty $25.00.

The idea of the play: The play draws a simple, eloquent, and reverent picture of the family of Jesus.

The director's suggestions: Family Portrait speaks to all mankind today in a most beautiful and dignified manner. Therefore, the director must not let the play become static. Keep it bright and alive—add characters and more action. For example:

1. We had a band of gypsies play the story.
2. During the street scene the women went to a well for water.
3. Insert a dance after the "Upper Room" scene of "The Crucifixion."
4. Play the scene with Judas very fast.
5. We played the opening family scene around a picnic table—a true family atmosphere.
6. The scene where Mary buys a scarf can be quite delightful.
7. Use several extras in the scene by the sea—strong men, virile.

Watch for the end lines on all the scenes, they should be carefully directed and timed.

The lighting for this play can bring about much excitement. The set need not be complicated, but merely suggestive.

> MRS. ARCH PEARSON
> Lon Morris College, Jacksonville, Texas

For *The Time Being*, W. H. Auden

A Christmas oratorio to be spoken; an open stage; 1½ hours; 20 speaking parts and a verse chorus; write Meridian Books (publisher), New York (play appears in *Religious Drama 1*); royalty $25.00 if no admission is charged.

The idea of the play: This is a long, vivid poem rather than a play in the sense that the term is usually used. It is one of the most profound restatements in our day of the meaning of the Incarnation, encompassing events from the Advent to the flight into Egypt. Distinguished development to show the profundity, the humor, the distaste, and the tenderness with which the gift of Christ is received by the waiting world.

The director's suggestions: *For the Time Being* is interesting in its stylized form, analysis of human culture, and understanding of meaning and function of God's act in the Incarnation. In the rehearsal schedule special attention must be given to study and discussion of the script and the perfection and variation of choral speaking effects.

It is really not a play at all; the real events in this script arise from the inter-action of ideas. The problem is to stylize this interplay with dramatic action, symbolic color and movement, and the pitch and pace of voices. There are actual episodes scattered through which may easily be given dramatic form— the shepherds in the fields, the coming of the Wise Men, the Nativity scene, the presentation of the child in the temple, the soliloquy of Herod. There are more stylized episodes which may be given illumination by the use of dance forms—the Annunciation, the temptation of Joseph, the flight into Egypt. The chorus provides the real fabric and setting of the play and may be used formally at times, and as participants in the action at others. The Nar-rator forms the link, both physically and ideationally, between the audience and the company.

The script is long, and breaking the performance not only gives the audi-ence a respite from hard thinking, but clarifies the process of logic:

Act 1: Advent, Annunciation, Temptation
Act II: Summons, Vision, Manger
Act III: Meditation, Massacre, Flight

The play should be performed by adults who have been prepared by read-ing or discussion of the script.

WAYNE R. ROOD
Associate Professor of Religious Education, Pacific
School of Religion, Berkeley, California

The Gardner Who Was Afraid of Death, Henri Brochét

30 minutes; no particular time or place; published by Longmans, Green and Company; royalty on application.

The idea of the play: An early Christian, Phocus, captured by two Roman soldiers summons the courage to meet death. He comes to realize that death itself has been conquered by the Christ he loves. The play is beautifully written.

The director's suggestions: "The actor who plays Phocus must understand that the entire drama is played within his own soul." This requires a strong actor.

I did the play in-the-round and felt it was a very satisfying venture. The lines of the play are so intimate that they seem to lend themselves readily to intimate staging.

Good lighting is essential. Costuming is important but in my judgement should not be identifiable with any specific time or place.

I would like to do it again in a small theatre with a proscenium setting. I feel the play is especially good for college students.

ARGYLE KNIGHT
Staff member, Division of the Local Church, The General Board of Education, The Methodist Church

He Came Seeing, Mary P. Hamlin

Biblical drama; 40 minutes; one interior (biblical); 3 m., 2 w.; Samuel French, Inc.; royalty $5.00.

The idea of the play: The play tells of a boy who, healed of blindness by Jesus, becomes a follower of the Messiah and discovers the terrible cost of seeing.

The director's suggestions: This drama is good for groups of many varying sizes because the lines are carried by five main characters and an additional group as extras, which can vary in number. The play is interesting because of the changes of pace—humor is injected at good places for relief. It is well suited to a service of worship and adaptable to chancel or stage—settings can be kept to a minimum.

Keep the staging simple. If it is done in the chancel, don't move the furnishings, except where they obscure the view of the players. Allow the imagination of your audience to function. A word on the program or bulletin saying that there is a window at the rear of the stage will suffice. The only props really necessary are two low benches, a copper bowl, loaves of bread, and Joab's staff. As in any drama requiring biblical costumes, these should be in good taste—avoid bathrobes. If the players are unfamiliar with biblical costumes and makeup, such as beards, let them use these things for more than one dress rehearsal.

The ending can be highly moving. This feeling should not be quickly interrupted by the closing of the curtain or by the exit of the players.

The play can be performed by senior high-school youth, older youth, and adults.

> Mathilda Cunningham Murphy
> Homemaker, minister's wife, Williamsport, Pennsylvania

He Who Says Yes and *He Who Says No*, Bertolt Brecht

"Learning pieces"; short one-acts; a chorus, 4 m., 1 w., 1 boy; stylized setting, very simple; published in *Accent*, Autumn, 1946 (translation by Gerhard Nellhaus); University of Illinois, Urbana, Illinois; royalty upon request to the publisher. (Opera version of *He Who Says Yes* [Der Jasager] with music by Kurt Weill is published by Universal-Edition A. G., Vienna, 1930)

The idea of the plays: The plays are "epic" and are among a series of short "learning pieces" (*lehrstueck*) which Brecht wrote for teaching purposes in schools and for other occasions. These are based on a Japanese Nō play, *Taniko*, using the characters, plot, and much of the dialogue of the original. The legend is that of a schoolteacher who is about to leave for a journey across the mountains where he hopes to bring back medicine with which to fight an epidemic. A boy whose mother is ill joins the party; he wants to consult the doctors in the town about her ailment. During the journey the boy becomes ill. The expedition will have to be abandoned if the boy is not to be left by himself in the wilderness. According to an ancient custom he is asked whether he consents to being left behind. He answers yes but asks to be killed rather than suffer a slow death. He is thrown into the abyss.

In *He Who Says No* the boy will not consent to die. He rejects the old custom; "I see the need for a new custom of thinking afresh in each new situation." The teacher and his party recognize the force of the argument, and turn back, taking the boy with them.

It is assumed that the two plays presented together will elicit a comparison of the two decisions. The author has suggested that discussion might follow the performance.

The director' suggestions: The plays are of special interest because of their direct approach to the didactic use of the theater. They are extremely simple, perhaps deceptively so. They demand a direct "objective" kind of presentation that avoids emotional overtones but embodies a kind of ceremonial dignity. Oriental trappings should be avoided, but some of the conventions of the Nō drama might be employed, especially if the opera version of the first play (Der Jasager with music by Kurt Weill) is presented. Here the chorus, which observes and comments, takes on special significance from the forceful music. Although the music is designed for student singers and orchestra, it is not simple. The idiom of Weill is severe and here his style is not a popular one as in The Three Penny Opera. If the plays are presented without music they may need special punctuation through the use of a drum, but they should not be given an impressionistic or highly stylized treatment. They should seem solid, realistic, and, at times, harsh. The realism of Brecht's work has been compared to the directness of Christian plays of the medieval period.

There are other plays by Brecht which employ similar conventions and have similar didactic or propaganda purposes—The Measures Taken, The Exception and the Rule. None of them are Christian, in fact they are frequently antireligious, but they lift up important social and moral issues in forceful terms. They are directly dialectical and perhaps suggest a kind of "use" of the theater from which the church might learn.

JAMES CARLSON
Director of the Theatre, Hamline University, St. Paul, Minnesota

Herod and the Kings (Coventry Cycle)
Medieval mystery play; approximately 30 minutes; at least 10 m., 4 w.; published by Meridian Books (Religious Drama 2); no royalty.

The idea of the play: Herod and the Kings combines the stories of the Magi before Herod, the Adoration, and the Slaughter of the Innocents. In this very fact lies its challenge and its special appeal.

The director's suggestions: At first, the contrast between Herod's scenes of broad comedy, the exalted seriousness of the King's worship, and the stark realism of the "Slaughter" may seem difficult to reconcile; but if you have a lively respect for the whole play and give each scene its full narrative value, you will find the variations refreshing and the whole story as consistent as life itself.

Have your group read Martin Browne's excellent introduction to the medieval plays in Religious Drama 2; it is, to me, essential to their understanding and successful production. You will realize that they were not composed for trained actors, but were made up and presented by ordinary people eager to tell the story in the light of their own experience—experience as soldiers, as mothers, as worshipers. Contemporary men and women who want to celebrate the birth of Jesus and bring the stories associated with it to bear on our contemporary lives will have comparable experience to contribute to the playing.

I would suggest reading the play aloud with a cast—though not, to be sure, the final cast. As the different individual members of the group read the roles they will come to life. Herod is a pretty obvious type—a tyrant, a bully, a show-off—a great part for Bottom the Weaver. (And there'll be a Bottom in every group!) But are the Kings just three slices off the same cake? Read them with three very different people and you'll begin to see how, within the kingly similarity, they can become three distinct people. Then, after that, they will suggest symbols. The fact that characterizations in the medieval plays are not rounded out in the psychological detail we have come to expect of dramatis personae shouldn't lead us to believe they were conceived, much less played, as abstractions.

Don't let the archaic language fool you, or floor you. The text has already been modified but you may find some further modification in order to assure its being intelligible to your audience. But do this sparingly! Many words and expressions that seemed "Greek" at first reading, come across, when the actors understand them. And there is a particular value in working for that understanding. The simplicity and forcefulness of Middle English can put the simple, forceful story from Scripture in a new light, evoke a shaper image than the one that's been softened by our more familiar, much-Latinized speech.

Herod's uninhibited style of writing calls for a most modern, presentational style of acting, with lively audience contact. At the same time, the play contains a certain formalism, inherent in liturgy, which makes it appropriate to the chancel. Our production, in Marsh Chapel of Boston University, was a play-within-a-play. A chorus costumed as medieval townspeople trouped down the center aisle caroling. The Herald addressed them and, beyond them, the modern audience. So did Herod. When he called for his musicians, a trio of recorders piped up, from their little gallery, above the organ. The Kings made their journey round the other aisles. The chorus used their full capes to curtain the stable, opening and closing them to the singing of carols. Capes, the long full capes of the Soldiers, were used again to curtain the brutal killing of the Innocents. We did, in fact, stylize this scene.

Although there was talent in our group, they were amateurs. Yet they gave an effective and moving performance and came, by common consent, to share a deep and refreshing experience of worship in giving the play. It is possible, and highly rewarding, to recapture from the fourteenth century a spark to illumine our modern faith.

CHOUTEAU DYER CHAPIN
Executive Director, BARDS East, Cambridge, Massachusetts

The Hour Class, William Butler Yeats

Poetic drama; one act; 5 m., 1 w., 2 children, extras; Samuel French, Inc. (published in *The Collected Plays of Yeats*); royalty upon request.

The idea of the play: A wise man comes to regret the disbelief he has instilled in others. Only the fool retains belief and saves him.

The director's suggestions: Interesting aspects of the play are the central problem, the freedom for space-staging, colorful costumes, and, above all, the language. Vaguely medieval costumes should be worn. Mild Irish ascents can give color to what might be a "talky" play. Let the students, wife, and children move vigorously.

Don't be disturbed by the tendency of some in the audience to laugh. The Scholar is mildly amusing. Be careful that the laughter is not at any aspect of the play, however. The Fool should be played as an "innocent," not as mentally retarded. The role dramatizes "blessed are the pure in heart."

This is more the director's play than you'd suspect at first reading. I like music on archaic instruments behind the angels, scenes and at the end.

It should be performed by older youth and adults.

AMY GOODHUE LOOMIS
Associate Professor of English and Drama, Vincennes University, Vincennes, Indiana

The House by the Stable and *Grab and Grace*, Charles Williams

Modern morality plays; Royalty $5.00 for each play. The plays may be produced by arrangement with Ruth Spalding of the Rock Theatre Co. Ltd. Write to Miss Spalding, c/o English Speaking Union, 37 Charles Street, Berkeley Square, London W 1, England. The plays are published in the collection *Seed of Adam* by Charles Williams (New York: Oxford University Press), and in *Religious Drama III*. (New York: Meridian Books.)

The Director's suggestions: I found these plays interesting chiefly for three reasons:

1. Charles Williams has given an old dramatic form—the medieval morality

play—new vigor. The vices and virtues have lost their abstraction and have acquired personalities. Hell, for instance, at one point in the play calls Gabriel "the old gossip of Heaven."

2. Moreover, Williams has been so bold as to approach the subject matter of his plays—the meaning of the Incarnation before and after the birth of Jesus Christ—in terms of comedy. There is great fun in both plays. The high comedy in *The House by the Stable*, and the sparkling farce in *Grab and Grace* is hard to equal in much of contemporary religious dramatic litera‑ ture.

3. Of his many talents as a writer Williams will probably be remembered first for his verse. These plays which are in verse reflect his extraordinary fer‑ tile and original imagination.

Things to watch out for in directing:

1. Don't force abstractions onto the characters. The more personable they become the more engaging the play.

2. Don't miss the fun. This may require a re-examination of the substance of some of your most cherished beliefs about Faith, Grace, et cetera, but that will be all to the good. In this connection, I believe that both plays work most successfully in contemporary clothes and setting.

3. Don't force the verse. Most of the time Williams captures the rhythm of our daily speech. There are some interesting interval rhymes, but there is no point in laboring them. Let the meaning cut across the beat and you'll find the rhythm exciting.

Chief difficulties: The plays need careful study before you begin to work on them with actors. All plays do, but these raise serious problems. For ex‑ ample, the scene between Man and Pride during Mary's recitation of the Magnificat in *The House by the Stable* will need special care in direction. It is worth reading something about Williams and his theology. (See "The Way of Exchange" and "The Way of Affirmation" in *The Image of the City*, some essays by Charles Williams, edited by Anne Ridler, Oxford Uni‑ versity Press, 1958.)

Audience reaction: The drunkenness and gambling in *The House by the Stable* and the knock about farce of *Grab and Grace* may be troublesome for persons who expect "religious" plays to be austere and pietistical. In some in‑ stances creative preparation and follow-up however should offset any resistance. In other instances the shock may be salutary. *The House by the Stable* is suitable for the chancel, but *Grab and Grace* is more effective on stage.

ROBERT E. SEAVER

Associate Professor of Speech, Director, Program in Religious Drama, Union Theological Seminary, New York City

It Should Happen to a Dog, Wolf Mankowitz

Serio-comic drama; one act; 2 m.; published by Meridian Books (*Religious Drama 2*); royalty upon request to the publisher.

The idea of the play: "*It Should Happen to a Dog* is a serio-comic strip, which those who know the story of Jonah will see is faithful to the original. If the characters speak as people we know personally, it is because there is no other way for us to know characters. If Jonah is somewhat familiar in his manner of address to the Almighty it is because one may assume that a greater intimacy exists between prophets and their source of instruction than does for the rest of us. As to the message of the story—"Why should I not spare Nineveh?" This is, one hopes, how God feels about man—unlike man who is less tolerant of himself."

The director's suggestions: The hilarious situations and dialogue in this modern setting of the Jonah story point up with great freshness and clarity our own efforts to escape God's direction for us.

In directing the play watch out that the dialect and character don't become a burlesque. Maintain Jonah's basic dignity and integrity in the midst of ludicrous situations. Point up his sharp, keen intelligence and wit. Work for naturalness and good timing. Maintain the fine balance of pace and timing the brilliant writing requires. Set the locales of the street, ship, inside the whale, the King's court, and the desert convincingly with a minimum of props. Keep up the tempo and light touch throughout the play.

Production suggestions:—Use coiled heavy rope for tub and shipboard. Throw rich cloth over platforms for a throne. Use a live "tree"—in a leotard with fringed burlap and branches attached—to hand Jonah paper and coconuts—burlap covered balls with curtain rings to slip over fingers. Using a child's scooter for the exit of the angel and Jonah can be very effective.

The play should be performed by youth sixteen years old and older.

MARGARET LIGHTFOOT
Assistant in Religious Education, Hollis, New York

The Journey of the Three Kings, Henri Ghéon

A humorous fantasy for Epiphany; 45 minutes; 8 m., 1 w., an angel, an elephant, a camel, an ox, an ass, slaves, (cast can be partially adapted to fit different needs); Baker's Plays; royalty on request.

The idea of the play: The familiar story of the journey of the three kings to Bethlehem, but richly embroidered by Ghéon with humor, fantasy, and written with reverence for the meaning of Epiphany—the manifestation of Christ as God's son.

THE DIRECTORS' PLAY LIST

The director's suggestions: While the story of the play is familiar to everyone, the play itself is not in the least a conventional retelling of the journey of the Epiphany Kings. The kings are delightful, disarming stargazers who are filled with excitement about their search for the new king. Bedecked in their finest array, escorted by a fantastically resplendent caravan of slaves and animals—the major part of which is never seen, so relax all of you directors of low-budget shows—the kings make their journey, guided by the most charming and efficient star in dramatic literature. One of the most humorous, and typically Ghéon-like, incidents is the embarrassing moment in Herod's palace when the kings barge in, making the dreadful mistake of thinking Herod to be the king they seek. Finally the child is found, and the Adoration is a strikingly simple, yet beautiful climax. The vital moment of the play occurs at the very end, however, when the kings realize, after having presented not only their gifts to the child but also the clothes off their backs, that it is definitely not clothes that make the king, for they are not recognized in their underdress by the night watchman who was so dazzled earlier in the play when they asked him directions.

To be sure, all of us welcome the simplicity of the play. But beware! It can be the unsuspecting director's Waterloo. The rather episodic nature of the play—12 short scenes—presents difficulty enough in maintaining a smooth, pleasant rhythm in the action. Don't try to elaborate on what is in the script, for if you do you will overwhelm the delicate simplicity and kill the story. Actors should have a sense of comedy, or they should be children—never doubt that they can do a topnotch job on this one—and they must be keenly aware of the particular rhythm of each scene and how each of these contributes to the overall movement and rhythm of the whole piece.

Now, for the director who might be a little squeamish about humorous treatments of Christian ideas, don't be! The first thing you should discover is that the play demands at once reverence from the audience and actors and laughter! Don't worry about trying to reconcile the two in your treatment of the play; the playwright did that for you. Make the most of it and your performance will be memorable in more ways than you can anticipate. When you begin preparation on the play, start with a fresh approach to the characters, especially the three kings. Don't be influenced by the pageant prototypes that haunt all of us. Get to know each of them; they are different, and their differences are extremely important for the play. If you don't take advantage of those wonderful animals you've missed the boat. (I made enormous papier mâché heads, dressed them in big, baggy, shapeless costumes, and they completely charmed the show.)

The play can be presented in almost any physical surrounding. I did it as an experiment in liturgical drama in the sanctuary of an Anglican church that is, naturally, accustomed to liturgical worship, and it was successful and seemed very much at home in the surroundings. The only set pieces that were used were two long poles which were held by two of the actors in the company who were not on stage in the particular scene, from which we hung different curtains to suggest different settings. We used a blue curtain with funny little painted stars for the journey curtain, a rich red one for Herod's palace, and a faded, ragged one for the stable. Each of these served as the backing for each of the scenes, moving with a certain amount of animation with the characters.

Use your imagination on the costumes and on the settings and particularly on the treatment you will give the play. The possibilities seem unlimited. (But watch out for that visual costume change during the Adoration when the kings have to present their clothes to the Child. You must have clothes that the actors can get off in a hurry. That's one thing Mr. Ghéon didn't allow time for in the dialogue.)

One of the nicest things about the play is that it is easily done by and for children or by and for adults. This is rare in the field of good literature for the theater.

WILLIAM THRASHER
Associate Director BARDS East, Boston, Massachusetts

A Match for the Devil, Norman Nicholson

Folk comedy in verse; full length; published by Faber and Faber (order from Baker's Plays); royalty on request.

The director's suggestions: This play was made interesting for me by the author's concept that the comic can be a part of the prophetic experience, by the excellent poetic dialogue, and by the three characters—Hosea, Amos, and Gomer.

The chief difficulty in the play is the point of view of the comedy. There is also a lack of action and the requirements of two full settings.

The problems in directing the play are how to establish sympathy for Hosea in his cuckolding, how to portray the emotional rantings of Amos without ridiculing the character, how to convey the idea that Gomer's return to temple prostitution is a normal act.

The audience must have some knowledge of Amos and Hosea and their prophetic mission, as well as an understanding of the religious life of the Hebrews at the time, in order to appreciate the playwright's point of view. The play should be performed by adults.

WILLIAM BRASMER
Chairman, Division of Theatre Arts, Denison University, Granville, Ohio

Murder in the Cathedral. T. S. Eliot
    Poetic drama; two acts; 10 m., 9 w.; interior of a cathedral; Samuel
    French, Inc.; royalty $35.00.

The idea of the play: *Murder in the Cathedral* depicts the temptations, sainthood, and martyrdom of Thomas á Becket. It is a play, eloquent in verse, revealing deep religious insight into man's sin, God's grace, and the mediation of the church.

The director's suggestions: It is impossible to do this play without an extremely fine actor to play Thomas á Becket. The other roles are not extremely difficult. The four tempters and the four knights need to be intelligent men who are able to deliver poetic lines with feeling and understanding, but they do not require great emotional depth or technical facility. Some groups may find casting the play to be no easy matter since it does require several men and no women in individual roles. However, one can use as few as ten or as many as forty women in the chorus as the women of Canterbury, and by picking out solo parts from the choruses one can create as many parts for women as seems necessary. In fact, the choruses lend themelves quite easily to solo reading.

Others have handled the chorus much more imaginatively than I did. I moved the women into the choir loft during the opening choruses of the play and had them remain there throughout the play. With rather inexperienced women and a choir loft that faced the congregation and dominated the chancel, this procedure seemed to be the best. In a Boston University production some years ago the movements of the individual members of the chorus were choreographed with a highly moving effect that added greatly to the visual interest of the play. This production was done, however, on a stage.

One of the great advantages of this play for church and college groups who might have a chapel in which to play is that it can be easily done in any chancel that looks even vaguely like a cathedral. It was necessary in the second act to introduce a writing desk and a chair, but these were brought in easily and naturally by some of the priests. The knights were able to make their drunken way down the center aisle and address the congregation from the chancel steps after the murder of the archbishop.

The greatest difficulty can become the chief source of satisfaction to the director—that is the fact that there is very little movement that must be done in terms of plot. The director can introduce as much movement as he chooses to point up speeches and symbolically represent the meaning of the spoken word.

Stripped of setting, a great deal of action, and the business that often either clutters up or saves some realistic drama, this play rests almost solely on the power and charm of the language. It need not become a talkathon, however, if the director gives proper attention to pacing and takes advantage of the humor and irony the playwright subtly provides for him.

A director who enjoys the sound of beautiful English, who has one experienced and mature actor, four others who read well, and a group of women who are willing to work hard can provide almost any audience with memorable theater.

JAY BUELL
Former Minister of Education, Church of Christ, Dartmouth College, New Hampshire

The Neighbors, Zona Gale

A comedy; 30 minutes; Baker's Plays; royalty.

The idea of the play: Excellent portrayal of lovable characters in a small town.

The director's suggestions: This comedy will always have appeal but the last time I did it, I thought it a little dated.

I have used this play with church and school groups of both youth and adults. The distinct character types afford opportunity for strong portrayals, but a director should exercise restraint. The characterizations should be strong, but a cast can easily go overboard on this one.

I have used this with what I felt to be genuine effectiveness as a play reading. It was done in a drama workgroup in a conference school of missions.

Audiences love it.

ARGYLE KNIGHT
Staff Member, Division of the Local Church, The General Board of Education, The Methodist Church

Noah, André Obey

Fantasy; full length; 5 m., 4 w., extras; 3 exteriors, biblical setting; Samuel French, Inc.; royalty $25.00.

The director's suggestions: The charm of this play is found in its delightful, earthy quality, its light touch, and its make-believe. I am in full accord with Francis Fergusson's view of it in his book Idea of a Theatre (pp. 215-22). I liked the challenge of making believable this simple story of Noah and the Ark.

As in all plays that move in a sequence series of episodes, the play must move—the director must have a clear idea of each scene's purpose and of the rise and fall in intensity or in involvement to carry along the focus on Noah's difficulties without repetition of effect and to make its appeals afresh in each scene.

Be certain the actor playing Noah believes in the simplicity, in the naïveté, in the old man's conversational acquaintance with God, in the old character's stubborn faith, and in his wavering moments as he reacts to the doubts of his family. It is important to get the whimsy, the poetic fantasy, and yet to avoid the temptation to:

1. Allow the animals to become so overly fantastic as to divert the purpose of the scenes.

2. Allow the dances to take on separate identity and not follow the flow of the scene.

3. Allow the setting to be any more than just suggestive.

I advise the person attempting to produce this play to read it through twice to get the continuity, then read it a number of times again to feel the sweep of the poetic movement of the play. Be convinced yourself that you can make the story live like the telling of a fable or fairy tale to children before you try to cast or direct it.

It should be performed by college age and older.

RAY E. HOLCOMBE
Director, MacMurray College Theatre, Jacksonville, Illinois

Our Town, Thornton Wilder

Drama (expressionistic realism); full length; 17 m., 7 w., extras; bare stage; acting edition published by Coward-McCann in cooperation with Samuel French, Inc.; royalty $25.00.

The idea of the play: Our Town depicts the life of a New Hampshire village—with humor, picturesqueness, and pathos—set against a background of centuries of time, social history, and religious ideas. As the Stage Manager says in the play, "This is the way we were in our growing up and in our marrying and in our doctoring and in our living and in our dying."

The director's suggestions: Our Town is considered by many critics one of the finest American plays. Studied in schools and colleges throughout the country, it is a play that is rewarding to produce and successful with audiences.

The acting version of this play is, in my opinion, one of the very best of all published plays. It is complete in every detail, and if the director follows instructions he cannot go far wrong.

This play is practically actor-proof. Just remember to keep the actors from acting. This is explained in the preface to the playscript. Here is a play that is always effective to an audience.

CARL GLICK
Assistant Professor [Emeritus] of Drama and English,
California Western University, San Diego, California

The Prodigal Son, R. H. Ward

Verse play; one act; speaking chorus; Baker's Plays; royalty upon request.

The director's suggestions: This is a provocative script. At our production the audience proved by their reaction that they had joined in the play. In directing the play be aware of the necessary balance of emotion and humor in the presentation. Much work must be devoted to the relationships of the characters.

In regard to the Presenters, expand the script's suggestions, using them as tempters and chorus. Stage them to incorporate formalized rhythmic movement and choreography.

It should be produced by adults.

MARIE L. ROPER
Director, Charleston, South Carolina

Roger Williams and Mary, Albert Johnson

Dramatic reading; 40 minutes; 2 m., 1 w.; an open stage; Friendship Press; royalty upon application.

The idea of the play: The play is a dramatic reading which tells of Roger Williams' fight for freedom and shows insights into the civil and religious problems of his day which have parallels in the world today.

The director's suggestions: *Roger Williams and Mary,* the first play written specifically for the drama-trio medium, has been in the repertoire of the Drama Trio from the University of Redlands since 1954—so has had hundreds of performances in hundreds of places, ranging from living rooms and church chancels to diverse television studios and the mammoth stage of Convention Hall, Atlantic City, N.J.

Conceived as drama for the chancel and as a mobile unit with "Have plays, will travel," the drama-trio medium relies on the power of the spoken word and the technique of pantomime.

The spoken word must be well spoken—that is, the actor must communicate the implicit meaning of the dialogue as well as the explicit meaning. Since much of the content of the play is lyrical, the players must project the image of the words. This is accomplished through a careful use of stress and rubato.

It is through the projected image and through the magic of movement, that the audience is able to see the scenery that isn't there, the props that don't exist, and the period costumes which the players are not wearing.

There is magic in movement when the director knows the dynamics of movement and can train his players to move with motivation, with rhythm, with grace, and with movement that is in rapport with textual content. This is, of course, true of the actor's gestures and changes in body position, as well as his movement from area to area.

Technique cannot substitute for emotional integrity and spiritual conviction, but spiritual conviction and emotional integrity are of little consequence if they do not communicate to those people out front. For this we need the word well spoken and the action suited to the word.

> ALBERT JOHNSON
> Director, the Little Theater on the Zanja, University of Redlands, Redlands, California

The Salzburg Everyman, Hugo Van Hofmannsthal

An ancient morality play; long one-act length; bare stage; large cast; available from M. Mora, 2 Residenzplatz, Salzburg, Austria. (There are several versions of the ancient morality play. See: *Everyman Today*, Walter Sorrell; *Everyman*, John Baird translation; *Everyman*, edited by John Allen, published in *Religious Drama* 2, compiled by E. Martin Browne, Meridian Books, Inc., New York.)

The director's suggestions: Interesting about this play:
1. It is always effective—has a real message.
2. It is easy to produce.
3. In modern version it is much more dramatic.

Action should be carefully planned to prevent actors from merely "standing around" with no apparent purpose.

The play does not really need scenery, but the costumes and properties can be as rich and spectacular as possible.

Everyman provides no real difficulties for a director, but with a little imagination and ingenuity in the production it can be even more effective and meaningful for all involved.

> DONALD EYSSEN
> Director of Drama, Ohio Wesleyan University, Delaware, Ohio

214   RELIGIOUS DRAMA: ENDS AND MEANS

Santa Claus, E. E. Cummings

Modern morality; 15 minutes; 2 m., 1 w., 1 child, crowd; published
by Meridian Books (Religious Drama 3); royalty $20.00.

The idea of the play: This is a morality play in modern form, the two
allegorical figures being Santa Claus and Death. The play suggests that knowledge without undertanding robs the world of love and that persons do not
exist apart from love.

The director's suggestions: This is a difficult, even "high-brow," one act
play. There are no real technical problems connected with the play, but the
difficulties exist within the content itself. The first problem is with the
dialogue which overpowers all else in the play. It is serio-comic and the players
must find that middle ground. They must not be allowed to "ham" it.

The second difficulty is in getting the subtleties of the imagery across.
It is often obscure, and while most of the bewilderment it causes is intended
by the author, it can be a probing thing and something that will stir imaginations if it is thoroughly understood and can be expressed to an audience.

The interconnection between the parts of the play that are played and
those that are imagined can also be confusing. This leads to a last statement
that without an experienced director and a mature group this play should
not be attempted.

It should be performed by adults.

ROGER ORTMAYER
Professor of Christianity and the Arts, Perkins School
of Theology, Southern Methodist University, Dallas,
Texas

The Sign of Jonah, Gruenter Rutenborn

Allegory; 1 hour; 9 m., 2 w.; action takes place in a theater in West
Berlin; Thomas Nelson & Sons; royalty on application.

The idea of the play: This is a powerful modern play coming out of post-
war Germany. It has subtle implications on three levels: That of the biblical
characters and events, their analogies to contemporary events, and the existential confrontation of each actor by the biblical and contemporary situations.
The play clarifies the typical human predicament of man's "refusal to meet
God at the place where God has come to meet him."

The director's suggestions: This play proved interesting primarily because
of its theological content and its contemporary theme. During most of the
play there are eight or more persons on the stage. Throughout the play
one is accused by the others. This should be staged so that it gets across

visually. The play can be difficult because the actors must drop their roles and become actors acting a role throughout the play. It is not a simple matter to know when the actor has assumed one role or another. Jonah's long prologue should be carefully paced in order to keep the interest and intensity. At the first production we presented the play intact. The reaction was a request to shorten the last scene, removing the explanatory lines. At a second presentation, however, it was suggested that the play be left intact for the sake of clarity.

If it is at all possible, present the play on two levels. This will simplify staging and communication to the audience.

It should be performed by college age and older.

VINCENT DE GREGORIS
Director of Drama, Andover Newton Theological
Seminary, Newton Centre, Massachusetts

A Sleep of Prisoners, Christopher Fry

Verse drama; full length (one act); 4 m.; interior of a bombed-out church in wartime; Dramatists Play Service; royalty $25.00.

The idea of the play: I liked the idea that Fry proposed: That man's differences and conflicts are often sprung from the façades behind which the true spirits of men are hidden. After studying the play I feel that Mr. Fry missed this proposal to some degree, but I believe that he moved into a greater truth—that all mankind, in spite of the outward divisions and the differences in each individual, is endowed with some of the element of God and that the great thought is the belief that the power of good in humanity is more powerful than evil if we abide by it. I was interested in the dream sequences and how each dream involved each of the prisoners. I find an interesting thing here. The men are soldiers trained to kill and maim, and their dreams are of killing, too—killing in anger, killing in defense, killing as sacrifice. The Bible stories are old and familiar and certainly more logical in this use than any of the Bible stories that speak of love and life. The departure from the useless slaughter comes with Abraham. Here we begin to see that killing is not part of God's pattern. The final scene of the men in the fiery furnace has great power and illustrates the need for belief in God and the power of good. Fry's line "the human heart must search 'to the lengths of God' " is, I believe, a great sermon.

The director's suggestions: Most important in this play is the actor's ability to speak Fry's language. Unless it is carefully interpreted, it can become just a jumble of words. Second, the members of the cast must be completely involved in the play and with each other. Reactions must be strong and well defined. Third, each dream sequence must be sharp and clear, yet the bridging from one to another has to be smooth. Fourth, "theatrics" such as sudden appearances of characters should be avoided. Play it simply.

I believe it is very easy to make this play enormously complicated. It must be kept simple and well paced. The bridging between dream sequences must be carefully worked out as to movement, position, and timing. Amateur actors might be inclined to overplay in several sections. Careful direction can control this. Above all, the cast must be adult and intelligent enough to work out and understand an interpretation of the play that will be mutually satisfactory to them.

I do not believe that any audience of this play will be completely satisfied. Some will get some of it, a few will get most of it, and there will be a few who will get none of it. I think that the quality of the actor's speaking, interpretation, enunciation, placement, and volume is what tends to make the play either good or bad for the audience.

I would advise using the bunk beds if at all possible. Have the actors get in and out of the bunks quite openly. Use spotlighting to pick up each dreamer as he starts his dream; then light up the playing area of the dream. Above all, study the play. Decide on its meaning for you and impart this meaning to your cast until all are in accord. Then play it. I believe you will be well rewarded.

It should be performed by adults only.

JOHN G. PATTERSON
Drama Director, First Congregational Church, Burlington, Vermont

Spark in Judea, R. F. Delderfield

Biblical drama; full length; 10 m., 3 w.; interior of Pilate's home; Baker's Plays; royalty $25.00.

The idea of the play: The leading characters in this play are Pontius Pilate and his wife Claudia Procula. It is about the crucifixion and the effect it has on Pilate—from his point of view. It is a play that is apparently not too well known. We stumbled on it by accident but found it to be very well written and an excellent vehicle.

The director's suggestions: This play requires a strong actor for the part of Pilate. There are a number of smaller parts which give an opportunity for excellent characterizations, but again must be chosen carefully.

It is a one-set show, so there is no worry about changing sets. The only production details which might cause any difficulty at all would be the properties—which are quite extensive—and the Roman and Hebrew period costumes.

Personally, I think this is an excellent play for the church. It tells the story of the crucifixion from a little different angle than we usually hear it. The fact that it requires only one set is a great help to the inexperienced director. And it does have some excellent characterizations, and moves at a good pace.

It should be performed by adults.

ALLEN G. RICHARDSON
Executive Director, Inglis Players of the First Congregational Church, Webster Groves, Missouri

This Way to the Tomb, Ronald Duncan

A miracle play; full-length; published by Faber and Faber (available through Baker's Plays); royalty upon request; music available from Boosey & Hawkes.

The director's suggestions: This is a miracle play divided into a masque, which is serious, and an anti-masque which is satiric. It is written in complex verse forms which are to be spoken to offstage liturgical music or sung and danced to an onstage jazz band.

This play has many qualities that make it interesting—superb poetic speech, a compelling portrait of the martyrdom of Saint Anthony, deft satire against pseudoliturgical forms in modern religions, and excellent music. However, the actors must be trained in poetic speech. They must be skilled in musical comedy acting as well as classical acting. The director needs an inventive choreographer and an excellent choral group.

The chief difficulties of the play are the outdated lyrics in the anti-masque and the resolution of the play which suggests a philosophic affirmation of the doctrine of the reincarnation. If the masque is played with compelling power, then the high jinks of the anti-masque are easily swallowed and theatrically effective.

It should be performed by adults.

WILLIAM BRASMER
Chairman, Department of Theatre Arts, Denison University, Granville, Ohio

A Very Cold Night, Dennis J. Winnie

An avant-garde sketch; 2 m.; a shack; 20 minutes; Baker's Plays; royalty.

The idea of the play: This short play—or, more appropriately, sketch—was the winner of the first prize in a competition for a new play on a religious theme sponsored by Union Theological Seminary in co-operation with the National Broadcasting Company. The author has been strongly influenced by Beckett, Ionesco, Proust, et al. The imaginative treatment of the descent from the cross and the economy with which Winnie has explored his theme enchance the play.

The director's suggestions: This is a play for two resourceful actors or for a director who knows how to release the untapped resources of less experienced actors. In this sense it provides excellent opportunities for acting and directing workshops. For the first performance at the seminary we approached the play in terms of improvisation, keeping in mind a taut line between the comic and serious overtones of the play. The play requires a good deal of invention in terms of business. Otherwise it will become static and dull.

ROBERT E. SEAVER
Associate Professor of Speech and Director, Program in Religious Drama, Union Theological Seminary, New York City

Why the Chimes Rang, Elizabeth McFadden (from the story by Raymond McDonald Alden)

Lords and Ladies, extras; a peasant's hut in a forest in Germany
A Christmas miracle-type play; 30 minutes; 2 m., 1 boy, 1 old woman, "long ago"; Samuel French, Inc.; royalty $5.00.

The idea of the play: The divine beauty of charity. After rich gifts have been offered in vain, a boy's small gift offered in love causes the miraculous ringing of the Christmas chimes.

The director's suggestions: This play was done to meet the needs of a Protestant-Roman Catholic chapel service. It is simple but profound and is especially suitable to junior-high and senior high-school youths.

It may be done simply or elaborately. In a future production I would keep it quite simple. I did, however, go all out for authencity of costume and setting perhaps because I did not know any better way at the time. I had the co-operation of a Catholic church where I was able to borrow complete altar furnishings.

Space or the illusion of space is an important consideration in the cathedral scene. It is suggested that theatrical gauze be used for the back wall of the hut and that the cathedral scene be set back of it. I used instead a divided back wall made of flats and mounted on coasters in a groove. The first scene dimmed down to the low embers of the fire in the hut as the walls parted and the lights came up revealing the cathedral scene.

The danger of a sentimental production may be offset in part by careful attention to the lines and the manner in which they are spoken. The physical movements of the boy will be an important consideration. The choice of person for this role will have much to do with the outcome.

ARGYLE KNIGHT
Staff Member, Division of the Local Church, The General Board of Education, The Methodist Church

The Zeal of Thy House, Dorothy L. Sayers

Poetic drama; long one act; 23 m., 1 w., 1 boy, choir and cantor, extras; published by Harcourt, Brace and World, Inc.; royalty upon request.

The idea of the play: This is the story of the building of Canterbury Cathedral by William of Sens, architect. His gift, his pride, his self-centeredness, and his final redemption are framed into a liturgical beginning and end.

The director's suggestions: These are interesting aspects of the play:

1. The central problem of the artist in the drama of Christianity.

2. The natural historic sequence of *Murder in the Cathedral*; the two plays being suitable for a season's study.

3. The use of the unadorned chancel as the setting.

4. The approach to Catholic tradition for a Protestant audience; the language.

Prepare your audience! Some explanation in advance of the play is imperative. This is a drama set in the full splendor of the Catholic tradition. The central conflict is moral and emotional, not theological. However, even in the sort of Protestant church where the play could be presented at all, some preparation will be necessary. Cutting the script won't solve the problem. The two confession scenes must stand.

William of Sens can be played with a slight French accent to give him additional color. Use good taste in the scenes with Lady Ursula, remembering the chancel setting. Don't be afraid of the comedy in the characterizations and in the lines; it is essential as contrast to the majesty of the final scene. The "big" scenes are almost operatic. Use everything you can get of color, movement, and mounting rhythms. The final scene between William and Saint Michael can be very moving when played by two good actors.

It should be performed by older youth and adults.

AMY GOODHUE LOOMIS
Associate Professor of English and Drama, Vincennes University, Vincennes, Indiana

SUPPLEMENTARY LIST OF PLAYS FOR PRODUCTION IN THE CHURCH

The Acts of Saint Peter, Gordon Bottomly
   Constable; royalty on application to the Religious Drama Society of
   Great Britain; 1 hr.; large cast and verse-speaking chorus.
   A difficult chronicle play in verse, on the life of St. Peter, written in a
highly formalized style.
Among Thieves, Helen M. Clark
   Baker's Plays; no royalty; 1 hr.; 6 m.
   A modern war-time setting of biblical events centering on the Jewish
revolt against the Romans. Christ is a "preacher" who tries to lead a band
of guerilla fighters away from their hatred and killing.
The Angel That Troubled the Waters, Thornton Wilder
   Coward-McCann, Inc.; production allowed only by written permis-
   sion of the publishers.
   One of the several three-minute vignettes written only for reading in the
collection by the same title. Intriguing sketches dealing with theological,
philosophical, and metaphysical ideas. (Out of print, but worth the search
to read.)
As Good As Gold, Lawrence Housman
   Baker's Plays; royalty $5.00; 15 min.; 6 m., 1 boy; available only in
   The Little Plays of Saint Francis, Lawrence Housman.
   A very short morality play about Saint Francis, dealing with greed. (Good
for all ages.)
At the Junction, Rachel Field
   Samuel French; royalty, $5.00; 10 min.; 2 m., 2 w.; modern costumes.
   A fantasy of a young girl who meets herself as a child on her way to
New York and who realizes what the future may hold for her and is inspired
by a greater courage in achieving success.
The Birth of the Song, "Silent Night," Florence French
   Baker's Plays; mechanical rights reserved; 30 min.; 4 m., 3 w.

A radio drama portraying the incidents in Gruber's life which lead to the writing of the song "Silent Night."

The Bishop's Candlesticks, Norman McKinnel
Samuel French; royalty $5.00; 30 min.; 3 m., 2 w.; nineteenth century French costumes.
A dramatization of the incident from Les Miserables in which a convict is softened through the benevolence of a bishop, yet who steals silver from the bishop, is caught, but freed by the bishop who informs the police the silver candlesticks were a gift to the man.

The Book of Job, Orlin Corey
The Children's Theatre Press, Anchorage, Ky. Application for performance to the publishers; 5 m. Chorus of 5 w.; biblical.
The text arranged by Mr. Corey is designed for choral presentation in an altar setting. Production given at the Brussels World's Fair in 1958.

The Boy Who Discovered Easter, Elizabeth McFadden
Samuel French; royalty, $5.00; 30 min.; 2 w., 1 m., 1 boy.
A man looses his son and is rescued from his overwhelming grief by a young boy from the slums who helps him gain a more vital faith. Sentimental.

Bread, Fred Eastman
Samuel French; royalty $5.00; 30 min.; 2 m., 4 w.; modern costume.
Based on the economic, personal problems of American farming people forced into dramatic situations which are fairly convincing. One of Eastman's best plays.

The Builders, Frances Dyer Eckardt
Baker's Plays; royalty $2.50; 20 min.; 5 m., 3 w., 1 boy, singing choir and verse-speaking choir if desired; simple to produce or to read.
A father grows to understand his son's desire to become a country preacher by revisiting the church of his childhood.

The Castle of Perserverance, arranged by Iwa Langentels
Baker's Plays; royalty on application; approx. 40 min.; adjustable cast.
The most ancient of the morality plays. Concerns the Norman conquest and the church's attempt to teach.
(See also: The Castle of Perserverance, arranged by Phillips E. Osgood, Baker's Plays.)

The Child of Peace, Edith H. Willis and Edith Ellsworth
Baker's Plays; royalty $5.00; 40 min.; 1 or 2 narrators, chorus (or solo voices); biblical costumes.
A narrative drama of the journey to Bethlehem and the birth of Jesus, presented in historical and geographical detail, and seen through the experiences of Mary, his mother.

A Christmas Carol, Charles Dickens, adapted for radio by Fred Garrigus
    Baker's Plays; radio rights reserved; ½ hr.; 18 characters (can
    double).
One of the simplest, yet most effective adaptations of the story.

Christmas at the Crossroads, Henri Brochét
    Baker's Plays (available only in Ghéon's collection, Saint Anne and
    the Gouty Rector and Other Plays); royalty upon request; 1 hr.;
    3 m., 4 w.; modern costume.
By the use of allegorical figures Brochét adds a novel touch to the meaning
of Christmas as it is realized by a small group of people in an inn.

Christmas Incorporated, Walter Kerr
    Samuel French; royalty $5.00; 35 min.; 7 w.; modern costume.
The story of a woman whose feelings about Christmas are destroyed by
the gross commercialism which has begun to characterize the season and
which are partially restored by a child whose feeling for Christmas, like
the earlier ones of the woman, have been too sincere to be destroyed even
by the large number of shabby Santa Clauses he sees.

The Cloak, Clifford Bax
    Samuel French; performance only through written permission of the
    publisher; 15 min.; 1 m. and 2 w., or 3 w.
A short, modern mystery play in which two spirits, An Unborn Spirit and
One Newly Dead, meet and are guided on their paths by an Angel who
relates the ideas and attitudes of the two spirits to those of the audience,
attempting to show what happens to human beings during the course of
their life on the earth. (Poetry is not extremely difficult, but requires some
experience.)
[Also available in Seven Famous One-Act Plays, edited by John Ferguson
Baltimore, Md.: Penguin Books, 1953.]

Confessional (or The Hour of Truth), Percival Wilde
    Baker's Plays; royalty $10.00; 3 m., 2 w.; 30 min.
A family play in which the honesty of the father in facing his past
achieves a healthier relationship within the family and a more vital realization of the importance for ethical standards. Revised as radio script.

The Death of Good Fortune, Charles Williams
    Oxford University Press (in Seed of Adam, and other Plays by
    Charles Williams); royalty $5.00 on request; 30 min.; 4 w., 4 m.
A Christmas verse play dealing with the Incarnation. The symbolic characters are used in the same way as in medieval morality plays.

The Devil to Pay, Dorothy Sayers
    Ann Watkins, 77 Park Ave., New York, N.Y.; royalty on application

to Ann Watkins; 1 hr., 40 min.; 13 m., 3 w., 20 extras; traditional medieval "mansion" settings; symbolic costumes.

A difficult retelling of the Faust Legend with strong emphasis on the theological implications.

Dust of the Road, Kenneth Sawyer Goodman
Baker's Plays; royalty, $10.00 if admission is charged, $5.00 if no admission is charged; 40 min.; 3 m., 1 w.; modern costume.

A Christmas play involving the story (legend) of the wandering Judas. Simple, yet requiring above average skill in character actors.

Everyman Today, Walter Sorrell
Dramatists Play Service; royalty $25.00; 10 min.; 10 m., 5 w.; modern costume.

A modern morality play patterned after the ancient morality play, written with reverence, humanity, and a little humor. (For adult actors.)

The Fare to Tarshish, Jesse Powell
Baker's Plays; royalty upon request; approximately 30 min.; 18 m., 1 w.

A stylized verse play, very much like a morality play, dealing with the character of Jonah and the difficulty of making significant decisions. (Cast can include more women in men's roles.)

The Figure on the Cross, R. H. Ward
Baker's Plays; royalty by arrangement with the author c/o the publisher; 1 hr. and 15 min.; 2 m., 1 w.

The seven words from the cross suggest seven contemporary incidents of "crucifixion" concluding with the Resurrection. A verse play which invites the audience to participate in an act of worship.

Finder's Keepers, George Kelly
Samuel French; royalty $10.00; 1 m., 2 w.; modern costume.

The story of a woman who refuses to return a purse and money which she finds, even after realizing it belongs to a friend. Her husband changes her mind through his action.

The Finger of God, Percival Wilde
Baker's Plays; royalty, $10.00; 20 min.; 2 m., 1 w.

Before committing a theft, a man is forced to face himself. The play points up the danger of running away from life instead of facing it realistically.

The Gifts, Dorothy Clarke Wilson
Baker's Plays; royalty $2.50 for all repeat performances, none for the first performance; 40 min.; 7 m., 2 w., 1 boy, a reader, voices of a crowd.

The story of what became of the three gifts of the Wise Men. Unusual. (Part of the boy makes casting difficult.)

Go Down Moses, Philip J. Lamb

Baker's Plays; royalty on application; 2 hrs.; 3 m., chorus of 4 w., chorus of angels.

A choral drama of theological and artistic depth with Moses as the central figure. Requires actors with good voices and ability to speak poetry. Suitable for chancel. (Excellent for Advent.)

Good Friday, John Masefield

Baker's Plays; royalty, $15.00; 1½ hrs.; 7 m., 1 w., crowds; biblical costumes.

A difficult dramatic poem on the incidents of Good Friday. Mob scenes are difficult and important, but forceful. Good for Lenten productions.

And He Came To His Father, Erna Kruckemeyer

Samuel French; no royalty; 20 min.; 4 m., 2 w., extras; biblical costumes.

A treatment of the return of the prodigal son, given additional dramatic interest by introducing a young girl in love with the prodigal. (For adult actors.)

It's Easter, Dr. Jordan, Sherwood Keith

Baker's Plays; no royalty; 30 min.; 1 m., 1 w.; no scenery.

The experiences of a young graduate nurse and a young surgeon set in a story similar to Pilgrim's Progress.

Journey to Judgement, Albert Johnson

Unpublished manuscript (write to Albert Johnson, University of Redlands, Redlands, California); no royalty.

A pageant of Luther, Zwingli, and Knox, their congregations and their renewal of faith. For Reformation Sunday.

The Just Vengeance, Dorothy L. Sayers

Ann Watkins, 77 Park Ave., New York, N.Y.; royalty on application to Ann Watkins; 2½ hrs.; 23 m., 10 w., 1 boy, 1 girl.

A study in verse and prose of the Christian doctrine of atonement by God through Christ. (Difficult.)

A King Shall Reign, Marion Wefer

Samuel French; royalty $5.00; 20 min.; 2 m., 4 w.; biblical costume.

The story centers around a mother whose child has been killed by Herod. She recalls the prophecy of the promised king of Israel and later ministers to him, unknowingly, as the holy family flees into Egypt. Her own grief is put aside in her realization that the young child whom she sheltered is the promised king.

Lamp at Midnight, Barrie Stavis
  Dramatists Play Service; royalty, $25.00; 2 w., 5 m. (as leads), 23
  extras (men); unit set.
  The story of Galileo and his intense conflict between reason and faith.
Difficult. (For Adult Actors.)
The Little Plays of Saint Francis, Lawrence Housman (Three Volumes)
  Baker's Plays; royalty $5.00 each play.
  Each of the plays in these volumes are short, playing between 10 and 20
minutes. They have humor, yet make a deep spiritual impact on actors and
audience. Fine literary quality.
The Lord's Prayer, Francois Coppee
  Baker's Plays; royalty $3.00; 30 min.; 3 m., 3 w.
  The play takes place during the French Revolution and is the story of
Rose, whose brother was shot by a soldier, who shelters a hunted soldier
out of the love for her brother.
The Man Born to Be King, Dorothy L. Sayers
  Harper & Brothers; royalty on application to Ann Watkins, Inc. 77
  Park Ave., New York, N.Y.
  This is a twelve-play cycle of radio plays on the life of Christ. They are
an attempt to translate into a modern idiom the major events of the life of
Christ. Fine literary quality with historically realistic characters and incidents.
*Under no circumstances should these plays be staged. They were written for
radio and are not suitable for staging.*
Nativity, Nora Ratcliff
  Baker's Plays; royalty on application; 1 hr.; 7 w., 12 m.; biblical or
  medieval costume.
  Similar to the medieval nativity plays, the story is simply that of the
biblical events from the Annunciation through the wise men, with a little
dialogue for each scene.
The Other Wise Man, Henry Van Dyke (adapted from the story)
  Dramatic Publishing Company; royalty $10.00; 1½ hrs.; 11 m., 14
  w., mob; 4 sets.
  An effective dramatization of the familiar short story of the fourth wise
man who discovers the meaning of self-sacrifice through the desire to save
his most precious gift for the Christ.
Our Lady's Tumbler, Ronald Duncan
  Faber & Faber, Ltd.; royalty on application to Margery Vosper,
  Ltd., 32 Shaftesbury Ave., London WI, England; 25 min.; 5 men;
  period costumes.
  A retelling of the familiar legend of Le Jongleur de Notre Dame, in

which an acrobat offers his skills as a gift to the Blessed Virgin. (Requires an actor with some ability both as an actor and more than average skill as a juggler.)

Parade at the Devil's Bridge, Henri Ghéon

Longmans, Green & Company; royalty, $10.00 if admission is charged, $5.00 if no admission is charged; 20 min.; 4 m., 3 w.

A relatively simple play with simplified production requirements. A comedy satirizing the pursuit of a noble end which may end in direct compromise with evil.

Pawns, Percival Wilde

Baker's Plays; royalty $10.00; 40 min.; 6 m., 1 narrator; easy production.

In spite of its somewhat contrived nature, the play is a rewarding study of the idea of peace.

Pull Devil, Pull Baker, K. M. Baxter

Baker's Plays; royalty on application to publisher (Religious Drama Society of Great Britain); 1 hr.; 4 m., 1 w., 2 choruses.

A verse mime with music which takes place between Heaven and Hell, showing the disturbance of church people when their parson tries to lead them to welcome the sinners from hell. (Production simple, but requires singing-actors.)

The Resurrection, Rosamond Kimball

Samuel French; no royalty; 12 m., 3 w., voice of Jesus.

An Easter service for a reader and tableaux.

The Rock, Mary Hamlin

Samuel French; royalty $10.00 if admission is charged, $5.00 if no admission is charged; 2 or 2½ hrs.; 6 m., 5 w.; biblical costumes.

An intensely dramatic study of Simon Peter.

Roger Williams, Marcus Bach

Baker's Plays; no royalty; 20 min.; 6 m., 3 w.; early American costumes.

The story of Roger Williams' struggle for freedom of conscience and his subsequent banishment by the intolerance of the American colonies. (Needs one good male and one good female actor for principal roles.)

The Sausage Maker's Interlude, Henri Ghéon

Longmans, Green, & Company; royalty $10.00 if admission is charged, $5.00 if no admission is charged; 20 min.; 5 m., 2 w., 3 children.

A comedy satirizing the machine age in which a machine, which man has made, turns against him and devours him.

Seed of Adam, Charles Williams

Oxford University Press; royalty, $5.00 each performance; 30 min.; 8 m., 3 w., 2 choruses.

A morality play rich in dramatic symbolism, centering around the moment of the Incarnation, when the history of man, from the creation through the highly civilized Roman empire, is brought before the audience as preparation for the coming of Christ. (Simple production, but poetry of the script requires some experience for successful performance.)

Simon the Leper, Dorothy Clarke Wilson

Baker's Plays; no royalty; 1¼ hrs.; 4 m., 4 w.; biblical costumes.

A development of the story of Jesus' curing of the lepers, one of whom, Simon, who did not return to Jesus to show his gratitude, later returns to the leper colony after the crucifixion to live with the lepers and show them the Christ.

Spreading the News, Lady Gregory

Samuel French; royalty $5.00; 30 min.; 7 m., 3 w.; Irish costume.

An Irish comedy showing the evils of gossip. (Simple except for the dialect.)

The Summoning of Everyman, adapted from the ancient morality play by John F. Baird

Samuel French; royalty $5.00; 22 symbolic characters.

A shorter version of the ancient morality play.

The Table Set For Himself, Elene Wilbur

Longmans, Green, & Company; royalty $10.00 if admission is charged, $5.00 if no admission is charged; 45 min.; 3 m., 5 w., 1 boy.

The Irish legend of Bridget Clancy who unknowingly entertains the Christ Child on Christmas Eve.

The Terrible Meek, Charles Rann Kennedy

Samuel French; no royalty; 30 min.; 2 m., 1 w.

The meaning of the events of the Crucifixion are discussed at the foot of the cross by a Roman captain, a soldier, and Mary, the mother of Jesus. (Requires good acting and imaginative staging and lighting for the last scene.) Should be cut.

Thor, With Angels, Christopher Fry

Dramatists Play Service; royalty $25.00; 1½ hrs.; 8 m., 3 w.

A poetically beautiful, but difficult, legend of Hoel, who introduced Christianity to the semi-barbaric Jutes in A.D. 6000.

Tobias and the Angel, James Bridie

Samuel French; royalty $25.00; 1½ hrs.; 5 m., 4 w., extras; 3 exteriors and 2 interiors in Mesopotamia and Northern Persia.

A comedy based on the Apocryphal Book of Tobit, telling how the Archangel Raphael, in disguise as a servant, assists the young Tobias, son of Tobit, on his journey to manhood. (Difficult acting and production.)

Too Little For Milo, Dane R. Gordon
    Abingdon Press; royalty on application to publisher; 3 acts, 1 hr.;
    3 m., 3 w.; modern costumes.

Two families living next door to each other lack communication. The son of one family and the daughter of the other strive to find ways to communicate and discover that when they do, they are suspected by their parents. Adults and high-school age.

The Traveling Man, Lady Gregory
    Samuel French; royalty $5.00; 20 min.; 1 m., 1 w., 1 child.

A story rich in Irish lore of an Irish woman who fails to recognize the King of the World when he appears as a common traveling man after she has waited for him for seven years. The simple truth that a child's heart reaches out to the real person when the adult is often blinded by externals. (Requires actors who can reproduce a good Irish brogue.)

The Undertaking, Patricia Vought Schneider
    Abingdon Press; royalty on application to publisher; 20 min.; 2 m.;
    modern costumes.

Two grave diggers burying a prophet discuss life and death and contemporary problems. Beckett style dialogue. Adults. Prize play of the Methodist Student Movement.

The Valiant, Holworthy Hall and Robert Middlemass
    Samuel French; royalty $10.00; 40 min.; 5 m., 1 w.

The sacrifice made by a young criminal to keep a knowledge of his deed from his family.

The Wanderer, Helen B. Bjorklund
    Abingdon Press; royalty on application to publisher; 15 min.; 9 m.,
    1 w.; costumes of no particular period.

A group of people living in a valley are forbidden on punishment of death to seek whatever is beyond the mountains. What happens to the Wanderer who went beyond the valley is the subject of the play. Adults.

The Way of the Cross, Henri Ghéon
    A. & C. Black; royalty on application; 50 min.; narrators, 2 m., 2 w.;
    the setting is the fourteen Stations of the Cross.

An extract from The Mystery of the Finding of the Cross, dealing with the Roman Catholic devotions related to the fourteen Stations of the Cross, in which actors portray themselves and the historical characters. (Difficult.)

What Never Dies, Percival Wilde

Baker's Plays; royalty $10.00; 40 min.; 1 m., 3 w.

A humorous play about unexpected charity. The story of three scrub women in a stockbrokerage, two of whom help the third whose son has lost his mother's savings by playing the market.

Where Love Is, B. Iden Payne

Baker's Plays; royalty $5.00; 30 min.; 3 m., 1 young w., 1 old w., 1 small boy.

A dramatization of a story by Tolstoy in which an old man learns that he is "receiving" Christ in aiding the poor.

White Christmas, Dorothy Clarke Wilson

Samuel French; no royalty; 40 min.; 4 m., 3 w., 2 small girls.

A missionary play dealing with the generous, but uninterested, giving of a wealthy family to foreign missions.

The Wise and Foolish Virgins, R. H. Ward

Baker's Plays; royalty on application; 25 min.; 2 m., 13 w., 2 angels; modern costume.

A contemporary expression of the biblical parable. Written with wit and with insight into our time.

The Wise Have Not Spoken, Paul Vincent Carroll

Dramatists Play Service; royalty $25.00; full-length; 16 m., 3 w.

The story of a boy and a girl and their struggles with the mores of society.

X=O (or *A Night of the Trojan War*), John Drinkwater

(Out of print, but can be found in *Pawns* by Wilde, or *Looking at Life Through Drama* by Deseo and Phipps.); royalty on application; 45 min.; 5 m.

A poetic treatment of the difficult subject of the tragic futility of war.

CHORAL DRAMAS

Auden, W. H., *For the Time Being*
Bogan, Gretchen, *Genesis*
Boiko, Claire, *Night Comes to the City*
Bradbury, Audrey, *The Vision of Sir Launfal*
Coyle, Rollin, *Unto Thy Doors*
Elicker, Virginia, *The Least of These*
Johnson, Albert, *Go Ye to Bethlehem*
Kromer, Helen, *They Made a Path*
Magee, Catherine, *Radio Jerusalem, The Story of Jesus*
Sliker, Harold G., *Unto the Living*

The Other Wise Man (adaptation
from the story by Van Dyke)
Swann, Darius, The Answers
The Crier Calls
I Have Spoken to My Children
The Circle Beyond Fear
A House for Marvin
Swann, Mona, Wonderful World

A LIST OF PLAYS FOR READING AND STUDY

THE FOLLOWING LIST OF PLAYS HAS BEEN SELECTED FROM A VAST BODY OF dramatic literature which represents the history of theatrical writing and is included in this text on the basis of its religious significance for modern times. It is listed in a general chronological manner and is divided into two major sections: Part I: Ancient and Classical Drama, and Part II: Modern Drama.

Part I identifies the plays by general period, country, and writer—when the writer is known. Part II only identifies the plays by the writers (listed alphabetically.)

PART I: ANCIENT AND CLASSICAL DRAMA

Pre-Christian Drama

GREEK

Aeschylus, *Prometheus Bound*
Euripides, *Medea*
       Electra
Sophocles, The Oedipus Trilogy (*Oedipus Rex, Oedipus at Colonus, Antigone*)

ROMAN

Plautus, *The Captives*
Seneca, *Medea*

HEBREW

(*The following are included in this list not because they are considered to be theatrical writings, but because*

of their dramatic quality and structure.)
The Book of Job from the Old Testament
The Song of Solomon from the Old Testament

INDIAN

Kalidasa, *Shakuntala*
(Anonymous), *The Little Clay Cart*

TIBETAN

(Anonymous), *Tchrinekundan* (a story of Buddha)

CHINESE

(Anonymous), *The Circle of Chalk*
S. I. Hsiung, *Lady Precious Stream* (translated from various sources).
(Anonymous), *The Lute Song*

JAPANESE

The Nō Plays of Japan.
(Nō Drama)
(Anonymous), *Taniko*
(*The reader is referred to an outstanding collection of Nō plays from the Japanese theater Arthur Waley's The Nō Plays of Japan.*)
(Kabuki)
Chikamatsu Monzayemon, *Fair Ladys at a Game of Poem Cards*

Medieval Drama
(*Christian Religious Drama*)

ENGLISH

(Anonymous), *Quem Queritis* (the earliest example of the mystery play)
(Anonymous), *The Castle of Perserverance* (one of the earliest morality plays)
(Anonymous), *Abraham and Isaac* (From the Brome Manuscript)
The York Cycle of Mystery Plays
The Coventry Cycle of Mystery Plays
The Chester Cycle of Mystery Plays
The Cornish Mystery Plays

DUTCH

(Anonymous), *Everyman* (early morality play)

GERMAN

(Anonymous), *Redentin Easter Play*

FRENCH

(Anonymous), *The Conversion of Saint Paul*

(*Secular Drama*)

FRENCH

(Anonymous), *Pierre Pathelin*

Early Renaissance Drama

ITALIAN

Machiavelli, *La Mandragola*

Tasso, *Jerusalem Delivered*

SPANISH

Lope de Vega, *The Star of Seville*

Calderón, *The Great World Theatre*

High Renaissance Drama
(Sixteenth Century)

ENGLISH

Robert Greene, *Friar Bacon and Friar Bungay*

Christopher Marlowe, *The Tragical History of Doctor
                                      Faustus*
                              The Jew of Malta

William Shakespeare, *The Merchant of Venice*
                                      The Winter's Tale
                                      Macbeth
                                      King Lear

(Seventeenth Century)

FRENCH

Pierre Corneille, *Le Cid*
                              Oedipe

Jean Racine, *Phèdre*

Jean-Baptiste Poquelin (Moliere), *The Bourgeois Gen-
                                      tleman*
                                      *The Imaginary In-
                                      valid*

(*Eighteenth Century*)

FRENCH

François Marie Arouet (Voltaire), *Oedipe*

ENGLISH

Richard Steele, *The Tender Husband*
Richard Brinsley Sheridan, *The School for Scandal*

GERMAN

Gotthold Ephriam Lessing, *Nathan the Wise*
Johann Wolfgang von Goethe, *Faust* (Parts I and II)
Johan Christophe, Friedrich von Schiller,
                                    The Robbers
                                    Maria Stuart
                                    The Maid of Orleans

(*Nineteenth Century*)

RUSSIAN

Nickoli Gogol, *The Inspector General*

GERMAN

Georg Buchner, *Danton's Death*
Friedrich Hebbel, *Maria Magdalena*
                Judith

PART II: MODERN DRAMA

(*Listed alphabetically by writer.*)

Albee, Edward, *The American Dream*
Anderson, Maxwell, *Winterset*
                Journey to Jerusalem
                Joan of Lorraine
Anderson, Robert, *Tea and Sympathy*
Andreyev, Leonid, *The Life of Man*
Anouilh, Jean, *The Lark*
                Becket
Ansky, S., *The Dybbuk*
Asch, Sholem, *The God of Vengeance*
                The Nazarene
Auden, W. H., *For the Time Being*
Bach, Marcus, *Roger Williams*
Barrie, Sir James, *The Boy David*

Barry, Philip, John
    The Joyous Season
Bax, Clifford, The Cloak
Baxter, K. M., Pull Devil, Pull Baker
Beckett, Samuel, Waiting for Godot
Benét, Stephen Vincent, A Child Is Born
Bernstein, Henry, Judith
Björnson, Björnstjerne, Beyond Our Power (Parts I
    and II)
Brecht, Bertolt, Galileo
    Mother Courage
    He Who Says Yes, and He Who Says
    No
    Saint Joan of the Stockyards
Bridie, James, Tobias and the Angel
Brieux, Eugène, The Red Robe
    False Gods
Brighouse, Harold, The Maid of France
Camus, Albert, Caligula
Capek, Joseph (and Karel), Adam the Creator
    The World We Live In
    (The Insect Comedy)
Capek, Karel, R.U.R.
Carroll, Paul Vincent, Shadow and Substance
    The White Steed
Chayevsky, Paddie, The Tenth Man
    Marty
    Gideon
Chekhov, Anton, The Cherry Orchard
    Uncle Vanya
Claudel, Paul, The Tidings Brought to Mary
Cocteau, Jean, The Infernal Machine
Coffee, Lenore, and Cowen, William Joyce, Family
    Portrait
Conkle, E. P., Prologue to Glory
Connelly, Marc, The Green Pastures
    Beggar on Horseback (with George
    Kaufman)
Coréy, Orlin, The Book of Job
Coxe, Louis O., and Chapman, Robert, Billy Budd
Cumming, E. E., Santa Claus

Dane, Clemence, Naboth's Vineyard
            Herod and Mariamn (from Hebbel)
D'Annunzio, Gabrielle, Martyrdom of Saint Sebastian
Delderfield, R. F., Spark in Judea
Dennis, Nigel, The Making of Moo
Drinkwater, John, Abraham Lincoln
            X=O (or A Night of the Trojan
            War)
Duncan, Ronald, This Way to the Tomb
            Our Lady's Tumbler
Dunsany, Lord, The Glittering Gate
Dürrenmatt, Friedrich, The Visit (translated by Mau-
            rice Valency)
Eliot, T. S., The Cocktail Party
            The Family Reunion
            Murder in the Cathedral
            The Rock
Ervine, St. John, Mixed Marriage
Flexner, Hortense, Voices
Forsythe, James, Heloise
            Emmanuel
            The Road to Emmaus
France, Anatole, The Man Who Married a Dumb
            Wife
Fry, Christopher, Thor, With Angels
            The Lady's Not for Burning
            The Firstborn
            A Sleep of Prisoners
            The Boy with a Cart
            Venus Observed
Gale, Zona, The Neighbors
Galsworthy, John, Justice
            Strife
            Loyalties
Ghelderode, Michel de, The Women at the Tomb
            Barrabas
Ghéon, Henri, Christmas in the Market Place
            The Mystery of the Finding of the
            Cross
            The Journey of the Three Kings
            Saint Anne and the Gouty Rector

An Enemy of the People (see Arthur
  Miller's adaptation)
  Ghosts
  Hedda Gabler
  The Master Builder
  John Gabriel Borkman
Inge, William, Come Back, Little Sheba
  The Dark at the Top of the Stairs
Ionesco, Eugene, The Lesson
  The Chairs
  Rhinoceros
Jeffers, Robinson, The Tower Beyond Tragedy
  Medea (adapted by Jeffers)
Johnson, Albert, Roger Williams and Mary
Joyce, James, Exiles
Kaiser, Georg, From Morn to Midnight
Kallen, Horace, The Book of Job as a Greek Tragedy
Kennedy, Charles, The Servant in the House
  The Terrible Meek
Kennedy, Cumming, Gillean
Kingsley, Sidney, Dead End
Komai, Felicia, Cry, the Beloved Country (verse adapta-
  tion of the novel by Alan Paton)
Lagervist, Pär, Let Man Live
Lamb, Philip, Go Down Moses
  Sons of Adam
Langer, Lawrence, Another Way Out
Laurents, Arthur, West Side Story (music drama)
  Invitation to a March
Lavery, Emmit, The First Legion
Lawrence, D. H., David
Lawson, John Howard, Professional
  Nirvanna
  Success Story
  Marching Song
Lorca, Federico Garcia, Blood Wedding
MacKaye, Percy, Jeanne D'Arc
MacLeish, Archibald, J. B.
  The Fall of the City
Maeterlinck, Maurice, The Blind
  Mary Magdalene

Mankowitz, Wolf, *It Should Happen to a Dog*
        The Bespoke Overcoat
Marcel, Gabriel, *The Man of God*
Masefield, John, *The Coming of Christ*
        Good Friday
        The Trial of Jesus
        Esther (Racine)
Mayakovski, Vladimir, *The Bed Bug*
Menotti, Gian Carlo, *The Saint of Bleeker Street*
        (Opera)
        Amahl and the Night Visitors
        (Opera)
Millay, Edna St. Vincent, *Two Slatterns and a King*
        Aría de Capo
Miller, Arthur, *Death of a Salesman*
        The Crucible
        All My Sons
Moody, William Vaughan, *The Faith Healer*
Mosel, Tad, *All the Way Home*
Nichols, Robert, and Brown, Maurice, *Wings Over*
        Europe
Obey, André, *Noah*
O'Casey, Sean, *The Plough and the Stars*
        Within the Gates
        Red Roses for Me
Odets, Clifford, *The Flowering Peach*
O'Neill, Eugene, *Lazarus Laughed*
        Ah, Wilderness!
        The Emperor Jones
        The Great God Brown
        The Iceman Cometh
        The Hairy Ape
Phillips, Stephen, *Herod*
        Nero
Pinero, Arthur Wing, *The Second Mrs. Tanqueray*
Pinski, David, *The Treasure*
Pirandello, Luigi, *The Mountain Giants*
Pollock, Channing, *The Captains and the Kings*
        The Enemy
Rattigan, Terrence, *The Winslow Boy*
Reid, Edith, *Florence Nightingale*

Rice, Elmer, *The Adding Machine*
          Street Scene
Richardson, Jack, *The Prodigal*
Saroyan, William, *The Time of Your Life*
Sartre, Jean Paul, *The Flies*
          No Exit
          The Devil and the Good Lord
Sayers, Dorothy, *Zeal of Thy House*
          The Man Born to Be King
          The Devil to Pay
          The Just Vengeance
Shaeffer, Peter, *Five Finger Exercise*
Shaw, George Bernard, *Saint Joan*
                    The Shewing Up of Blanco Posnet
                    Androcles and the Lion
                    Major Barbara
                    The Devil's Disciple
                    Arms and the Man
                    Pygmalion
                    Back to Methuselah
                    Man and Superman
Shaw, Irwin, *Bury the Dead*
Sheldon, Edward, *The Nigger*
Sherriff, R. C., *Journey's End*
Sherwood, Robert, *The Road to Rome*
                  Abe Lincoln in Illinois
                  There Shall Be No Night
Shevill, James, *The Bloody Tenet*
Sierra, Gregorio Martinez, *The Cradle Song*
                          Holy Night
                          Kingdom of God
                          The Two Shepherds
Steinbeck, John, *Of Mice and Men*
Strindberg, August, *The Father*
                    Easter
Sudermann, Hermann, *John the Baptist*
                    Magda
Sweig, Stephan, *Jeremiah*
Synge, John Millington, *Riders to the Sea*
Tagore, Rabindranath, *Chitra*

Sacrifice
Toller, Ernst, *Man and the Masses*
No More Peace
Tolstoy, Leo, *The Power of Darkness*
The Light Shineth in Darkness
Turner, Philip, *Christ in the Concrete City*
Cry Dawn in Dark Babylon
Van Dyke, Henry, *The Other Wise Man* (adapted by the author from the short story)
Vane, Sutton, *Outward Bound*
Ward, R. H., *The Prodigal Son*
The Figure on the Cross
The Holy Family
The Wise and Foolish Virgins
The Lost Sheep
The Builders
Werfel, Franz, *Paul and the Jews*
The Eternal Road
Wexley, John, *They Shall Not Die*
Wilde, Percival, *Confessional*
The Finger of God
Pawns
Wilder, Thornton, *Our Town*
The Skin of Our Teeth
The Angel That Troubled the Water (see all plays in this collection by this title)
Flight Into Egypt
Pullman Car Hiawatha
Williams, Charles, *The Seed of Adam*
House by the Stable
Grab and Grace
Cranmer
Williams, Emlyn, *The Corn Is Green*
Williams, Tennessee, *The Glass Menagerie*
This Property Is Condemned
Yeats, William Butler, *The Hour Glass*
Purgatory
Calvary
The Resurrection
Zangwill, Israel, *The Melting Pot*

A LIST OF PLAYS WRITTEN FOR DISCUSSION PURPOSES

THE FOLLOWING PORTION OF THIS LIST IS DEVOTED TO THE PLAYS OF NORA Stirling, published by the National Association for Mental Health, 10 Columbus Circle, New York, N. Y. (There is a special price for a packet containing a script for each cast member, which also gives royalty information.)

Scattered Showers
    3 young women, stage manager.
    Subject: Three mothers and how their preschool children act in crisis when each has been reared according to different methods of discipline.

Fresh Variable Winds
    1 man, 1 woman, a ten-year-old boy and girl, stage manager.
    Subject: A situation between a father and his ten-year-old son and a neighbor's child shows the difference between a healthy "mischief maker" and a spoiled brat, and also demonstrates the importance of the father's role in the family.

High Pressure Area
    1 man, 1 woman, 2 teen-age girls, stage manager.
    Subject: Two teen-age girls are tempted to take part in a questionable escapade with men they don't know. Each girl's final decision shows the influence of her parents' attitudes.

Random Target
    2 women, 1 man, eleven-year-old boy.
    Subject: The need for youngsters to express feelings of anger and hostility if they are to grow into mature adults, and the realization that unless there is understanding of this, the child's buried resentments may cause him to lash out at any "random target" rather than the actual cause of resentment.

The Case of the Missing Handshake
    2 women, 1 man, one ten-year-old, stage manager.
    1 act—30 minutes
    Subject: "Good manners" in preteen-agers and what adults really have a

right to expect from this age. Deals with the difference between personal integrity and manners.

Tomorrow Is a Day

5 women (may be combined to 3), 1 teen-age girl, 2 teen-age boys (may be combined to 1), stage manager.

Subject: A mother who fails to understand her shy daughter and the particular love and help she needs, until a more understanding and perceptive neighbor helps her.

And You Never Know

1 woman, 1 man, one twelve-year-old girl, stage manager.

1 act—30 minutes

Subject: Jealousy of the twelve-year-old for her sister, with the family— for the first time—talking over the problems that arise and coming to understand reasons and feelings back of the problem.

The Room Upstairs

3 women, 1 man, stage manager.

Subject: The problem of old and young people living together; the things which cause resentment and the honesty, patience, and sympathy needed by all for the solution of this problem.

Point of Beginning

1 woman, 1 man, one ten-year-old boy, 1 teen-age boy

Subject: Parents discover that due to their own "cutting of moral corners" in practice and their blindness to the needs of their own child, they almost falsely accuse another of their own child's actions. They feel that to begin again to develop a family, the church may be their "point of beginning." Publisher: General Department of United Church Women, 175 Fifth Avenue, New York, N. Y.

The Ins and Outs

3 teen-age boys, 2 teen-age girls

Subject: This deals with the "ins"—those who belong to a group—and an "out," who tries to belong, but is excluded. The sketch shows the same scene twice; once as it did happen and once as it might have happened had true feelings rather than group pressures been expressed. Especially fourteen-age groups.

What Did I Do?

Order from: Human Relations Aids, 1790 Broadway, New York 19, N. Y.

2 women (one about 35, the other 22), one eleven-year-old girl

Subject: How parents feel about their influence on their children and how they can achieve a healthy balance in assuming enough but not too much responsibility for shaping their children's personalities.

Ever Since April

Order from: Plays for Living, The American Association of Retired Persons, Dupont Circle Building, Washington, D. C.

1 man (65), 1 woman (65), 1 woman (50s), 1 man (35-40), Stage manager.

Subject: The problem of mandatory retirement based on chronological age, the effect on the individual and on his family, the employer, and those younger individuals planning their futures.

Eve of the Hurricane

Order from: Plays for Living, Family Service Association of America, Inc., 215 Park Avenue, South, New York 3, N. Y.

1 man, 2 women, one ten-year-old boy, stage manager

Subject: The role of a family caseworker in helping a family whose equilibrium is being threatened by the disturbed behavior of one of its members —the ten-year-old son.

The Green Blackboard

Order from: Plays for Living, Family Service Association of America, Inc., 215 Park Avenue, South, New York 3, N. Y.

2 men, one seventeen-year-old boy, 1 woman, stage manager

Subject: The child who enters the first grade before the legal age of entrance; the inappropriate and premature pressures on children and the damage these can cause.

The Daily Special

Order from: Human Relations Aids, 104 East 25th Street, New York 10, N. Y.

5 actors

Subject: How to handle situations in which conflict with the rights and wishes of some members of the family conflict with the rights and wishes of others in the family.

Help Wanted, Marjorie E. Watson and Irving M. Brown

Order from: Human Relations Aids, 104 East 25th Street, New York 10, N. Y.

6 actors

Subject: The family reaction to the subject of working wives and mothers, the situation in this play being a mother who does not need the money, yet who wants the emotional satisfactions of working. The many facets of this problem are examined one by one.

New Fountains, Lee Gilmore

1 woman, 2 teen-age girls, 1 teen-age boy, stage manager.

Subject: The adjustments of a paralytic to home and school situations, and the special insights needed by adults.

Publisher: General Department of United Church Women, 175 Fifth Avenue, New York, N. Y. Scripts free from publisher.

The Sign of Jonah, Gruenter Rutenborn

Order from: Thomas Nelson & Sons, 18 East 41st Street, New York 17, N. Y.

"A powerful, modern play, coming out of post-war Germany. The play deals with the human predicament of men's refusal to meet God at the place where God has come to meet him. The biblical and contemporary confrontations for each character have great implications as to the role of the church today. Difficult, but excellent for study and discussion."

Take a Giant Step, Louis Peterson

Order from: Samuel French, Inc.

"A drama dealing with the problems of Negro teen-ager learning the narrow lonely path he must walk in a racially mixed school and community situation—on one hand his parents who believe he must 'learn his place,' and on the other, his own need for self-respect and acceptance. The play contains a great deal of profanity, but real depth of understanding."

A Neighbor and Friend, Nevin E. Kendall and Samuel A. Rulon

Order from: Westminster Press, Young Fellowship Kit, Volume 15

"A Negro family, ejected to make way for new building project, finally rents a house outside of 'Negro neighborhoods.' The owner of the house and her minister urge the family to move in even though other white neighbors begin a telephone campaign to keep the Negro family from moving. The play develops with unusual sensitivity and insights into the feelings and reactions of the Negro family."

Cry, The Beloved Country, Felicia Komai

Order from: The Friendship Press

"In blank verse, this is a powerful dramatic adaptation of Alan Paton's novel of South Africa. All or parts can be used for reading and study. The recording of 'Lost in the Stars,' the Broadway musical production of the same book, can assist a study group and intensify the emotional impact."

Family Life Plays, Nora Stirling. Association Press, 291 Broadway, New York 7, N.Y. A collection of plays on problems relating to family relationships.

APPENDIX G

COLLECTIONS OF RELIGIOUS DRAMAS

Brown, Thelma Sharman. *Treasure of Religious Plays*. New York: Association Press, 1947.
Plays are: *The Birth of the Song*, "*Silent Night*" (F. F. French); *A Christman Carol* (C. Dickens); *White Christmas* (D. C. Wilson); *The Shepherd's Story* (H. G. Grover); *A Child Is Born* (S. V. Benét; *No Room in the Hotel* (D. C. Wilson); *It's Easter, Dr. Jordan* (S. Keith); *The Symbol of the Cross* (M. B. Shannon); *The Cloth of Sendony* (E. H. Emerson); *Where Love Is* (L. Tolstoy); *The Captains and the Kings* (C. Pollock); *The Curtain* (H. B. Flanigan); *The Coming of Light* (M. Bach); *Roger Williams* (M. Bach); *To Speak of Freedom* (G. New); *Empty Hands* (H. M. Clark); *The Builders* (F. Eckardt); *Sentence* (L. Carmichael); *Speaking of Pictures* (M. Wefer); *Among Thieves* (H. M. Clark).
Browne, E. Martin, editor. *Religious Drama 2: Twenty-one Medieval, Mystery, and Morality Plays*. New York: Meridian Books, Inc., 1958. A representative collection of mystery and morality plays.
Plays are: *The Creation of the Heavenly Beings: The Fall of Lucifer* (York); *The Creation of Man* (York); *The Garden of Eden* (York); *The Fall of Man* (York); *Noah's Flood* (Chester); *The Sacrifice of Isaac* (Brome manuscript); *I. David Takes the Shoots to Jerusalem* (Cornish) and *II. David and Bathsheba* (Cornish); *The Parliament of Heaven: The Anunciation and Conception* (Hegge); *The Birth of Christ* (York); *The Plays of the Shepherds* (Wakefield); *Herod and the Kings* (Coventry); *The Temptation of Christ* (York); *The Woman Taken in Adultery* (Hegge); *The Second Trial Before Pilate: The Scourging and Condemnation* (York); *The Crucifixion* (York); *The Harrowing of Hell* (York); *The Three Marys* (Cornish); *The Ascension* (York); *The Last Judgment* (York); *Everyman*.
Cawley, A. C. *Everyman and Medieval Miracle Plays*. New York: E. P. Dutton & Company, 1959. (Paperback.)
Plays are: *The Creation and The Fall of Lucifer* (York); *The Creation of Adam and Eve* (York); *The Fall of Man* (York); *Cain and Abel* (N.

246

COLLECTIONS OF RELIGIOUS DRAMAS

Town); *Noah's Flood* (Chester); *Abraham and Isaac* (Brome manuscript); *The Annunciation* (Coventry); *The Second Shepherd's Pageant* (Wakefield); *Herod the Great* (Wakefield); *The Woman Taken in Adultery* (N. Town); *The Harrowing of Hell* (Chester); *The Resurrection* (York); *The Judgment* (York); *Everyman; The Death of Pilate* (A Cornish trilogy).

Doyle, John W. *Adam.* Sydney: Shakespeare Head Press, 1948.
The text and a study of the anonymous medieval play.

Eastman, Fred. *Modern Religious Dramas.* New York: Henry Holt & Company, 1928. (Out of print.)
Plays are: *The Neighbors* (Gale); *Confessional* (Wilde); *What Men Live By* (Church); *The Valiant* (Hall and Middlemas); *Bread* (Eastman); *The Deathless World* (Tompkins); *El Cristo* (Larkin); *Dust by the Road* (Goodman); *The Color Line* (MacNair); *The Golden Rule in Courtship* (Cook); *Modern Magi* (Brown); *The Christmas Pageant of the Holy Grail* (Bowie); *America's Unfinished Battles* (Eastman).

Ghéon, Henri and Brochet, Henri. *Saint Anne and the Gouty Rector and Other Plays.* New York: Longman's Green & Company, 1950.
A collection of plays by one of France's foremost literary figures of the century. Plays modeled on medieval mystery and miracle forms are modeled to contemporary characterizations and current problems. Production notes accompany the plays. Plays are: *Saint Anne and the Gouty Rector; The Gardener Who Was Afraid of Death; The Sausage Maker's Interlude; The Poor Man Who Died Because He Wore Gloves; Parade at the Devil's Bridge; Christmas at the Crossroads; Saint Felix and His Potatoes.*

Greenberg, Noah, and Auden, W. H., editors. *The Play of Daniel: Thirteenth Century Musical Drama.* New York: Oxford University Press, 1959.
A valuable edition of the medieval musical play with notes on costuming and production.

Halverson, Marvin, editor. *Religious Drama 1.* New York: Meridian Books, Inc.
Plays are: *For the Time Being* (W. H. Auden); *The Firstborn* (C. Fry); *David* (D. H. Lawrence); *The Zeal of Thy House* (D. Sayers); *The Bloody Tenet* (J. Schevill).
Religious Drama 3. New York: Meridian Books, Inc., 1959.
Plays are: *The Last Word* (J. Broughton); *The House by the Stable* and *Grab and Grace* (C. Williams); *Santa Claus* (E. E. Cummings); *Let Man Live* (Pär Lagerkvist); *It Should Happen to a Dog* (W. Mankowitz); *Billy Budd* (L. O. Coxe and R. Chapman); *The Gospel Witch* (L. Phelps).

Housman, Laurence. *Little Plays of Saint Francis.* 3 vol. London: Sidgwick & Jackson Ltd., 1947. (Available through Baker's Plays.)

Hussey, Maurice, editor. *The Chester Mystery Plays.* New York: Theatre Art Books, 1957.

A study of the Chester medieval drama through the plays adapted for this volume. Valuable addition to the limited material available on the actual texts of mystery plays.

Osgood, Philip. *Old Time Church Drama Adapted.* New York: Harper & Brothers, 1928. (Out of print.)

One of the early books introducing contemporary audiences to the historical background of medieval drama through certain plays. Introductory chapter is valuable as a historical survey. The remainder of the book contains the following plays with notes: *Melchizedek, Abraham, and Isaac* (Chester); *The Nativity Cycle of the York Mystery Plays; The Summoning of Everyman.* The section of adapted oratorios to be used as sung miracle plays includes: "Elijah" (Mendelssohn); "Judas Maccabeus" (Handel). Also included are ancient dramatic services: "The Feast of Lights" (Greek, from the fourth century); "*The Burial of the Alleluia*" and "*The Burning of the Palms*" (Gothic, eleventh century); "The Boy Bishop" (French and Saxon, eleventh century); "The Quem Quaeritis" (Gothic, tenth century).

Pollard, A. W. *English Miracle Plays, Moralities and Interludes: Specimens of the Pre-Elizabethan Drama.* Rev. ed. New York: Oxford University Press, 1927. (Out of print.)

Purvis, J. S. *The York Cycle of Mystery Plays.* New York: The Macmillan Company, 1957.

A collection of all extant manuscripts of the plays in the York cycle.

Williams, Charles. *The Seed of Adam and Other Plays.* New York: Oxford University Press, 1948.

Four plays by one of England's outstanding literary figures: *Seed of Adam; The Death of Good Fortune; The House by the Stable; Grab and Grace.*

Prize Plays. Nashville: Abingdon Press, 1961. (Methodist Student Movement Playwriting Contest, 1961.)

The Undertaking (Patricia Vought Schneider); *The Wanderer* (Helen B. Bjorklund); *Too Little for Milo* (Dane R. Gordon).

BIBLIOGRAPHY

The books listed here are the chief publications on drama and its history and production. Many are out of print but are listed for library reference. Those marked with an asterisk are most suitable for the average church group. Notations under others tell why they are included.

History

Appia, Adolphe. *The Work of Living Art* and *Man is the Measure of All Things.* Coral Gables, Fla.: University of Miami Press, 1960.
For the first time in English here is the whole mature theory of the pioneering Swiss designer-director.

Bates, Katherine Lee. *The English Religious Drama.* New York: The Macmillan Company, 1917. (Out of print.)
One of the early standard works on what Miss Bates calls "the miracle play." A chapter on the Latin Passion and saint plays and a concluding chapter on "moralities." Good material.

Bieber, Margarete. *The History of the Greek and Roman Theatre.* 2nd ed., revised and enlarged. Princeton, N. J.: Princeton University Press, 1961.
Theatrical productions, acting, buildings, and popular entertainment illustrated with pictures of costumes, settings, masks, et cetera.

Bowers, Faubion. *Broadway, U.S.S.R.* New York: Thomas Nelson & Sons, 1959.
A book on the theater in the U.S.S.R. that reminds one of the great need for us to know each other and exchange ideas.

Chambers, Edmund. *The Medieval Stage.* 2 vols. New York: Oxford University Press, 1903.
The scholarly, accepted, basic book on the medieval drama. Difficult but rewarding in its thoroughgoing analysis of plays and their performances. Traditional theory of liturgical drama origin.

*Cheney, Sheldon. *The Theatre.* Rev. ed. New York: Longmans, Green & Company, 1959.

A sweeping history that covers in a condensed fashion the long history of the theater.

Clark, Barrett, and Freedley, George. *A History of Modern Drama*. Rev. ed. New York: Appleton-Century-Crofts, Inc., 1947.
A history by two of the conversant writers on drama. Balanced judgment.

*Coggin, Philip A. *The Uses of Drama*. New York: George Braziller, Inc., 1956.
A historical survey of drama and education from ancient Greece to the present day. Excellent. Recommended for its readability.

*Craig, Hardin. *English Religious Drama of the Middle Ages*. New York: Oxford University Press, 1955.
The origin of religious drama and a thorough study of the medieval stage; a full treatment of the Chester, York, and Wakefield plays; chapters on miracle and morality plays; the Reformation, renaissance and medieval religious drama. The best one-volume treatment of the subject.

Driver, Tom F. *The Sense of History in Greek and Shakespearean Drama*. New York: Columbia University Press, 1960.
An analysis of the way in which drama reflects history. Chapter I as well as Chapter IV on the "Problem of Dramatic Form" are especially pertinent to this book.

Ernst, Earle. *The Kabuki Theatre*. New York: Oxford University Press, 1956. Evergreen paperback.
An introductory book on this important part of Japanese theater that ought to be read along with Faubion Bowers' *Japanese Theatre*.

Freedley, George, and Reeves, John A. *A History of the Theatre*. New York: Crown Publishers, Inc., 1955.
A standard history by an authority whose familiarity with drama comes out of long association with the New York City Public Library.

Garten, H. F. *Modern German Drama*. New York: Oxford University Press, 1959.
Historical and critical account of contemporary German drama. Exhaustive treatment of expressionistic and epic theater.

Gassner, John. *Masters of the Drama*. New York: Random House, 1953.
A well-balanced history from the Greeks to the present day.

Gassner, John, and Allen, Ralph. *Theatre in the Making*. Vols. 1 and II. Boston: Houghton Mifflin Company, 1962.
Documents, arranged chronologically, on the classic, medieval, renaissance, and modern theater and drama. A source book for the study of the Western theater.

Gaster, Theodore, H. *Thespis, Ritual, Myth, and Drama in the Ancient Near East*. New York: Henry Shumann, 1950.

One of the few available books on this little-understood period. Background book throwing light on Western dramatic history.

Ghéon, Henri. *The Art of the Theatre*. New York: Hill and Wang, Inc., 1961.
Ghéon's concept of dramatic art in historical perspective. A stimulating book of real value from one of the truly religious spirits writing drama.

Gorelik, Mordecai. *New Theatres for Old*. New York: Samuel French, Inc., 1940.
The theater as a public institution is considered in its various styles and periods as reflecting the social and political changes.

Hartnoll, Phyllis, editor. *Oxford Companion to the Theatre*. 2nd ed. New York: Oxford University Press, 1957.
Source book for drama and theater. A wealth of material makes this an invaluable source book on almost all aspects of the subject.

Hewitt, Barnard. *Theatre U.S.A. 1668 to 1957*. New York: McGraw-Hill Book Company, 1959.
A history that depends mainly on source material. To be used as background for understanding rather than interpretation of chronological history.

*Hughes, Glenn. *The Story of the Theatre*. New York: Samuel French, Inc., 1928. (Out of print.)
A readable history that has been a standard text for a long time.

MacGowan, Kenneth, and Melnitz, W. *The Living Stage: A History of World Theatre*. Englewood Cliffs, N. J.: Prentice-Hall, Inc., 1955.
A textbook written by theater persons who have also taught; enlivened with tables and charts.

Murray, Gilbert. *Five Stages of Greek Religion*. Garden City, N. Y.: Doubleday & Company, 1955. Anchor book.
A study of the religions from which the tragedies derive, using drama as the chief source of reference.

Nagler, A. M. *Source Book in Theatrical History*. New York: Dover Publications, 1959.
A scholarly probing that makes fascinating reading for theater addicts.

Nicoll, Allardyce. *Masks, Mimes, and Miracles*. New York: Harcourt, Brace & Company, 1931. (Out of print.)
One of the early books by one of the best-informed writers on drama.

————. *World Drama*. New York: Harcourt, Brace & World, Inc., 1949.
Authoritative statements about drama in a historical analysis.

Priestly, J. B. *The Wonderful World of the Theatre*. Garden City, N. Y.: Doubleday & Company, 1959.
One of the "Wonderful World Children's Series" and an excellent brief

history of the development of the theater. One of the largest selections of illustrations of theatrical history to be found.

*Prosser, Eleanor. *Drama and Religion in the English Mystery Plays.* Stanford, Calif.: Stanford University Press, 1961.
The religious doctrines with special attention to the Redemption in a careful study of some of the plays.

Quinn, Arthur M. *A History of the American Drama from the Beginning to the Civil War,* Vol. I, 1936. *A History of the American Drama from the Civil War to the Present Day,* Vol. II, Pts. 1 and 2. Rev. ed. New York: F. S. Crofts & Company, 1943.
These are outstanding books on the history of American plays and playwrights.

Salter, F. M. *Medieval Drama in Chester.* Toronto: University of Toronto Press, 1955.
Shortened analysis of the rise of medieval drama and a lively description of the plays and performances in Chester. Scholarly work with discussions of origins and dates.

Scott, A. C. *An Introduction to the Chinese Theatre.* New York: Theatre Arts Books, 1959.
An illustrated text showing the uniqueness of the Chinese classical theater in combining dance, speech, music, and costume.

Southern, Richard. *The Medieval Theatre in the Round.* New York: Theatre Arts Books, 1958.
A detailed study of the wide use of the circular theater in medieval England. The most detailed study of English medieval staging practice that has appeared; contains new insights and detailed analysis of a complete performance of *The Castle of Perserverance* around 1425.

*Speaight, Robert. *The Christian Theatre.* New York: Hawthorne Books, 1960.
One of the volumes in the *Catholic Encyclopedia.* Christian values and influence on drama since the Middle Ages including contemporary France and Germany.

Waley, Arthur. *The Nō Plays of Japan.* New York: Grove Press, 1953.
A book of nineteen plays that form an introduction to the literary form of the world's most "highly civilized" theater.

Introduction to Drama, Theory, Criticism, Reviews

*Artaud, Antonin. *The Theater and Its Double.* New York: Grove Press, 1958. Evergreen paperback.
A provoking book that presents the arousing purpose of theater as irritant. Essential for mature drama students.

Bentley, Eric. *In Search of Theatre*. New York: Alfred A. Knopf, Inc., 1954. Vintage Books.
Essays on drama and theater that clarify sound concepts. Stimulating writing.

*————. *The Playwright as Thinker*. New York: Meridian Books, 1955.
Provocative essays that make the reader think because the author has thought about the work of intelligent playwrights.

————. *The Dramatic Event*. Boston: Beacon Press, 1954.
An excellent collection of criticism that contains some of Bentley's best writing.

————. *What Is Theatre?* Boston: Beacon Press, 1955.
A companion volume to *The Dramatic Event* that is opinionated and shows the author's prejudices.

*Clark, Barrett, editor. *European Theories of the Drama*. Rev. ed. New York: Crown Publishers, 1947.
Standard work of criticism containing well-selected excerpts of dramatic criticism from the Greeks to the present. Revised edition contains American criticism.

Clurman, Harold. *Lies Like Truth*. New York: Grove Press, 1958. Evergreen paperback.
A series of essays on almost all aspects of the theater drawn from the experience of a long association with the theater.

Coggin, Philip A. *The Uses of Drama*. New York: George Braziller, Inc., 1956. See "History."

Craig, Edward Gordon. *On the Art of the Theatre*. New York: Theatre Arts Books, 1956.
The great book of prophecy, the testament of new principles of twentieth-century theater. A study of the theater as one unified art rather than as a haphazard assembly of many crafts.

Downer, Alan. *The Art of the Play*. New York: Holt, Rinehart & Winston, Inc., 1955.
To illustrate what the author has to say about the drama he has chosen these plays: *Ghosts, Prometheus Bound, Doctor Faustus, Anthony and Cleopatra, Tartuffe, The Sea Gull, The Emperor Jones, The Sheep Well*, and *Oedipus Rex*.

Else, Gerald F. *Aristotle's Poetics: The Argument*. Cambridge, Mass.: Harvard University Press, 1957.
Scholarly work that is useful for students of Aristotle's theories. Each paragraph of *Poetics* is retranslated and interpreted. A reference work.

*Fergusson, Francis. *The Human Image in Dramatic Literature*. Garden City, N. Y.: Doubleday & Company, 1957. Anchor book.

An excellent study that will be particularly rewarding for study groups in churches.

————. *The Idea of a Theatre: A Study of Ten Plays.* New York: Doubleday & Company, 1953. Anchor book.
Sound analysis by one of America's best critics and teachers.

Fowlie, Wallace. *Dionysus in Paris.* New York: Meridian Books, 1960.
A guide to contemporary French theater.

Gassner, John. *Theatre at the Crossroads: Plays and Playwrights on the Mid-century American Stage.* New York: Holt, Rinehart & Winston, Inc., 1960.

*Jones, Robert Edmond. *The Dramatic Imagination.* New York: Theatre Arts Books, 1941. Fifth printing.
Invaluable comment on the theater as a unity in which all aspects work toward an organic whole. A basic book.

McCollom, William C. *Tragedy.* New York: The Macmillan Company, 1957.
One of the most useful books on the subject written with engaging scholarship.

*Mitchell, Roy. *Creative Theatre.* New York: The John Day Company, 1929. (Out of print.)
The aesthetic principles of good theater analyzed and criticized. A highly inspirational treatment.

Nelson, Robert J. *Play Within a Play.* New Haven, Conn.: Yale University Press, 1958.
An attempt to isolate a given dramatist's controlling conception of the theater and to trace major movements of Western literature as they have been reflected in the theater.

Parrott, Thomas Marc. *William Shakespeare, A Handbook.* New York: Charles Scribner's Sons, 1934.
A brief and valuable introduction to Shakespeare and his times.

Peacock, Ronald. *The Poet in the Theatre.* New York: Hill & Wang, Inc., 1960. Dramabooks.

Rice, Elmer. *The Living Theatre.* New York: Harper & Brothers, 1959.
Appraises the theater in terms of social and economic forces which have shaped it.

*Rowe, Kenneth Thorpe. *A Theater in Your Head.* New York: Funk & Wagnalls Company, 1960.
A complete dramaturgy from the experiencing of the play by visualization of the production while reading to the final pleasure of its criticism.

Saint-Denis, Michel. *Theatre: The Rediscovery of Style.* New York: Theatre Arts Books, 1960.
The classical tradition in the theater related to new, effective styles in

every phase of theater—acting, directing, and scenic design. Theater as a domain of spirit, imagination, and faith.

*Selden, Samuel. *Man in His Theatre*. Chapel Hill, N. C.: University of North Carolina Press, 1957.

A simple and direct presentation of the author's personal views on the important connections between myth, ritual, and drama, and the significance of these connections for an understanding of the theater.

Sewall, Richard B. *The Vision of Tragedy*. New Haven, Conn.: Yale University Press, 1959.

An illuminating publication on the tragic form for the student of dramatic theory who is suspicious of neat definitions, weary of Freudian interpretations of Greek and Elizabethan plays, and distrustful of deductive applications of the *Poetics* to contemporary works.

Sobel, Bernart, editor. *The Theatre Handbook and Digest of Plays*. New York: Crown Publishers, 1940.

An attempt to form an encyclopedia of information about the theater. Valuable listing of plays to be found in various anthologies.

*Styan, J. L. *The Elements of Drama*. New York: Cambridge University Press, 1960.

Stimulating and rewarding introduction to the art of theater for playgoers, amateur actors, and students of literature. The consideration of plays in stage terms. Recommended.

*Whiting, Frank M. *An Introduction to the Theatre*. Rev. ed. New York: Harper & Brothers, 1961.

Excellent for a basic all-around understanding of theater. Good as text for beginning student.

*Wright, Edward A. *A Primer for Playgoers*. Engelwood Cliffs, N. J.: Prentice-Hall, Inc., 1958.

The responsibilities and tasks of the playgoer with ten commandments which are necessary for critical judgment on the part of the audience. Intended for cinema, stage, and television. Recommended.

Young, Stuart. *The Theatre*. New York: Hill & Wang, Inc. Dramabooks.

Essays on various aspects of theater by one of America's most literate critics.

Playwriting

Archer, William. *Playmaking*. New York: Dover Publications, 1959.

A complete discussion of the art of dramatic writing.

Baker, George Pierce. *Dramatic Technique*. Boston: Houghton Mifflin Company, 1919. (Out of print.)

The product of years of experience in training writers in the "47 Workshop." Great numbers of references to Elizabethan plays. For advanced students.

*Busfield, Roger M., Jr. The Playwright's Art. New York: Harper & Brothers, 1958.
A practical text giving the advice of successful writers and exercises compiled with the help of many teachers of playwriting.

Cole, Toby, editor. Playwrights on Playwriting. New York: Hill & Wang, Inc., 1960.
Statements by the artists themselves in what might be called credos; good for practicing playwrights and drama students.

*Egri, Laos. The Art of Dramatic Writing. Rev. ed. New York: Simon and Schuster, Inc., 1960. Paperback.
A down-to-earth discussion of dramatic techniques with a view to selling the play in the commercial theater. Recommended.

Hopkins, Arthur. How's Your Second Act? New York: Samuel French, Inc., 1931.
A small book containing some excellent analysis by one of the veteran play producers.

Kerr, Walter. How Not to Write a Play. New York: Simon and Schuster, Inc., 1960. Paperback.
Some perceptive opinions about plays from one of Broadway's leading newspaper critics. Opinionated but provocative.

Langner, Lawrence. The Play's the Thing. New York: G. P. Putnam's Sons, 1960.
A stalwart of the Theatre Guild writes out of his long experience of reading and selecting plays for Broadway. Practical advice for the professional playwright.

*Lawson, John Howard. Theory and Technique of Playwriting. New York: Hill & Wang, Inc., 1960. Dramabooks.
One of the standard books on playwriting now made available in paperback. Good.

Matthews, Brander. Papers on Playmaking. New York: Hill & Wang, Inc., 1957. Dramabooks.
The famous Columbia University professor who gave distinction to university drama work knew plays and how they were made.

Rowe, Kenneth Thorpe. A Theater in Your Head. New York: Funk & Wagnalls Company, 1960. (See Introduction to Drama, Theory, Criticism, Reviews.")

Selden, Samuel. An Introduction to Playwriting. New York: F. S. Crofts Co., Inc., 1946.
An excellent text by a professor who has helped to develop writers.

Directing

*Brown, Ben W. *Upstage-Downstage: Directing the Play.* Boston: Walter H. Baker Company, 1946.
The playing area defined and stage movement illustrated in a practical, easy-to-follow book.

Brown, Gilmor, and Garwood, Alice. *General Principles of Directing.* New York: Samuel French, Inc., 1936.
One of the early books on directing by practitioners of the Pasadena Playhouse. Simple and suggestive.

Cartmell, Van H. *Amateur Theatre.* Princeton, N. J.: D. Van Nostrand Company, 1961.
A simple, chatty guide for the amateur director and others who look upon theater as a hobby.

*Cole, Toby, and Chinoy, Helen, editors. *Directing the Play.* New York: Tudor Publishing Company, 1957.
How to do it by those who do it. A variety of suggestions by directors.

Dean, Alexander. *Fundamentals of Play Directing.* New York: Holt, Rinehart & Winston, Inc., 1941.
The most comprehensive treatment of play directing by the late Yale Drama School director. Directing by carefully blocked, anticipated action.

Deitrich, John E. *Play Direction.* Englewood Cliffs, N. J.: Prentice-Hall, Inc., 1953.
A practical book that can be understood and followed by the student. Recommended.

*Dolman, John, Jr. *The Art of Play Production.* Rev. ed. New York: Harper & Brothers, 1946.
A section on directing in one of the best books on theater practice.

Franklin, Miriam A. *Rehearsal: Principles and Practice of Acting for the Stage.* 3rd ed. Englewood Cliffs, N. J.: Prentice-Hall, Inc., 1950.
Simple and easy to follow; this book is designed to save time and worry throughout the production of a play.

Klein, Ruth. *The Art and Technique of Play Directing.* New York: Holt, Rinehart & Winston, Inc., 1953.
A study of the art of directing with analysis of the principles in practice. Good.

*Mutual Improvement Associations. *Play Production Handbook.* Salt Lake City, Utah: Deseret News Press, 1959.
A delightfully illustrated booklet that condenses much common sense wisdom into a short space. Good for church groups.

Young, John Wray. *Directing the Play: From Selection to Opening Night.* New York: Harper & Brothers, 1958.
Primarily for community-theater directors. Like many books on directing, dogmatic and individualized in advice but provocative for experienced directors.

Acting

Alberti, Eva. *A Handbook of Acting.* New York: Samuel French, Inc., 1932.
A theory of acting is supplemented by exercises designed to aid teachers. One of the old standard books.
*Albright, H. D. *Working up a Part.* 2nd ed. Boston: Houghton Mifflin Company, 1959.
Practical approach for the beginner; analysis of the role from rehearsal to performance. There are ten scenes for rehearsal and informal presentation.
Baldwin, J., and R. P. *The Fun of Acting!* Boston: Walter H. Baker Company, 1951.
A simple book for those who do not take their acting too seriously.
Boleslavsky, Richard. *Acting, the First Six Lessons.* New York: Theatre Arts Books, 1933.
Brief introduction to the Stanislavski method. Difficult but worthwhile for the serious actor.
Calvert, Louis. *Problems of the Actor.* New York: Henry Holt & Company, 1918. (Out of print.)
A veteran actor gives the results of a life of acting experience. Stimulating reading.
Cole, Toby, editor. *Acting: A Handbook of the Stanislavski Method.* New York: Crown Publishers, 1955.
Cole, Toby, and Chinoy, Helen, editors. *Actors on Acting.* New York: Crown Publishers, 1949.
Actors write on the art of acting. Excellent.
*Crafton, Allen, and Royer, Jessica. *Acting.* New York: F. S. Crofts & Company, 1934.
One of the best texts for college use. Practical and workable methods for the student. Recommended.
*Dolman, John, Jr. *The Art of Acting.* New York: Harper & Brothers, 1949.
This book combines the technique and experience of working with students. Recommended.
Franklin, Miriam A. *Rehearsal: Principles of Acting for the Stage.* 3rd ed. Englewood Cliffs, N. J.: Prentice-Hall, Inc., 1950.
Goodman, Edward. *Make Believe: The Art of Acting.* New York: Charles Scribner's Sons, 1956.

Directed primarily at the beginning actor in a school organized to prepare actors for the professional theater.
*Lees, C. Lowell. *A Primer of Acting.* Englewood Cliffs, N. J.: Prentice-Hall, Inc., 1949.
A creative approach to acting with exercises for the student.
Lewis, Robert. *Method or Madness.* New York: Samuel French, Inc., 1958.
A sensible and entertaining explanation of "the method."
*McGaw, Charles J. *Acting Is Believing.* New York: Holt, Rinehart & Winston, Inc., 1955.
Based on the Stanislavski method. Treated as actor and himself, actor and play, and actor and production. Detailed exercises. Recommended.
Moore, Sonia. *The Stanislavski Method, the Professional Library of an Actor.* New York: The Viking Press, 1960.
The essence of "the method" by a pupil.
*Selden, Samuel. *A Player's Handbook.* New York: Appleton-Century-Crofts, Inc., 1934.
The theory and practice of acting with considerable detailed information for the student. Recommended.
Stanislavski, Constantin. *Building a Character.* New York: Theatre Arts Books, 1949.
This book deals with the technical and external part of Stanislavski's concept of acting.
————. *An Actor Prepares.* New York: Theatre Arts Books, 1936.
Stanislavski's theory of acting.
————. *Creating a Role.* Edited by Hermine Isaacs Popper. New York: Theatre Art Books, 1961.
Three plays are used to show how systematically a role is brought to life. Prepared from notes made by Stanislavski.
*Strickland, F. Cowles. *The Technique of Acting.* New York: McGraw-Hill Book Company, 1956.
A "method" that contains suggestions for making the actor create for himself. Well documented. Good for stimulation.

Production

*Adix, Verne. *Theatre Stagecraft.* Anchorage, Ky.: Children's Theatre Press, 1956.
A logical choice for a beginning stagecraft course. Presents the basic theories, materials, and processes involved in the work of the designer-technician of the noncommercial theater.
Albright, Harry D.; Halstead, William P.; and Mitchell, Lee. *Principles of Theatre Art.* Boston: Houghton Mifflin Company, 1955.

An excellent book justifying the art process by which plays are translated into theatrical terms. Recommended.

*Bailey, Howard. *The A.B.C.'s of Play Producing: A Handbook for the Nonprofessional.* New York: David McKay Company, 1955.

A practical work containing lists of plays for production by high schools, colleges, community theaters, and church groups.

*Barber, Philip W. *New Scene Technician's Handbook.* Rev. 1953. Bound with John Gassner, *Producing the Play.* New York: Holt, Rinehart & Winston, Inc., 1953.

Buerki, F. A. *Stagecraft for Nonprofessionals.* Madison, Wis.: University of Wisconsin Press, 1956.

An excellent manual fully illustrated. Reasonable and worth owning.

Burris-Meyer, Harold, and Cole, Edward C. *Scenery for the Theatre.* Boston: Little, Brown & Company, 1938.

Burris-Meyer, Harold, and Mallory, Vincent. *Sound in the Theatre.* New York: Radio Magazines, Inc., 1959.

An authoritative book on sound and how to produce and control it.

Carey, Grace. *Stagecraft for Small Drama Groups.* Edinburgh: The Albyne Press, 1948. Modern Stage Handbook # 5.

Cornberg, Sol, and Bebaur, Emmanuel L. *A Stage Crew Handbook.* Rev. ed. New York: Harper & Brothers, 1957.

Standard reference for technical workers in the nonprofessional theater. All aspects of staging plays. Best for beginners.

Cotes, Peter. *A Handbook for Amateur Theatre.* New York: Philosophical Library, Inc., 1957.

Elementary book dealing with most of the varied problems found in amateur theater.

*Dolman, John, Jr. *The Art of Play Production.* Rev. ed. New York: Harper & Brothers, 1946.

One of the best all-around, standard texts on play production. Recommended.

Gassner, John. *Producing the Play.* Bound with Philip Barber, *New Scene Technician's Handbook.* New York: Holt, Rinehart & Winston, Inc., 1953.

*Hake, Herbert V. *Here's How! A Basic Stagecraft Book.* Rev. ed. Evanston, Ill.: Row, Peterson and Company, 1958.

Text and illustration on facing pages in a practical treatment of the essentials of stagecraft. Recommended.

Heffner, Hubert C.; Selden, Samuel; and Sellman, Hunton D. *Modern Theatre Practice.* 4th ed. New York: Appleton-Century-Crofts, Inc., 1959.

The means involved in the effective staging of plays. A standard text that is particularly good for class discussion.

Hewitt, Barnard; Foster, J. F.; and Wolle, Muriel. *Play Production, Theory, and Practice.* Philadelphia: J. B. Lippincott Company, 1959.
A text that comes out of teaching experience and that is written for the beginning student.

*Jones, Robert Edmund. *The Dramatic Imagination.* New York: Theatre Arts Books, 1941. (See "Introduction to Drama, Theory, Criticism, Reviews.")

*Lees, C. Lowell. *Play Production and Direction.* Englewood Cliffs, N. J.: Prentice-Hall, Inc., 1948.
Practical text.

*Mutual Improvement Association. *Play Production Handbook.* Salt Lake City, Utah: Deseret News Press, 1959.
(See "Directing.")

Nelms, Henning. *Play Production.* Rev. ed. New York: Barnes & Noble, Inc., 1958. College Outline Series.
A guide book for the student of drama and a handbook for backstage work. Recommended.

Phillipi, Herbert, *Stagecraft and Scene Design.* Boston: Houghton Mifflin Company, 1953.
A comprehensive discussion of every element of modern theater, suitable both for the beginner and the more advanced technician.

Santos, Louisa. *Projected Scenery for the School Stage.* Boston: Walter H. Baker Company, 1949.
Simple but valuable discussion of the uses of projected scenery and the different methods by way of which it is done.

*Selden, Samuel, and Sellman, Hunton D. *Stage Scenery and Lighting.* 3rd ed. New York: Appleton-Century-Crofts, Inc., 1959.
A text for a semester course which condenses much practical experience in scenery and lighting. A standard book.

Simonson, Lee. *The Stage Is Set.* New York: Harcourt, Brace & Company, 1932.
Critical and philosophical insights into the problems and aesthetics of theater from the viewpoint of scene designing.

*Smith, Milton. *Play Production.* New York: Appleton-Century-Crofts, Inc., 1948.
Another one of the basic handbooks that is a good all-around treatment. Recommended.

*Southern, Richard. *Stage Setting for Amateurs and Professionals.* New York: Theatre Arts Books, 1960.
Good for production suggestions for rooms other than picture-frame stages. Suggestions for simple settings and the use of folding screens.

Lighting

*Bowman, Wayne. *Modern Theatre Lighting*. New York: Harper & Brothers, 1958.

A topnotch handbook for use in the school and community theater which is suitable for beginners and those who have some knowledge. A practical and comprehensive volume.

Fuchs, Theodore. *Stage Lighting*. Boston: Little, Brown & Company, 1929.

The most comprehensive book on stage lighting but in need of revision.

*————. *Home Built Lighting Equipment for the Small Stage*. New York: Samuel French, Inc., 1939.

Designs for building various types of stage lighting equipment at the lowest possible cost which will provide good results.

*Hake, Herbert V. *Here's How*. Evanston, Ill.: Row, Peterson & Company, 1958.

Pictorial explanations of basic lighting instruments with photographs of scenes of actual productions to illustrate their use.

Knapp, Jack Stuart. *Lighting the Stage With Homemade Equipment*. Boston: Walter H. Baker Company, 1933.

Methods of lighting without the use of expensive or elaborate equipment. For the low-budget group.

McCandless, Stanley. *A Method of Lighting the Stage*. New York: Theatre Arts Books, 1954.

A complete and thoroughgoing presentation. Difficult but worthy of study.

*Mutual Improvement Association. *The Play Production Handbook*. Salt Lake City, Utah: Church of Jesus Christ of the Latter Day Saints, 40-50 North Main Street, 1959.

Through the use of cartoon drawings all aspects of play production are treated, with one section especially devoted to lighting the play. Simple and too brief but clear and easily understandable. Good use of color in illustrations.

Say, M. G. *Lighting the Amateur Stage*. Modern Stage Handbook #6. Rev. ed. Edinburgh: The Albyn Press, 1956.

The aesthetic value of lighting too often neglected by the small company, and how it may be achieved with a minimum of technical difficulty.

*Selden, Samuel, and Sellman, Hunton D. *Stage Scenery and Lighting*. 3rd ed. New York: Appleton-Century-Crofts, Inc., 1959.

A handbook for nonprofessionals. A practical and comprehensive text for study as well as for the person seeking solutions to specific production problems.

Costuming

Barfoot, Audrey. *Discovering Costume*. London: University of London Press, 1959.
For the stage designer with no previous experience. A good introduction to dress and its relationship to history.

*Barton, Lucy. *Costuming the Biblical Play*. Boston: Walter H. Baker Company, 1937.
A useful, short book for persons who don't know much about the craft of costume and yet are called upon to design costumes for the biblical play.

————. *Historic Costume for the Stage*. Boston: Walter Baker Company, 1935. A standard text for classes in stage costuming.

Bruhn, Wolfgang, and Tilke, M. *Pictorial History of Costume*. New York: Frederick A. Praeger, Inc., 1956.

Chalmers, Helena. *Clothes On and Off Stage*. New York: Appleton-Century-Crofts, Inc., 1928.
A history of dress from the earliest times to the present day.

Davenport, Millia. *The Book of Costume*. New York: Crown Publishers, 1941. One-volume edition.

*Gorsline, Douglas. *What People Wore*. New York: The Viking Press, 1952.
A basic book for the dress designer, theater costumer, and research student. A comprehensive, visual history of dress from ancient times to the twentieth century in detailed line drawings with accompanying historical surveys.

Hansen, Henny Harald. *Costumes and Styles: The Evolution of Fashion from Early Egypt to the Present*. New York: E. P. Dutton & Company, 1956.
The main historical periods are covered with information on the basic tendencies in style and the wearing of clothes. The most important part of the book is the section of excellent illustrations in color of seven hundred figures.

*Healy, Daty. *Dress the Show: A Basic Costume Book*. Evanston, Ill.: Row, Peterson & Company, 1948.
A simple book dealing with costume construction for the inexperienced costumer. Contains well-drawn illustrations, exact patterns, and simple directions.

Houston, Mary G. *Ancient Greek, Roman, and Byzantine Costume and Decoration*. 2nd ed. New York: The Macmillan Company, 1956.

————. *Medieval Costume in England and France, 13th, 14th, and 15th Centuries*. New York: The Macmillan Company.

Houston, Mary G., and Hornblower, Florence. *Ancient Egyptian, Mesopotamian and Persian Costume and Decoration*. 2nd ed. New York: The Macmillan Company, 1954.

A new edition of the *Ancient Egyptian, Assyrian, and Persian Costume* with much new material. Clear, well illustrated with helpful diagrams.

Kohler, Carl, and von Sichert, Emma. *History of Costume.* New York: David McKay Company, 1928.

A good translation from the German. The chapters on ancient dress, especially Hebrew dress, are particularly valuable. Good diagrams.

Paterek, Josephine. *Costuming for the Theatre.* New York: Crown Publishers, 1959.

Primarily for the costume designer. Discusses the use of color, accessories, and the importance of studying the character thoroughly, so that costumes will be suitable.

Saunders, Dorothy Lynn. *Costuming the Amateur Show.* New York: Samuel French, Inc., 1937.

A handbook well illustrated with diagrams and patterns.

Tilke, Max von. Costume Patterns and Designs. New York: Frederick A. Praeger, Inc., 1957.

————. *Oriental Costumes, Their Designs and Colors.* Berlin: Ernest Wasmuth, 1923.

Contemporary but virtually timeless costumes of Palestine and other countries. Especially helpful because of the rich variety of patterns.

Tissot, J. U. *The Old Testament.* Paris: Brunoff, 1904.

Written by one who knows a great deal about the costumes of the period. Valuable for its authenticity rather than for its information on costuming.

Wilson, Lillian. *The Clothing of the Ancient Romans.* Baltimore, Md.: The Johns Hopkins Press, 1938.

The reference in this area. May be used for New Testament Romans with confidence about accuracy.

*Wright, Marian. *Biblical Costume.* New York: The Macmillan Company, 1937.

The most complete description of biblical costumes with patterns and drawings.

*Zirner, Laura. *Costuming for the Modern Stage.* Urbana, Ill.: University of Illinois Press, 1957.

An interesting and important little book dealing with the relationship of costumes to dramatics. The author's development and interest in convertible costume units make the book especially significant.

Makeup

*Baird, John. *Make-up.* Revised ed. New York: Samuel French, Inc., 1930.
Basic book for amateurs. Illustrated.

Corson, Richard. *Stage Make-up.* 3rd ed. New York: Appleton-Century-Crofts, Inc.
Detailed, comprehensive, and standard text.
*Knapp, Jack Stuart. *The Technique of Stage Make-up.* Boston: Walter H. Baker Company, 1942.
A practical manual for the use of Max Factor's theatrical makeup. "Max Factor's Hints on the Art of Make-up" is the basis of this book. Book integrates material.
Melvill, Harald. *Magic of Make-up.* New York: Citadel Press, 1957. Written with authority and simplicity. The author deals with the practical problems of makeup in contemporary theater. Based on the premise: "The less apparent the make-up, the more effective it will be, and the simpler the materials employed the easier the means whereby it can be achieved."
*Strauss, Ivard. *Paint, Powder, and Make-up.* New York: Barnes & Noble, Inc., 1938.
A well-illustrated manual for the amateur.
Strenkovsky, Serge. *The Art of Make-up.* New York: E. P. Dutton & Company, 1937.

Arena Staging

*Boyle, Walden P. *Central and Flexible Staging.* Berkeley, Calif.: University of California Press, 1956.
Hughes, Glenn. *The Penthouse Theatre: Its History and Technique.* Rev. ed. Seattle, Wash.: University of Washington Press, 1950.
The experience of the director of one of the most successful small, arena stages.
Jones, Margo. *Theatre in the Round.* New York: Rinehart & Company, 1951.
The experience of one of the most creative and independent spirits of the revolt against the picture-frame stage.
*Southern, Richard. *The Open Stage.* New York: Theatre Arts Books, 1959.
The author is concerned not only with the historical aspect of the open stage but chiefly with its use in practice; he examines critically the exciting liberties which it offers to certain theaters today and tomorrow.
————. *The Medieval Theatre in the Round.* New York: Theatre Arts Books, 1958.
A detailed study of the wide use of the circular theater contrasted with the wheeled pageant wagon in fifteenth-century England. The most detailed study of English medieval-staging practice that has yet appeared. Includes an analysis of a complete performance of *The Castle of Perserverance* done about 1425.

Speech

Brodnitz, Friedrich S. *Keep Your Voice Healthy.* New York: Harper & Brothers, 1953.

Karr, Harrison M. *Develop Your Speaking Voice.* New York: Harper & Brothers, 1953. A formal textbook presentation of speech.

*Levy, Louise, and Mammen, Edward W. *Voice and Diction Handbook.* Englewood Cliffs, N. J.: Prentice-Hall, Inc. 1950.
The only inexpensive (paperback) volume among speech handbooks. An older but popular and practical book.

*Manser, Ruth, and Finlan, Leonnard. *The Speaking Voice.* New York: Longmans, Green & Company, 1957.
A good standard text for beginners. The best handbook. Clearly written with cartoon illustrations. Formal approach.

Choral Speech

*DeBanke, Cecil. *The Art of Choral Speaking.* Boston: Walter Baker Company, 1937.
Discusses the voice, selection of a choir, the ways of presenting readings, and gives many practical suggestions.

*Gullan, Marjorie. *Choral Speaking.* Boston: Expression Company, 1936.
A standard work by an authority in this field.

*————. *Speech Choirs.* New York: Harper & Brothers, 1937.

Loomis, Amy Goodhue. "Choric Speech Resources in the Bible." In manuscript form only. Write Amy Loomis, Vincennes University, Vincennes, Ind.

Sanson, Clive. *Choric Drama.* London: The Talbot Press. Religious Drama # 11. S.P.C.K.

Swann, Mona. *An Approach to Choral Speech.* Boston: Expression Company, 1934. Techniques and methods effectively worked out.

Dance

Andrews, Gladys. *Creative Rhythmic Movement for Children.* Englewood Cliffs, N. J.: Prentice-Hall, Inc., 1955.

*Fisk, Margaret Palmer. *The Art of the Rhythmic Choir.* New York: Harper & Brothers, 1950.

*————. *Look Up and Live.* St. Paul, Minn.: The Macalester Publishing Company, 1953.

Hays, Elizabeth. *Dance Composition and Production for High Schools and Colleges.* New York: A. S. Barnes & Company, 1955.

*H'Doubler, Margaret Newell. *The Dance and Its Place in Education*. New York: Harcourt, Brace & Company, 1925.

Hering, Doris, editor. *Twenty-five Years of American Dance*. New York: Dance Magazine, 1951.

Hughes, Russell Meriwither. (By La Meri, pseud.) *Dance as an Art Form: Its History and Development*. New York: A. S. Barnes & Company, 1933.

Humphry, Doris. *The Art of Making Dances*. Edited by Barbara Pollock. New York: Holt, Rinehart & Winston, Inc., 1959.

Morgan, Barbara. *Martha Graham*. New York: Duell, Sloan & Pearce, Inc., 1941. Album of photographs.

*Murray, Ruth. *Dance in Elementary Education*. New York: Harper & Brothers, 1953.

Sachs, Curt. *World History of Dance*. New York: W. W. Norton & Company, 1957.

Pageantry

There are no books in print dealing specifically with pageantry. Histories of drama refer to the form, and numerous articles have been written about the pageant renaissance in Virginia, North Carolina, and Kentucky in the historical, out-of-doors performances of *The Lost Colony, Horn in the West, Unto These Hills, Wilderness Road*, et cetera.

Bates, Esther Willard. *The Art of Producing Pageants*. Boston: Walter H. Baker Company, 1925. (Out of print.)
A handbook for those just beginning the art of pageantry; a textbook for schools and colleges. Designed as an elementary text, it stresses the need for continuous training and study needed to improve the quality of production. Covers the complete process of organizing and producing pageants.

Miller, Madelaine Sweeny. *Church Pageantry*. Cincinnati: The Methodist Book Concern, 1924. (Out of print.)

Russell, Mary M. *How to Produce Plays and Pageants*. New York: George H. Doran Company, 1923. (Out of print.)

Creative Dramatics

Allstrom, Elizabeth. *Let's Play a Story*. New York: Friendship Press, 1957.
An easy-to-follow handbook especially conceived for the church-school teacher.

*Andrews, Gladys. *Creative Rhythmic Movement for Children*. Englewood Cliffs, N. J.: Prentice-Hall, Inc., 1954.
This author skillfully encourages children to create through patterns of movement.

*Brown, Corinne. *Creative Drama in the Lower School.* New York: Apple-ton-Century-Crofts, Inc., 1929.
One of the early books on dramatic play with young children.

Brown, Jeanette Perkins. *The Story-Teller in Religious Education.* Boston: Pilgrim Press, 1951.
Clear and practical advice on what stories to tell and how to tell them. Fifteen complete stories included.

Buehler, Bernice. *Let's Make a Play.* New York: Friendship Press, 1944.
Techniques of informal dramatization stated briefly with a story on Burma used as an illustration. Lists good stories to be used for dramatization.

Burger, Isabel. *Creative Play Acting.* New York: The Ronald Press, 1950.
The author's procedure is to develop formal plays with children and young people by means of creative dramatic techniques.

*Cole, Natalie. *The Arts in the Classroom.* New York: The John Day Company, 1940.
The essence of creative teaching in the arts.

*Dixon, Madeleine C. *High, Wide, and Deep.* New York: The John Day Company, 1938. (Out of print.)
Creative heights, social widths, and depths of wonder are the motivation of this book which stresses the important social adjustments which come through the dramatic play of nursery-school children.

Durland, Frances C. *Creative Dramatics for Children.* Yellow Springs, Ohio: Antioch Press, 1952.
The author traces her steps in guiding children to develop a creative-drama project into a formal play.

*Haaga, Agnes, and Randles, Patricia. *Supplementary Materials for Use in Creative Dramatics with Younger Children.* Seattle, Wash.: University of Washington, 1952.
Concrete illustrations of procedures in creative dramatics with little children.

Hartley, Ruth E.; Frank, Lawrence K.; and Doldenson, Robert M. *Understanding Children's Play.* New York: Columbia University Press, 1952.
Two chapters of this book are devoted to the study of healthy personality development through dramatic play.

Hartman, Gertrude, and Shumaker, Ann. *Creative Expression.* Eau Claire, Wis.: E. M. Hale and Company, 1939.
Section on "Creative Expression Through Dramatics" gives views of several people on secular education use.

Kilpatrick, William H. *Foundations of Method.* New York: The Macmillan Company, 1925. (Out of print.)
A basic book for the teacher of creative dramatics.

Mearns, Hughes. *The Creative Adult.* New York: Doubleday & Company, 1940.

*————. *Creative Power.* Rev. ed. New York: Dover Publications, 1958. The sub-title of this book, "The Education of Youth in the Creative Arts," suggests the book's wise usefulness in all fields of creative teaching. A definite book in the field.

————. *Creative Youth.* New York: Doubleday & Comapny, 1928.

Mendelowitz, Daniel. *Children Are Artists.* Stanford, Calif.: Stanford University Press, 1953.

Merrill, John, and Fleming, Martha. *Play-making and Plays.* New York: The Macmillan Company, 1930. (Out of print.) Both formal and informal drama are discussed and illustrated in this book which came from the work of the Francis Parker School of Chicago.

*Niebuhr, Hulda. *Ventures in Dramatics.* New York: Charles Scribner's Sons, 1935. (Out of print.) Dramatic projects carried on with older children in New York City's Riverside Church School.

Osborn, Alex F. *Applied Imagination.* With an instruction manual. Rev. ed. New York: Charles Scribner's Sons, 1953.

Sawyer, Ruth. *The Way of the Story-teller.* New York: The Viking Press, 1942. The leading book in this field which has grown from years of story-telling experience. Author includes eleven of her own stories.

*Siks, Geraldine, and Lease, Ruth. *Creative Dramatics for Home, School, and Community.* New York: Harper & Brothers, 1952. A book for parents, teachers, and community leaders on the guiding of children in creative dramatics.

Slade, Peter. *Child Drama.* New York: Philosophical Library, Inc., 1955. The leading English work on creative drama. A comprehensive and important book.

*Ward, Winifred. *Drama with and for Children.* (Creative Drama, Children's Theater, Bulletin 1960 # 30.) Washington, D. C.: U. S. Department of Health, Education, and Welfare, 1960. The result of a joint concern felt by the Office of Education and the Children's Theater Conference for the apparent lack of easily available material on creative dramatics. To offer guidance in the art of creative drama *with* children; and to give some assistance to organizations wishing to give plays *for* children.

*————. *Playmaking with Children.* 2nd ed. New York: Appleton-Century-Crafts, Inc., 1957. A new version of the earlier book by this title which is directed to the class-

room teacher of small children. One of the outstanding, practical, and com-
prehensive texts in the field by an outstanding pioneer in creative dramatics.
Willcox, Helen L. *Bible Study Through Educational Dramatics.* New York:
The Abingdon Press, 1924. (Out of print.)
One of the earliest books on informal dramatics. Though long out of print,
it is well worth procuring from libraries.

Children's Theater

Chorpenning, Charlotte. *Twenty-one Years With Children's Theatre.*
Anchorage, Ky.: Children's Theatre Press, 1954.
A creative director of formal plays tells her philosophy and techniques as
playwright and director of a children's theater.
*Davis, Jed H., and Watkins, Mary Jane. *Children's Theatre, Play Production
for the Child Audience.* New York: Harper & Brothers, 1960.
A comprehensive book on children's theater directed and produced by
adults for the child audience.
Fisher, Caroline, and Robertson, Hazel. *Children and the Theatre.* Rev. ed.
Stanford, Calif.: Stanford University Press, 1940.
This book discusses formal theater as it benefits the child participant.
*Ward, Winifred. *Theatre for Children.* Rev. ed. Anchorage, Ky.: Children's
Theatre Press, 1958.
The first authoritative book on children's theater written out of the ex-
perience of directing the pioneering venture in Evanston, Ill.
*————. *Drama with and for Children.* (Bulletin 1960 # 30.) Washing-
ton, D. C.: U. S. Department of Health, Education, and Welfare, 1960.
A pamphlet written for the Office of Education of the United States De-
partment of Health, Education, and Welfare. In sixty-four pages it covers
the field of creative drama and theater for children. Excellent bibliography.

Drama in Education

*Adult Education Association. *How to Use Role Playing.* (Leadership Pamphlet No. 6.) Obtainable through the Board of Education of The Methodist Church, Box 871, Nashville 2, Tennessee.
*Coggin, Philip A. *The Uses of Drama.* New York: George Braziller, Inc.,
1956. From the viewpoint of the community spirit giving birth to drama
and the dramatic instinct inherent in man, a historical survey of drama and
education from ancient Greece to the present day.
Curtis, Eleanora Whitman. *The Dramatic Instinct in Education.* Boston:
Houghton Mifflin Company, 1914. (Out of print.)

Highet, Gilbert. *The Art of Teaching.* New York: Alfred A. Knopf, Inc., 1950.

*Mearns, Hughes. *Creative Power.* 2nd rev. ed. New York: Dover Publications. 1959.
One of the foremost books on education. The progressive approach to the teaching of the creative arts. The statement of Mearns' methods which now are considered among the most effective and valuable approaches to the teaching of creative arts yet formulated.

Ommaney, Katherine, and Pierce C. *The Stage and School.* 3rd ed. New York: McGraw-Hill Book Company, 1960.

*Overton, Grace Sloan. *Drama in Education.* New York: The Century Company, 1926. (Out of print.)
A good historical analysis.

Russell, Mary. *Drama as a Factor in Social Education.* New York: George H. Doran Company, 1924. (Out of print.)
One of the pioneering books on the subject.

Wise, Claude Morton. *Dramatics for School and Community.* Cincinnati: Stewart Kidd Company, 1923. (Out of print.)
Discussion of the meaning and rise of the little-theater movement. Sketchy information on production aspects and somewhat dated; bibliographies compose major part of book.

Psychodrama, Sociodrama, and Plays Used for Discussions

Haas, Robert B. *Psychodrama and Sociodrama in American Education.* Boston: Beacon Press, 1949.
Presents various applications of role-playing.

How to Use Role-playing Effectively. New York: Association Press, 1959.
The two pamphlets that are used as the text for this book are about the only simple guides available on the subject.

*Moreno, J. L. *Psychodrama and Sociodrama.* Boston: Beacon Press, 1946.
A basic text by an authority.

Simos, Jack. *Social Growth Through Play Production.* New York: Association Press, 1957.
An author trained in education and social work discusses the process of producing a play, bringing to light the creative process inherent in the relationship between teacher or director and the emotional development of all participants. Drama is viewed not only as a form of beneficial recreational activity but also as a rich source from which to draw knowledge of human behavior.

Weiss, M. Jerry. *Guidance Through Drama.* New York: William Morrow & Company, 1954.

Six plays that are good for high-school students to be used as departure points for discussion. Texts of the plays are given. There is a chapter on the discussion leader and some suggestions for discussion points.

Community Theater

Gard, Robert E. *Grassroots Theatre: A Search for Regional Arts in America.* Madison, Wis.: University of Wisconsin Press, 1955.

*Gard, Robert E., and Burley, Gertrude. *Community Theatre: Idea and Achievement.* New York: Duell, Sloan & Pearce, Inc., 1959.

Thirteen interviews with community-theater pioneers and leaders help to illustrate that drama is a dynamic part of community life across the nation and that our local theaters, albeit not commercial, are not professional.

MacGowan, Kenneth. *Footlights Across America.* New York: Harcourt, Brace & Co., 1929.

The most complete record of the little theater movement in America.

*Young, John Wray. *The Community Theatre and How It Works.* New York: Harper & Brothers, 1957.

A practical discussion of the community theater and what makes it successful if not distinguished.

Wise, Claude Morton. *Dramatics for School and Community.* Cincinnati: Stewart Kidd Company, 1923. (Out of print.)

Religious Drama

Meaning and Development

*Balmforth, Ramsden. *The Ethical and Religious Value of the Drama.* New York: Greenberg Press, 1926. (Out of print.)

One of the early books to set forth the meaning of religious drama and to illustrate it by way of the great religious plays of the world.

Butler, Sister Mary Margarete. *Hrotsvitka: The Theatricality of Her Plays.* New York: Philosophical Library, Inc., 1960.

An evaluation of the tenth-century nun with a detailed discussion of two of her plays.

Cargill, Oscar. *Drama and Liturgy.* New York: Columbia University Press. 1930. (Out of print.)

An attempt to refute the long accepted theory that later medieval drama was the work of artists and had not developed out of the liturgical drama.

Chaigne, Louis. *Paul Claudel: The Man and the Mystic.* New York: Appleton-Century-Crofts, Inc., 1961. A biography of one of the greatest contemporary religious playwrights in which space is given to his struggle to find the meaning of faith. An excellent analysis of Claudel's plays.

*Coggin, Philip A. *The Uses of Drama.* New York: George Braziller, Inc., 1958. See "History."

Ehrensperger, Harold. *Conscience on Stage.* New York and Nashville: Abingdon-Cokesbury Press, 1947. (Out of print.)

Glover, Halcott. *Drama and Mankind: A Vindication and a Challenge.* London: Small & Company, 1924. (Out of print.)
A general discussion of the values of drama.

*Young, Karl. *Drama of the Medieval Church.* 2 vol. Rev. ed. London: Oxford University Press, 1933.
Volume I deals with the history of the church of Rome, the dramatic aspects of the liturgy, the Resurrection and Passion plays. Volume II deals with plays associated with the nativity, legends, and subjects of the Bible. Much of the illustrative text is in Latin and the volumes are scholarly. They contain detailed notes and references.

Handbooks on Production in the Church

*Bates, Esther Willard. *The Church Play and Its Production.* Boston: Walter H. Baker Company, 1938. (Out of print.)
Production material stresses liturgical and chancel drama. Sound thought and worthy material.

Chapman, Raymond. *Religious Drama: A Handbook for Actors and Producers.* Boston: Walter H. Baker Company, 1959. London: S.P.C.K.
A small book written from a British point of view. Suggestive.

*Eastman, Fred and Wilson, Louis. *Drama in the Church.* Rev. ed. New York: Samuel French, Inc., 1961.

Ehrensperger, Harold. *Conscience on Stage.* New York and Nashville: Abingdon-Cokesbury Press, 1947. (Out of print.)

Moseley, J. Edward. *Using Drama in the Church.* Rev. ed. St. Louis: The Bethany Press, 1955.
A small book and therefore a necessarily limited treatment.

Use in Religious Education

*Deseo, Lydia Glover, and Phipps, Hulda Mossberg. *Looking at Life Through Drama.* New York: The Abingdon Press, 1931. (Out of print.)
A thoroughgoing analysis of plays for study and discussion.

Edland, Elizabeth. *Principles and Technique in Religious Dramatics.* Cincinnati: The Methodist Book Concern, 1926. (Out of print.)
One of the pioneering texts on the subject and still amazingly good.

Ferris, Anita B. *Following the Dramatic Instinct.* New York: Missionary Education Movement of the United States and Canada, 1922. (Out of print.)

An early statement that remains a sound one.

Loomis, Amy Goodhue. *How to Dramatize Your Meeting.* Philadelphia: Baptist Youth Fellowship, 1703 Chestnut Street, 1930. (Out of print.)

Taylor, Florence. *Drama in Religious Education.* London: The Talbot Press, 1944. S.P.C.K.

*Ward, Winifred. *Playmaking With Children.* 2nd ed. New York: Appleton-Century-Crofts, Inc., 1957.

Contains an excellent chapter "Playmaking in Religious Education."

*Wood, W. Carleton. *The Dramatic Method in Religious Education.* New York: The Abingdon Press, 1931. (Out of print.)

For a long time the authoritative text written by a religious educator.

Biblical Material

DeJong, Meindert. *Bible Days.* Grand Rapids, Mich.: Fideler Company, 1948.

Authentic pictures and descriptions of life in ancient Palestine.

Duce, Robert. *Steps in Bible Drama.* London: Independent Press, Ltd., 1955.

*Miller, Elizabeth Erwin. *The Dramatization of Bible Stories.* Chicago: University of Chicago Press, 1918. (Out of print.)

Still the standard work on the subject.

Raine, James W. *Bible Dramatics.* New York: The Century Company, 1927. (Out of print.)

Smither, Ethel L. *A Picture Book of Palestine.* New York and Nashville: Abingdon-Cokesbury Press, 1947.

One of the leading books for stories to be told or played for fifth through the seventh grades.

*Willcox, Helen L. *Bible Study Through Educational Dramatics.* New York: The Abingdon Press, 1924. (Out of print.)

Good theory and practice.

Worship

*Meland, Bernard E. *Modern Man's Worship.* New York: Harper & Brothers, 1934. (Out of print.)

A suggestive treatment. Highly recommended for study groups and leaders.

Palmer, Albert W. *The Art of Conducting Public Worship.* New York: The Macmillan Company, 1939.

Best book on this aspect of worship.

————. *Come, Let Us Worship.* New York: The Macmillan Company, 1941.

A manual of worship for the small church. Practical and helpful.

Seidenspinner, Clarence. *Form and Freedom in Worship.* Chicago: Willett, Clark & Company, 1941.
Provocative and thorough treatment. Practical.

*Sperry, Willard. Reality in Worship. New York: The Macmillan Company, 1939.
Thoroughgoing, sound, and suggestive.

Steere, Douglas V. *Prayer and Worship.* New York: Association Press, 1938.
Last chapter contains excellent suggestions for devotional readings. Good bibliography.

*Underhill, Evelyn. *Worship.* New York: Harper & Brothers, 1957. Torchbooks.
Scholarly and complete discussion of the meaning and purpose of worship. Historical development.

*Vogt, Von Ogden. *Modern Worship.* Rev. ed. New Haven, Conn.: Yale University Press, 1927.
A thorough study of the subject of worship and treatment of worship as a celebration of life.

APPENDIX I

ADDRESSES OF DRAMA ORGANIZATIONS

American Educational Theatre Association
  Religious Drama Project
  # 18 71 Bay State Road, Boston 15, Mass.
Bay Area Religious Drama Service (BARDS)
  1798 Scenic Avenue, Berkeley, Calif.
The Bishop's Company
  Box 424, Santa Barbara, Calif.
Boston Area Religious Drama Service (BARDS—East)
  61 Sparks Street, Cambridge, Mass.
The Broadway Chapel Players—Broadway Congregational Church
  Broadway and 56th Street, New York City, N. Y.
The Christian Drama Council of Canada
  71 Bloor Street West, Toronto 5, Canada
The Drama Trio
  University of Redlands, Redlands, Calif.
The Lutheran Foundation for Religious Drama, Inc.
  Broadway and 93rd Street, New York 35, N. Y.
Manhattan Division of The Protestant Council
  71 West 23rd Street, Room 1816, New York 10, N. Y.
The Methodist Church
  1. Department of College and University Religious Life
  2. Division of the Local Church, The Board of Education
    Box 871, Nashville 2, Tenn.
Mutual Improvement Associations of the Church of Latter-Day Saints
  (Mormon)
  40-50 North Main Street, Salt Lake City, Utah
National Catholic Theatre Conference
  142 Laverack Avenue, Lancaster, N. Y.
National Council of Churches of Christ in the U.S.A.
  1. Department of Worship and the Arts

276

2. Division of Christian Education—Religious Drama Workshop
475 Riverside Drive, New York 27, N. Y.
The Protestant Episcopal Church
Department of Christian Education
28 Havermeyer Place, Greenwich, Conn.
The Religious Drama Society of Great Britain
166 Shaftesbury Avenue, London, W. C. 2, England
The Southern Baptist Convention
Sunday School Board
127 Ninth Avenue, North, Nashville, Tenn.
The United Presbyterian Church in the U.S.A.
Commission on Ecumenical Missions and Relations
475 Riverside Drive, New York 27, N. Y.

LIST OF PUBLISHERS AND ADDRESSES

(Order all plays and books through your local bookstore if at all possible)

Abingdon Press, 201 Eighth Avenue, South, Nashville 3, Tenn.

American Theatre Wing Community Plays, 351 West 48th Street, New York, N. Y.

Anti-Defamation League of B'nai B'rith, 515 Madison Avenue, New York 22, N. Y.

Anvil Books (see D. Van Nostrand Co.)

Apex Books (see Abingdon Press)

Appleton-Century-Crofts, Inc., 35 West 32nd Street, New York 1, N. Y.

Association Press, 291 Broadway, New York 7, N. Y.

Augsburg Publishing House, 426 South 5th Street, Minneapolis 15, Minn.

Avon Book Division, Hearst Corporation, 959 Eighth Avenue, New York 19, N. Y.

Baker's Plays, 100 Summer Street, Boston 19, Mass.

Ballantine Books, Inc., 101 Fifth Avenue, New York 3, N. Y.

Bantam Books, Inc., 271 Madison Avenue, New York 16, N. Y.

A. S. Barnes & Company, 11 East 36th Street, New York 16, N. Y.

Barnes & Noble, Inc., 105 Fifth Avenue, New York 3, N. Y.

Beacon Press, 25 Beacon Street, Boston 8, Mass.

British Book Centre, Inc., 122 East 55th Street, New York 22, N. Y.

Children's Theatre Press, Cloverlot, Anchorage, Ky.

Christian Education Press, 1505 Race Street, Philadelphia 2, Pa.

Compass Books (see Viking Press)

Coward-McCann, Inc., 200 Madison Avenue, New York 16, N. Y.

Dell Publishing Company, Inc., 750 Third Avenue, New York 17, N. Y.

Dodd, Mead & Co., 432 Park Avenue, South, New York 16, N. Y.

Dover Publications, Inc., 180 Varick Street, New York 14, N. Y.

Drama Book Shop, 51 West 52nd Street, New York 19, N. Y.

Dramabooks (see Hill and Wang)

Dramatic Publishing Company, 179 N. Michigan Avenue, Chicago 1, Ill.
Dramatists Play Service, Inc., 14 East 38th Street, New York 16, N. Y.
E. P. Dutton & Company, Inc., 300 Park Avenue South, New York 10, N. Y.
Evergreen Books (see Grove Press)
Everyman Paperbacks (see E. P. Dutton)
Faber & Faber, Ltd., 24 Russell Square, London W. C. 1, England
Samuel French, Inc., 25 West 45th Street, New York 36, N. Y.
Friends Book and Supply House, 101 Gusher Hill Drive, Richmond, Ind.
Friendship Press, 475 Riverside Drive, New York 27, N. Y.
Galaxy Books (see Oxford University Press)
Grosset & Dunlap, Inc., 1107 Broadway, New York 10, N. Y.
Grove Press, 64 University Place, New York 3, N. Y.
Harcourt, Brace & World, Inc., 750 Third Avenue, New York 17, N. Y.
Harper & Brothers, 49 East 33rd Street, New York 16, N. Y.
Harvest Books (see Harcourt, Brace)
Hill & Wang, Inc., 141 Fifth Avenue, New York 10, N. Y.
Holt, Rinehart & Winston, Inc., 383 Madison Avenue, New York 17, N. Y.
Houghton Mifflin Company, 2 Park Street, Boston 7, Mass.
John Knox Press, 8 North 6th Street, Richmond 9, Va.
Longman's Green & Company, Inc., 119 West 40th Street, New York 18, N. Y.
The Macmillan Company, 60 Fifth Avenue, New York 11, N. Y.
Mentor Books (see New American Library)
Meridian Books, Inc. 2231 West 110th Street, Cleveland 2, Ohio
Modern Library (see Random House)
Muhlenberg Press, 2900 Queen Lane, Philadelphia 29, Pa.
National Association for Mental Health, Inc., 10 Columbus Circle, New York
    19, N. Y.
New American Library of World Literature, Inc., 501 Madison Avenue, New
    York 22, N. Y.
The Newman Press, Westminster, Md.
Noonday Press, 19 Union Square West, New York 3, N. Y.
W. W. Norton & Company, Inc., 55 Fifth Avenue, New York 3, N. Y.
Oxford University Press, Inc., 417 Fifth Avenue, New York 16, N. Y.
Penguin Books, Inc., 3300 Clipper Mill Road, Baltimore 11, Md.
Phoenix Books (see University of Chicago Press)
Pocket Books, Inc., 630 Fifth Avenue, New York 20, N. Y.
Prentice-Hall, Inc., Englewood Cliffs, N. J.
Random House, 475 Madison Avenue, New York 22, N. Y.
Reflection Books (see Association Press)
Religious Drama Society, 166 Shaftesbury Avenue, London W. C. 2, England
Charles Scribner's Sons, 597 Fifth Avenue, New York 17, N. Y.

The Seabury Press, Inc., Fawcett Place, Greenwich, Conn.
Signet Books (see New American Library)
Simon and Schuster, Inc., 630 Fifth Avenue, New York 20, N. Y.
Theatre Arts Books, 333 Sixth Avenue, New York 14, N. Y.
Tudor Publishing Company, 221 Park Avenue, South, New York 3, N. Y.
UNESCO, 2201 United Nations Building, New York 17, N. Y.
Universal Library (see Grosset & Dunlap)
University of Chicago Press, 5750 Ellis Avenue, Chicago 37, Ill.
D. Van Nostrand Company, Inc., 120 Alexander Street, Princeton, N. J.
The Viking Press, Inc., 625 Madison Avenue, New York 22, N. Y.
Vintage Books (see Random House)
The Westminster Press, Witherspoon Bldg., Philadelphia 7, Pa.
Yale University Press, 149 York Street, New Haven, Conn.

INDEX